Immortal Justice

by

Faith V. Smith

Immortal Justice

Contact Information: info@thewildrosepress.com

Cover Art by *Tamra Westberry*

The Wild Rose Press
PO Box 706
Adams Basin, NY 14410-0706
Visit us at www.thewildrosepress.com

Publishing History
First Faery Rose Edition, 2011
Print ISBN 1-60154-979-2

Published in the United States of America

"Ye willna be needing a weapon, I will protect ye."

His statement irritated Abby, but at the same time a part of her was just a tiny bit thrilled. It seemed immortal or not, a man always had the attitude of protecting the little woman—whether they needed it or not. Of course to be fair, he had saved her butt from the demon, but he needed to know she wasn't some frightened babe in the woods.

"I beg to differ. If I'd had a knife I could have done some serious damage, and besides, you can't protect me twenty-four-seven, Darach."

"Ye will be protected at all times, Abby."

"You're missing the point. Maybe I don't need a keeper. I have managed to take care of myself for over…" Abby decided he didn't really have to know she was over thirty. "And what about when you're asleep? You do sleep don't you?"

Darach frowned, but answered, "*Aye*, I do sleep, but 'tis usually during the daylight hours. However now I will be sleeping at night in your bed with ye."

Praise for Faith V. Smith

"Again, Faith Smith has wowed me with her heartfelt words. *GIDEON'S HEART* is an intricate love tale of the purest form.

~Angela, Nocturne Romance Reads (5 Hoots)

~*~

"Readers will love the latest novel [*SEMPER FI MAGICK*] by Smith. Full of laughter and passion."

~Sabrina Cooper, Romantic Times Book Reviews (4.5 Stars)

~*~

"Sexy, dark, and irresistible. *DUNBAR'S CURSE* blends danger and scorching passion into a fast-paced, wicked hot story. Faith V. Smith writes vampire heroes to die for. But be warned...readers who enter her paranormal world won't want to leave!"

~Sue-Ellen Welfonder,
USA Today bestselling author

~*~

"When reading this story [*VIKING, GO HOME*] this reviewer couldn't help but think of another excellent time travel, Jude Deveraux's *A Knight in Shining Armor*."

~Cindy Himler, Romantic Times (4 Stars)

~*~

"*KENSINGTON'S SOUL* is a wonderfully written, tender and thoroughly enjoyable book by Faith V. Smith. It has everything in it. The plot of the story is superb."

~Eaim, Night Owl Reviews (5 Stars)

~*~

"*BEWARE WHAT YOU WISH*...Time Travel fans take note of this short, sassy, sexy and highly entertaining debut by an author to watch."

~Kathe Robin

Dedication

To my Rick who is in Heaven.
May your days be filled
with all the blessings on high!
To my daughter Amanda,
again my heartfelt thanks for making it easy
for me to write.
To all my critique partners who helped me
with this work, you know who you are,
may you know I love each and everyone of you!
And to God be the glory!

Acknowledgements

I never thought I would write a book about demons. I decided to write *Immortal Justice* because a publisher was telling me what was hot, and some of the stuff I couldn't wrap my beliefs around to write. I have to write what I can believe. Yes, I know I don't really know if vampires are real (most of my fans know I write vampire romance), but I do know there are a lot of different creatures in this world—some I don't want to know. However, I do know there are demons that inhabit the mortal body of mankind at some time or another. It may be they possess them or it could be an evil spirit.

Regardless, once I put my imagination to work, I felt there was no reason that Michael the archangel, working under God's directions, could not create a band of immortals who fight demons. So there you have it. This book is the story of one man who died before his time but was given a chance to fight evil on earth. I like to think all of us as God's creatures deserve a chance to do it better, or in Darach's case to live out the destiny that should have been his.

A heartfelt thank you to Sarah Hansen, my editor, for believing in this book as much as I did. Special hugs to Eliza March, Sandi Morris, Sky Purington, Alicia Dean, April Moss, and Kelly McCrady. And please forgive me if I left someone's name off—it's not because I don't love you, but I only have so much space.

Additional note: I used the city of New Orleans or NOLA as you've seen in the book because of its unique history. I researched my facts, and if anything is not quite right, then please forgive me.

Love to all my readers! Thank you for loving my work!

From the fall of Lucifer, one of the most beautiful angels ever created by God, evil has reigned on earth. Only the pure of heart and those filled with courage will sway the hold his demons have on mortal man.

From the desk of Michael/Archangel to God

Chapter One

Blood seeped from his numerous wounds onto the rush-strewn floor. Darach gazed around the great room of his home, searching for the sound of whimpering that seemed to resonate inside his head. His wife Briene lay huddled in a fetal position. His brow furrowed with the pain radiating from his chest, thigh, and sword arm as he tried to rise. He couldn't see his son, Jamie. Where was Jamie?

An uttered cry—quickly cut off, caused him to turn his head. His cousin held the not quite two-year-old babe by his arm. Angus turned his gaze toward Darach and smiled before thrusting a knife into Jamie's heart. A roar tore a path from Darach's chest to his lips and beyond.

"Nay!"

He tried to crawl to his lifeless son, but one of Angus's men kicked him in the ribs. Darach collapsed on the stone floor within feet of his wife. Her chest rose and fell, briefly giving him hope she could be saved. Then the reality of what she would endure before Angus would be satisfied caused the hair on his arms to stand on end. He cursed his inability to fight.

Again, his cousin turned his head and smiled

before moving to Briene's body. Darach watched as he lifted her skirts and knelt between her thighs. Rage marched in time to the pulse beating within him, sending more of his crimson blood spurting onto the floor.

"Pity's sake, mon, have ye not done enough? She will be a widow, childless, and without a home."

"Nay, cousin, I have waited ages to take back what should hae been mine. Now, I will help meself to the soon-to-be widowed MacRath."

Angus's men stopped Darach's attempt to reach his wife. They held his head in place, forcing him to watch. Even without their coercion he would not have closed his eyes. He wanted—no, needed—to take the image of his sweet wife's rape, his son's death, with him to the grave. For if there were any way to haunt Angus MacRath for his deeds, then Darach would strike a bargain with the devil himself to get that chance.

What seemed like hours later, his wife breathed her last, and Angus swaggered to where Darach lay, still cursing him. The sword his cousin carried was the MacRath battle sword, Darach's father's sword, given to him when he was barely a man.

"'Tis time ye joined your family, cousin. May hell open its doors for ye in a timely manner."

Darach spit at Angus's feet. The blood-flecked spittle landed on his leggings and footwear. The fire in his cousin's eyes went from gloating to hate. Angus raised the jewel-encrusted blade high. The sword swung downward.

"I will see ye in that same hell one day, Angus."

Darach jerked with the blow, but welcomed the pain. He closed his eyes and reached for the welcome arms of death.

****

Darach jerked awake from the nightmare. His body as well as the bed was drenched in sweat. God's teeth, it had been months since he'd dreamed of that long-ago night in Scotland. A night when his entire world caved in around him. Instead of waking up in Heaven with his wife and child, as he'd been taught, he'd awakened on a different plane. It was there, while his mind was still accepting the fact he was alive yet his family was dead, the archangel Michael told him why he'd been denied the right to a heavenly home and reunion with his loved ones.

"Your death was untimely. These events were not supposed to happen. You were meant to do wondrous things for your clan. However, Lucifer used your honorable traits to hasten your death and prevent those acts of goodwill toward your fellow man. He interrupted God's plans for you. Now you have been chosen to be a part of a group of immortals."

"I didnae ask for this, and I dinnae think I want it. I would prefer to be reunited with my family."

"It is not in my power to grant you your wish. I *can* give you an immortal body. One that will be almost impossible to kill. It would take a powerful demon to take your life, or if you step out of God's grace and go rogue, then I will do the honors. Until then, you will be an emissary of justice."

"I suppose I dinnae have a choice?"

Michael shook his head sending locks of hair, black as night, flying. The smile on his lips told Darach the angel was amused.

"No, you don't. Once chosen by God for a job, it is best you just do it, or…"

Darach grunted. "I ken you will be giving me the facts of what I will be doing."

"Yes."

****

Darach tossed back the sheet and climbed out of bed. The rest of what Michael told him was simple: "Prevent as many crimes as you can and render justice to evil mortals and demons alike."

After several decades of training with other immortals, he'd been sent to Earth once again. For over a thousand years, he had followed Michael's edict, moving from city to city, country to country, until he had been assigned to New Orleans.

As he brushed his teeth and prepared for a shower, he wondered if immortal executioners ever got a vacation. He was tired—tired of death and tired of being incapable of preventing rapes, tortures, and murders. Although an emissary of God, he still couldn't be in more than one place at a time.

The water hit his body in a soothing pattern. It was early, but some crimes started before sunset, and he needed to be on the streets to prevent them. After toweling off, he slicked a hand through his hair and pulled on a pair of black pants and a loose tunic-like shirt. True, it was a bit old-fashioned for this day and time, but it allowed him free range of motion. Something he needed when he ran up against demons and other paranormal beings.

Of course *mortals* were the least of his problems. He usually glared at them and they ran, but more and more, the Devil commanded his minions to possess the bodies of mortals—men and women alike. Those who coveted evil and had even performed evil deeds in their past, and those who possessed an ever-present need to hurt others. That made it a lot harder to take them down. And Michael's order to try and preserve the soul if possible, in case the human happened to be an innocent used by Satan, was oftentimes hard to do.

Darach pulled on a long coat, and grabbed his weapon. The special loop on the inside of the material held his sword and concealed it as well. In bygone days, he'd worn the sword for all to see, but no longer. Modern day police authorities frowned on a weapon that could decapitate with one swing.

****

Abigail Dupree woke from the short nap she allowed herself after her day job, and before she went to her night job as a singer in the French Quarter. The dream she'd had still disturbed her. The young woman's screams echoed in her head. She'd fought with her attacker, and Abby knew from the woman's thoughts, she hoped help would arrive.

It wouldn't.

Abby knew that. All her dreams and visions entailed crime scenes where the victims were brutalized or murdered.

She ran a trembling hand across her sweat-beaded forehead. Grandmere knew about her visions, and it had helped to know someone else understood what she went through, but her beloved and only grandparent had died during Abby's last year in college. She'd inherited the old colonial house that sucked up money faster than the bayou soaked up mud. One of the reasons she'd taken a second job, and now, she needed to get up and get ready for that night job at a dinner club on Bourbon Street.

As she went through the motions of showering, layering on makeup, and fixing her hair, she converted the ordinary admin assistant persona into a nightclub singer. Casting a glance at the picture on her nightstand, she mumbled, "Grandmere, I miss you."

It had helped to have her grandmere to come home to after a date gone badly. And most of her dating forays turned out that way. She'd stopped going out her freshmen year at LSU. The taunts of one of the most popular jocks there still made her cringe. Of course back then she'd been full of the marvels of being with peers who didn't know anything about her.

Abby turned off thoughts of the past as well as all the lights except for the one leading into the entryway of her two-storied home. She pulled the heavy oak doors closed and then locked them both. The moon was on its way across the night sky, and she needed to hoof it to get to the club on time. Starting tomorrow, the Thanksgiving holiday would give her almost a week off from both her jobs.

She knew just what to do with her time. Nothing!

****

Darach materialized near Bourbon Street, one of his favorite haunts. Since he'd arrived in New Orleans a decade earlier, he'd had his share of natural disasters to contend with, as well as dealing with crime waves.

He strolled down the street passing Antoine's Restaurant, and made his way to a bar near the riverfront. Once inside, he took a seat at a table near the back.

"Evening Darach, your usual?"

"Yes, thanks Rae."

The Highlander Bar reminded him of taverns back in the day he was laird of his clan, before he married Briene and became a family man. Those were the good times he could think about without wanting to slash and hack to pieces everyone in sight. Even after a millennium, he still couldn't get the picture of his wife's and child's murders out of his head. Since becoming an immortal, Michael had given him plenty of gifts. Offerings that allowed him to take care of his needs. Even a created executioner needed a place to rest his head and at least two meals a day. Of course, the best gift of all had been the cessation of the nightmares he'd experienced night after night the first fifty years or so. Now, they came infrequently and for that Darach was grateful.

The waitress brought him a ginger ale spiked with whiskey. Michael wouldn't approve, but the archangel wasn't here dealing with the chaos of crimes.

"Anything else I can get you?" Rae shook her blonde hair back from too-slender shoulders and gave him a tired smile. The lass worked entirely too hard to support her lousy husband and three cute kids.

"No, I'm good." Darach reached into the pocket of his pants and pulled out a twenty-dollar bill.

"Still trying to buy a date, Darach?" Her flirtatious question was always the same whenever he tipped her.

"A mon can only hope." He pushed the bill across the table to Rae.

The smile she gave him told him how much she appreciated the tip before she started back to the bar.

"Rae, could ye wait just a moment?"

The waitress turned around, the hopeful gleam in her eyes dimmed a bit when Darach spoke. "Have you seen or heard of any strangers frequenting this bar or any others in the area?"

"I don't think we've had any new faces in here, not for a while anyway. I can't speak for some of the other places, but I can check with a friend of mine who works down the street."

Darach gritted his teeth. "If ye do, will ye let me know?"

Rae studied him for a moment, and then she blew a strand of bangs out of her eyes. "Sure thing, darling."

"Thanks, Rae."

"You're more than welcome, handsome. Now, if there's nothing else, I've got a couple of tables that need clearing."

Darach fished out another twenty and stuck it into the low-necked top Rae wore. "Put it away for the kids, okay?"

She caught his hand, kissed it, and then started

clearing the tables.

This pub was always his first stop at night.

It was as good a place as any to fish for information, and it reminded him of his long ago home and all he'd lost. Shaking off his thoughts, he finished his drink. Dark came early with winter and mischief and mayhem would abound tonight as it did every night.

****

Angus allowed the woman to slump to the floor, her lifeless and soulless body a reminder of what he'd missed after dying and being sentenced to hell. Her brief struggle before she succumbed fired his blood and lust, but could not satisfy his quest for vengeance—a retribution that could not come quickly enough to suit him. He instructed his demons to dump the body in the bayou. He wasn't ready to show his hand to his cousin.

Mortals lived in a world of fantasy, sin, and hope. For those who cried out for help, it was Michael's job to do all he could to keep them safe until they made a choice of commitment to grace or not. A job that became harder and harder every millennium.

Chapter Two

Abby pulled on her jacket, slid her purse strap over her shoulder, and pushed opened the door of the Night Owls' Club. She'd finished her second show, and it was past time to be at home. Thirty seconds out the door, she felt the cold of winter down to her bones, and the arctic tendrils turned her feet into cold blocks of ice in her non-practical high heels.

Her steps beat out staccato taps as she walked briskly along the path to her house. The evening carried an eerie feel to it, much like the dreams she'd had for the last several nights. Dreams were usually a forewarning of what was to come for Abby, and she hated them. Her life would be so much better if she didn't have the dreams and visions popping up at every turn. They manifested themselves in fragmented pieces of detail like a disjointed puzzle that could come to her asleep or awake. Yes, she hated them, and she hated herself for allowing one man, no, Jason had been just a boy who wanted to be grown, to make her feel she was a sideshow exhibit because she was different. And since that night, she'd made sure that no man got close to her again. If one even looked her way she froze him out and would continue to do so—no man was worth the agony of self-doubt and the guilt that came with her baggage.

She crossed over to the other side of the street where the streetlights glared brightly on the cracked sidewalks. A bit of the foreboding disappeared. About to breathe a sigh of relief, the air trapped itself in her lungs as one by one the brilliant orbs above her head winked out. Under different circumstances, she'd call it strange, but she knew better.

Her vision blurred and then kaleidoscoped into a sharp image. A young woman, the same one she'd dreamed about, lay supine on a dirty alley floor. Her round, terrified eyes struck a chord of horror inside Abby. She knew what was coming next. A man—no, a demon with eyes the color of blood would savagely rape and then kill his victim, sucking the very soul of the woman into his lungs. Abby shook her head, stomped her cold feet, and began to run.

Not this time! Abby might not want the visions but she was sick and tired of being a third party in another death and not do something about it.

She arrived in the alley a few blocks from where she'd had the vision. The woman lay on her back—Abby couldn't tell if she was dead or alive. Her attacker, a man in his forties or so with dank, dirty-blond hair, hovered over his victim.

Abby skidded to a halt about five feet from the man. His head turned slowly toward her, and she could see the blue of his eyes quickly change to crimson.

"Well, well, it looks as if I'll have two for the price of one tonight." The grin he gave her sent chills down her spine.

"I don't think so, demon. It's time you learned how to behave in public." Though her words were brave, Abby's hands shook as she fished a can of mace out of her bag and sprayed a steady stream straight into the flame-flickering pupils.

"OIEEEEE." The tortured scream would have curled her hair if she weren't running on adrenaline. She knew he would not be incapacitated for long, so she lifted her leg to kick him where it hurt. Man or demon they all screamed like girls when that part of their anatomy came under attack. Before she could kick the daylights out of him, the devilish entity slapped her across the face with so much force the pain ripped a flag of fire beneath her eye.

He'd recovered too quickly. The clout sent her body flying, and her head ricocheted off the ground. She saw stars.

Way to go, Abby, now you've done it. Made it mad and you without another weapon.

When her vision cleared the demon hovered over *her*. She drew her body in close to avoid touching the nasty piece of vermin. She didn't look forward to the physical contact, death, or to having her soul sucked from her body. What she needed now was a huge miracle to avoid becoming his next victim.

She raised her hands and curled her fingers into a weak attempt at a weapon. Maybe her nails would do a bit of damage before he killed her.

The demon leaned closer. The human body he'd appropriated carried the mingled odors of alcohol, smoke, and urine. He reached out a human hand that quickly changed to a scaly mass of tissue with claws attached.

Yuck. If she got out of this alive, Abby swore she'd start carrying a knife or a box cutter—anything sharp to cut off repulsive limbs. It'd been months since she'd confronted a demon face to face. And that last time she'd barely gotten away with her life. The almost invisible scar she carried on her upper thigh reminded her daily how vicious and poisonous a swipe from a demonic claw could be.

"Hey Ugly, don't you have anything better to do with your time than harass women? Or can't you get one without using your demon powers?"

When he leaned closer, she brought her knee up and kicked out with the pointed tip of her shoe.

The monster roared, but it didn't stop him from circling her neck with the gruesome appendage. Abby felt the slight drip of blood his touch caused. He squeezed tighter, and her vision blurred. Dammit, this was so not the way she planned on dying. Against her will, her lids began to close as she opened her mouth trying to suck in air. She grabbed his hand with both of hers and tried to pry it loose, she used her upper body in an effort to throw him off. Nothing worked.

Then a miracle happened. One moment his hand squeezed tighter, the next he was gone.

Abby slowly sat up, threw off the pain of being slam-dunked, shocked and scared spitless, and looked around. The demon lay, seemingly unconscious, about ten feet away. She didn't know what had happened, but it didn't matter. What did, was she now had a chance to get the young woman some help. After staggering gingerly to her feet, she realized one heel was broken. Abby tossed the useless shoes and approached the demon's prospective victim, all the time skirting as far as she could around his frame.

"Can you walk?"

The woman didn't answer. Her eyes were now closed, not like in her vision, and she looked unconscious. Abby dug her cell out of her purse. Her finger was on the first 9 of 9-1-1 when a mist shimmered across from her. As she watched, it morphed into the most enthralling, sensual man she'd ever seen.

Another demon?

Should she run?

Even as she stood frozen in place, Abby couldn't help but look in awe at the man before her, at least she hoped he was human and not demon.

Six-foot-six, or thereabouts. Without her shoes he looked even taller. His eyes were almost black but as she watched they went molten silver. Skin a golden bronze, the body of a pro-wrestler, and the face of an aged cover model completed the package. As she continued to stare and commanded herself not to drool, the black-haired avenger, for want of a better word, raised a sword. Where it came from, she had no idea. He approached the demon, but then stopped and glanced at her.

Abby felt like a bug as the giant of a man stared at her, his countenance a strong visage of determination. As she waited, the demon jumped to his feet and attacked the man. Again, the demon met the ground with what looked like a distinct lack of effort on the rescuer's part. The man now checked the woman on the ground. He touched her face with a gentle hand before turning back to the demon. The giant's furious gaze brimmed with metallic fire, and for one moment, it seemed as if he conveyed regret. One second he was motionless, the next his sword a blur of silver as he struck the attacker through the heart.

The demon's body turned into molecules of dust. And as she watched, a thin vapor floated toward the sky. Possibly, the soul of the human he'd inhabited.

So quickly did it happen, Abby's scream remained trapped in her throat as the man approached, his eyes now a soft onyx. When he sheathed the sword into a holder inside his long coat, she noticed the black shirt he wore hugged his muscular chest, and the leather of his pants and boots were silent as he drew near.

"Who are you?" she asked. Her question came out in a slow croak.

The young woman's question took Darach back as much as she seemed to be taken by him. When he'd sensed what was happening, he zeroed in on the scene before actually materializing. His resolve to stop the crime before the demon went further deepened when he realized there were two women involved. He'd been in danger of swallowing his tongue when this young woman came to the other's rescue. She had fought to protect the victim. Something you didn't see that often—one mortal helping another.

Not only fought but also tried to give as good as she got. But by the looks of her face and the circle of blood droplets around her throat she should have stayed out of it.

Now he was in a quandary. Never before had there been a witness to his executions. Fie, he should have put the woman in a deep sleep before he unleashed his sword.

Yet, for some reason, the petite but generously curved woman flustered Darach. It couldn't be her silver-blonde hair, nor could it be the softness in her eyes, the color of the lake by his birthplace—blue and vibrant. Possibly it was her courage, albeit misguided.

He looked toward the heavens and waited for some type of signal from Michael. What should he do with his witness? When no answer came, he made a snap decision.

He moved closer but stopped within a foot of her. "I ken what ye've seen is strange, but 'tis nothing but a dream. Ye will return to yer home, retire for the night, and then remember nothing in the morning." Darach reached out to touch the woman, but she jerked away.

"Get real, this isn't a dream."

Startled, he stepped back. Instead of doing as he asked, she seemed immune to his forceful suggestion. The concept astounded Darach. He punched in 9-1-1 on his cell phone, spoke a few words, and then grabbed the woman by the arm. He needed to do some damage control.

"We need to talk. Now, close your eyes."

Abby fought his touch, she didn't plan on going anywhere with this whatever he was, but the ground dissolved, and the air around her twirled in a dizzying dance. When all was still once more, she opened her eyes and found herself in an ornate size room with her rescuer...or would that be *kidnapper* now?

"Who are you, and how and why did you just snatch me out of that alley to this place?" She pulled herself from his arms and backed away just a bit, but then stood her ground.

His soft rasp of laughter shot straight to her heart and other regions. The sound of his amusement was so potent, the man or whatever he was, could rev a dead motor. And she didn't like that, not one bit. Handsome men could not be trusted. Especially not one who materializes out of thin air and carried a sword almost as long as her body.

"Ye were interfering with me job."

His accent was mesmerizing, yet the edge to his words caused Abby to see red. She'd been through enough tonight, and wasn't going to take any lip from Mr. Hot-but-Spooky.

"Oh please... What type of job allows you to go about killing demons and kidnapping people?" He moved a bit toward her, but she didn't back up nor would she back down.

"How did ye know he be a demon?" His question was a rapid command of sound.

When she didn't answer, he spoke again. "Ye might as well tell me, I'll be finding out one way or another."

For the first time, Abby felt a frisson of fear travel deep down her spine.

"And what does that mean, pray tell?"

He moved closer. To heck with bravery. Abby backed away a few feet.

"Okay, before something bad happens, don't you think I should at least know your name?"

"I dinnae see the need, but 'tis Darach MacRath. And I be not going to hurt ye. Your face and neck need to be looked after."

His accent thickened enough this time that if it weren't for all the Scottish romance novels Abby devoured in her spare time, she wouldn't have a clue as to what he just said.

"Nice to meet you. I'm Abby Dupree, and I'm fine."

"I wish I could say the same, but yer meddling may have caused more than a bit of trouble."

For a second he cocked his head, and it seemed as if he was listening to or for something. His brogue seemed to be back under control. A pity really, she could melt inside the butter-soft tone.

The Highlander reached out and touched her forehead before closing his eyes. Abby waited for something to happen, and when it didn't, against all common sense, she reached up and touched his palm.

"Okay, what's your game? You touch my forehead and what, I turned into a pumpkin?"

Darach opened his eyes. "Strange, 'tis not working. Ye should not be aware of anything that's happened since the alley."

"Oh, your touch is supposed to wipe my memory away?"

"Aye, something like that."

Strange how his accent seemed to resurface when he was a bit upset. "So, what now? You're going to let me go, tell me what's going on?" She waited but Darach remained silent.

Darach's puzzlement ran deep. Never before had he failed to wipe a memory. Still, this woman was different. She actually knew the attacker was a demon. Maybe if he tried to insert another memory it would work.

"Not yet." Again he reached out and touched the silken skin of her forehead. Nothing! The trouble could lie in the fact he was immensely attracted to the woman—something that never happened when he dealt with women. He wouldn't allow it—not after Briene.

"Okay, now that you've done the hocus-pocus thing and it didn't work, I want to go home."

Puzzled did not describe his feelings. Why was this woman taking everything he said in stride? If nothing else, she should at least be curious if not down right frightened by the night's events.

"Ye dinnae have any questions about what's happened?"

Abigail flung her hair forward and began to braid the mass of blonde strands falling around her face. "You mean the demon or you?" Her laughter was as musical as her soft southern accent.

"MacRath, I've lived in New Orleans all my life. I've been having visions since before I got my first bra. I'm not a stranger to fighting demons, although, I have to admit watching you do your appearing act and then spiriting me here was a bit unnerving, but hang around NOLA long enough and you see all kinds of things that would spook ordinary people." She fisted her hands on her hips. "I'm not one of them."

"Ye make a habit of accosting demons?" The woman was just a wee bit touched.

Again, Darach sent up a mental S.O.S to Michael. Still no answer. What choice did he have? He had to tell her the truth, swear her to secrecy, and hope she kept her word.

"Then I willna be telling ye a pack of lies. Have a seat, and I'll explain what I am and what I do."

"Fine." His guest took a seat on the high-back bench that served as a rough and uncomfortable couch.

Darach pulled the footstool from underneath the piano and placed it in front of Abby before seating himself.

"Would ye care for anything to drink?"

"Only if it's got a lot of liquor in it. It's been one heck of a night." Her laughter bubbled forth again. This time it caressed his insides with a warmth he'd forgotten ever existed.

"I can get ye some whiskey."

"That would work, but I think I'll wait until after your story." She cocked her head to one side. "Not only do you have an impressive Scottish accent, but your speech is definitely old-fashioned. Only it seems to come out in spurts, like you don't always use it."

Darach wished for a drink himself. The woman would probably think him mad. And what sane person wouldn't?

"'Tis complicated, and ye will probably think me a bit loony, but I fear I have no choice." He cleared his throat, and then allowed the words to flow.

"I was born over a thousand years ago in Scotland. I lived and died there also."

****

He gnashed his teeth as he reviewed the report one of his committee brought to him. The woman who had interfered was interesting, but the man who saved both her and another from Baras made him want to retch. A thorn in his side for what seemed like an eternity was stronger than he'd been told. It would be hard to bring Darach down, but he would and it would be a fitting and final end.

Note to self: I must remember not to interfere in what happens in the mortal world. All will work as it should by grace.

From the desk of Michael/Archangel to God

Chapter Three

Darach paused to see how Abigail was taking his words.

Her eyes opened wider, and her hands trembled slightly where she held them in her lap. The soft material of her dress caressed her thighs. Darach wondered if she bespelled him for he wanted to be the covering on her body. Sex was not something he'd thought of often since he'd awakened from the dead, and not something he and his boss Michael had ever discussed. Would he be breaking any rules if he did indulge with the beautiful Abigail?

"You died there?"

"Aye, me cousin Angus slaughtered my family and myself. I know 'tis hard to believe, but I was chosen to be an immortal. To stop crimes and punish those who commit them, not to mention ridding the world of demons. The archangel Michael gave me no choice in the matter. And that's what I've been doing ever since."

Abigail stood up and began to pace the room's circumference.

After a bit, she stopped and turned toward Darach.

"You certainly know how to fabricate a good story. Did you pull your text from a romance novel? I mean, immortals, really?"

"I do not lie." He stood up also and moved to the cupboard where he kept a few bottles of scotch. He supposed it had been too much to hope she'd believe him. After pouring several fingers of the golden liquor into a silver goblet, he allowed himself the pleasure of taking a few deep gulps.

"I'd go easy on the booze, Mr. Immortal Man, I would think the *archangel* might not be happy with your indulgence."

"A sheep's testes on what he thinks."

Almost to an instance of his last word being uttered, Darach found himself in the presence of Michael.

"You forget who holds your life in their hands, Highlander."

Michael's eyes glowed with a fiery gold blaze. Perhaps he *should* have kept his mouth shut and then again…

"I forget nothing, Michael. Not the deaths, the executions, nor the fact I asked your advice and ye ignored me."

"I was in conference with *my* boss, and he comes way before you do, Darach."

Darach, angry as he was, could not dispute that fact.

"Agreed. Now would ye mind telling me what I'm supposed to do with that woman?"

"Not what you want to do."

Heat burned on his face as well as inside his body when he realized Michael had ascertained his lust toward Abby.

"If ye stayed out of me mind, ye wouldn't know this."

"Right again, immortal man, as she called you, but I have to know what is going on inside your head. And while I'm happy something has finally creased the machine you've become over the centuries, you will not act upon your lust for Abigail Dupree."

"Why not?" He knew he was taking his life in his hands, and only an hour before he would have welcomed the chance to die but something about Abigail made him want to explore the essence that made her who she was.

"Abigail seems to be one of a kind in her city. Although, we know there are others who can see what normal mortals can't, she is the only one willing to admit or act upon it. And she is an innocent in the ways of men. Leave her alone."

Darach shot Michael a look that could get him more than an admonishment.

Michael continued without acknowledging. "She is already under surveillance by the demon world. You are to protect her only. To show more will be a red alert to Angus and his kind. You do not want him to touch her as he did Briene."

"Angus? Angus is dead!"

"Technically he is, but he's also a demon."

"How can that be? I saw his grave. He should be smoldering in hell." Darach was so agitated his hands shook.

Michael smiled slightly. "He *was* in hell. It seems he begged Satan for a chance to prove himself and now he's topside."

Before Darach could assimilate that information, Michael spoke again.

"Now he's after you."

"Why? As far as he knows I *am* dead. Remember, he killed me and why be I just finding this out now?"

"Yes, of course I remember." Michael's tone was a symphony of sympathy and a bit of ire. "You have to remember, Darach, demons have been dying by your hand and other immortals' for centuries. You have exceeded what I thought you could do. In doing so, you have earned the hatred of all of hell's minions. And as for Angus, I just got the memo myself. He's only been out a couple of days, but he's already wreaking havoc.

Rage escalated and fought to be released inside Darach. His fists clenched, and his teeth ground together to keep it under control.

"Darach, we can't mess this up. Abby is important because of her gift, and she is special—more special than I am at liberty to say for the moment. Do all you can to keep her safe.

"I know that you have for the most part abstained from the urges of a man since I've known you or if you haven't you've been discreet, but I need you to keep your mind on Abby's protection. Try not to give in to your baser needs. That's an order from higher than me."

"Michael, why me? Can't ye get another immortal to protect her?" He dreaded to hear Michael's answer. If he said yes, then Darach would not be able to see her. And since his fellow friends and immortals were devastatingly handsome to the female mortal population or so the rumors went, he'd rather not have them guarding Abby. And if the archangel said no, he would be in a world of hurt trying to keep his lust under wraps.

"No, it has to be you. You've dealt with more demons then some of the other immortals. And to pull you away from NOLA at this time would just raise suspicion. Besides, Abby will be the instrument you will need to capture Angus."

"Capture? Not kill?"

"Correct."

Rage over being denied a chance to even the score with Angus ignited something deep inside Darach. He would not stand by without seeing Angus pay for what he did to his family, his life, and to so many others—now that the piece of scum was a demon and on his turf.

"Judgment for Angus will come from elsewhere, not you, Darach. You are to take him down and then bring him to me."

"And if I should find and capture him, how do ye suppose I get him here without killing him?"

"You will have to decide that for yourself." Michael stood up and moved from behind his desk. "In the meantime, you need to make certain you keep Abigail safe. Stick with her every possible moment."

"I willna allow him to kill another woman because of me." His anger ebbed, replaced by terror and loathing at the past possibly resurrecting itself.

"For the reasons I've already disclosed to you, you will do as you've been instructed. Guard the mortal woman, capture Angus, and if you need my help, then call me. That is all, Darach."

Before he could respond, Darach was back in the room with Abby. By her frantic and disbelieving stare, he could have only been gone a few moments.

"What happened? Where did you go?"

"Ye wouldna believe me if I told ye."

"Try me." Abby refused to allow the quaking inside her limbs to manifest in her hands. This was not a time to show the terror she'd experienced when Darach disappeared. She didn't know where she was or how to get home.

"Michael took umbrage with me remark about the sheep's balls. He wanted to have a chat."

"Ahh. Tell me what he said."

"That I'm to capture a demon and keep me hands off of ye in the bargain."

Abby's lungs expelled a gulp of air, and she forced her trembling legs to walk back to the bench she'd vacated earlier. Once there, she looked up at Darach. "Why would he mention me, and how does he know me?"

"Believe this, Michael knows everything about everybody."

"How could an angel even mention something about you keeping your hands to yourself. I mean, it's preposterous."

"What is? That he could know, or that I have been indulging in lustful thoughts about ye?" Darach's grin was magnetic, although a bit wolfish. And definitely dangerous. *Remember, Abby, he's dark, handsome, and not to be trusted.*

After his disappearing act, she was prone to believe he was possibly what he said he was—an immortal but still…

"Both." How she got that one word past her lips, she had no idea. But for some reason, the second part of her question was far more important than the first. She wondered if he would lie.

"As I said before, he knows everything. He has God's ear or so he says, and I believe him. As for the thoughts about ye, he be right."

Abby's mouth opened to ask more, but Darach moved in a blur of dark and light. His lips were now centimeters away from hers.

Michael, you owe me this one thing before I do as you ask. His lips barely touched hers…

Darach! The warning came a second before Darach's body went sailing across the room. The landing wasn't all that hard, but a lesson. Michael could kill him without blinking an eye. For the moment, the archangel was just irked.

Darach peeled himself away from the dented wall, shrugged his shoulders, and then moved to Abby.

"Come, I will take ye home. I'm not sure why, but it seems we will be housemates."

"I don't think so, MacRath."

The fire in her gaze re-kindled the one Michael so successfully put out.

"Ye have no choice. Michael says ye are to be protected, and I can only do that if we be together."

Abigail drew back from his touch. He couldn't blame her. She'd had a lot thrown at her in the last hour.

"Our living together is so *not* going to work."

"I agree, but ye will just have to trust me when I say, I promise to keep me hands to myself."

"Look, as far as I'm concerned, you're certifiably insane. I'm still not sure I believe your cock-and-bull story about being an immortal." The woman paused for breath, and the movement expanded her diaphragm and caused her breasts to rise and fall. "Who is it you're supposed to protect me from?"

His black eyes turned silver. She wondered if they went that beautiful color when he made love.

"From a demon that loves nothing better than to rape and kill women and children."

Abby's heart froze for a beat and then restarted. "Please tell me this has nothing to do with the man that killed your family."

Darach reached out and pulled her close.

"Hey, what happened to no touching?" Her lips trembled with fear and desire.

"Do ye want the truth or a lie?" His words were terse, and the mesmerizing stare he gave her told her he would answer whichever way she preferred."

She knew she should probably say lie, but if a demon was after her, Abby would rather know what was going on and take measures to stop it.

"Truth."

The look he gave her was one of respect.

"Very well, then ye shall have it. According to Michael, ye have drawn the interest of a few demons. Why? It could be because ye have visions and because ye chose to take on a demon yourself earlier. At the moment, Michael's main concern is to make sure ye stay safe."

"Great, the first time I get involved in a long time, and I draw the attention of a demon. Not what I had in mind at all." Abby knew her words were a bit hysterical, but geez, it had not been a great night.

"Ye will be okay. I will make sure Angus cannae touch you." His words helped some but not a lot. After all he was an immortal or so he said.

"Thanks, but how can I believe you're who you say you are? I mean I know there are other things in the world besides demons. Entities most people can't see, but how do I know you're one of the good guys?"

Darach's laughter took her by surprise. Instead of frowning at her like she just knew he would, he seemed to find it amusing.

"Hey, this is not funny!" She tried to free herself from his grip.

"Relax, I'll let ye go in a few minutes. I kin what I've told ye and what you've seen if only by watching me fly across the room, that ye kin there is a force directing me. Aye, it sounds preposterous, and to be honest, if I be in your shoes, I'd feel the same way."

Abby watched the amusement disappear from his dark gaze. "If I wasn't a good guy, first off, you'd already be naked in me bed, and second, worst case scenario, you'd be dead."

The breath left her lungs about the same time he tightened his grip on her waist.

"I need to get ye home. Any other questions can wait until later."

Abby's open-mouthed stare drew Darach's attention to her lips. He wanted to... Instead he nuzzled the soft swath of her hair with his chin, and allowed himself a moment of pleasure wondering about the what-ifs before waving his hand and his body prepared itself for the teleportation.

His mumbled, "I be not sure if this woman will be the death of me or not," was met with a loud feminine, "Hmmp!"

Darach's smile came unbidden at Abby's ferociousness. A smile that disappeared as the vortex of transference took him and Abby, and did not resurface when they entered her home.

Someone had been there. The sulfuric stench caused a feeling of dread to roil up inside his belly.

The demon underworld had wasted little time in tracking Abby. Michael's words came back to haunt him. Angus was probably not far behind and would do all in his power to strike against another innocent.

Darach pushed away the thoughts of Briene and Jamie. He would need more than his wits about him to do his job. And do it he would, just maybe not the way Michael wanted. He had been cheated out of revenge centuries ago, but if he got the chance to kill Angus for what he'd done, then Michael would have to exact justice on Darach for he would not just turn over Angus for judgment. And God have mercy on Abigail if he failed.

****

Angus clasped his hands together in glee. His sources should be reporting in soon on Darach's whereabouts. His cousin had disappeared without a trace, but he would find him, and if it took a while, then he had other plans in mind to keep himself occupied and to flush his despised kin out into the open.

Michael tossed his quill pen down, a holdout before mankind created more up-to-date writing utensils. He supposed he could get a computer, be savvier as some of the younger angels teased him, but he liked the old ways the best. Besides, tonight he was not in the mood to pen a note in the journal he kept—Satan's demons were planning something, and he wanted to know what it was.

Chapter Four

"What's wrong?" Abby hesitated to ask the question, but Darach's frozen form scared her spitless. The man could put down a demon without blinking one of those gorgeous dark eyelashes, but as soon as he transported them to her house, he went all arctic.

"Can ye not smell that?" His eyes were still glacial orbs, and his countenance looked like it would crack if he smiled.

"Smell what?" All she could smell was the delectable aroma of sandalwood and musk oozing from the man's pores. At his impatient wave toward the circumference of her living room, Abby sniffed deeply.

"Stinks like rotten eggs a bit, but odors are ripe here in New Orleans. With the bayous and the marshes not that far away, and a good breeze we get all kinds of scents."

Darach spoke again as he moved out into the hallway, and Abby followed on his heels. "Aye, but there's only one way to get a true sulfuric smell, and that's from a demon."

She stopped so quickly she almost lost her balance. "Are you trying to tell me there was a demon in my house?"

"No, I'm telling you there were at least two if not three by the combined and slightly different odors."

"So…what do we do? We need to do something." She hated the slight tremor to her words, but knowing demons had invaded her home—her sanctuary against the world—gave her the shakes. Abby would much rather fight them off her home turf. How had they found her?

"*We* do nothing. I will make sure they are no longer here, but ye are to stay put."

She opened her mouth to tell him to bite her only to have him close it with a gentle grip on her chin.

"I mean it, Abigail. Ye cannot jump into the thick with these creatures. They will kill ye and…"

"Yes, I know. Take my soul, but Darach, they were or are in my house. I will not allow them to stay without a fight."

He tugged her closer and slid his arms around her. "Aye, ye be a right brave lass, but 'tis better at times to wait." Tears came unbidden and she blinked them back. She would not give into her rage and fear. Besides like it or not, she now had a keeper.

A keeper who unsettled her almost as much as the demons.

"Everything will be all right, Abigail. I willna let them hurt ye—ever."

With her face muffled against his chest, she could only nod acknowledgement of his promise. She knew she shouldn't feel this way, and he was totally not the type of guy she could ever entertain real emotion about, but she wanted to stay in his arms forever. For the first time since losing her grandmere, she felt a kinship with another. She reveled in the feeling, but then he pushed her away.

"Darach?"

"Although, I be sure they probably left when we arrived, I need to check the house, and then we'll talk."

Before she could say another word, he was gone. Poof, no warning, no nothing. After a moment or two she heard footsteps overhead.

Not sure what to do now or how long Darach would be, Abby decided to head to the kitchen, but first... She darted into the downstairs bathroom and tugged off her ruined panty hose. A quick wash with a cloth removed some of the dirt from her abused feet, and then she went in search of sustenance. Did Darach eat food? If so what kind?

She was slapping ham and cheese on top of a hoagie bun when the man in question popped up right in front of the oak kitchen table.

Abby almost swallowed her tongue but managed to keep the scream begging to escape inside her throat.

"I wish you wouldn't do that."

"Why?" Darach's mood seemed to have lightened if the cocked eyebrow and half-smile on his sensual lips were any type of indicators.

"Because I could have thrown this knife at you." She held up the serrated blade resting beside the sandwich fixings to make her point.

"It wouldn't kill me, so—"

"What do you mean?"

"I'm immortal, remember?" Darach looked like he wanted to smirk.

"Yes, but...even immortals have an Achilles' heel right?"

"Ye watch too much television, Abby, but the knife would have hurt a bit, so thanks for not throwing it." He tossed her a full-fledged grin.

She wanted to be just a bit incensed at his smug

attitude, but couldn't. For some reason, his teasing caused a flicker of warmth to spread from her toes to between her thighs, before finding a home inside her heart.

"I read more than I do anything, and I only watch one television show."

"Probably the one where a Highlander gets to cut off people's heads, but is always in danger of losing his."

Her face heated as she realized she had thought Darach to be a true-to-life Duncan McLeod in some ways. "Well, I, uh..."

"It's okay. I know how strange this is for ye, and God's truth, for me also. You're the first mortal that I actually can't wipe my memory from their mind."

Abby finished putting together the sandwiches, sprinkled a glob of chips on each plate, and then motioned for Darach to sit.

"I'm assuming you can eat?"

"Yes, immortals can eat."

"Good, then after you finish, I want to hear about why I'm different, and about what you do as an immortal."

****

Darach finished the last bite of his sandwich, and washed it down with a deep gulp of iced tea. Abby had finished her food a good five minutes before. Anticipation of learning more about the sensual, exciting Highlander had caused her to choke her food down like a starving rat.

He, however, ate with the niceties you would expect from a royal personage. She wished he would get on with it. Curiosity was beating a fast refrain inside her brain.

"Are ye ready for me to begin?" The smile he sent her was positively full of mischief. Darn the man, he knew she was on the edge of her seat, literally.

"If you don't, I'm liable to conk you on that big Scottish head of yours."

"Ye have a bit of a violent streak, Abby. Something I saw earlier tonight with the demon. Which reminds me, ye should never go after a demon with mortal weapons. And ye never did clean your throat."

Abby wanted to pull her and his hair out. "Okay, I'm a bit impetuous, so why don't *you* tell me what type of weapons I should have with me in the future. As to my throat, I will take care of it, but not now."

"Ye willna be needing a weapon, I will protect ye."

His statement irritated Abby, but at the same time a part of her was just a tiny bit thrilled. It seemed immortal or not, a man always had the attitude of protecting the little woman—whether they needed it or not. Of course to be fair, he had saved her butt from the demon, but he needed to know she wasn't some frightened babe in the woods.

"I beg to differ. If I'd had a knife I could have done some serious damage, and besides, you can't protect me twenty-four-seven, Darach."

"Ye will be protected at all times, Abby."

"You're missing the point. Maybe I don't need a keeper. I have managed to take care of myself for over..." Abby decided he didn't really have to know she was over thirty. "And what about when you're asleep? You do sleep don't you?"

Darach frowned, but answered, "*Aye*, I do sleep, but 'tis usually during the daylight hours. However now I will be sleeping at night in your bed with ye."

The moment the words left his mouth, Darach knew he was in trouble. Not only Michael's faint yell from above signaled he'd said the wrong thing, but the thunderstorm brewing in Abby's blue gaze foretold he would be in for a fight.

"Think again, Mr. Immortal Man. I sleep alone."

When he opened his mouth to ask why, she continued. "By choice, and I'm not happy you've been assigned to stick to me like gum on a shoe, but I do understand the need—for now. However, we need some ground rules." Abby shot him a look he could only interpret as stubborn.

"And number one, you will be sleeping on the couch not in my bed."

Darach could think of a lot of reasons to be in Abby's bed. The most important was he yearned for her as he hadn't lusted for a woman in a thousand years. Whether or not it was because she knew what he was and wasn't afraid, or the fact she was not an ordinary woman, or the fact she gave as good as she got, it didn't matter. The bottom line was she fascinated him.

And although, he didn't plan on taking her to bed that way, he would welcome the chance to hold her close during—

God's teeth! What was he thinking? He had a job to do, and his newly awakened emotions had no place in his quest to keep Abigail safe or to find and capture Angus. *And most importantly, kill him.*

"Besides, if you're that concerned, why can't you do some type of magic? Protect the house from demons without you having to sleep here?" Abby's voice broke into his thoughts.

"I can do that—"

"Then there's no need for you to be sleeping anywhere near me. You can just pop back home."

"But I won't." Darach finished the sentence Abby had interrupted. However in truth, it would be for the best if he didn't stay with her. The temptation of being close to her while she slept, if not squashed by both Abby and the archangel, could get him into real trouble.

"What do you mean, you won't? You said you could do some hocus pocus thing and I'd be safe inside the house. So why on Earth would you insist on spending the night here?" Abby's question ended in a shrill treble.

"Look, I have a boss, who says I have to stick to ye like white on rice, so that's what I'm going to do." He held up a hand to stop what would be another argument but it didn't stop Abby. He wondered if anything would except for an act of God.

"Well, you're not staying in my room."

"Fine by me, Ms. Stubborn-as-a-Fence-Post." His breathing grew rapid as he tried to quell the anger her words caused. You'd think he was a monster. But then again, she could see him that way. "Now, why don't ye show me where I *can* sleep."

Darach crossed his arms and waited on Abby to acknowledge his words or do something.

Although, she'd gotten what she wanted, Abby couldn't decide why she felt a bit ticked. He'd given in way too easy for her self-esteem. A bit of an argument would have been nice. Maybe Michael had something to do with it—then again, it could be he just decided she was a job and nothing else. And anyway, it didn't matter. She did not need or want a man in her life, especially not someone who fought demons for a living. She would much rather keep the female legacy in her family for fighting the creatures on the downside.

Still, it seemed they were stuck with one another, and since she didn't want to live in a war zone in her own home she decided to take the high road.

"Tomorrow's Thanksgiving. I plan on cooking so I'll be up fairly early. Is there anything you want in particular for breakfast?"

For just a split second his black gaze went silver. Not sure what that was about, Abby decided to get the couch made up and then hit the bed before her guest changed his mind about their sleeping arrangements. She had a lot of questions about how he came to be an immortal, but they could wait until the morning. Her eyes were gritty from lack of sleep, and her body was beginning to ache big-time from her encounter with the demon. A hot shower, and then a few hours of shut-eye would make her a new woman.

"I'm be not fussy about food. Anything ye prepare will be fine with me."

"Well, then, great." Abby turned her back and moved to mount the stairs. She removed a sheet, blanket, and fresh pillowcase from the linen closet and then grabbed a pillow off of her bed before returning downstairs to Darach.

The immortal reached to take the items from her, but he was a guest in her home even if she didn't want him to be and her grandmere had taught her manners.

"I've got it. It'll just take a minute to get everything ready."

And in that same time frame, Abby smoothed the pillow out and laid it on the couch. "There's a bathroom right off the kitchen if you need it. It has fresh towels and a shower." For the first time since she started making the bed, she looked him in the eyes.

"I'm going to grab a shower myself. Make yourself at home, Darach. I might not be happy about you being here, but I do appreciate you wanting to protect me."

She turned to leave, but Darach caught her hand. "Abby, Angus willna stop at nothing to get back at me. I truly am here to keep ye safe."

"I know, but I can't quit living my life because of fear."

"And ye shouldna. Just allow me to make sure ye stay safe until Angus is caught."

The look in his gaze sent tendrils of warmth

throughout her body. He really seemed to care. Again, dangerous territory.

"Fine, but you have to allow me to go about my business. I can't stay locked up. I need to go back to work after the holiday."

"As you wish. We can talk about that in the morning."

"Good night, Darach."

He placed a kiss on the top of her hand before letting it go. "Good night to you too, Abby."

****

Darach punched his pillow once, twice, and then a third time. Nothing seemed to help. He couldn't sleep. It was a pity neither he nor Abby had taken into account that his body was longer than the couch.

After an hour of tossing and turning, he'd tried sleeping on the floor, still no rest in sight. Even with being an immortal his body still required all the normal things a mortal man did. Sleep was not something he took for granted. Although he was nigh on invincible, he needed to stay as sharp as possible in his fight against demons. Angus in particular.

From the moment the man had arrived at MacRath Castle, claiming to be a cousin on his father's side, he'd been a thorn in Darach's side. Always arguing over how to defend the castle, which raids to go on, who to accept as allies, Darach was at the point of asking him to leave when he was called away to handle business several clan territories away. It was then, Angus tried to take over the lairdship. Upon returning, Darach banished Angus from MacRath lands. For a while there was peace, he and Briene married and even after Jamie's birth and the years following, Angus stayed gone from their lives.

Darach punched the pillow harder this time. He

had been a fool. He should have known Angus would not give up his fight to take all Darach held dear—as he did that cold winter night.

He shook off thoughts of the past and climbed off the couch. He needed to move, to think about where Angus could be, and what he would do in reference to Abigail.

Chills dotted his naked arms as he forced back the vision of his son and Briene's murder, the rape with Abigail becoming the victim.

He headed to the kitchen. He needed coffee to clear his mind, and to wake him up to the early hues of sunrise. A few moments later, he found what he needed, and soon coffee poured into the glass carafe of Abigail's coffeemaker.

Darach took a sip of the dark chicory-vanilla bean mix and sighed. Michael should have let another immortal guard Abigail. Then he would be free to hunt Angus without the fear that he would lead him straight to her.

He wondered if he implored Michael for another face-to-face meeting if he could change the archangel's mind.

"Darach?" Abigail's soft tone cut his thoughts in two.

"I'm in here."

He heard the lighter-than-down pads of her feet as she moved toward the kitchen.

"Morning. What are you doing up so early?"

A smile he couldn't stop found its way to his lips. Abigail dressed up as she was the night before was indeed a sensual delight, but this softer version made him want to tug her close and hold her beneath his heart.

Her silver mane of hair was tousled, her blue eyes held the remainders of sleep, and her cheeks were rosy from her slumber.

The pink robe she wore over her nightdress

reminded him of cotton candy, a delicacy he'd discovered a few decades before. Her feet were encased in bunny slippers making him think of a child on Christmas morning.

Yet, when she moved closer to grab a cup from the cupboard, the womanly scent of musk and jasmine drove home the fact she was a beautiful, sensual woman. One he needed to distance himself from.

"I decided to make coffee." His excuse was lame even to his ears.

Abigail's body moved a fraction closer to him as she poured her coffee, and then rooted in the cabinet for a small packet of sugar.

Darach moved to the table, pulled out a chair, and straddled it—ignoring the hard bulge inside his pants.

"You don't exactly strike me as the domestic type."

"Ye have no idea what type of immortal I am or the type of man I was." Darach's lust rode him hard and his words were clipped, almost harsh, but he didn't care. Abigail Dupree was a job, nothing more—he dared not allow her to be anything else. His goal was to find Angus and exact his revenge.

Abigail bit her tongue to keep from lashing out at Darach. His words were cutting, but she'd glimpsed just a bit of hurt in his gaze. Strange, how his eyes would go from black to almost silver in sequence with his mood.

He'd told her earlier, that his family had been killed. Maybe he needed to talk about what happened. She shook her head; the past was over a thousand years gone, if his story was true. Would it still bother him after all this time?

She added the sugar to her coffee and then seated herself across from Darach. Before she spoke, she took the time to admire his naked chest. Lord, he was put together so fine and she so wanted to touch the flesh his missing shirt had covered, but that was ludicrous. The immortal was her bodyguard, nothing more.

"You're right, so why don't you tell me about the real Darach—before and after you were changed into an immortal."

For a moment, she thought he hadn't heard her request. He took another sip of coffee, placed the mug on the table, and then cleared his throat.

"'Tis not a pretty story, Abigail. Ye would be better off letting the past die. We all would."

She could do that, probably should, but something inside Abby needed to know what made Darach tick. If he truly did mean to guard her day and night until Angus was caught, then it would help to know more about him.

"And somehow I don't think you have let it go. I truly want to know about your lives, Darach. Maybe it will help you to talk about it."

His snort came right before a harsh laugh.

"Nothing helps the pain of what happened."

Sorrow turned his eyes into a silver pool and made Abby want to yank out her tongue. Who was she to ask him to relive the horror of the past?

"Look, I'm sorry. I should never have asked. It's really none of my business."

As Darach continued to gaze at her, it looked as if he fought and then won a battle within his mind.

****

Angus loved the holidays of mortals. They tended to let their guards down. Full of goodwill, they tried to make up for the other days of the year when they were slothful, vindictive, and allowed themselves to be directed by his boss.

This year he planned to have his own celebration.

Taunting Darach had always been fun, but now

he would give the Highlander a warning he could not ignore.

In doing so, he hoped to unleash the inner beast of the immortal for his own gain.

Do not allow the tragedies of mortals to sway me from my tasks. I cannot change the past, nor can I direct my immortals to always do what is prudent. After all they do have free will just like any creature created by God.

From the desk of Michael/Archangel to God

Chapter Five

"No, ye be wrong. It's because of my past that ye are now drawn into the aftermath." He took another sip of coffee and with the cup still in his hand he spoke again.

"I was groomed to take over as laird from the time I was old enough to read. My mother believed in all her children knowing how to write, read, and cipher. I know my people have been depicted as being a backward and wild bunch of barbarians in history, but that's not the case of my home life."

Abigail held her breath as Darach paused, looked down at his now cold coffee, and then back at her.

"My childhood was a good one. I learned from me da about taking care of the needs of our clan before my own. From me mother, how to teach those who would become the future of the clan. By the time I reached marriage age, I was more than a bit finicky about the type of bride I wanted by my side.

"Briene was a vision of loveliness even though she never thought herself to be beautiful. I courted and won her hand in marriage, and spent the first year of our life together teaching her she was beautiful inside and out." Darach cleared his throat.

"You see, she wasn't as fortunate as I was to be raised by a family who loved her. Her da was mean spirited and showed it in ways that reduced my bride into a shy, insecure person when it came to anything, especially having a man love her. Finally, I convinced her she was the most important thing in my life. I reveled in her first hesitant smiles, then the full-bloom of happiness as she realized the truth about herself. When she told me she carried our child, I couldna hae been happier than if I had been handed the moon."

Abby pushed aside her cup of coffee and slid her hands under the table. She clasped them tightly together to keep them from shaking. The being sitting across from her was indeed a man. One who had loved and lost but continued to try to protect others. She dreaded to hear the remainder of his story, but she needed to know everything. Maybe then she could help him. For no matter what he said, his past was still very much a part of his present and like it or not, she was involved.

"Jamie was born and my heart rejoiced in having an heir to carry on the clan's name. Ye see, me da had died just a few months after Briene and I were wed. Me mom still lived but she loved me da so much, it was not long before she followed him through death's gates. For almost two years, Briene and I loved, laughed, and dreamed of having more children. As we watched Jamie take his first steps, speak his first words, we couldna been more blessed."

"Where does Angus come into this? Did he live with you and Briene?" Abby held her breath after asking.

Darach's sigh assaulted the air with a warm breath of vanilla.

"Not at that time, not anymore. He came calling

a few months before me da's death. He claimed to be a cousin on me da's side of the family. Although, me da couldna recall the kinship Angus claimed, he be not the type of man to toss him out into the cold. By then his health had grown precarious, and I had taken over the reins in everything but the title of laird.

"Angus argued with me on every facet of the clan's business. He wanted war and I wanted peace. When I journeyed to neighboring clans, he made his move. With my da bed-bound, there was no one to stop him from involving himself in the daily running of MacRath Castle. When I returned, I found me kinsmen up in arms, Angus ensconced in my da's chair, giving orders that could lead us into battle."

"So what did you do?" Even though it was way too early for a drink, Abby wished for one. The more Darach talked the more she knew in her heart Angus was a demon she never wanted to meet face to face.

"I tossed him off MacRath land. I didnae care where he went as long as he never returned to our clan. In the interim, I married Briene and Jamie was born. One night during Yuletide, Briene and I were sitting in the great hall. We were talking about how much Jamie would love this season of good cheer. While we watched him sleep in the small bed I made for him for when he was in the hall, I heard the sound of fighting at the doors of the castle. Before I could see what was happening, Angus and his men broke into the great hall. There were fifty of them if not more. Too many for the rest of my men to fight, for I had sent several of our men to deliver Yuletide gifts and food to the needy on the outskirts of our land..." Darach closed his eyes for a moment.

Should she call a halt to his story or allow him to finish?

He took the matter into his own hands when he

opened his eyes and reached across to brush a tear from her cheek.

"'Tis not a tale for the meek and gets worse, Abigail. If ye prefer, I can stop."

"It's your call. I don't want to cause you more anguish." Her words were a mere whisper, but he heard them all the same.

"The anguish is knowing Angus has broken free of hell's domain and is out to hurt another innocent. So I will finish what I have started."

She laid her hands on the table. She wanted something more sturdy then her lap to grip. Darach caught one of them in his.

"Angus and his men surrounded us, separating me and Briene from our son, and then from one another. I yelled at him, asking what he wanted, but before I could get an answer, his men forced me to my knees. I could hear Briene screaming, struggling to get free. Our son was now awake and crying.

"I fought my captors but there were too many. Of course, Angus didnae allow them to do his dirty work. He took great delight in stabbing me with my own sword. Three times he stabbed me and left me lying on the rush-strewn floor."

The grip on her hand tightened, and Abigail turned her grimace into a moue of shock. Not hard to do, since his entire story was horrendous. How could one person wreak such pain on another? And how had Darach survived, but then again he hadn't.

"The blood loss worsened as I continued to try to break free of Angus's men. Briene had turned deathly pale, and she was now on the floor—stretched out like an offering for Angus. I fought harder, and his men used the flats of their swords to keep me down. I tried to find Jamie. I knew if I could help him, Briene would fight. Though what good it would have done any of us if we had gotten free I didnae kin.

"My men were dead or dying, the others too far away to return in time. Finally my gaze found me son. I looked right into his frightened eyes and witnessed the exact moment Angus cut the life from his body."

Darach stopped and took several deep breaths. Abby tried to gulp in air and almost strangled on her horror. How much more could there be?

"Angus then moved to Briene, all the time making sure I witnessed his every movement. He raped her, then gave her to his men. She died and I couldna do nothing to stop it. By that time, I didnae care if I lived or not. I just wanted a chance to take Angus to hell with me. I was denied that wish, for coward that he be, even with me being wounded, he wouldna fight me as a man. He again used my family's sword to send me to death."

"Oh, Darach, I'm so sorry. Nothing I can say will help. I'm sorry to have put you through this." Tears stung Abby's cheeks, and the sobs she held back had a chokehold on her throat.

"Ye did nothing it's all in the past. I just want ye to understand Angus is all that is evil. If it means going through ye, to get to me he will. That is why I must stay here. He was conniving as a mortal and will be even more so as a demon."

"Surely, he won't trouble himself with me. You and I just met. There'd be no reason for him to come after me." She prayed that was the truth.

"The only reason he needs is the slightest hint that ye could be important to me."

Abby wanted to scream. Coming on the heels of Darach's terrifying tale, the knowledge that Angus might do the same thing to her as he had Briene scared the daylights out of her. If she was smart, she'd leave NOLA until Darach and Angus killed one another.

No...she couldn't.

To take the easy way out would be to deny her heritage. A heritage of many generations of her family's women helping others, fighting demons when they could.

"Then wouldn't it be better if you left me alone?"

"I wished it could be that easy, Abby. I dinnae ken how Lucifer knew about your gifts or how Angus got out of Hell. Knowing him, he promised Satan something in return. I can guess what that something was."

Abby withdrew her hand and stood up. "Look, none of this makes any sense to me. You're immortal, you told me that yourself, so what's the point of Angus going after you?"

"True, but I can be injured and in some cases, very unlikely cases, I could be killed. I do not recover as quickly as some of the paranormal beings you see on television, so while I recover, you could be at risk. Angus will do all he can to catch me off guard—I know the mon, and I'm sure he has a plan that will try to bring about my downfall one way or the other. Although, I dinnae know what that is just yet."

His brogue had thickened, telling Abby he was more than a bit upset about what Angus might do.

"So, I guess we're stuck together."

"It looks that way."

Abby moved to the fridge, pulled it open, and took out a pitcher of juice. She poured two glasses and handed one to Darach. Finding out he could die was not giving her a warm and fuzzy feeling. Quite the opposite. She prayed he was right and Angus could only try and not succeed. And although he'd blown into her life and thrown her a marathon of a curve, she couldn't help but be drawn to him. But attraction aside, although he knew she had visions, he would freak out if he actually saw her having one. History had proven that to Abigail. Men could be anything, but women were expected to be different—

normal.

"Well, then I suppose I should start the turkey for dinner. I have a feeling we're going to need all the comfort food we can get in the next few days."

"Abby, I'm sorry."

"For what? Having your family killed, becoming an immortal, or for Angus targeting me through you? Don't you see, Darach, sooner or later the demons would have found me without you. Then where would I be?"

"I promise, I willna let anything happen to ye."

"Thank you for that, but we both know we can't always keep our promises. You'll do your best and that will be enough. Now, help me get this turkey into the sink. I don't want to be eating too late. I promised I'd take a plate to one of the teachers at my school. He's all alone for the holidays."

Darach could only stand and marvel at the courage of the woman before him. Even in the midst of being stalked by demons she was willing to help her fellow man. It just reiterated more why he would keep her safe.

What he'd told Abby was true, every bit. After training with other immortals, and a second lifetime of fighting demons, he wasn't worried about what would happen to him.

Abigail, however, was mortal. Did she not realize just by stepping out the door, she could be a target? He opened his mouth to tell her just that but at the look in her eyes, instead, he pushed her gently back, took the Thanksgiving bird from the rack, and placed it in the sink.

"I need to make a few calls, let me know when ye be ready to put the turkey in the oven. I'll do it for ye."

She gave him a slight smile. "Thanks, I'll hold you to it. Now, since I think both our appetites were ruined for an early breakfast, I'm going to concentrate on getting the rest of the dinner pulled together once I've got the turkey cooking.

****

Later, after listening to Abby rattle pots and pans, hum several old gospel songs, and talk to herself, Darach decided to vacate the premises. He now made a circumference of the outside of Abby's home. It was magnificent in the bright rays of the noonday sun

He stood in amazement looking at the two-story stone house with a wraparound porch and two matching columns sitting on opposite sides of the double front doors.

With the sun hitting the exterior, Abby's home resembled a golden oasis. It must have taken months if not years to gather matching stones to build the place. Shutters that were once painted white but were now dingy beige were the only eyesore he could spot. The building set on about a half-acre of land, butting up against the canal. Trees tangled with moss, although bare with winter's bite, seem to make the house part of the landscape.

Darach scanned the area. There were several houses near Abby's but they seemed deserted. It could be due to the holiday or some of the natives had relocated after the hurricane and flood. The solitary surroundings left a lot to be desired in his opinion. Too much could happen to a lone woman before aid arrived.

"Darach, you out there?"

He jumped the three steps, closed and then bolted the door Abby had left open. He also laid his hand against the door to ward off demons.

"I'm here, Abby." The scent of baked turkey, dressing, and a combination of more enticing smells filtered out into the hallway. For the first time in a long time, he was looking forward to celebrating a holiday.

"Oh good. Lunch is almost ready." Abby's smile was contagious despite his worry about her safety.

"Do I have time to pop back home? I'd like to take a shower before we eat." He hated to delay her plans but he'd missed the chance to get cleaned up before their early morning talk, and since then he'd been too busy.

"Sure, I'll just turn the oven off and you can help me get the turkey and dressing out after you get back." Abby started toward the kitchen. "Hurry up now, I'm starving."

Darach teleported to his house, grabbed a fresh T-shirt, some jeans, and briefs before stripping down to nothing and heading to the bathroom. He hastily turned on the water, stepped in, and wet his body. Shampoo ran in rivulets through his hair, and he rubbed it in quickly before sticking his head under the stream of water. He applied soap in the same manner. Although he'd reset the safety guards, he didn't want to be away from Abby for long.

Five minutes later, shaved, dry, and dressed, he teleported back to her house. He made his way to the kitchen, pushed open the door, and then rushed toward Abby. He caught her in his arms before she hit the floor.

****

Angus drummed his fingers against the desk he sat behind. Soon, he would have the first peg nailed in the coffin that would result in Darach's downfall from grace and his destruction.

He would never understand how such a goody-two-shoes ended up working for an archangel. He should have been the one working side by side with the big guns of Heaven. He should be the one gathering riches, instead he'd spent the centuries since his death shoveling coals onto the brimstone that burned day and night in Hell—except for one of two brief excursions into the mortal realm.

But that was now over. Once he delivered Darach into Satan's hands, the king of the underworld would raise Angus up as his right-hand demon.

Michael stared down through the veil separating Heaven and Earth. So many good mortals still inhabited the planes of God's creation. And as many as there were good, there were those who were evil. If only he could do more, but he could only do what he was directed to do...and God in his mercy would set things right.

Chapter Six

Darach's heart pounded so hard he thought it would explode. Abby's eyes were wide-open, horror etched into her blue-eyed gaze. What had frightened her? He lifted her limp form and carried her to the living room. After laying her on the couch, he smoothed a hand down one paper-white cheek, as he inhaled but found no sulfuric stench inside the walls of her home.

Yet, something had scared her into an almost comatose state. His other hand fisted into a symbol of his own upset at not knowing what was wrong. As he knelt by her side, her eyelids closed, and she took in several audible breaths of air.

He held his breath in anticipation of Abby opening her eyes again. One long minute passed before he let his breath out. The look in her eyes now was one of confusion. Her beautiful lips trembled as she looked around and then her gaze lit on him.

"Oh no...oh God please, no." Abby jerked away from his touch and pressed her back as far into the couch as she could. Please, please, let Darach not to have witnessed her having a vision.

"Abby, what's wrong?" The immortal's question contained concern, but she wasn't buying it. He probably had to put on a good face because he worked for an archangel. She knew all too well what happened when someone was a party to one of her episodes.

"Go away, please."

"No, I'm staying right here with you. Ye scared me to death, woman." Darach caught one of the hands she was wringing and settled it against his chest. As agitated as she was, she couldn't help but admire how broad and muscular that part of his anatomy was.

"Look, I'm sorry. I didn't mean… I mean, you never should have seen…"

"Seen what?" His anxious tone drew her eyes away from his chest and to his face.

"Nothing, it's not important." Abby's voice trembled.

"'Tis something, Abby. You were out like someone in a coma." Darach's sooty brows drew together, before he took a deep breath. "Did ye have a vision, lass?"

Oh God above, why would he ask that? And what should she say? Abby struggled to think, but came up with only one answer. This was do or die time as far as she was concerned. The last hot looking guy to see her like this viewed her as a freak.

"Yes." She prayed he wouldn't run away in horror.

"Then 'tis okay. I feared ye saw a demon."

So amazed he wasn't pushing her away in disgust, she blurted out, "You're not scared, repulsed, any number of things most men would be?"

"Fie, lass, I kill demons for a living, visions dinnae frighten me." Darach's smile did amazing things to her heart.

"Now, why dinnae ye tell me what ye saw." His tone was patient, almost as if he were talking to a child. She should resent that, but instead it made her feel all squishy inside.

"Blood, lots of blood. I don't know where it was, and that usually means I've never been there before, but it was not good, Darach."

"That's okay. Visions could mean it's already happened as ye know or a portent of something to come." He tugged lightly on her hand and pulled her into a sitting position. "For right now, why don't ye go wash your face, and then I'll help you get everything out of the oven. Then if you want to, over lunch, we can talk about what you saw a bit more, okay?"

"Sure… I can do that." She knew she sounded a bit off, but Darach's easy acceptance of what he'd seen and how well he was taking her lapse into zombie status really threw Abby. Could this handsome, oh so sexy man, actually be blasé about something most people looked at as a curse, a disgusting trait that made her lesser than human?

She slid off the couch and headed for the downstairs bathroom. One thing Abby did know, she wasn't going to look this particular gift in the eye, but she would wait and see if Darach truly meant what he said.

****

"Here, take these into the dining room and set the table, please."

"Why dinnae we just eat in here?"

Abby turned and looked at the Highlander. He truly looked puzzled.

"Well, ever since I can remember, my grandmere always made sure we ate at the dining room table for holidays. I don't always cook for the holidays, but when I do I make sure I follow her customs."

"Oh…I see."

"It's okay, it's probably been awhile since you actually got to take Thanksgiving off." Abby grabbed a couple of goblets and motioned for Darach to precede her. "I mean, I know you're working guarding me and all, but to actually..."

Darach smiled. "You be right. It has been a long time since I actually sat down for a real home-cooked holiday meal, or any meal to tell ye the truth."

"Well, then I'm glad I could cook it for you. Now, if you grab the turkey, I'll get the rest of the side dishes and we can pig out."

Darach did as she asked and exited the kitchen before Abby.

She knew her good spirits were forced. Ever since Darach told her the story of what happened to his family and to him, she'd not thought of anything else. And now she had the vision's repercussions.

The food she cooked would probably sit in her stomach like bayou mud, but she had to make an effort. Darach's smile seemed genuine. Lord knew the man or immortal had gone through Hell on Earth when he was alive, but there was no point in making him feel bad for telling her.

She wanted him to be happy, to actually experience a bit of time when he wasn't on guard. Lord knew she knew how that felt. A respite from care for even a few minutes was more than what he'd had before. The immortal who killed the demon in front of her, spirited her to his home, and then the man who lost everything, was a hardened warrior.

Less than twenty-four hours since they met, and she'd barely seen him show any type of mirth.

Arms laden with dishes, she returned to set them in the center of the table. Darach stood near one of the chairs. She moved to the head of the table, and he pulled her chair out.

"Thank you. Now please sit."

Darach did as she asked and then at her request

carved the turkey. Once their plates were filled with meat, dressing, mashed potatoes, and string beans with tiny onions, Abby said grace.

She took a bite of turkey, and watched as Darach did the same. As he chewed the morsel, it seemed his gaze lost some of the hardness she had grown use to.

"'Tis good, Abby. Thank you."

"Hey, you're my bodyguard, so I want you to eat up and stay strong." The moment the words left her mouth, she wanted to call them back. His features hardened again.

"Darach, please, I'm sorry. Let's try to not think about anything but this dinner and our blessings."

"I want to talk about your visions, the one ye just had in particular. I need to ken how often ye have them and if ye have any warning before they occur." His face remained carved into a hardened mask.

Abby almost strangled on the sip of tea she'd just taken.

"Why do you need to know?"

"Because it would help me if I ken more about what ye see in your visions and if I have some type of guideline to get ye to safety and out of the public's eye if it happens while we're out."

When she raised her glass to her lips again, her hand trembled slightly. Darach didn't seem to care that she had visions, just what they were about, and to protect her when they happened. She couldn't believe it. Someone or the only one since her grandmere who didn't look on her as a pariah for her gift. And maybe it was time she thought of it as a gift. If she hadn't had the vision last night, that young woman would probably be dead.

"Okay, I saw a dark room with lots of blood inside. I don't know where it was or anything else. It's like I get tunnel vision, and I zoom in on that one scene. I have no idea what happens to me after that."

Abby pushed back her plate, got up from the table, and pulled out a bottle of tequila. She opened it and poured some in a clean glass before moving back to the table.

"When I was in college, I had a vision that hit me at a school dance. The guy I was with told me my eyes rolled back and I got this strange look on my face. Then he said I kept repeating the word demon."

Darach didn't even flinch at her words. "So what happened next?"

"You mean before or after he shoved me into a wall and started calling me a freak and witch?" She knew her words were bitter, aimed at the incident in her past that made her leery of trusting anyone with her secret, but she couldn't help how she felt.

"That son of a bit—" Darach broke off the obscenity but it didn't prevent the rage in his gaze from burning Abby. The emotion went straight to her heart. He actually was angry that someone had hurt her.

"So, there you have it. One minute we were dancing, the next I zoned out. The only warning I have is like everything freezes." Abby kept her tone light as she continued, "I guess that's not much help, huh?"

"Dinnae worry about it. I will make sure no one ever does that to ye again." Darach's words made her feel more than a bit warm and fuzzy. She felt like she could dance on the roof. The smile she gave him reflected just that.

****

An hour later, the food was stored in the fridge, dishes washed and left to drain, and Abby grabbed her coat.

"So where does this teacher live?" Darach held the material as she slid her arms into the sleeves.

"Cecil lives a few miles from here. But don't worry, we can catch the St. Charles streetcar and be there in about ten minutes." She finished buttoning her coat.

"I could get us there faster." Darach didn't smile. It was as if he was just stating a fact and nothing remotely about being able to transport through space.

"Thanks but no thanks." Abby smiled and then carefully picked up the box she'd packed the food in. "It might be less noticeable if we do it the mortal way."

She made her way to the door. "Have you ever ridden on a streetcar?"

Darach's eyes widened for just a second. "No, I haven't."

"Well then follow me, Immortal Man, you'll love it." Abby laughed at his expression as he opened and then closed the door.

"Hey, wait a minute, I left my keys in the house."

"You won't need them, no one will pass the thresholds I set."

****

A scant three minutes later, seated on the streetcar, Abby wasn't sure how Darach could be certain no one would break into her house, but it made her feel a whole lot safer knowing he was on the job. Of course, he made her think of a lot more than protection when she was near him. It truly was a shame that a man, oops, make that immortal, who looked as hot as Darach, had no clue of what he did to a woman just by giving her a brooding look. What she wouldn't give for just a taste of his lips. Just to see if he could melt every bone in her body like she feared he could. And for the first time since she met him, she felt it was okay to feel that way. He had seen her in the throes of a vision and hadn't run screaming into the night or day.

"Abby?"

It took her a moment to refocus her thoughts but when she did, Darach was staring at her. Here's hoping he still couldn't mess with her mind.

"Yes?"

"Would ye like for me to carry the box?"

"No, I'd prefer you have your hands free if you need them…you know if we run into any red-eyes."

"Red-eyes?"

"Yeah, you know, demons."

Darach didn't know whether to laugh or curse. Michael would probably have his head if he let loose with some of the words he'd learned over the centuries. How could the woman be so matter-of-fact over creatures that would do anything they could to get to her? Her penchant for taking demons in stride, not to mention fighting them would have to stop.

"I ken demons, Abby. They're dangerous, in case you have forgotten. I would also suggest ye rethink ever fighting one again."

The car began to slow, and he gave her no time to reply before he jumped off. If she did, she trusted him completely and would do as he told her, but if she hesitated…no…he did not want to think that way. He wanted, needed her to trust him.

Abby laughed out loud and then flung herself in his arms. Her breath came in little puffs of cold air. Her magnolia skin glowed with the wind's touch. Her breasts pressed against him, and he continued to hold her close…closer. He leaned down. Before he could place his lips against hers, common sense struck hard. He needed to keep his distance. His main goal should be only protecting Abby.

"Uh, Darach, you're smashing the box."

Abby's eyes were full of laughter but he also saw what he hoped was the same disappointment riding his body. God's teeth, he just couldn't seem to help himself. She was a little girl and a woman rolled into one. He was drawn to her in so many ways—ways that he needed to tamp down if he was to do his job right.

He released his arms from around her and slowly backed up. "Which way to your friend's house?"

"Whoa, did someone take away your toys, MacRath?"

"I dinnae ken what ye mean." He knew it for a lie, but he hoped Abby would not call him on it.

"Sure you do. You wanted to kiss me, so don't act like I dumped on your parade. You stopped—I didn't stop you. Is it the fact I have visions? I thought you were okay with that."

He could feel his cheeks burn with the truth of Abby's words. He did want to kiss her and badly...and she wanted him also—more grounds for distancing himself. Maybe when Angus was caught...no, then there'd be no reason to be around Abby. Yet, he could not let her think she repulsed him.

"I didnae stop because of your visions. Now, let's get your errand over with. Ye need to be home before dark."

Abby pointed down the block, and Darach allowed her to lead the way, but he stayed one step behind her, constantly scanning the street, the trees, and any moving or parked cars for anything out of the ordinary.

He saw nothing, and he didn't get any inkling that Angus or any demon had been near the three-story frame house where Barrett lived. As soon as he got Abby home safe, he would hit the streets, shake up some of the local demons that came out at night, and then launch his search for Angus.

Darach scanned the boarding house Abby's

friend lived in and the area around it as Abby walked up the steps to the porch.

"Which floor does he live on?"

"Cecil told me the top one. His wife died last year, and after paying the funeral costs, he had to give up their home. He's a nice man."

Abby's concern for the teacher made Darach want to take back his terse attitude. It wasn't her fault he wanted to make love to her.

"Abby, I'm sorry I was such a—"

"First class jerk, royal ass when it came to your attitude about holding me?"

He wanted to laugh, but didn't dare. He was grateful she was speaking to him at all.

"Aye to both. Ye make me think all kinds of thoughts about what I would like to do to ye."

Abby's eyes lit up, showering him with a brilliant hue of tantalizing blue.

"Really, what type of things?"

Darach dropped an arm over her shoulder and then kissed her on the nose before he gently pushed her away.

"Maybe I'll explain it to ye, after ye get finished with your visit."

"Count on it, MacRath. And I want all the details. And just so you know, I forgive you." She gave him a saucy smile and then entered the building.

He quickly followed and caught up with her. "Forgive me for what?"

"For being so bossy. I don't like being told what to do." This time her smile was tightlipped.

"I ken that, but ye have to ken I only do it for your own good." When Abby didn't respond Darach waited. A second later she opened her lovely mouth.

"I don't see an elevator so I guess we'll have to hoof it up to Cecil's."

"Ye want a ride?"

"You and your transport thingy. Maybe another time. I don't really like being dizzy." Abby softened her answer by patting his arm.

She hoped he understood, but traveling by having your insides twisted seven ways to Sunday wasn't her idea of fun. It ranked right up there with flying in an airplane. And she wasn't yet ready to be held in his arms again. She still wasn't happy with his dictatorship even if he did couch it in such a sensual tone.

Darach remained silent as they made their way up to the third floor. Was he upset about what she said, or was it their almost kiss? Did he regret putting a move on her? The man was giving off mixed signals, and she wanted to slap him silly. He needed to make up his mind to bypass Michael's warning and make love to her, or stop making her think he wanted her like she wanted him.

Of course, it signaled how crazy she was to be developing any type of feelings for someone she'd just met the day before. Ludicrous was only the beginning of an explanation for her actions. Why on earth would she even want to hook up with a man who fought and killed demons, even if he did understand her? It was a dangerous job, and sure he said he couldn't die or probably couldn't, but there was a time to live and die for everyone, wasn't there?

"What room number, Abby?" Darach's husky baritone sent shivers deep to her core, but she ignored them. He was right, there were things they needed to do, and truthfully things they needed to talk about.

"Apartment eight. It should be just around this next corner."

Abby knocked on the door and waited. No answer. "Cecil, it's Abby. I brought you some dinner." When that got no response, she looked up at Darach.

"I don't understand. He should be here. I talked to him last night before I went to work. Cecil was looking forward to me coming over. You don't suppose something happened do you?" Her apprehension was not unfounded. Cecil, while not the oldest teacher at the school, was somewhere around sixty.

Darach tried the doorknob, and it slowly turned under his grip.

"Something's wrong. Cecil would never leave his door unlocked even expecting company."

"I'll check, ye stay here." Darach's words were spoken low, almost a whisper but not quite.

"No way I'm I going to wait. Cecil might be hurt. I can help." She answered him in kind, but her whisper was defiant all the same.

His grunt signaled his displeasure, but Abby ignored the man's snit. She was used to doing things on her own, and immortal or not, she planned on continuing the same way.

"Well, then, make sure ye stay behind me."

Oh yeah, Darach was not happy.

"Fine, now can we go in?"

Darach pushed the door until it swung open halfway. Abby tried to see around him, but it was impossible. The man filled the entire doorframe with his body. She resisted the urge to push him out of the way. One, she wasn't quite sure what he would do if she followed through on her inclination. Two, she doubted she'd be able to move his impressive and handsome bulk.

Apparently satisfied nothing was going to loom out in front of them, Darach pushed the door open all the way. He turned slightly, gave her a look she could not misunderstand, and then stepped over the threshold.

Abby waited for what seemed an eternity after Darach disappeared from view. When he returned, he motioned her inside.

"Did you find, Cecil?"

"You don't have to whisper. No one's here, Abby."

She exhaled loudly. "That makes no sense. He knew I was coming by. Did he leave a note?"

Abby moved around Darach, intent on searching for a message from Cecil. Maybe he got a better offer for dinner or had to run out for a moment. If so, then it might possibly be why he left the door unlocked, if he just left thinking they would be there any moment.

"Your friend didnae leave a missive."

Darach's thickened brogue sent out warning bells to Abby. When his Scottish tone turned into an imitation of molasses it always meant something affected him strongly.

"Out with it. What's happened to Cecil?"

"I dinnae kin."

"Well, then he could be okay, right?"

"Nae, just because 'tisn't a body, dinnae mean he could be all right."

Abby didn't like where this was going.

"Again, out with it. What did you find?"

"You dinnae need to see it, Abby. I'll call the police and report Cecil missing."

Something bad had happened. She knew it, and the fact he didn't want her to see it made her blood run cold.

"No, I won't be protected. Cecil was…is my friend."

Abby detoured around him, but Darach caught her hand and followed her to a room off the living area they stood in. The bedroom was small but more than adequate for one person. The bed was unmade, but that could mean Cecil got up and left in a hurry. A chair lay on its side, and Abby wasn't sure she could rationalize a reason for that one.

Darach kept hold of her hand until they stood on the opposite side of the bed. A large circumference of something dark marred the fibers.

"That's blood, isn't it?"

"Aye, and it's several hours old. Whatever happened probably took place not long after Cecil got up."

"He's dead isn't he?"

"We dinnae know that for sure, Abby. I'll call a friend of mine on the NOLA police force."

Abby's mind spun. "Does he know what you are?"

"No, he doesn't. Over the centuries, I've found it better to keep that information to myself. The only reason you ken is because I couldn't wipe your memory away or replace it with another."

"I see. Well, I say let's call your friend…and…"

"And after that, ye are going back home where it's safe."

Abby stopped Darach's movement to call the police. "Do you think it could have been a demon?"

"I don't smell any sulfuric fumes, so probably not. Still, the demon world can and will use mortals to do their bidding."

"But why Cecil? He's harmless, he never bothers a soul."

Abby watched Darach's eyes. They went from ebony to silver in less than a second.

"Oh no…if demons were behind this attack, it's because of me."

Horror that her actions in any way could cause another harm, made Abby bend double at the waist to gulp in much needed air. Realization that she'd seen this before hit—seen Cecil's blood in her vision. As she grappled with that horror, time froze for a moment. Another vision creased her brain, black spots danced before her eyes, and she prayed she wouldn't pass out.

****

Angus watched as his minions dragged and then dropped the old one, who was a friend of Abby's, on the floor. He would unwittingly help Angus get the justice he craved when it came to Darach.

A thorn in his side while he was alive and mortal, Darach had gained a name as one of the best immortals to come out of Heaven's gates. Even if he didn't have a score to settle with his soon-to-be dearly departed cousin, for the second time, he would want to take him down for being the cause of so many demons deaths. His goal as always, to have Lucifer's ear, and the riches he was cheated out of on earth.

Michael made his way from God's throne room back to his office. His mood was fractious, not at all what an angel of God's should be, let alone an archangel, but he couldn't shake it off. Events were unfolding, put into play by Lucifer, that could injure a man he claimed as friend, although, he wasn't at all sure Darach would feel the same way. He'd pushed the immortal time after time to be the best, but all the training in the world could not control the heart and soul. Michael shrugged his shoulders before sitting down behind his desk. Patience was a virtue he needed badly at the moment, and something his boss just told him to find in spades, for he'd been warned not to interfere no matter what.

Chapter Seven

Darach laid his precious burden down on top of her bed. He stripped her coat off and then stood looking down at Abby. She'd almost frightened him out of his immortal skin when she'd fainted. Probably for the best; it enabled him to transport her back to the house without any protests.

He needed to get her out of her jeans and sweater. Would Michael slap him with a lightning bolt? Darach decided to take a chance—she needed to be comfortable. Footwear first, then he'd go from there. He unlaced her shoes, pulled off the thermal socks next to her skin, took a deep breath, and sighed.

Undressing Abby would not be easy. So far, she'd been an instrument of lust for him while fully clothed. Even her nightwear made him hard as the rocks lining the shore of the lochs in Scotland.

"Stop being a ninny. Ye can do this." After his brief and not very inspiring words, Darach set to work. He eased to the head of the bed, grasped the heather-colored material at her waist, and brought it upward; however, he met with a problem. The material would not go past her chest. The firm mounds of flesh he glimpsed under the sweater's hem beckoned him to touch them. He closed his eyes against the temptation.

Not only would Michael zap him into the next room, he would probably put him to work cleaning swords. Gradually and with hands that shook so badly he dropped the offending garment twice, he was finally able to pull it off her head,

The material cupping and enticing the view of her breasts could stay where it was. He was only a man, regardless of being immortal. Besides, if he got anywhere near the taut pink nipples playing peek-a-boo between the lace, he would not be answerable for any of his actions.

After several more deep breaths, Darach undid the button to her jeans, and slid the zipper down. His breath stalled in his throat, and his manhood went from rock consistency to concrete. The same peach material covering her breasts caressed her slender but slightly rounded belly, hid her mons. He wanted to see what lay beneath the material so badly he shook with lust.

No. He would never take advantage of someone in his care. Darach finished his task, but stopped when he saw the scar high on Abby's thigh. He wondered how she came by it. Not sure if he would ask her or not, he pulled a blanket lying at the foot of the bed over Abby. He forced himself to leave her and made his way downstairs. He needed to call his contact at the police department. And it might be a good idea to talk to Michael, but given his lustful thoughts—maybe not.

****

Abby woke to the sound of a phone ringing somewhere in the house and to find herself in her own bed. How had she gotten there? Her brow creased as she tried to remember. Oh no! Cecil.

She sat up so fast her head spun just as it did right before she passed out. Something she'd never done before and never wanted to do again. Then it hit her. She'd had another vision. Chills dotted her flesh. Abby tried to still her rapidly escalating breath. Darach had been in the vision. Not only that he starred in it and if her vision was correct, he would die.

Her heart ached at the thought. She closed her eyes and tried to remember what she'd seen. The background playing across her lids was not familiar to her, nor was the ornate blade being thrust into his body. As she watched Darach stopped fighting, his eyes closed, and then nothing. Oh Lord, when and where would it happen, and could telling him prevent his death?

So many questions warred inside her head. Foremost she needed to see Darach. Where was he?

Abby pushed the blanket aside and then stopped dead still.

Why was she only in her underwear? How did her clothes get removed? Darach? Oh Lord, she hoped not. Just the thought of him looking at her naked sent heat spiraling through her body and not all of it was due to her attraction to him.

Okay, enough. She needed to get dressed and get downstairs. No matter how much she wanted to daydream about her and Darach being together that way, Cecil was missing and the possibility of harm to Darach bothered her greatly. She prayed the blade represented Darach's death in the past, but there was no way of knowing. Right now she needed to know if Darach was all right and second if he'd found out anything.

She threw her clothes on, not bothering with shoes, and hurried downstairs to run right into the man in her thoughts.

"Slow down before ye get hurt." Darach sounded tense.

"I'm sorry, I was in a hurry. Who was on the phone? Did you talk to your friend?"

"Aye, Sean says he will check out Cecil's apartment."

Abby wasn't pleased with that answer. "Is that all? Can't he do something else? Cecil could be dead."

"Abby, he could be, and if he is there's not going to be anything Sean can do or ye or I for that matter." He took her by the elbow and her attempt to shake him off was futile.

"Come and sit down. I know 'tis not what you want to hear, but that's—"

"That's what?" She succeeded this time in jerking free of his light grasp. She was so not in a mood to listen to him. "Policy for policemen, immortals? What?"

"What has ye in such a mood?"

"Try my friend disappearing, a policeman who acts like nothing can be done, and a man I hardly know undresses me down to my unmentionables. I'd say that's enough to put anyone into a mood." Abby could have bitten her tongue. She had not meant to voice that last thought only to keep him from asking more questions. She wanted to keep the vision from him.

"I swear I only wanted ye to be comfortable. I didnaee even look..."

When his voice trailed off, Abby gave him a cocked eyebrow and a stare she hoped would singe his hair.

"Well, I didnae look much." The heat climbing his cheeks almost made her laugh, but Darach still wasn't off the hook.

"You shouldn't have looked at all." A slight smile crept onto her lips against her will.

"Abby, even a saint couldna keep his gaze off the lovely sight of your bonny body."

Zap! He burned the last of the angst out of her with his words.

"Thank you…I think. Now that we have that out of the way, what are *we* going to do about Cecil?"

Darach closed the distance between them before speaking. "I will take care of this, Abby. Ye can do nothing."

"I beg to differ, big man. I can help look."

"No, ye need—"

The phone rang silencing the rest of his sentence. Abby grabbed the phone from its charger before Darach could beat her to it. It might be the lieutenant calling back.

"Hello."

"Abby, this is Chaz. I need you to come in to work."

"Chaz, no…I'm off until the middle of next week. You promised." Abby did nothing to disguise her aggravation.

"Look, I know I promised, but Lisa is sick, she caught something from one of her kids and can't work. We need you. I need you." Her boss's tone was sugary sweet, but Abby wasn't buying it, nor did she believe his story about Lisa. She probably had a date.

"Hey, we both know what she's likely doing, and I don't want to work."

"You don't work and you don't have a job."

There it was—the tone she knew. Abrupt and uncaring.

"Fine." Abby clicked off and slammed the phone

back down.

"What's wrong?"

"I have to go to work."

"'Tis a holiday, I thought ye were off."

"Yeah, well, so did I. But if I don't go in, I won't have a job. And without this second job, I won't be able to keep the house." Abby was so mad she wanted to scream.

"I can help with that, Abby. I have—"

She caught the hand he extended, patted it, and then let it drop. "Thanks, but I have to stand on my own two feet. You won't always be around...check that, you will be around, but not necessarily here. I have to be able to take care of myself, without anyone doing it for me."

"I want to help, and besides ye don't need to go out tonight."

"Darach, I appreciate your offer, your being here to protect me, but you are not my keeper. I have to keep going as I plan to after you're gone. So, I'm going to the club. You can come with me or not, I don't care."

****

Darach, if he could, would pull out his teeth one by one. It would be no worse than trying to talk sense to a woman who refused to listen.

The short walk to the club had consisted of more than the bite of weather. Abby's demeanor had been icy as well. Just because he didn't think she needed to wear so much face paint. Not to mention, the dress she wore revealed too much of the body he wanted no other man to see.

They reached the side door of the club, and Abby turned to face him. "Look, I know you don't like this, but it's my job. Try to behave, please."

"I willna not promise something I be not sure I can deliver."

"Oh please, stop with the brogue already. I don't

care how sexy it sounds, it's not going to work. I'm going in there and do my job. I don't strip, I sing. I'm fully clothed and the tips and my salary help pay bills."

Darach's eyes were glued to Abby's buttocks as she turned and pushed through the door. The woman was going to kill him. And did she really think his brogue sexy? He'd been an immortal for so long, he hadn't realized he'd retained some of his Scottish accent. Now, he couldn't help the full-fledged grin pulling his lips apart.

Almost at the same instant, it faded. Abby was in there alone, and he needed to be stuck to her side like a lamb with its ma. Only he had no feelings of familial affection toward the woman. He wanted her like a man wanted—no, needed a woman.

Darach pushed through the door, allowed his eyes to adjust to the smoke-filled room, and then his gaze found Abby.

She stood talking to a man he supposed was Chaz, the manager, and looked none too happy about it. Neither did Chaz. A moment later, she marched up the steps of the stage, nodded to the guy on the keyboard, and closed her eyes.

The memorable notes of "The Rising Sun" echoed throughout the bar. Patrons stopped drinking, eating, and talking. The haunting tale, and the picture Abby made as she sang mesmerized Darach himself. Her eyes, now open, glowed an unfathomable blue, her lips were round and sensual as she sounded out each syllable, and the thrust of her breasts against the low, round neck of her emerald green cocktail dress drew the eyes of every man present.

He didn't like it, not at all.

"Can I get you a drink, mister?"

"Scottish whiskey, straight up." Darach gave his order without taking his eyes off of Abby.

"You got it, sugar."

When the waitress returned, he handed her a couple of twenties. "I'll be in that corner, bring me another in a bit."

"You want ya change back?"

"Keep it."

"Sure thing, mister, thanks."

Darach made his way to a table secluded from the ones lining the stage. The corner offered a dim light that suited his mood. With his back against the wall, he concentrated on watching the crowd as they watched Abby.

Bugger it; he didn't like her job at all. She was too close to too many desperate men. And he was one of them. Trying to keep his mind off of making love to Abby was harder than trying not to breathe. He was certain Michael knew what it was doing to him, and probably why he hadn't gotten the usual notes the archangel liked to send out to his immortal team.

His life had been so simple for a millennium. Although, he hadn't lived as a monk, his sexual encounters had been few and far between. In fact, the last time he'd been with a woman was during Desert Storm.

It had taken Darach centuries after he became an immortal to even bed a woman. His heart bled for Briene for so long he felt to do so would betray her and Jamie's memories. The long years hadn't erased his guilt or hurt, but the once sharp pain had turned into a dull endless ache.

He not only wanted to bed Abby, he wanted to hear her laugh, watch her eyes sparkle with mischievousness, and to always keep her safe.

Abby's second set had barely started when the waitress brought him another drink. The whiskey burned his throat but didn't faze the flames burning below his waist.

The song was a combination of sensuality, love gone wrong, and revenge. The patrons were eating it up. As she went through several of the same type of lyrics, he gritted his teeth, and slugged down the rest of the liquor.

His hand tightened around the glass until he feared it would shatter. Just when his self-control was at an end, Abby laid the microphone down and walked off the stage.

Darach was on his feet and on his way to meet her when one of the men gathered around the stage stopped her. Abby's blue eyes widened, and she tried to take back the hand the man had appropriated. Instead of knocking men and women out of his way, as was his inclination, he bided his time until he reached her side.

"Release the lady." His words were icicles of sound. The man turned toward Darach and looked up.

"And if I don't?" The burly fisherman, for he carried the scent of a long day on the gulf, sneered at Darach.

He resisted the urge to slam Abby's admirer across the room. "Well, I didnae plan on getting me hands dirty, but if it's a fight ye seek, then you're welcome to throw the first punch."

The man hesitated just a second before punching the air where Darach had just stood. Now at the man's side, he threw an arm over the shorter man's shoulders, leaned down, and whispered.

"Abby Dupree is my woman. I willna hesitate to hurt ye in ways ye can only imagine. Now, run along like a good little mortal."

Whatever the man saw in Darach's gaze must have put the fear of God in him, for his eyes rolled back, he began to tremble, and then he ran for the exit.

"Darach, I told you I didn't need your help. I'm

more than capable of taking care of myself." Abby's hand massaged a red place on her wrist. He should have mangled the man's bones for hurting her.

"Not another word."

"But, I—"

"Silence."

Darach grasped Abby's arm, but made sure his grip wasn't hard. He tugged her to the corridor near the bathrooms, pulled her against him, and then sealed her protest with his lips.

****

Angus sneered at the broken and lifeless man at his feet. When he'd been mortal, men were made of stronger stuff, even the aged soldiers. The teacher had not even put up a fight while being tortured. No fun at all for Angus, but his next victim would be more of a challenge.

And soon, very soon, he would attain the confrontation he wanted more than a drink of water when he first arrived in Hell's realm.

Reminder: No matter how much I want to, I cannot zap Darach with a lightning bolt. To give in to my emotions would put me on the same level as the immortals I trained. Never show feelings is my motto. I cannot persevere in the fight against evil if I give in.

From the desk of Michael/ Archangel To God

Chapter Eight

Darach slammed his hands on either side of Abby's head—sandwiching her between him and her bedroom wall. She should be scared but she wasn't. The man had some serious issues but hurting someone weaker than him wasn't one of them.

And she certainly was weak since he'd kissed her senseless back at the club. Still, she didn't like being pinned into a corner.

"Darach—"

"Unless you want more than you bargained for, stay quiet."

His words sounded tortured. Gruff, pained, and pleading. What on earth was wrong with him?

"What's wrong with you?" Her question ended in a squeak as he captured her lips again. Time stopped as his tongue sought and then gained access to the inner circle of her mouth. Darach teased and taunted her until she could do nothing but kiss him back.

When she did, it seemed to open a floodgate within the immortal. The kiss continued and her knees went weak, her bones went fluid, and she wanted to be closer to the man driving her to a lust she'd never experienced before.

She tugged on the T-shirt he wore, and welcomed the warmth of his body against hers. The press of his hard exterior against her breasts, stomach, and the distinct hardness pressing against her lower extremities.

"Abby..." Her name was a groan on his lips as he nipped the sensitive line of her neck. She grasped his arms to keep her legs from buckling.

His hands moved to the neck of her dress, one sliding inside the lace of her bra. She moaned as he tweaked one nipple. The rush of heat pooled between her thighs. Her desire for him grew.

Abby knew they shouldn't be playing with fire. Michael had warned Darach about this, yet she wasn't sure what the archangel would do to him. She prayed it wasn't death—for she wasn't sure if even that would stop Darach from touching her. Not that she wanted him to. His touch felt too good, awakening a deep need inside she didn't know she had. It eased the loneliness of the past years.

Darach's other hand moved below her waist, and she held her breath. Would he touch her there? Would his touch quench the blaze beginning to burn out of control?

He slowly pushed her dress up until it was at her thighs, and then higher. Her breath released in a moan of anticipation. No one had ever touched her like this before; she'd never allowed them to, not that the few dates she'd had tried often. Her visions seem to derail that part of her life. Darach more than made up for her celibacy. He made her body hum with tendrils of desire.

When his fingers found and pushed under the lace edge of her panties, her knees buckled.

"Steady Abby, it will only get better."

"I'm not sure I can take much more."

"Aye ye can, and ye will embrace our lovemaking."

She didn't know how she got the faint chuckle out of her mouth with his hand climbing closer to the heart of her desire, but she did. "And how can you be so sure?"

"Because I will embrace it with ye. And I'm not without some experience."

Her giggle turned into a guttural moan when he touched her hard feminine nub. The only thing holding her up was the wall. First one and then a second finger caressed her until her eyes almost crossed. She could feel her body spiral higher and higher.

Right on the peak of what, she didn't know, she waited as the spirals grew tighter, her legs stiffened, and then—

God's angels! Darach jumped when his cell phone went off. He tried to ignore the musical tones of "Spirit in the Sky" but it continued to ring. Finally it stopped. He took a deep breath and focused his attention back on Abby.

Abby who was just as sweet and succulent as he knew she would be. Her warmth, wetness, and escalating desire made him ache with a need fast becoming a torment.

Her skin waxed a pale rose with her desire, and he touched her face; first her cheek, then the slightly swollen contours of her lips. Lips he wanted to drown in.

He caught her whimper inside his mouth, and began caressing her soft feminine center again. Her desire coated his fingers, his kiss deepened, and he felt Abby's body tense. Her release was near. A moment more and he felt the vibrations of her body as it rippled and then contracted just beyond what he couldn't breach.

How he wanted to slide his fingers deep inside

her essence. To push through her virginal barrier, to claim her as his own.

Darach shook with the emotion. When had he allowed the feeling he'd sworn never to have again creep up on him? To love someone only brought heartache. They would die, he would live, and his life would once again be a lonely and work-driven force. Did he want to go through that again? Could he live through another loss?

Before he could decide the answer, his cell phone rang again. He pulled away from a satisfied Abby, supported her limp weight with his arm, and eased her down on the bed. It was a good thing he'd teleported to her bedroom.

His phone continued to bleat loudly. He yanked it from his pants pocket, flipped it open, and slapped it to his ear. "MacRath here."

"Sean Black here. I need you to come to 743 Clint's landing. I have a DB. It could be your missing teacher."

"I'll be there in five."

"Five? Where are you?"

"At Abby's house."

"That's a twenty minute drive by car. No way." The lieutenant's skepticism almost made Darach laugh.

"I have a really fast mode of transportation."

"Like what, a rocket? See you when you get here." The lieutenant clicked off and so did Darach.

"What is it?" Abby's question flowed out on a series of quick breaths. He wanted to hold her, to keep her close until her body relaxed, and she slept but he couldn't.

"Nothing. I need to go out for a bit." The moment he finished his sentence, he knew he'd made a mistake. Abby pulled her body up straight and gave him the *look* he was coming to know as her *no way, not without me*. He knew if he left her at home, she might take it in her head to try and find him anyway, and with demons enjoying the nighttime, he couldn't take a chance. But to take her to a crime scene didn't seem right.

"Oh no. I know what you're doing, and it's not going to work. Who was on the phone, Darach?"

"Abby, 'tis not something ye need to be exposed to."

"Look, I'm totally over passing out. It won't happen again. I'm not a child, though not nearly as old as you are, but I can handle whatever I need to." Her tone went from firm to almost pleading.

"I dinnae think it's a good idea."

Abby stood up, straightened her dress and then moved to the bureau. She yanked the drawer opened, pulled out a pair of jeans and a shirt. "I'll be ready in a minute."

She hoped Darach would not say anything else. The evening wasn't ending quite how she'd like, but as her grandmere would say, *"Life is life, you live it, accept it, or get over it."*

The explosion of release he'd given her with just his hands had been totally off the charts. The only thing comparable would be if he'd actually taken her for his. Instead, he went from strong, sensual, almost lover, to dominant, all male, immortal—protecting-the-little-woman.

"Abby, I—"

"Have you forgotten that Michael said you're to protect me?"

"Nay, I didnae forget. And if ye stay here with me safeguards in place ye will be protected."

"Yeah, right. Well I've got news for you, I will do anything I can to get out of this house safeguards or not if you leave me behind." Abby pulled the jeans on under her dress and then turned her back to pull the dress off and the pullover on. Strange after how he'd pushed every sensory button she had, she felt shy in dressing in front of Darach.

"Okay, I'm ready. How far do we need to go?"

"Woman, ye are too stubborn for your own good." Darach growled the words.

Abby merely smiled. "See that you remember that, it might save us both some trouble in the future. So again, how far is it we need to go?"

"Distance willna be a problem. We will travel my way."

Abby wanted to groan. "Why can't we grab a cab?"

"I told Lt. Black I would be there in five minutes, and more than half of that time is gone. Now come here."

She forced her feet to move, allowed him to lock his arms around her waist, and then closed her eyes. "All right, do it."

****

Abby welcomed Darach's tight grip as her body rematerialized in one piece. She shook off the dizzy spell and then carefully stepped out of his embrace when his arms dropped to his side. The scene in front of them was bizarre. Several cops stood around a cloth-covered body. Against her will, Abby's feet carried her closer. It was like she couldn't stop the macabre curiosity. This time when she shook her head, she reinforced why they were there. Someone had died. That someone could be Cecil.

"Great, you're here. That *was* quick." Lt. Black closed his phone and moved to stand in front of Abby. "You must be Ms. Dupree."

"Yes, I am." Abby eyed the tall, slender built man with blond hair and green eyes. "Is it Cecil?" She prayed it wasn't, but the sympathetic look in the lieutenant's eyes told her the body could indeed be her friend.

"Abby, why dinnae ye wait and I'll do what needs to be done." Darach's voice should have irritated her, a command within a request, but it didn't. Too many things had happened in the last twenty-four hours. Visions were one thing but up close with death and violence was different, still...

"I'll be okay." She took the arm he offered and as a trio they moved to the body. The lieutenant did the honors or the horrors by pulling back the sheet. Cecil's face was battered almost beyond recognition, except for his sightless eyes rimmed with bruises, and the cuts on his naked chest. Whoever had done this horrific act had left him with no dignity when they stripped him of his clothing.

"It's him." Abby's voice caught.

"You're positive?" The lieutenant spit out the words so quickly she was startled.

"Yes, it's Cecil." Abby rubbed her arms in an up-and-down motion. She wanted to be back home, to be safe, to be normal. Something she'd never been her entire life.

"Abby, I ken this be hard. Give me a few moments, and then I will take ye home."

Lieutenant Black looked back down at Cecil's remains as Abby watched. A second later, he glanced up, and she almost swallowed her tongue. His eyes glowed red. The officer who was supposed to protect, serve, etc., was a demon.

"Darach, get back, he's a demon!" Before she could decide to run or jump in front of Darach, he pushed her behind him. Although the immortal didn't bring out his sword, maybe because of the crowd of mortals around, he did grab Lt. Black by the arm.

"What are ye?" Darach's tone was low but deadly sounding.

"I'm a person fast losing patience, trying to do my job." The lieutenant/demon sounded equally upset.

"No...you're not human." Abby's whispered

statement brought both men's gazes back to her.

The look Sean Black flashed Abby wasn't evil, just harsh. "I will explain something I should not have to after I'm finished here."

The lieutenant looked at Darach, shook his grip off, and spoke again. "We can meet at Ms. Dupree's house or anywhere else you want."

"Abby's house in one hour. If ye dinnae show up, I will come for ye."

"Deal, but I have some questions of my own I want answered."

****

Abby walked the carpet like a soldier on duty, while Darach practiced twirling and doing intricate moves with his sword.

"I don't know why you're pitching that thing about, you can't kill a police lieutenant—no matter what he is."

"Dinnae tell me how to do me business, Abby. I dinnae plan to stab him through the heart or lop off his head." His black eyes smoldered, making her think of the exact shade of silver he'd exhibited during their interrupted lovemaking.

Abby stayed out of range of the four-foot-long blade. "Fine, so what do you plan to do?"

"Talk to the mon. I've known him for several years. There must be a reason I didnae pick up on him being a demon."

Vacating the living room and the topic for the moment, Abby went to the kitchen, pulled out the fixings for a margarita, and then swirled her way to a bit of nerve settling.

"What are ye doing?" Darach's silent approach almost caused her to drop her just filled glass. It made her even more testy.

"What does it look like? Why do you always sneak up on people?"

His chuckle warmed her insides, but didn't do

much to tame the almost feral look in his eyes. The immortal seriously needed to chill. He looked like he was going to do some severe damage to someone, and Abby wasn't at all sure she wanted to be around when it happened. Oops, she couldn't go anywhere without the big man guarding her. Yeah right.

"I will try to give a warning next time."

The cheeky grin he fed her turned her insides to melted Jell-O. Did he have any idea what he did to a woman? Not to mention what he'd already done to her.

"See that you do. Now…" Abby checked the clock on the wall. "We have ten minutes until the lieutenant gets here. Do you have a game plan?"

Darach's breath of air ruffled the lock of hair falling over his brow. "I told ye already, I plan to talk to him."

"I get that, Mr. Immortal Man, but what happens if he goes all demon on us?"

"I will kill him."

Abby slapped a hand to her forehead. It was that or slap Darach senseless—if that was even possible.

"You can't. Don't you think the NOLA police department would have something to say about that?"

"Well, then Michael would need to fix it." Darach pulled open the fridge, took out a pitcher of water, and poured a glass.

"Just like that? The archangel is going to make it as if it never happened? I mean that is what he would have to do, right?"

"Aye."

"You know, this entire thing is nuts! Cecil is dead, we don't know who killed him, you've got a demon as a lieutenant, and I'm running around with a man that's lived almost a thousand—"

"Over."

"Excuse me?"

"I'm over a thousand years old if ye count my mortal years."

Abby slung her body down into a chair and gulped half her drink. "Great, can we say the age difference is not helping me either, since we almost made love."

Darach hid his grin and a bit of apprehension. They'd never got to discuss what happened before Lieutenant Black called. He knew he'd satisfied her, but he wasn't sure how she really felt about him taking advantage. Sure, she'd participated, but he'd not given her much of a choice. He'd used his experience to entice her. And if the phone had not rung, he would probably have taken her maidenhead—even if it meant Michael would punish him severely.

He pulled out a chair next to Abby. Her posture went from despondent to stiff. Not good for him, but maybe he could make her understand why he'd touched her. Did he really understand it himself? As much as he hated to admit it, the woman got under his skin in ways he wasn't sure he wanted or needed. Again, he reminded himself, once Angus was stopped, he would need to leave Abby alone. She would no longer be his assignment.

"Age has nothing to do with two people loving…" His voice trailed off when she gave him a look.

"In that way. Physical attraction is not something ye can turn on or off at will."

"Really? Well I beg to differ. You seem to be able to go from red-hot lover to immortal man in less than five seconds."

"Do ye really think it was that easy for me? I wanted to sink deep inside ye, make ye a part of me, but…"

"Duty called. I get that." Abby's tone went a bit shrill. "What I don't get is how you can turn your emotions on and off. Is this something you've learned over the centuries as a killing machine?"

Her words hurt Darach deeply. Did she truly see him as a machine? Only Michael had spoken about his habit of keeping things close to his chest. He locked his feelings deep inside in order to do the job he was chosen to do. So many times, he'd arrived too late to save a victim, and then his goal was simply to take out the demon responsible for the senseless death.

Did that make him a machine? And when did he begin to care what other people thought? Only now with Abby did he wish to be open. By telling her the truth, it seemed he pushed her away.

"Nay. That's not it at all. I dinnae ken if ye can understand or not, lass. I was given a new body, but my emotions were locked deep within me. Although, mortal time moves at a snail's pace, in Heaven 'tis a blink of an eye."

Darach stood up and walked to the counter where he'd left the glass of water. He took a deep gulp before turning back to Abby. Her beautiful eyes were staring back at him; with what he didn't know.

"When I woke up from death almost at Michael's feet, for me Briene's and my son Jamie's deaths had just happened. I was filled with grief, rage, and finally a stony acceptance that I couldna change anything. All I could do was fight to stop others from being killed."

Tears leaked from Abby's closed lids. He wanted to go to her, but he needed to tell her more. "Abby, ye have been the only one that has made me think of more than killing."

Her lids flew open. "Darach—"

The doorbell droned through the house.

"Dammit!" Darach's curse shocked him as much as it seemed to astonish Abby. Since becoming an immortal, he'd cleaned up his language a good bit.

Cursing in any form was not something Michael tolerated.

"I'll get it." Abby stood and moved toward the living room.

"Nay. I would prefer to be in front of ye until we find out what type of demon Lt. Black is, and his reason for working with the police."

For the second time in a minute, he received a shock when Abby did not argue. Was that a good sign or a bad one? Who could tell with women, whether they be from the eleventh century or present day.

****

Angus left the mortal woman who'd satisfied his need. She was someone his minions brought to him for enjoyment. When she awakened, he'd have them take her somewhere, use her if they desired, and then dispose of the body. She'd help to calm his impatience as he waited for news Darach had discovered the body. It shouldn't be long now, but it might take a while for him to realize Angus had been behind the murder. In that case, he would take delight in delivering more hints to point his cousin in the right direction.

Michael dropped his head onto his desk and closed his eyes. Darach's evening's activities could get him more than a slap if his boss found out, and of course he would. Michael would take the brunt of the sermon, but his immortal needed to learn to curb his appetites—all of them—or be prepared to suffer the consequences.

Chapter Nine

Abby stood behind Darach as he opened the door. His bulk prevented her from seeing Lieutenant Black at first, but then he moved forward over the threshold. Her breath caught. She wasn't sure how she'd missed his impressive build before. His shoulders were not as wide as her guard dog's but were still imposing. And speaking of eyes, the red flames she'd seen earlier had reverted to the loveliest shade of emerald she'd ever seen—much darker than before. His blond hair seemed a bit longer than it had last time, but that was impossible—wasn't it?

"MacRath, Ms. Dupree."

"Lieutenant." Darach's tone matched that of the just slightly shorter man—or would that be demon, more than a bit icy.

She'd had enough. There were questions that needed answers, and the men were standing there like two dogs getting ready to fight.

"Enough, you two. Come in, Lieutenant Black." She didn't quite succeed in pushing Darach back an inch but he got the message all the same.

"Didnae I tell ye to stay behind me?" His gruff and sulky tone reminded her of a little boy's.

"Yes, and if I did as you told me, we'd be standing here until Gabriel blows his horn."

The lieutenant's snicker brought an almost smile to Darach's stony demeanor.

"Why don't we head to the kitchen and get something to drink. That is if you are off duty, Lieutenant."

The lieutenant gave her a smile that lit up his face enhancing the tan contours. She managed one of her own—earning her a scowl of major proportions from Darach.

"Okay, gentlemen, and I expect you both to act as such, follow me." Abby led the way and once they were all seated with the drink of their choice, she decided to put in her two cents again.

"Lieutenant Black, I—"

"Sean, call me Sean."

This time Darach's scowl became a snarl. Before matters got totally out of control, Abby planned to put a stop to their battle.

"All right, let's chat. Darach, you've known the lieutenant for how long?"

"Around a decade. Why?" His expression was one of confusion warring with the angst still prevalent in his gaze.

"Well, have you ever known him to do anything demonic?" Her question caused both men to stop glaring at one another.

"Nay, I haven't."

"Lieutenant Black, did you have any idea that Darach was an immortal?"

The lieutenant's eyes grew wide, and the crimson flame came back, burning low—not quite obscuring the green of his irises.

"No. The Highlander kept his secret well."

"As did you, demon." Darach's shoulders

bunched as if he planned to spring over the table at Sean.

"Half-demon, and don't forget it, Highlander."

"Oooh, if you two could keep the testosterone under control, then maybe we could get a few more answers. I know I still have questions. Darach?" Her question was aimed to diffuse the situation, but her immortal didn't look like he wanted to diffuse anything. She reached out as far as she could with her foot and kicked him.

"Wheesh, woman, ye kicked me in the shin." His pained expression looked disgruntled as well.

"Well, crap, I was aiming higher." Abby allowed some of her own temperament loose.

Sean's chuckle brought both their gazes back to the lieutenant who raised his hands in the air.

"Don't kick me, I couldn't help it." The demon/mortal shot her a smile that was infectious.

"Darach, settle down. He's not going to jump my bones right here."

"Aye, ye can count on that."

Abby took a sip of her margarita, and resisted the urge to spit it out when Darach glared once more at Sean.

"Sean, why don't you tell us about yourself, if you don't mind. It could go a long way toward making Darach more mellow."

Darach's eyes turned silver as he directed his gaze at her.

"Then again, maybe not, but go ahead, please." Abby smiled at Sean.

Darach wanted to smash something, preferably the lieutenant. And when he was finished, he wanted to jerk Abby across his knees and paddle the daylights out of her for making him so jealous he could kill. He counted to ten and then twenty silently before he seconded Abby's request for the demon's story.

“Well, I guess you probably want to know how I can be both mortal and demon. And before you,”—he glanced at Darach—“go off the deep end, I'm not a bad guy. I've been working to help the innocent for a long time—a very long time.”

“Oh, wow, are you as old as Darach? He's like a thousand plus.”

“Give or take a few decades I am.” Sean moved a strand of hair that had fallen across his face. “I come from Ireland. My mother was raped by a demon one night, and although it's not common, I was the result.”

“Wow. That must have been hard on you both.” Abby's soft whisper soaked into Darach's ears. He'd been an ass to Sean, and the man had probably lived through torture like none other with his paternal parentage.

Sean's eyes blazed red for just a moment, but Darach kept still. He didn't think it was the demon in him but rather emotion.

“Hard enough. My mom worked to take care of us, but when I was ten, she died, and I was placed in an orphanage, which”—he looked at Darach—“you know in those days was pretty much a death sentence. I managed to survive, but I didn't even know what I was until I turned twelve.”

Again the demon stopped. “I need something a bit stronger than the stuff you're drinking, Ms. Dupree.”

“Call me Abby or Abigail. I'm afraid I don't have anything else in the house.”

Sean sent her a smile and then grinned at Darach. “Not a problem.” He waved his hand and a bottle of Irish whiskey appeared on the table with two ancient looking goblets.

“Care to join me, Highlander?”

“It'd be a sin to let you drink alone.”

The men laughed, at what she wasn't sure.

Some male bonding probably. Go figure. Half-demon mortal and an immortal executioner.

"All righty then, now that you boys have your drinks, you want to finish your story, Sean?"

Both exchanged another grin before Sean turned to Abby.

"A bit over a decade I was, and not the largest kid in the orphanage, not by a long shot, but I'd earned a rep for being able to take care of myself. One night, I heard one of the smaller girls crying. I crept out of bed and went to her. I found a couple of the older boys, bullies to be sure, trying to rape her."

Again his eyes glowed crimson. "Well, after being the product of rape, I couldn't stand the thought that another innocent, for that was what my mother was before it happened, would be assaulted."

Sean took a swig of the whiskey and then looked down at the table. "I lost it. Completely lost it. I jerked the boys away and almost beat them to death before I was stopped. I guess my emotions: rage, fear, you name it, brought out my demon side. I was cast out of the orphanage that night, and told if I ever tried to return, I would be labeled a disciple of Satan and burned alive."

Tears scalded her eyes as she reached across and caught his hand. "I'm so sorry. How could anyone do that to a child?"

"Thank you, Abby, but you forget this was a time, Darach can tell you, where people were ancient in their beliefs. The headmistress only followed what she was taught."

He squeezed her hand. "And I am part demon, so not at all an innocent."

She gripped his hand tighter before speaking. "What a bunch of cow crap. You didn't ask for what happened, so forgive me if I don't agree."

"Don't try to argue with the woman, Sean, she is an extremely stubborn woman." Darach lifted his goblet.

"I'm getting that."

"Enough. Finish, please."

"Yes, ma'am. Well, once I realized I could take care of myself, I made sure to stay away from grownups. I found work, ate like there was no tomorrow, and waited for the day I would grow up."

Darach poured another spot of whiskey. "So what did you do when you grew up, and did you ever find out who your sire was?"

"I soldiered, worked as a mercenary, and studied anything I could get my hands on pertaining to the law until I could become a police officer. From there it was a short jump to lieutenant. As for my sire, I don't know, and I don't want to know."

"I wanted to... Look, I just have to ask. When I first saw you with Cecil's body...you seemed to be a lot smaller in build and your hair wasn't this long." Abby hoped he wouldn't think her crazy, but she just had to know if she was delusional.

Sean grinned. "Your woman is very astute."

"I'm not his—"

Darach leaned over, lifted her hair off her neck, and placed a kiss over her pulse beat. "Aye, ye are, and soon I will prove it."

She could feel the heat in her cheeks. Not to mention the fire beginning to burn in her body.

"Stop." Abby wiggled as far away from Darach as he'd allow which wasn't much. At least it gave her a bit of breathing room.

"So, I'm not crazy. How did you do it, Sean?"

"I glamoured myself. It's something I learned in my third decade. It comes in handy. I think people want to see what makes them comfortable. So, I conform to what I think they want to see in an officer of the law."

"It's a shame you can't bottle it. You'd make a fortune just on the women who purchased it."

Both men laughed, and finally Abby joined in their merriment until she remembered the reason for their meeting. "Do you have any idea who killed Cecil or why?"

"No, nothing at the scene gave us any clues." Sean turned to Darach. "I didn't smell a demon, so it's pretty safe to say it was a mortal crime."

"I think so too. I can usually smell the sulfur when demons are near, except in your case."

"Don't feel bad, Highlander, even my sire's kind have a hard time picking me out, so don't stress over it." For a moment, the lieutenant's eyes took on the flames of fire.

"That reminds me, Abby, how did you know, how could you tell what I was?"

"Your eyes turned red."

"Did you see the same thing, Darach?"

"Nay. But I can see them now. I be not sure why. Now, Abby, however, seems to have a gift for discerning demons. As well as having visions about crimes committed by Satan's minions before they happen."

"That's an interesting talent." The lieutenant exchanged glances with Darach. "And the only reason I can think of for you being able to see my eyes change is that I've dropped my glamour."

She didn't need to read their minds to know they both thought it was dangerous, and they were right.

"So, Highlander, how did you become an emissary of God?"

Abby half listened as Darach repeated the story that tortured her heart every time she thought or heard it. So much heartache. How had he survived the mental anguish to retain the endearing qualities he kept locked inside? A lesser man would be raging against the fates or using his God-given talents for something other than humanitarian purposes.

"...so this Michael of yours, is he hardnosed?

Would he want you to kill me because I'm part demon?"

Abby waited to see what Darach would say before she put her input in play.

"I know what ye be asking, but I am supposed to kill demons committing crimes. I dinnae see ye doing that."

"So I take it we can continue to work together?" Sean leaned forward as did Darach.

"Aye, as long as ye stay on the side ye are on now, I willna have to kill ye."

Sean laughed. "And that could be harder than you think, but…" He paused as Darach snarled. "I will be a good demon/mortal. Seriously…"

His eyes remained green as he took a couple of deep breaths. "Truth, I would like to meet this Michael someday. If he's as reviled as I've heard he is in the halls of Hell, then he must truly be a soldier for God. And I will need all the aid I can get when or if I give up this body. I'm not really sure what happens to me if I die."

"Michael might be able to answer some of those questions."

"Would you mention it to him?"

Darach chuckled. "Knowing the archangel, he is already privy to this conversation."

The sip of margarita Abby took almost went down the wrong way. She managed to get out, between having Darach and Sean pat her on the back, one important question. "Does that mean he could know what happened earlier?"

The immortal gave her a wolfish grin.

"Count on it, but he won't blame ye. It'll be me head on the chopping block."

"Well, at the moment, I wouldn't mind doing a bit of chopping myself."

She ignored both men as they doubled over with laughter. Her mood turned sour quickly. Cecil was dead—his murderer free and possibly never to be caught. And there was still that last vision she'd had… Abby glanced at the clock. Three o'clock in the morning. Time for bed.

"Look, I'm going to bed. Stay up for the rest of the night, I don't care, but clean up the mess you made. I'll take care of mine in the morning.

"Abby…I didn't mean—"

"Save it, Darach. It's been a long day and night. I'm tired. Sean, please let me know if you find out anything."

Sean stood to his feet as Abby pushed back her chair. She ignored the hand Darach held out, and guarded her heart against the hurt look in his gaze as she left the room, leaving a piece of herself behind. It would do no good to dream about a future with a man who could be dead if her vision was correct.

****

Darach bit his lip so hard he tasted blood. The commiserating look the lieutenant gave him only made him feel worse. He'd embarrassed Abby. Of course, over the last two nights, he'd done so much more. Although he'd found her at the scene of a crime fighting a demon, he had brought her into some of his world. And if things did not improve, she would see even more of the dark side of life and death.

"So, you just going to let her go to bed upset?"

"Truth?"

"Sure, I always prefer that to lies." Sean chuckled.

"If I go to her now, I will take her. I cannot, Sean. She has been through way too much, and if Angus gets his hands on her, it will be a nightmare.

"Are you sure he's around?"

"Michael says so, and—"

"He knows. I get it, but there ought to be some

halfway ground for you two. She's falling in love with you, you know?"

Darach knew his mouth flew open, but before he could deny Sean's words, or think about what they meant, his cell phone rang. The strains of "How Great Thou Art" showered the kitchen.

"Cool tune."

"Well, you can bet your arse, it'll get hotter in a few. It's Michael." Darach spit out the words.

Sean's eyes flashed red and then green in a split second.

"You really think he knows what you've been doing, and that I'm here?"

Darach glanced down at the phone's screen. The angelic wings that usually accompanied his boss's call were no longer a Heavenly white, they were beginning to turn a bit gray.

"Oh aye, he knows. Excuse me a minute, I have to take this call." He flipped the phone open. "Michael?"

"Don't act so surprised, Highlander. We both know you knew it was me. I believe you have some explanations you want to tender?"

"I suppose ye want them now? Can they not wait until tomorrow?"

"No. You forget I have a boss too, and he's not really thrilled that you've been drinking whiskey with the enemy."

"Sean's not the enemy. He's a victim, just like I was, just like Abby is."

Michael's exhalation caused a shard of lightning to brighten the sky right outside the kitchen door.

"Look, you need to stay focused on Abby. Stay out of her bed. I mean it, and tell Sean he has free choice just like the rest of you mortals and immortals. His choices decide where he resides after he dies."

Darach looked at Sean and gave him a slight

grin before turning his attention back to the call.

"So, how much trouble am I in?"

"Not much, if you keep to the course. I have a bad feeling that things are lining up that could cause you and Abby some serious hurt if you're not careful."

"Can ye give me a hint of what might be coming?"

A second exhalation shook Abby's home with the vibration of thunder.

"I understand, ye can't or won't. So, I'll just keep guarding Abby." Darach's sigh was not nearly as theatrical.

"Good night, Darach. I'll be in touch."

Darach closed his phone before opening his mouth to speak, although he knew Michael could hear him anyway.

"Keep in touch he says, like I dinnae already know he watches me night and day."

Sean laughed but it sounded forced. "Did he say anything about me?"

"That ye would be in control of your own destiny or something like that by the choices you make."

Sean remained silent for a second before he nodded. "Thanks."

For the rest of the night they talked about Angus, where he might be, and who had murdered Cecil. By the time they staggered to the living room, Darach was more than a bit flummoxed by the whiskey he'd consumed. He needed to remember for future references, never drink with a half-mortal, half-demon companion. They could drink a man, even an immortal, under the table.

Something he needed to make sure didn't happen in the future. His goal to find and kill Angus as well as keep Abby safe could not be derailed by anything.

****

Angus viewed the photograph of Abigail Dupree one of his minions had gotten from her school. She looked a bit too boring for his taste, but then another photo fell out of the manila envelope. The woman staring back at him was a far cry from the meek woman façade. What a difference makeup could make.

Her silver-blonde locks and blue eyes were just what he liked in a woman. Of course, he liked most women. They served a purpose, and having this woman beneath him would be a slap that Darach would never forget.

When dealing with immortals who do not listen, remind myself not to let off steam. It tends to make the wallpaper in my office peel. Also, remember to get information on Sean Black.

From the desk of Michael/Archangel to God

Chapter Ten

Abby awakened to weak sunshine creeping through her bedroom window. She'd left the shutters open before falling into bed. Normally they were locked tighter than a virgin's knees in church, but with Darach as a houseguest she figured she'd be safe from any mortal break-ins or demons as long as she stayed inside.

After stretching, she lay there for a moment more before jumping up. A few seconds later, a quick shower poured more life into her mentally tired brain. She should have asked Sean when Cecil's body would be released. He and Elaine had not had any children, and as far as she knew there were no next of kin. She wanted to help plan the funeral and with expenses if possible.

First things first, though. She needed fuel for her body's system. Coffee and then a quick slice of toast with jelly. She didn't have to worry about cooking lunch, not with the leftovers from yesterday's feast.

She barreled down the staircase in jeans and an old sweater. Her sneakers made little noise as she left the carpeted treads and traversed the hardwood floor toward the kitchen. She detoured through the living room, and stopped dead in her tracks.

Darach lay sprawled on the floor, a blanket barely covering his naked chest and arms. A scant distance away, Sean dozed in one of the armchairs. His long legs were stretched out, and his booted feet rested on the coffee table.

She had no idea what time the men called it quits after she went to bed, but by their comatose state it had to be pretty late. Late? Shoot, her bedtime was late; theirs must have been close to dawn.

Deciding to leave them to their rest, she continued to the kitchen. When she pushed the door open, she was pleasantly surprised to find the evidence of their late-night gabfest was gone. The blender stood upside down in the drain rack, and the glass she used rested next to it. The antique goblets and the whiskey bottle had disappeared. Probably whisked back to wherever they came from.

She shook her head at how easily she'd accepted the magic Sean had displayed, not to mention having a half-demon and an immortal in her home. Life had certainly taken on a surreal taint. And her solemn vow never to get involved with a man again had fallen into the hole of resolutions she repeated every year on New Year's Day. Abby could no longer dismiss the fact Darach was fast becoming her ideal man. His lovemaking turned her inside out, and his slow appraising looks and sensual smiles simply made her want to tie him up and keep him with her forever. Of course that couldn't happen. Darach was an immortal, and would move on when his assignment was over. She just hoped it wasn't through death.

Her stomach rumbled and Abby took her mind off of what would never be, and began to think an omelet would be a better start to her day. There was a lot she wanted to get accomplished. First she wanted to go back to Cecil's and see if he left any clue as to what or who had killed him. She needed to eat quickly and get moving. No telling how long her protector would sleep.

However, once she glanced over the fridge's contents she remembered she'd used the last of the eggs in the dressing. The kitchen clock highlighted the hour. There was still a bit of time to go to the store before she would have to contend with people vying for sidewalk space and after-holiday sales.

She knew Darach would have a cow if she went out, but it was broad daylight. Surely any demon would be getting their ugly sleep, and if a mortal bothered her, she'd kick him where it hurt. While she was trying to decide what to do her cell phone rang. She didn't use it all that often, but the school had it on file.

Abby dug it out of her briefcase and popped it to her ear.

"Hello."

"Abigail?" The voice on the other end sounded familiar, but she couldn't place it.

"Yes, who's calling please."

"It's me, Jim Dobbs."

Abby ran the name through her memory banks and then it clicked. One of the teachers at the school. She should have known him right away but he never called her. It could be he'd heard about Cecil.

"Oh, hi, Jim. How are you?" She glanced at her watch, she really wanted to go to the store or at least the corner bakery.

"Not good. I heard on the news about Cecil. A few of us—me, Nathaniel Chase, Meg Henderson, thought we'd see if you wanted to get some coffee. I know you and Cecil were fairly close."

She could hear the sympathetic tone but also the curiosity lapping at his words.

"Yes, we were. Uh, I have houseguests, so—"

"Please, Abby, it might help us wrap our heads around what happened."

Lord, she so didn't want to rehash what happened not with everything else she had on her mental list, but she could probably do a ten-minute chat, grab something for breakfast, check out Cecil's apartment, and be back before the men woke up. And so what, even if she didn't, Darach's job was to protect her, not keep her a prisoner, no matter what he thought.

"Okay, can ya'll meet me at the coffee shop at the end of Canal Street?"

"Yes, that would be great. What time?" The relief was prevalent in Jim's voice.

"I can be there in five."

"All right, see you in a few, and thanks, Abby."

Abby said goodbye, and then backtracked to the living room. Snores greeted her ears. Good, maybe she wouldn't get chewed out if she hurried. After grabbing her handbag, she tossed the cell phone inside, and sprinted for the front door. Thank God for sneakers, they were great for making a silent getaway.

Exactly five minutes later she arrived at the shop, which was pretty much empty at the moment.

"Hi Elle, can I get a latte and some beignets?"

"Sure thing, Abby. You want me to fix up a box for you to take home?"

"Yeah, that'll be great. I've some guests, and it'll save fixing breakfast."

"I heard you had a great big hunk of sex staying with you." Elle winked as she brought the latte to the counter. "Go ahead and take a seat, I'll bring your beignets over, and fix you up a nice box of goodies."

Abby's face stung with heat. Lord, did everyone know Darach was staying at her house? And how had they found out?

"Thanks, Elle. Oh...by the way, how did you know my guest was male and sexy to boot?"

The owner/waitress propped a hand on her hip, leaned over just a fraction, and grinned. "Honey, everyone around these parts knows Darach. He's the man everyone goes to when they need something. He's not only hot but has a good heart."

"I guess I forgot how much our neck of the woods keeps up with everything." Abby took a quick sip of her mocha and almost burned her mouth.

"It's cause we care, sugar. When Grandmere Dupree passed on, all of us natives were worried about you. Just fresh out of college and all alone. You've got friends, Abby, even if you don't realize it."

Abby glanced up into the concerned brown-eyed gaze of a woman she'd known most of her life. Looking at her brown hair tipped with gray, the slightly stooped posture, and the tired smile, she wondered how much she'd missed by keeping to herself.

"Thanks, Elle. I guess I've been a bit clueless since Grandmere died."

"Oh honey, you've just been caught up in life, and sometimes that's enough to break anyone."

Abby squeezed the hand Elle held out, sniffed just a bit when the woman walked away, and then tried to pin on a smile when Jim and the rest of his entourage entered the shop.

Abby remained silent as Jim, Meg, and Nate, as some of his peers called him, took seats beside and across from her in the booth. Jim spoke before she could get even a hello out.

"Thanks for meeting us, Abby. I think I speak for all of us when I say Cecil's death was a shock."

She tried to smile but his words brought back the upset and frustration of the last twenty-four hours.

"I know. It was quite a shock for me too."

"Do you know if he suffered? We saw some of the television footage. You looked shocked." Meg's usually brisk transplanted northern tone was low.

What could she say, that she'd seen the blood he'd lost, she'd seen his battered face? No, the news reports would have been bad enough.

"I don't know. I pray he didn't."

Nate spoke up for the first time. "I wonder who they'll get to cover his classes after the break. And do you know anything about funeral services?"

Abby breathed a sigh of relief, this was something she could talk about. "I'm sure Principal Caldwell is already on it. As for the arrangements, I will be talking to the lieutenant today about when they might release Cecil's body."

Once the other three sat nursing lattes, and Abby sipped the last of her vanilla mocha, the silence was a bit daunting. She'd worked with this group, but had never been close to any of them. Maybe that was what Elle meant. She needed to allow others in more.

"Once I find out about the arrangements, I can let ya'll know."

"Thanks that would be great. Maybe next time we could meet for coffee under happier circumstances." Meg's offer was tentative, but Abby grabbed it anyway.

"That would be nice. I'll look forward to getting together."

****

Darach woke with a pounding head, and a mouth that tasted like some of the bayou had crawled into it while he slept. An obnoxious noise hit his ears, causing him to clamp his hands over the abused appendages before looking around to see where it came from.

Sean lay sprawled out in one of the chairs seemingly dead to the world except for the God-in-

Heaven awful noise erupting from his mouth and nose. Darach pulled on his discarded shirt, caught up one of his boots from the floor, and tossed it square into the lieutenant's chest.

"Wha—who—"

"Do ye have any idea how bad ye snore?"

"I don't snore."

"Trust me, ye do. What time is it?" Darach waited for Sean to check the watch on his wrist.

"It's about eleven-thirty. I have to be at work at three."

Sean sat up, rubbed a hand over his bristled brow, before standing up. "Gotta find a bathroom. After that, you think Abby would cook me something to eat? The whiskey is sitting like C-4 in my belly."

Darach groaned, Abby would more than likely throw a frying pan at the both of them. "Maybe, if she dinnae kill us first."

"Kill us, for what?" Sean stopped and turned back to face the living room.

"For keeping her up half the night, drinking, embarrassing her, ye name it. And for pity's sake keep your voice down. Me head is splitting."

Sean grunted and then disappeared. He returned a couple of minutes later with his hair shorter, a fresh suit on, clean-shaven, and looking like he'd never had a drop to drink.

"Not fair, halfling. Ye should have to go through the rites of getting clean like the rest of us mort…immortals."

Sean grinned. "Not my fault you have to do things the old way. Talk to Michael and see if he can give you a bit of power to go along with your longevity."

"I'm rather fond of me hide, so I'll keep that to myself." Darach stretched to a series of snap, crackle, and pops as he straightened out his spine and stood up.

"Getting old, Highlander?"

"No, not that it's any of your concern. Now move, I need to find Abby."

Sean's grin turned a bit evil. "Not trying to tell you your business, but you might want to shower first."

Darach quickly brought his arm up and sniffed. Good, he didn't stink. But the halfling was right, he did need a shower in a bad way, and probably a razor to his face wouldn't hurt any before Abby saw him.

"All right, but when you see Abby tell her I'll be down in a few minutes."

"Sure, take your time. I'd love to chat her up." Sean's smile this time was positively wicked.

"Chat better be all you do, halfling."

Darach wasted no more breath on Sean, but transported himself to his house for some fresh clothes, then back to Abby's and into the shower. He was rinsing his hair and body when someone banged on the bathroom door.

"Highlander, your woman's disappeared." Sean's voice was sharp, and a second later, Darach stood in the hallway with a towel around his waist.

One hand reached out to grab Sean around the neck, but he sidestepped Darach.

"What do ye mean, she's disappeared? What did ye do to her?"

"Chill out, MacRath, I went looking, but I couldn't find her. I thought she might be outside, but no go."

Darach's heart did freeze, as did the rest of his body with fear. Why would Abby leave? Did she leave on her own? Who had her? Was she at the mercy of Angus?

"Ye be sure?"

"Yes. Why don't you get dressed, and I'll check outside again. Do you have any idea where she might go if she went out?"

Darach cursed his ignorance about Abby's daily activities. He knew she left for school when it was in session, but not the time, he knew she went to the club at night to sing, but he didn't have an inkling of where she went during the day when she wasn't working.

"Nay, I just met her the night before Thanksgiving."

"Well we'll find her, don't worry."

"I have to worry. Michael believes Angus could target Abby because of me."

Several quick seconds later, both Darach and Sean stood on the sidewalk. If Abby didn't plan on being gone long, she would probably take the streetcar.

"She may have taken the trolley. I'm going to teleport to some of the shops that run up and down the trolley line."

"Okay, I'll meet you there." Sean moved off at a fast clip, and Darach allowed his body to embrace the teleportation process.

He rematerialized on a side street opening out to the main thoroughfare. He scanned the passersby and the openings to shop entrances. Nothing but clothing and Mardi Gras paraphernalia on one side. He turned his gaze to the opposite side and a door opening caught his attention.

Abby!

He resisted the urge to rush across the street and pull her into his arms—for all of one second.

She stood in the midst of two men and a woman. They seemed to be mortal. He wondered if they were.

Sean stepped into stride beside Darach. "They are not demon."

God's teeth, did the halfling have the ability to read people's minds?

"No, I can't read minds." Sean's lips almost carried a smile as they moved closer to the quartet. "Anyone could read what was on yours. Your facial expression said it all."

Darach didn't argue, but he would take care in the future to keep the stony expression he'd always worn before first meeting Abby in place.

"Abby." He enjoyed the look of surprise and then guilt lacerating the deep blue of her eyes.

"Darach, hi. I thought I'd be home long before you woke up."

"Introduce me to your friends, my love."

Surprise was quickly replaced with shock, a glimmer of happiness, and then sadness. What was it about his words that would make her feel sad?

"Uh, this is Jim, Meg, and Nate. They're teachers from my school, and they heard about Cecil."

He hooked his arm around her trim waist and pulled her to him. "Nice to meet ye. I'm Darach MacRath. Abby, it's time to go."

"But we were making plans to get together before Cecil's funeral." Abby looked around and her eyes widened when she spotted Sean.

"Lieutenant Black, can you help us out here?"

Sean stepped next to the group. Darach watched as he shook hands with the teachers. Once he stepped back he looked at Darach. "I was right. No problem."

Abby began to look increasingly agitated. Not something he wanted, but it couldn't be helped. At least not at the moment.

"What can I do to help, Abby?"

She cleared her throat. "Do you have any idea when Cecil's body will be released? We want to plan a wake before the funeral."

"It's going to be several days. The body was shipped to Baton Rouge to the crime lab this morning."

"I don't understand, why was he sent there?"

"Any time there's a violent death, the SCL, short for State Crime Lab, has to autopsy the body. I'm sure it won't be much more than a week."

"Oh... Well, thanks, Sean." Her words were low but when she turned back to the group with her, Darach watched her square her shoulders.

"Hey, it's going to be a week or so before we can do anything to honor Cecil, so I can let you all know after school's back in session."

"Cool, thanks Abbs." The other woman in the group of teachers patted Abby on the arm. "I'm heading out. I promised my family I wouldn't be gone long."

Her words seemed to galvanize the other two, and soon it was just Abby, Darach, and Sean.

"Let's go home, Abby."

"Actually I had another errand to run."

"Well, I'll go with you." Darach's gaze brooked no refusal.

"Darach, I hate this. I hate not being able to go out on my own in broad daylight without it causing a red alert." Her words came tumbling out, and she shoved a pastry box into his hands, before spinning around and walking off.

He looked at Sean who did nothing helpful but give him a look of pure innocence. Darach in turn gave him the pastry box and barely heard his, "Oh good, I can eat now," before he hurried after Abby.

"Abby, please, ye cannae just go traipsing off on your own."

"I'm not alone, there are a lot of people out, it's daylight, and I'll be fine."

"Maybe, but maybe not. I cannae take a chance on something happening to ye." He gently gripped her arm.

"Why do you even care?" Her question felt like

she'd stabbed him in the heart.

"I care, all right?"

"Highlander!"

Darach jerked to a stop causing Abby to stop with him. Sean hurried up.

"What is it?"

"The PD found another body. This time it's a woman."

****

Angus didn't grieve over his dead bedmate. She'd lasted longer than others he'd had. So what if things had gotten a bit out of hand. She was a woman and deserved to be used. It wasn't his fault she couldn't take his type of bed sport.

Michael pushed the reading glasses up onto the bridge of his nose. No, he should not have to wear glasses. After all, he was an archangel, but after millenniums of paperwork, his eyes did get a bit tired. Not that he couldn't see twenty-twenty, he just had so much work to do. As he perused the biography of Sean Black, he marveled at how the halfling, as Darach called him, managed to survive with a sense of justice still intact. Perhaps, the man might be of some use to his immortal.

Chapter Eleven

Abby waited for Darach to tell her he was taking her home again, but when he didn't she glanced up at his face. Gone were the tiny laughter lines from around his mouth and eyes she'd glimpsed in the last couple of days. His face once again resembled a piece of marble, albeit a beautiful and breathtaking vision of a conquering warrior, but she wanted the Darach she was coming to know.

"Ye will have to come with us."

"Really?"

"Aye, I dinnae like it, but there be no help for it. I willna leave ye alone." Darach looked at Sean who shrugged his shoulders.

"Don't worry, between the both of us, we'll make sure she stays safe."

"Thank you. Where do we need to go?"

"Bourbon Street. You can do your thing or we can catch the streetcar," Sean replied.

"Streetcar, please." Abby almost yelled her

preference. Darach's face unfroze long enough to give her a brief glimpse of a smile before etching itself back into an uncompromising visage. He gently tugged her toward the streetcar. Sean followed. Conversation remained absent. Abby's thoughts didn't. Someone else had died. Could it be the same person who'd stolen Cecil's life?

The trio that got off on Bourbon Street was subdued. Abby didn't know what to say to break the silence and wasn't sure she wanted to. The situation was not of her making, but she hated it all the same. As soon as Darach heard it was a woman, both he and Sean had gone on what she'd call red alert. They'd edged her in on the streetcar, and on the walk to and now from the transportation stop.

What were they afraid of?

"Sean, over here." A street cop held up the yellow crime tape surrounding a Dumpster. The closer they got to the crowd surrounding the body, the more Abby wanted to go back home by any transportation possible. Sean went under the tape first, helped her under, and Darach quickly followed. She so did not want to go through this again. Her lips were open to ask Darach to take her home, when the uniform deep human barrier parted.

Sean must be deserving of quite a status with the NOLA PD. They parted like grass in a high wind. And miracles of miracles, neither she nor Darach were stopped as they followed the lieutenant.

"What do we have?"

"Woman, mid-twenties or so, bled out from several wounds to her torso and upper thighs. There are bruises around her neck, like someone choked her."

Sean pulled on a pair of gloves and knelt by the blonde-haired woman. Thank God she lay on her side. Abby did not want to see the death mask on her face.

She and Darach watched as the lieutenant reached out and lightly touched the abrasions. His eyes flared, his posture stiffened, and he stood up so quickly, Abby almost got whiplash watching. He ripped the gloves from his hands, tossed them into the Dumpster, and then turned their way.

"Darach." Sean jerked his head to the right, and Darach followed him, leaving Abby standing on her own. Something was up. Probably something she wasn't going to like.

"Abby." She tore her gaze from the paramedics lifting the body onto a stretcher.

"That didn't take long."

"No, but we need to make haste." Concern overrode his hard facial expression.

"Why?"

He grimaced but remained silent.

"Are you going to tell me anything or what?"

"We'll talk back at your house."

Abby got nothing else from him until they were clear of the crowd and stood in an alley.

"Come." Darach held his arms out. She knew what was coming.

"No."

"Yes." His black eyes went silver.

"Do I have a choice?"

"No."

Abby walked into his arms and closed her eyes.

****

Darach watched as Abby moved around the homey-style kitchen, warming up food for lunch. She'd been quiet since their arrival home. He wasn't sure if she was waiting on him to explain or if she felt the emotional impact of the morning.

She took a covered plate out of the microwave and sat it in front of him before pouring tea into a glass.

"Give me a minute to warm up my plate, and then I want to know what you and Sean found at the crime scene."

He welcomed the few minutes of respite. She would not be happy when he told her what he had to in order to keep her safe.

"Okay, shoot."

Darach looked up from his untouched food. Abby was now seated across from him. The expression in her blue gaze screamed she wanted the truth and nothing else.

"The young woman that was murdered was touched by a demon."

Abby sat her glass of tea down so carefully, Darach knew she was trying to control her shock.

"I don't suppose ya'll could be mistaken?"

"Nay, I wish we were, but Sean is certain."

Her gaze speared him with its compassion and slight fear.

"That poor girl. How awful."

He clamped his teeth together. Awful did not touch on what the woman had endured. Rape, torture, and finally death by the hands of one who reveled in causing harm. There was no point in telling Abby all the details if he could avoid it. Nor that he was certain Angus had been part of the crime.

She didn't say anything else, and so they concentrated on eating. Ten minutes later, he watched Abby push the same piece of turkey around her plate again. Her appetite seemed to disappear just like his had, only he forced the food to his lips and beyond. His body needed fuel to function, and tonight he would be out hunting the monstrosity who'd killed the young prostitute. It was a plan he and Sean had come up with while they briefly spoke at the scene, and one that would not earn him any points with Abby.

He took the last bite of food from his plate and then pushed it back. Abby, as if waiting for a signal, got up and scraped their plates into the garbage before putting them in the sink. She ran water into one side and squirted liquid soap into the swirling depths.

Darach wondered if she was still in shock. Her movements were stiff, not at all like the fluid grace he loved. Loved? There was that word again. An emotion he could not afford to have.

"Abby, we still need to talk."

She kept her back to him as she rinsed and then placed the dishes, cutlery, and glasses in the drain-rack. Only after drying her hands did she turn to face him.

"Finally, we get to the reason your face has reverted back into a stone sculpture."

"What are you talking about?"

"Come on, Darach, ever since you found out about this woman's body, you've turned back into the emotionless man I first met."

"I dinnae think we need emotions to cloud the issue." He wished he knew what Abby was talking about. He'd been more open with her than he had with anyone since his mortal death.

"So you think showing feelings has no place in this situation or when you are dealing with me at all?"

"Ye are putting words in me mouth. What I think is that we both need to remember ye could be a target. And emotions can make clear thinking murky."

Abby's eyes went from a wide-eyed blue to a tempestuous indigo. He was not sure what he'd said to make matters worse, but he would need to choose his next words wisely.

"Let me see if I have this straight. You think we need to leave off any type of emotions when dealing with one another. Or do you mean you regret allowing your emotions to make love to me, or whatever you want to call it?"

A knife would have been better used to cut off his manhood. The blow she delivered made him want to groan. How on earth could one woman come up with such a bedlam twist to what he'd said?

"I didnae say that, Abby."

"Really? Well you've been acting like an ass, Darach."

The ass had just about taken all he be going to take. First she slandered their lovemaking and then she called him names. Emotional involvement be damned.

"Dinnae call me an ass, Abby."

"And what are you going to do to stop me?"

Abby didn't like the way his lips turned up into a smile. It looked more like a smirk to her. A promise of retaliation coated his now silver irises.

As she tried to decide to stand her ground or run, he stood up. His delectable body looked like a piece of meat to a starving animal, and muscles rippled as he moved around the table. His legs drew her attention as they ate up the short distance between them.

His arms slid around her waist and she almost screamed, no, make that melted, as one hand slid downward to cup her butt. No fair, he was so totally not playing by the rules. They should be in a totally satisfying war of words which would leave them both feeling like the air had been cleared—not this sensual battle of male versus female hormones.

"Take it back, Abby."

"Take what back?" At the moment, she was having a hard time remembering what she'd said as his hand slid around to the front of her jeans. A flip of a wrist and the button opened like magic. The teeth of the zipper parted like the Red Sea, and she was lost to anything but the touch of his fingers grazing her center.

"Take back calling me an ass."

Abby pulled her mind back from the sexual bliss beginning to mark her body as his. What harm would it do to apologize? *Fight it Abby, you know if you give in, the man will hold it over your head for a lifetime.* Her mind clashed with her body's pleas and lost.

"Fine, I take it back."

His low rumble of laughter caressed her ears, and made her want to climb inside his body. When Darach was a poster child for a warrior come to life, he was hot, but when he laughed he sent her desire meter to the top of the charts.

"And..."

His thumb found and thrummed her sensitive nub. She forced back the keening cry begging to be released and tried to think about what else he wanted.

"And what?" Her words were a husky whisper of sound. Her frustration on being denied the pleasure she craved, as he stopped his bone-melting motion, echoed in her question.

"Throwing aspersions on our previous lovemaking."

Despite the situation she was in, or because of it, Abby wanted to laugh. Men were so dense, especially when it came to matters of the male ego. Here he was making love to her again, she was a puddle of melted bones, and he continued to think she'd found fault in his lovemaking.

"All right, if it makes you feel better, I'm sorry. You are not an emotionless clump of dirt when you touch me. Okay?"

His laugher was full of satisfaction, but she didn't care as long as he assuaged the need deep inside her body.

Abby's breath caught when he did just that. As the spirals built into a crescendo of want, she felt the arm around her waist tighten. Good thing, too, for she would hit the floor if he turned her loose. His thumb continued to work magic on her needful flesh and then her body exploded into a thousand pieces.

She closed her eyes and barely felt when Darach lifted her off her feet. However, she was grateful he took the mortal way to her room. As he gently laid her on the bed, she opened her eyes, glimpsed the silver tone of his gaze, and held her hand out.

Darach followed her down to the bed, pulled her body next to his until her backside spooned against his hardness. He ran his hand down her still trembling body. How he wanted Abby. To take her, make her his. Should he? Or would it be best to leave her be? Of course, if he planned to do just so, then he would never have touched her in the first place.

His hand shook slightly as he followed the contours of her hip to below her knee. He traveled the path again, reversing his movements before resting his hand on her waist. His fingers trembled just a bit as he contemplated stripping her bare and pushing himself deep inside her. If he did would he finally be able to quench the fire just being near her always brought.

A brief twitch of her backside, a soft snuffle of sound, and the room filled with the sounds of Abby's soft but feminine snores.

Darach groaned inwardly, and then relaxed his tense body. It was probably for the best. He still had to tell her about their evening plans.

****

Abby slid out from beneath the warm arm holding her captive. She wasn't sure how long she'd been down for the count, but the sun streaming into her bedroom window warned she didn't have long, if she wanted to go out, before it became dark.

She held her breath as she tiptoed across the room and down the stairs. Washing her face and brushing her teeth could be handled in the downstairs bathroom. She wasn't taking a chance the water would wake up Mr. Hot-and-Sexy *and please let him continue to sleep.*

Abby washed the cobwebs out of her eyes, brushed the fuzz off her teeth, and ran a comb through her tangled hair. She then grabbed her bag and headed to the front door. Hopefully, as earlier today, the safety guards were just there to keep demons out and not her in.

The door opened easily enough and she stepped out onto the porch. When a lightning bolt didn't send her hurtling back into the house, she let her breath escape. A few minutes later she caught the trolley to Cecil's apartment.

The stairs were just as tedious as before, and she stood catching her breath when she hit the landing that lead to his apartment. Abby was brought up short when she rounded the corner and spied the yellow crime scene tape across Cecil's threshold.

Crap. She forgotten this would be considered a crime scene. Well nothing for it, even if the police had already gone over the apartment, she wanted to search also. Abby thanked God the door opened inward and made nary a sound as it completed its arc backward. She slid carefully under the crossed yellow streamers and then closed the door almost all the way shut.

As she looked around the living area, she decided to start with Cecil's work desk. The police, why she didn't know, had not taken his computer so she'd start there. Abby seated herself in the desk chair, and ignored the chill moving up and down her spine as she thought about how the last time Cecil had used this desk he'd been alive. Just maybe she could find out a timeline for what happened.

The aged laptop with its scratches and dents booted up slowly but nicely. The welcome screen glowed blue and then she was looking at the icons. What to check first? E-mail? Documents? Did he have a schedule he kept?

Abby gave up trying to get into Cecil's e-mail after the tenth time of invalid user ID and password. The sky was already beginning to get darker. She needed to wrap this up. Hopefully, Darach still slept, if not they would probably have another fight.

The document folder held nothing more interesting than student papers from Cecil's history class. Abby search and found a partial schedule denoting plans for their Thanksgiving visit, but nothing else on that day. She was on the verge of searching the day before for information when a slight sound in the hallway startled her. A second later, the door was pushed open and she stared into the blood-red eyes of Lieutenant Black.

****

Darach awoke to Abby's raised voice, and Sean's unmistakable baritone. One moment sleep fuzzed his brain, the next he was on his feet. Something had happened.

"Absolutely and totally not gonna happen, Lieutenant."

"If you don't tell the Highlander, I—"

"Oh, that's great, threaten me. I should have known you'd react this way." Abby's voice sounded angry and frantic.

"Abby, he has a right to know. You never should have—"

"Don't tell me what I should or shouldn't do. It's not your place."

Darach materialized right outside the living room. He could hear Abby's stomping steps. She was the only person he knew who could make her bare feet slap like she was garnering for battle.

"Be reasonable. It's for your own good." Sean's tone had gone to pleading.

"I don't think so. I've done perfectly fine without a keeper, and guess what, if Darach thinks he can make love to me in an effort to get me to go along with his asinine idea, he has another thing coming and it ain't what he thinks."

"Make love?" Darach heard the amusement in Sean's voice. The halfling had better tread lightly.

"How interesting. I didn't think the immortal had it in him to be so devious."

"Well just goes to show what you know about immortals, demon man."

"Ouch. Abby, darling, you don't have to take aim at me. I'm only doing my job, and I'm following the Highlander's directions."

"Enough!" Darach stepped into the room and gauged Abby's reaction. Immediately her spine seemed to turn into iron, her eyes flashed blue sparks, and her lips turned up in a snarl. Not good, but he could turn this thing around. Or at least he hoped he could.

"Oh, gee, look, it's the mighty warrior come to put his foot down. Well, let me clue you in, MacRath, I answer to no man."

"And I'm not just a mon. I'm your protector, an immortal, and I'm getting fast irritated with your misplaced anger." He advanced a few steps toward Abby, who in turned moved a fraction closer to Sean. A movement that did nothing to eclipse Darach's own growing anger. He turned to Sean. "What did she do?"

"Oh please, why does it always have to be my fault? And how can you say 'misplaced'? You've turned my entire life into chaos."

"Hush Abby, it wasn't by my design. Ye placed

yourself into danger and a demon's path by choosing to follow a vision. Ye insisted on being there when both bodies were found, and going to work when ye should have stayed home. All of these reasons have brought about your present circumstances." Darach eased forward a bit more. "And let's not forget, ye were a willing participant when I made love to ye."

"Like I had a choice." He could almost hear the silent *Take that.*

"Abby, are you saying Darach took you against your will?"

Sean's question rained into Darach's head. Did the woman truly believe he would make love to her against her will, and when he didn't even have the pleasure of attaining his own release.

"Well, no, but he kissed me senseless, and I..."

"Hell no!"

Both their comments came out at the same time. Sean looked to Darach who turned his gaze back on Abby after a look of warning to the lieutenant.

"Okay, then, why don't ya'll work out what we *are* going to do tonight, and I'll get back to you."

"No, I need to know what she did. What does she need to tell me?" Darach knew he'd have to drag it out of Abby. The woman's face was a testimony of her refusal to do anything he wanted. Her blue eyes flashed, her lips were set in a grim line, and he hated the way she tapped her foot on the wood floor.

Sean turned back, gave Abby a pitying glance, and then spit out. "Your woman, whom you need to control better, was at the first crime scene. I found her going through the victim's computer." Having dropped that bomb, the halfling left the room, but Darach was too stunned to acknowledge his leaving other than a grunt. Abby kept silent.

His anger grew stronger, egged on by fear that ripped his inner organs to shreds.

"Do ye really believe I didnae leave ye a choice?"

Abby's cheeks reddened just a bit and then she shook her head.

"Good, now answer this question. Why in all that be holy did ye go out and to a crime scene?" His words were low but ferocious.

"Because I thought maybe I could find something." Abby sounded defensive, as she should be.

"Well that was the most ignorant move ye have made so far. Whoever killed Cecil could have returned to the scene of the crime." Darach's hands fisted together. He was close to having a coronary.

"What did you want me to do, Darach? Just wait and see if they find who killed him?"

"Dammit, aye! I dinnae want anything to happen to ye." At her disbelieving look he added, "And it has nothing to do with following Michael's orders." As he watched, her look changed to chagrin.

"I'm sorry. I just feel helpless sitting here. Besides, it was daylight when I left. I'll be more careful next time."

Darach frowned. The woman still didn't get it.

"Stop looking like Mr. Gloom-and-Doom. I'm fine. Now let's talk about what you have planned for me tonight."

Hell, he hoped she'd forget about that. He should have known better.

"Sean and I are going out and looking for demons. Ye cannae go with us. 'Tis not—"

"Well I don't cotton to being put in protective custody, while you two go off and act the heroes hunting human and demon murderers. That wasn't what I had in mind for tonight."

"What *did* you have in mind, lass?"

A blush bloomed on her cheeks and then darkened. "I thought we could stay home and continue what you started earlier."

Lust ran rampant throughout his lower body, as

his brain tried to assimilate the bomb she'd dropped on his head. Women, although adorable, could be the most confusing people alive.

Darach closed the distance between them and pulled her close. "I think that idea has merit, but not tonight, Abby. We have to find who is doing the killing or ye willna never be safe."

"I'm warning you right now, I'm not going to spend the night in jail."

He dropped his head to rest on top of her silky silver mane, and inhaled the jasmine scenting the air.

"Don't worry about it, we'll work something out."

****

Angus laughed. Everything was going much better than he planned. If all went well tonight, then he could have Darach in his grasp and dead before the next few sunrises. He loved it when everything fell into place. It made his life so much easier. And once he had Darach out for the count, he would still go after Abigail. The woman was a prize he would love to lay open.

Michael closed the ledger of notes he'd made on Sean Black, checked off what he could use on his notepad, and then turned his attention to Darach. He'd closed the cloud opening earlier in order not to see the immortal violate what he'd been told. He wanted to call him forth from Earth and give him more than a wingful of admonishment, but Abigail Dupree was not fighting Darach's touch. Could it be she felt something for his warrior?

Chapter Twelve

Abby walked beside Darach, so closely tucked to his side, she could almost crawl under his skin. The wafting fragrance of his cologne tickled her nose, and she wanted so badly to drag him back to her house.

His way of working it out was for her to be installed at a bar where he would leave her with someone he knew. He and Sean would be in the area and all Abby had to do was call him. Of course that facilitated having to buy a cell phone for Abby. She didn't really think she needed a new one, but Darach insisted he wanted something more up-to-date.

"Almost there. You'll like Rae."

Rae? That was a woman's name!

"Who is Rae?" She hoped the tinge of jealously burning in her heart didn't coat her tongue.

"She's a waitress. I've known her since first coming to NOLA. She works at the Highlander Bar."

Abby had heard of that place, and not all good things either. A place where some of the meanest ex-cons, lowlifes, and other sorts who bided their time until their next fix or crime hung out.

If a woman waited on tables there, she'd have to be one tough lady. Probably old looking with a body that had seen better days, and wrinkled to boot. No need to be jealous—no need at all.

She squeezed the hand encircling her waist. "I'm sure I'll love Rae."

Bourbon Street housed a lot of bars and restaurants, some fancy, some not. The more seedy types were established on the lower end. Soon, the bar came into sight. It didn't look so bad on the outside with its medieval-type front doors, dormer windows, and an old-fashioned lantern lighting up the exterior. The building itself was made of some sort of sturdy-looking wood, with concrete blocks reinforcing the foundation around it.

Darach opened the door, motioned Sean inside, and then pulled Abby across the threshold. The room was a semi-dark cavern filled with a variety of bodies. Some were clean and some stank just a bit.

Sean stepped back and allowed Darach to take the lead and he led them both to a booth in the back of the room. After he scooted in, Abby slid in beside him, and then Sean. Now she felt like the filling of a sandwich.

"Darach, I missed you for the last few nights. Where have you been?"

The lilting voice belonged to a woman in her early thirties. Blonde hair was pulled back into an intricate design on top of her head, with a few loose bangs, drawing attention to the high cheekbones and green eyes of the waitress. She wore a low-cut peasant blouse like she was born to it, and the short flared skirt showed off more than enough of her legs.

Abby hated her already. This had to be the infamous Rae, since she didn't see any other women in the place.

"Rae, darling, 'tis good to see ye. I've been a bit busy lately. Could you bring a round of drinks for me and my friends?"

Abby listened as he ordered a beer for himself and Sean after conferring with the lieutenant, and then a margarita for Abby. The camaraderie between the immortal and the barmaid was hard to watch. It didn't take having a satellite fall out of the sky onto her head for her to know Rae was in love with Darach.

The woman finally moved off to fill their order, and Darach turned to Abby. "What did I tell ye? Rae is an angel, isn't she?"

At his question, even Sean's mouth opened a bit. Was Darach blind as well as dumb as a piece of clay? Couldn't he see what was going on?

"Well, I'll take your word for it, since I just met her and all."

"Rae is not like a lot of women who work in this district."

Oh, and just what type of woman is she? Abby wanted to scream.

"She works here at night to bring in money for her children. During the day, while her kids are in school, she does the same. Her husband is a slimy piece of offal. I've tried to convince her to leave him, but she's afraid he'll try to take her kids."

Oh great, the fact the woman was a jewel of a person made it worse.

Rae brought their drinks, and Darach pulled a bill from the vicinity of his pants pocket. Sean followed suit.

"Hey, that's way too much for the drinks." Rae's features looked stunned.

"I always tip, ye know that, Rae."

"Yes, but your friend is giving way too much also. I don't want a handout, Darach."

Now the woman deserved a gold metal. Even

Abby couldn't keep pretending there was something wrong with Rae.

"Consider it payment for doing us a favor."

Now Rae's green eyes slanted a bit in probably curiosity and confusion. "Look, you don't have to pay me for doing you a favor. Without you... my kids might not have what they need for school."

Darach closed Rae's hand around the two bills. "Keep it, ye have no idea how much trouble this job can be."

"Really, now that sounds intriguing."

Abby didn't care for the insinuation that she was trouble, but decided to keep quiet for now.

"Okay, what's the job?"

Darach cleared his throat. "I need ye to watch Abby here, while Sean and I take care of some business."

"What's wrong with her that she can't stay by herself?" Rae's tone, to be honest, was curious, but Abby chose to take it entirely in a different way.

"Okay, that's enough. I'm a grown woman, and I don't need a keeper. I'm so out of here." As before when she tried to move the mountainous bulk of Darach she didn't succeed. Now, she tried pushing her way past Sean. Another roadblock, one she was not happy with—not at all.

"Abby, settle down for a minute. This is for your own good."

"Oh please... you did not just pull the I-know-what's-best-for-the-little-woman routine, did you?" Rae's caustic tone caused Abby to swing her gaze that way.

"Rae, there be a reason Abby needs to stay here, and she knows what it is."

"Your charming accent won't work on me. You can't go around treating women like underlings." Rae stared him down.

Now it was Darach's turn to be on the hot seat,

and Abby was going to enjoy it with a vengeance.

"Rae, how can ye say that? I've always treated you as a—"

"Woman? Yes, and when you do every so often it smacks of *I know better than you do.* So why not leave it up to Abby to decide if she wants to stay here or not. I'm sure she has some sense of what she feels is right."

Abby's estimation of Rae continued to climb. If only the woman didn't wear her heart on her sleeve when it came to Darach. Of course, he must seem like a knight in armor to Rae.

"Well, thank you for asking me, Rae. I don't want to be here, but I don't want to be in the way either. If they"—she motioned to the men—"had bothered to ask and not just tell me this is what we're going to do, then I might have been more amenable to this solution in the first place."

Darach's expression as well as Sean's was confused to say the least. Men! She and Rae exchanged glances and even grins at the men's continued dumbfounded looks.

"So ye will stay put while I go out?" His question sounded awfully tentative to Abby. She wondered what he would do if she said no.

"Fine, I'll stay here. Just make sure you two supermen don't get into any trouble."

The look he leveled on her this time took her breath. The cocked eyebrow, silver-gilded gaze, and the sexier-than-hell cast of his lips as he leaned over and whispered in her ear made her want to climb his body like a cat up a tree.

Rae slid into the booth after the men left.

"So what did he say?"

Abby wasn't sure if she wanted to tell the woman Darach told her she was the only trouble he wanted.

"Let's just say, he's not upset anymore."

Rae laughed, and then her expression turned serious. “You in some kind of trouble?”

“Not the kind you think. You know about the teacher found dead?”

At Rae’s nod, Abby continued. “He works at the same school I do. I was with Darach when they found the body. Now, he’s afraid someone is targeting me.”

“That’s so not good.” Rae caught Abby’s hand and gave it a light pat. “Listen, you’ll be safe here. And just so you know”—she gave Rae a woman-to-woman look—“Darach has never looked at me like he does you. He’s been an incredible friend. My husband…” Rae stopped for just a moment and took a deep breath. “He tries hard, but he’s…he’s…”

“Abusive?”

“Yeah, but he looks after the kids at night, so I can’t divorce him, not now. Once I get finished with school and get a real job, then I can take care of my children all by myself.”

“Rae, if you need a bolt-hole, you could stay with me.” Abby wasn’t sure who was more surprised her or Rae. She’d never asked anyone to stay in her home. She valued her privacy and with the visions and dreams, she scared herself sometimes when she woke up screaming.

“That’s really kind of you, and if I need one, I promise I’ll call you.” Rae blinked back tears and then stood up. “Listen, can I get you anything to eat? I’m not sure how long they’ll be gone, but the bar’s open until six a.m. It could be a long night.”

“I’m fine for now. Thanks for asking. Hey, I don’t suppose you have a paperback novel I could read or something to pass the time?”

“I sure do! Give me a few and I’ll bring it out.”

“Thanks!”

****

Several hours later, Abby was deep into *Witch*

Of Air and Fire, by Eliza March. She munched her way through a bowl of mixed nuts, had another margarita, and an order of fries. The book was good—hot, and a bit more than what she was used to in a romance, but she loved the characterizations. The sex scenes made her want Darach in a truly erotic way, but she tamped those thoughts down.

Abby thought about what would happen after her life settled back down to normal.

She knew Darach could not be a part of it, but it didn't stop her from wanting it to work or from dreaming about the what-ifs. The more she studied their situation, the more she realized she just did not want to let him go. He made her feel like a woman, someone worthy, not just a fractured loner who scared off people by what she could see.

Normal people tended to shy away from those not so normal.

So now, she had a decision to make. Take what she could get from Darach and act like it didn't bother her when he moved on, and he would have to sooner or later, or shut it down now.

Her heart, soul, mind, and body screamed *no* to the latter solution. At the moment, she wanted to tell all four to shut up, but then that would make her as crazy as she felt at times.

Deciding she could solve nothing tonight, she went back to her book. Right in the middle of the sentence describing the Trinity Ceremony the strains of "How Great Thou Art" greeted her ears. She snatched her coat off the seat and unearthed Darach's phone. He must have dropped it out of his pocket when he slid out. Should she answer it? The old gospel song seemed to get louder, and some of the patrons in the bar looked in her direction.

"Hello?"

"Abigail?"

"Yes, who is this, please?"

"Ah, you have Darach's phone." The deep baritone on the other end sounded like an angel. She wondered who it could be.

"Yes, he must have left it when he went out."

"I see. I assume he's out hunting demons?"

Abby's heart stopped. How did this person know what Darach did? Was he friend or foe?

"I am a friend, or to be exact, Darach's boss."

The cell phone dropped from her suddenly nerveless fingers. Oh my gosh, it was Michael, the archangel.

"Abigail?"

Abby fumbled for the phone. Her thumbs were like cotton balls. Finally, she had it back to her ear. "Yes, sorry, I dropped the phone. I guess I'm a bit nervous."

The deep rich laughter coming through the phone bathed her in a pool of calm. "I tend to make a lot of people nervous. Your immortal included."

"Yes, Darach does seem to have a healthy respect for you."

"If it would only last more than a few minutes at a time, I would be most grateful."

"Is there something I can tell him? I know you can do the mind thingy or whatever it is when you communicate with Darach but…"

"I called to tell him to be especially careful tonight. There are several demons on the streets. More than there have been. I don't like it, and I think it has a lot to do with what's been going on."

Abby tried to quiet her fast-beating heart. "You think Angus is behind all this, don't you?"

"You are a bright mortal. Yes, I do."

"I don't know how to get in touch with him. Wait, I could probably track down Sean."

A sigh greeted her statement. "It might be for the best. Thank you, Abigail."

"You're welcome, your…" Lord, how on earth did

you address an archangel?

"Michael will be fine. Good night."

Abby closed the phone, and propped an elbow on the table. Could her life get any stranger? Talking to an archangel. Wow. And she needed to try to get in touch with Sean.

Doing a quick flip of the phone again, she dialed 9-1-1 and asked for Sean. After being chewed out a bit for not having an emergency, she was connected to the department. A few moments later, an officer said he would try to reach Sean by cell.

Now, she just had to wait and see if he would call her back. A bare minute later, the cell rang.

"Sean?"

"Yeah, Abby, what's up? I'm a bit busy."

"I know, but Michael called looking for Darach."

"Michael as in leader of God's army, Michael?" The awe in Sean's voice echoed what she'd felt.

"Yes, he said there are a lot of demons out tonight and for Darach to be extra careful. Angus could be behind this."

"Why didn't he call Darach?"

"He left his phone here, and I don't know why he didn't just communicate with him another way. Maybe there's a rule. Who knows, but please let Darach know if you see him?"

"Will do. Stay put, okay?"

"I plan on it. Thanks!" Abby hung up the phone, but instead of feeling comforted that Sean would look for Darach, she felt a shiver of fear. The vision she'd had Thanksgiving Day still rode her mind. What if something had happened to Darach? What if he was dead? Again, could he die?

****

Angus smiled. He'd found someone who could get close to Abby and bring her to him. Once that happened, he would enjoy himself as he hadn't since he'd taken Briene.

Michael hoped he would not get his wrist slapped. He'd interfered as much as he could without crossing the line. He could guide his immortals but he could not direct them in all they did. He just prayed his warning would be received in time. Yet, he had an ominous feeling things could turn deadly.

Chapter Thirteen

Darach had been following the same trail of sulfur since he'd split off from Sean after leaving the bar. His mind had been on and off again with the demon he hunted.

Abby's words were well taken. He should have asked her what she thought. After all, it was her life in danger. Of course after thinking she was correct, his mind shifted the other way. Why was it so wrong that he wanted to look after her?

The alleyway he walked through was like fifty others he'd traversed tonight. It was getting on toward morning. The bar would close soon, and he needed to get Abby back home. Of course after the scathing set-down she'd delivered, she would probably say she could do it herself.

And to think Rae sided with her. It was confusing to say the least. That was one of the reasons he couldn't quite keep his mind on the task at hand. A scuffling to the right of the alley preceded several rodents running from the debris. Strange how even the smallest of creatures didn't like paranormal beings.

Were they running from him or a demon?

The alley narrowed before it took a slight turn to the right. Darach moved with it, but measured his steps. He wanted to surprise Satan's minion, get the job done, and get back to Abby.

"Well, lookee here. You are a bit off your bounds aren't you, executioner?"

The oily voice matched the face of the demon standing in front of him. Darach couldn't be sure but he felt like the creature had used glamour to disguise his form and not taken over a mortal's body. 'Twould make the killing much easier.

"Nothing is off bounds to me in NOLA. 'Tis my territory, demon, and ye are not wanted."

The demon moved closer and Darach could make out the bleak contours of his face, the amber gaze that could not quite hide the flames of Hell, and the sharp fangs pushing his bottom lip down. Slight of build, he must be a lower demon, but he still needed to be dispensed.

"What, nothing to say before I send ye back to Hell?"

His foe laughed, the sound a raucous belching of noise. Darach wanted to flinch but kept his eyes on the demon. He was either braver than most of his peers or he had something up his pointed tail.

"I think that it will be you who dies tonight, immortal."

Darach felt the first hint of apprehension cross his spine. He'd bet his power to teleport that this was a well-sprung trap, and he knew Angus was behind it.

"Well, dinnae just stand there, demon. Show me what ye have before I kill ye."

Again laughter fell from the creature's snarled lips. Another bad sign.

Darach drew the sword out of his coat, and raised it in the air.

"Come ye, son of Satan."

The demon seemed to fly forward on a breath of hot air blowing through the alley. Its clawed hand sported a knife. If that was the best the creature had, then Darach could more than handle him.

He brought his blade down and blocked the smaller weapon in its downward spiral. The demon snarled, showing uneven fangs, before retreating.

"Time be wasting, come let me finish this night's work." Darach taunted him in the hopes he would oblige. He was more than ready to see Abby.

Again the demon laughed. "You are too sure of yourself, immortal. This night's work will belong to the one who craves your body and soul."

"Then he should be here fighting and not his lesser demons."

"Right you are, and that is why he sent a few others to help me with this task."

Darach felt the air current at his back change. He couldn't tell how many demons were behind him without turning around. And then he breathed a sigh of relief as two of the creatures joined the first.

He relaxed somewhat. Three he could take if he was careful and kept his head, and God prayed he did for that would mean he could get out of this without more than a scratch or two.

The first demon still bided his time, the smirk he wore grated on Darach's nerves.

One of the later arrivals moved toward Darach and then as he brought his sword to bear on the demon's head, his face changed into Abby's image. Darach pulled back. He knew it couldn't be his Abby, but it threw him off stride.

As he watched the face warped back into the creature, but before he could swing his sword again, he felt a sharp fiery pain in his back thigh.

He could feel the blood running down his leg. Darach turned to face his attacker and found three more of the monsters behind him. His odds of surviving just went down a notch, but he'd faced harder battles before and won. His gaze scanned the alley and found an open space where there was no debris. If he could make it there, he could use the brick wall to protect his back while he fought the demons face to face.

And he knew just the way to do it—transport. Darach concentrated on the back wall, willing his body to turn to molecules. A part of him wanted to dissolve, collect Abby, and run for Canal Street, but the executioner in him would not allow him to leave without taking as many demons down as he could.

He felt the first beginning of the molecular change radiate throughout his body when the demons attacked in mass. One caught him a glancing blow to his sword arm, but he brought it to bear on the creature's chest.

One down and five to go. Blood dripped from his arm in tandem with the wound in his thigh. A third fanged creature struck Darach a blow to his other leg, dropping him to his knees. The odds had just turned in favor of Satan's minions. He struggled to stand—he had to get to his feet and fight. If he didn't he could very well die this night, and Abby would be left at Angus's mercy.

A blow to the back of his head, no telling from what, caused Darach to see constellations. His eyes began to close despite his fight to keep them open. He could not give up—he would not give up.

A quick thrust of something sharp slid under his ribcage into his chest area. Blood flowed freely as he fought the dizziness threatening to take him under.

He fell backward and the view from the alley floor only made him wish he'd stayed home with Abby. More demons had gathered. A smaller demon moved in close, probably to gloat at Darach's impending death.

He brought the sword up one last time and

severed the head from the demon. Then darkness moved in to gather like a storm over his head. He prayed that Michael would dispatch someone stronger than he'd been to protect Abby.

****

Abby looked at the bar's clock for what seemed the hundredth time in the last hour. Six o'clock was fast approaching and still no word from Darach. She was so afraid something had happened. And she so wanted to yank her bitchy tongue out of her mouth.

Why had she fussed so much about staying at the bar? Come to think of it, she'd been a witch more than once since Darach had come into her life. Yes, maybe it was due to the fact he'd scared her spitless, or that she knew he could get under her guard, making her almost quiet life into something she wasn't ready to embrace.

What type of woman was she, to allow a man to play her body like he owned it, to ache for his touch, and then turn on him like a bayou reptile?

Abby took a sip of the water Rae brought to her while warning her the bar would soon be closing. It tasted like bracken to her. She should have waited instead of pouncing on Darach like a shrew.

"Abby, I've gotta close up, hon. Bill, the owner, says you can stick around until I get things squared away, but then you'll have to leave." Rae cocked her head to one side, making her now slightly disheveled hair list to the left.

"Have you heard anything at all from Darach?"

"No." The word sounded hollow just like it had the last several times she'd repeated it in answer to Rae's queries.

"What about the lieutenant?"

"No, not since he said he'd try to find Darach."

"Oh honey, I'm sure Darach will be okay. He's a strong man, and I'll say a prayer for him and you."

"Thanks. I appreciate all you're doing for me."

"Not a problem, even if I didn't hold Darach in such high respect, I would still do it. You're in love with him, and he deserves someone good."

Abby felt the burn of tears in her eyes. How could she have been so blind? The emotions she'd tried to push off could be moved no longer. She wasn't sure when it happened but Rae was right. She did love Darach.

"I'll be back in a bit, then if you don't hear anything I'll walk you to the streetcar."

"Thanks, Rae."

She looked at the clock again and willed the door to open, for her phone to ring, anything that would tell her where Darach was and if he was okay.

When the phone did ring, Abby jumped. She grabbed it off the table and slammed it to her ear.

"Hello!"

"Abby, I need you to get to the emergency room as soon as possible. Darach's hurt bad." Sean's words touched off a fear so strong in Abby she wanted to pass out.

"What happened?"

"No time to go into details. I'll meet you there."

Abby closed the phone, grabbed her coat, and looked for Rae who was coming out of the back room.

"I have to go. Darach's hurt. I need to get to the hospital."

"Oh, sweetie, I'll start those prayers now. I'd go with you, but I need to get home to the kids."

"Thanks for the thought," Abby called over her shoulder as she pushed the door opened and hit the street running.

God in His merciful Heaven, it must be bad since a half-demon was worried. She ran for the streetcar as she wondered if she could get in touch with Michael. Then she shook her head, silly thought, he was an archangel he had to know. Then a germ of thought popped in her brain, why, if he knew, had he not stopped it from happening?

Sean was nowhere in sight when Abby blew through the ER doors. She spotted the help desk and ambushed the woman sitting behind the glass barrier.

"Hi, I'm here to see Darach MacRath. He was just brought in."

The woman looked up from her paperwork, gave Abby a tired smile, and then bombarded her world.

"Are you a family member?"

"No, I'm…a…friend."

"Then, I'm sorry, you cannot see the patient."

Abby wanted to pull her hair out and yank the nurse over the desk.

"Can you at least tell me how he is?"

"Again, I'm sorry, I can't give out pertinent patient information without a release from the patient directing me to do so, unless your a family member."

"Please, I just want to know if he's okay."

"Abby!"

She spun around at the sound of Sean's voice and walked into his hug. "How's Darach?"

"Not good. The doctors are prepping him for surgery as we stand here."

"Oh my Lord, what happened? He's almost indestructible."

Sean walked her over to one of the vacant seats and helped her sit. He lowered his body next to hers.

"I was out hunting him, had been since I got your call. I was about ready to call it quits when I heard the sound of fighting. By then I could smell the stench of demons—a lot of them.

"I found Darach in an alley alone. The demons must have fled almost to the instant I arrived. He had several deep cuts, and was bleeding badly. I got no response when I tried to wake him up, and his pulse was almost non-existent." Sean raked a hand through his hair.

"I'm sorry, Abby. I didn't know how to help him. I know he's an immortal, but the wounds weren't closing like I thought they should have. I was afraid if I didn't get him professional help he wouldn't live long enough for you to see him."

Abby slumped in the chair. "And now it still may be too late."

"I should have looked harder."

"Sean, you did what you could. In fact, you're not obligated to help Darach or me."

For just a moment, she saw the red leap into his eyes before he replied. "I am obligated. I'm not like the demons that attacked Darach, nor am I like Angus. I don't believe in death for the sake of just killing."

"I'm sorry. I just meant… Oh Lord, I don't know what I meant. I haven't since Michael called.

"It's okay. You've been through a lot lately."

"Don't excuse my behavior, I snarled at you, at Darach. I've done everything I can to fight him on what he thinks is right. I should have listened to him. To tell him I was wrong. To admit…"

"That you love him?"

Her opened mouth must have clued him into her shock.

"Abby, if that hard-headed Highlander hasn't already realized you love him, then he's not as smart as I think he is. And you should know he is feeling the same for you."

"Strange, Rae said a lot of the same things tonight. How could both of us be so blind?"

Sean laughed. "Well in your case, you're excused because you're human. But Darach isn't, so I think once he gets well you should hold his feet over the fire for not admitting his love."

Abby giggled just a bit, but quickly realized there was nothing funny about the situation at all.

Darach could die…

Both she and Sean sat there for what seemed like hours before a physician came into sight. He looked like he'd just come from the OR. As she waited, he spoke to the nurse she'd wanted to throttle earlier before making his way to where she and Sean were seated.

"Lieutenant Black?"

"Yes, and this is Abigail Dupree, Mr. MacRath's fiancée."

With Sean's words, the surgeon turned to Abby. "I'm Dr. Jackson. Mr. MacRath is in recovery, but it doesn't look good. He lost a lot of blood before we got our hands on him."

"Will…he…"

"Make it? I don't know, Ms. Dupree. The fact he survived the surgery is a miracle in itself. One of my staff will keep you posted and let you know when you can see him."

Sean thanked the doctor for both of them while Abby sat there with her eyes closed. She could feel the tears leaking out from under her lids, but could do nothing to stop them. Darach could die, and there was nothing she could do to stop it.

****

Angus' hand banged against the wall so hard, the concrete cracked. He cursed the fact he didn't have a woman with him. He needed an outlet for his rage.

Darach should be here now in his power. Why couldn't the minions he used do as they were told? Why were they so weak they ran from a half-breed demon?

Dawn sailed across the night sky, and he rose from his chair to cross to the bedroom. He was tired of playing games. The next move he made would be one Darach could not mistake for anything but what it was—a gauntlet of demonic war.

Michael viewed Earth far below and zoomed in on the hospital where Darach lay fighting for his life. Had he done wrong so many years before by taking away his mortal death? Now when he'd finally found love again, although against the rules for executioners, he stood the chance of losing what he'd had stolen from him by Angus. Yes, best not to interfere again.

Chapter Fourteen

Abby rubbed the back of her neck trying to dislodge the crick that had sprung up over night. Darach had still not awakened from surgery. She, as well as Sean, pleaded and won the battle to stay in his room. ICU rules dictated short visits at specific times of the day, but she couldn't live with those. She needed to be near him.

If, God forbid, he died, she did not want him to be alone. In the telling of his mortal death centuries before he'd not addressed the fact that he'd died without any loved ones there. Of course, she could argue the fact that the ones he loved the most were in the same room, but for Abby it wasn't the same.

She prayed he'd awake up, and if he did, and she had to believe he would, then she wanted to be close enough to tell him what she should have before. She loved him.

"Abby, you really need to try and rest. I could take you home."

Sean started to move his long legs off of Darach's bed.

"Stay put, Sean. I'm not leaving. Besides, Darach would say it wasn't safe, and after what happened to him, I have to agree."

His smile lacked its usual warmth but she appreciated it all the same. Both of them were worried sick. Sean had a killer running loose, plus now a possible demon explosion on his hands, and Abby just wanted to crawl into the bed with Darach and hold him. Something the nurse said would not be tolerated when she'd done just that last night.

Not that she would have disturbed him. He lay like a corpse, his normally bronze face pale, his torso and arm covered in bandages. She didn't have to see under the bedspread to know his thighs were swathed the same way. He'd been stitched up with enough thread to hem a dress.

God help her, what if Darach did die? Could Michael make him an immortal a second time? Dare she ask—no beg—the archangel to do so if worse came to worse?

"Abby, I don't suppose you've heard from you-know-who?"

She wondered how Sean seemed to read her mind. It was a bit disconcerting at times.

"No. I even tried to star 69 the number he called from but it said number not available."

"Well, I'm sure—"

"Hi, may I come in?"

The woman standing in the doorway looked like a model for a glamour magazine. Her auburn hair hung almost to her tiny waist. A waist Abby would love to have. In fact, Scarlet O'Hara would be envious. The black sweater she wore was a perfect foil for a magnolia complexion. Not a blemish in sight. And the sweater emphasized a set of boobs Abby couldn't carry off with her height even if she could afford the surgery.

The sound of Sean's boots hitting the floor

caused Abby to turn her head. The lieutenant looked like someone had punched him in the gut.

Looking at him and then back at their visitor, she would say they were almost the same height. Could have something to do with the fact the woman was wearing five-inch heels.

Regardless of her extraordinary looks, Abby needed to remember her manners. The woman was here for a reason. She pulled herself out of the recliner the staff placed in the room for her and started for the door.

Before she could get there, Sean jumped in front of her. "Hold on, Abby. We don't know this woman or even what she is."

"Sean, you're being rude."

"And you're overstepping your bounds, demon. Now get away from her." The woman snarled in answer to Sean's words.

Well, looks like she could get out of introducing herself, but she'd still like to know who the woman was and how did she know Sean was part demon?

Instead of moving, Sean got closer, and the woman stepped over the threshold.

"Uh, look you two, why don't we take this out into the hall. Sick man here, remember?" Abby inserted.

The woman glanced at the bed, and concern beat inside her gaze for a second, before she once again took a step.

"I mean it. Darach is...he could die...and he needs to stay quiet." Abby put on a false manner of bravado, and stepped between the bristling duo.

The woman immediately grabbed her by the arm and pulled Abby behind her.

"Now, demon, we fight."

"Fine by me, but I have to warn you I don't go down easy." Sean's eyes glittered red, sending Abby's temperature down a few notches.

"First, I would like to know the name of the one I kill." Sean's statement caused the woman to bristle.

"My name is Arianna, and you will be the one to die."

The more Abby stood there watching Sean and the woman posture their dislike and animosity, the madder she became. She again inserted herself between the two would be combatants.

"I don't care what you two do to one another, but do it somewhere else." She gave Sean a look that had his eyes flaring a deeper red before he gave a quick nod. Abby then turned to the woman. "As for you, I don't care what your name is, if you disturb Darach, you will answer to me."

Arianna's cheeks turned a light pink. "Forgive me, I should have given you more information. I was a bit startled to find you in the company of that demon." A bright-red-tipped finger pointed toward Sean.

"He is—"

"I am not a demon."

"Really, then why can I smell sulfur in this room?"

"Please you two, not again. Sean is a halfling. And you still have not stated your business."

"Michael sent me to guard you until Darach gets back on his feet or…"

"Don't you dare say it, he is not going to die!"

"Sorry again. Look, are you cool with being here with this…this…creature?"

"I am a man, not a creature. Now why don't you just give your archangel a call and ask him. He knows who I am." Sean bristled.

Arianna cocked an eyebrow, but pulled out her phone. "If you are brave enough, whatever you are, then why not follow me out to the waiting room while I make that call."

Sean huffed but removed himself from Darach's room. Abby fought and won her battle against the tears that had threatened ever since she'd first seen Darach look so helpless, lifeless almost. What if he didn't make it? What would she do? He was the first man she'd given her heart to, and Abby didn't think she could live without him. Crazy as that sounded, she didn't want to give him up. He'd brought so much into her life. And if he did pull through, she promised she would make up how she spoke to him the last time. She should have told him about her vision, then maybe this wouldn't have happened.

Darach's phone rang somewhere deep inside her purse. Something that shouldn't have happened, she was sure she'd turned it off per hospital instructions. Yet, the unmistakable chimes of Michael's number caressed her ears.

"Hello."

"I see you are watching over our immortal."

"Yes, but I have a few questions for you, Michael."

What sounded suspiciously like laughter was turned into a quick cough.

"And what would those be?"

"Why did you do nothing to keep Darach from being hurt?"

Michael cleared his throat before responding. "Darach had free will to go into that alley. And just as all creatures have free will, he chose to do his duty. I did try to warn him, and in the process got my wrist richly slapped for my interference."

"I don't understand. God is merciful. Why would he be upset about your warning?"

Again, she heard him clear his throat.

"All I can tell you is there were events set in place long before even I came into existence."

Abby wanted to scream that was not an answer.

"I know, but it's the only one I can give you. But

ask yourself, if Darach had arrived back at the bar last night safe and hearty, would you have realized just what he meant to you?"

Before she could reply she heard a soft click. She tossed the phone back in her purse and hoped it broke. Which probably wouldn't happen since it worked regardless of being turned on. She was sure having it smashed to smithereens wouldn't keep it from going off again.

Abby slid the chair closer to Darach's bed. She gently eased her fingers into his. Such strong hands to be lying so still. She closed her eyes and remembered what it felt like to have them run over her body with a scorching touch, to have them swipe her hair out of her eyes, or just hold her. Would she ever feel those things again? Would Darach wake up from the coma the physician said he could remain in for an indefinite time? She hated herself. If he hadn't been so set on protecting her, he could have stayed home. She never should have hunted the demon that night. She should have let life happen and then even though she would never have met him, probably, then at least he would be safe and well.

"Ms. Dupree."

She forced her attention away from Darach's almost non-existent breathing. Arianna had returned without Sean. She hoped they had taken their battle outside.

"Yes."

"Do you mind if I sit down? It was a long flight from LA."

"I didn't think you immortals got tired. And couldn't you just teleport?"

"Not often, but it does happen. And I thought I'd do it the mortal way for a change. Dumb idea." The executioner sent her a quick smile. "Look, I'm sorry for what happened before. I was just surprised to see a demon alive in Darach's room."

That was the second time she'd used his given name. Had she known him before now?

"Did you know Darach before?"

"We met when I attended a training session he gave. To say he wasn't happy dealing with a bunch of newbie executioners would be putting it mildly."

"I thought Michael trained all of ya'll."

Arianna laughed. "Well, he was suppose to, but I think he made Darach do it as punishment."

"He probably spouted off to Michael."

Abby glanced back at Darach's chest—he still breathed—before looking at the other immortal.

"I hope you didn't kill Sean."

A snarl very much reminiscent of what she was use to from Darach erupted from the woman's lips. "No, but he got on my everlasting nerve. Who is this halfling? Why is he someone Michael would say is safe?"

"Michael didn't tell you?"

"Tell me what?" Her curiosity forced the woman's body to lean forward giving Abby a glimpse of fine lines around her eyes. She might look like a million bucks in most ways but something or someone had put those marks on her face.

"That Sean saved Darach's life. If he hadn't been hunting him to give him a message from Michael, Darach would have bled to death in that alley." Just saying the words caused Abby's stomach to revolt into a painful tension knot. Her heart began to hammer so fast she almost couldn't catch her breath.

"Hey, you all right? Should I call a nurse?"

"I'm…fine…just give me a moment." Abby took several deep breaths, but it didn't keep her hands from trembling as she eased her hand from beneath his and smoothed the already wrinkle-free bed-covering.

"I didn't realize the demon saved his life."

"Well, from what I've learned of Sean Black, he keeps things pretty much close to his heart. He and Darach have been acquaintances since Darach was assigned here a decade ago. He called Sean when my friend went missing."

"I'll try to keep that in mind when dealing with the halfling."

"Why don't you call him Sean? It might make the dealing easier."

Arianna's amber eyes twinkled, before she retained the somber expression Abby figured most immortals wore.

"I'll see what I can do."

"Thank you. There's already enough violence without you two inventing more."

Abby turned her attention back to Darach. He should have already awakened. His body was receiving fluids and nutrients from the IVs inserted in both his arms. She prayed they would do their work and keep him alive until he came back to her.

"Do you want me to go get you anything to eat or drink, Ms. Dupree?"

"No thank you, and please call me Abby. It's what I'm used to."

"Okay, I'm a bit curious, do you mind telling me how you met Darach?" Arianna's tone was friendly, and yes a bit curious as she said, but she wondered if the woman just wanted to keep her from jumping off the deep end like she so wanted to do.

"It's a pretty short story. Mortal woman fights demon, immortal executioner saves her butt..."

****

Darach woke to the sound of voices. Where was he? The last he knew the demons were closing in for the kill. He inhaled and his chest exploded with pain. He slowed his breathing, and in doing so he recognized the scent of antiseptic, the smell of bandages, and above all the heavenly aroma of jasmine.

Slowly and extremely carefully he tried to turn his head toward the sound of her voice. Darach wanted to see Abby, but couldn't make his limbs do what he wanted. His body felt like frozen slush. The same with his eyelids. When he tried to raise them, they remained shut. Whatever damage his body sustained it seemed it would take a while to heal.

Tired from his efforts, he just listened to the sound of Abby's voice. It bathed him in peace. If he could do nothing else for the rest of his immortal life, then he would be content.

"...And now I'm in love with Darach."

His heart skipped one beat, then two, before the rhythm evened out. Was it possible? Could Abby truly love him? And what if she did? What type of life could he give her if he died? What type of life if he lived? Yet, he wasn't sure if he could live without her.

Darach's pulse slowed down to a crawl as his body began to wear down just from being awake.

He allowed the silken threads of darkness to envelope him. When he was stronger he would make sure Abby knew he felt the same way.

****

Abby paced the small confines of the hospital room. One day had turned into four. Still Darach did not stir. The doctors would tell her nothing, and that in itself said too much. They didn't think Darach would recover.

It was surreal. He should not be able to die. He was immortal. Why didn't they make rules that would keep him safe? Why couldn't there be laws that said he couldn't die because he was good?

And speaking of good, she'd tried to reach the archangel several times over the last forty-eight hours, but to no avail. Sean was out hunting the killer, Arianna was here for a bit and then gone as needed to help search for the demons who attacked Darach.

"Abby..."

So softly spoken was her name, she thought she imagined it. Still she turned toward the sound. Darach's lids flickered once before they opened to reveal dark spheres of confusion and pain.

"Darach?" She whispered his name—almost afraid she was hallucinating.

"Abby, dinnae cry." His voice was hoarse from disuse, but Abby didn't care. He spoke, he lived, he would make it.

"Oh Darach, I thought I'd lost you."

The slight chuckle emitting from his throat was a poor imitation of the rich baritone she loved, but she'd take what she could get.

"Nay, I fear ye will be stuck with me fer a verra long time."

****

Angus made sure to keep to the dark side of the street, downwind from the new immortal and the demon. What a strange combination. One who was almost Satan's minion working hand in hand with the archangel's executioner. He'd not planned to be out this late, but there had been no media news about Darach's attack. He needed to know if his cousin would live or die before he made his next move.

Reminder: Archangels do not shed tears over what happens in the mortal realm. It would be fruitless since he would never get any work done if he allowed his hardened shell to crack. As he reached for a golden cloth and wiped his eyes, he repeated, archangels do not shed tears.

Chapter Fifteen

It had been three days since Darach awoke the second time. Seventy-two hours stuck in the bed because the mortal doctor would not believe he was doing much better. He hated lying there, instead he should have been spending his time in a better way. Four-thousand-three-hundred plus minutes he could have been holding Abby in his arms.

Enough was enough. Abby, who had dozed in fits and starts during his sojourn between the sheets, had finally fallen into a deep sleep. It was time. The nurse would not be around for at least thirty minutes. Darach carefully removed the IV from one arm and then the other. He prayed an alarm would not be triggered; he didn't have time to explain how his body was completely healed from his wounds, that the numerous sutures needed to stitch him up had disappeared and only pale pink scars showed the results of his escape from death. Soon they would be gone also.

He needed to get to his house, get some clothes, and then talk to Sean. All before Nurse Ratchet arrived to shove more unwanted pills down his throat. His body, which at first lacked the ability to heal itself immediately, had finally done just that. The doctor would see it as a miracle, Abby as a blessing, and for Angus, who he was sure was behind the attack, as the signal to try again. Without leaving the bed, he concentrated on his home. When the teleportation began, he breathed a sigh of relief before his body became molecules.

A moment later, he stood in his bedroom, and a moment after that he was dressed and headed for the NOLA PD.

****

"I need to speak with Lieutenant Black, please."

"Sir, he's in a conference with the chief. He'll be out in a moment."

"Thank you." Darach nodded to the frazzled redhead behind the front desk, and moved back. By his estimation, he'd been gone from the hospital around five minutes. Still time to get back. He just hoped Abby didn't wake up first. He watched as Sean exited a room in the inner sanction of the station, and was hailed by the receptionist. The halfling turned his head in Darach's direction, and then strode to where he stood.

"Highlander, are you crazy? You should be in the hospital."

"Good to see you too." Darach grinned. "I hear I have ye to thank for saving my arse."

"Yes, and believe me I'll cash in on that favor one day."

"Good enough. Now listen, I dinnae have much time." He drew Sean further into the corridor leading to the cells.

"I need ye to get Abby out of that room for a bit, tell Arianna I said so, and then I need to talk to ye."

Sean stared at Darach's clothing like he wanted to see under the material to the wounds beneath.

"Look, I'm healed completely. But, in order to catch Angus, no one else must know."

The halfling's eyes glowed red for a moment. "You got it. I'll try to get by no later than seven tonight."

"Thanks."

Darach said nothing more as he turned and exited the way he'd come in.

Five minutes later he was back in bed in the despised gown and with the IVs hooked up once more. Abby still slept but her now restless movements could mean she would wake anytime. At least he'd made it back. Now, if his plan worked, he would bring Angus down and hopefully without anyone else dying. He also needed to talk to Michael. He'd rather do it in person and would if things played out like he wanted them to tonight. He loved Abby, and now that he ken she loved him, he would make sure she was taken care of no matter what.

****

Darach purposely kept his eyes shut when he heard Arianna return. If Sean contacted her then it would be better if Abby thought he was sleeping.

"Hi Abby. I've come to take you to dinner."

"Thanks but no thanks, Arianna. I can't leave Darach."

"Yes you can. Look, he's asleep." She motioned toward the bed and Darach quelled his escalated breathing.

"And I know he doesn't expect you to stay cooped up in here twenty-four-seven. You need some fresh air and food that doesn't come from a tray. Now, we can do this one of two ways." Darach could hear the humor in the immortal's tone. She was a good kid, about half his immortal age, but a proven warrior of justice.

"I can just teleport us to the restaurant but I thought you might want to freshen up. You know, for dinner and for when Darach wakes up again."

He almost busted a rib trying to keep from

chuckling. After easing one lid open, he had to control his amusement as Abby rushed to the mirror over the sink and then turned back to Arianna.

"Oh no. Why didn't you tell me I looked like I went through a briar patch?"

"Well, it didn't really seem important while Darach was in the coma, and right after he first woke up. I actually think it was sweet of you to not care about the way you looked while at his side."

Darach's ribs hurt so badly, he thought he might have punctured a lung. Arianna had surpassed taunting Abby into leaving. She was now in overkill.

"Okay, so we won't be gone too long?"

"Naw, we'll go by your house, let you change and whatnot, and then go to dinner. Two hours tops, three if the restaurant's busy." The immortal looked his way as Abby grabbed her purse, and winked.

He winked back, and then steeled himself to lie still when Abby's sweet, sweet lips kissed his.

No later than five minutes after they left, Sean darkened the doorway.

"I see Arianna did her thing."

"Aye, thanks for talking to her for me."

Sean slid into the chair Abby had vacated. "So, what big plan do you have?"

Darach grabbed the bed controls and raised himself to Sean's eye level. "You mean after I get some food that willna make me feel like a day-old bairn?"

Sean laughed long and loud. "Yeah, we can fix that. What do you want?"

"Just grab something, my plan will be better if I'm not seen outside this hospital."

"Okay, you want to teleport where?" Sean waited patiently, but Darach needed to think. His house as a meeting place would be best.

"My house."

"Okay, give me the address." Sean jotted it

down.

Once Sean had what he needed and Darach's order for a large steak with all the trimmings, he left. Darach decided to keep the short tail hospital gown on, it would make getting back easier. He teleported and was sitting on the couch wearing a robe to hide his bare arse when Sean arrived.

He dropped the takeout boxes on the table and gently placed a six-pack of beer on the marble surface.

"I figured we might as well be comfortable while you fill me in."

"Good idea, I need something that will get me through the next week."

Sean's green gaze was puzzled. "Why, if you're so much better, don't you just tell the doc and then check yourself out?"

"I thought about that, but then Angus will learn I'm one hundred percent again. I dinnae want that."

Sean grabbed one of the boxes, flipped the lid back, and tucked in. After chewing a bite of steak, he asked, "Why not?"

"Because if he thinks I be at death's door, he willna expect me to be hunting him." Darach grab a box of his own and reveled in the tender steak. He grabbed a handful of fries and tossed them in his mouth, before chasing it with a deep draft of beer.

The halfling dropped his now empty plate onto the table, reached for some of Darach's fries, and earned himself a hand slap.

"Hey!"

"Leave me food alone. I'll have to eat Jell-O and pudding, and other gruel tomorrow."

"All right, you win. You couldn't pay me to eat that stuff." Sean said all that while snagging another beer. "When you get through stuffing your face, Highlander, I want to hear that plan."

"Didnae ye listen? I told ye."

"You mean you plan on sneaking out of the hospital every night just to hunt Angus? Ain't gonna work, man."

Darach set his Styrofoam plate down, inhaled a deep breath. "I am more than a bit full."

Before the last word was out of his mouth, Sean had the plate in his hand. Darach grinned at how the mortal-demon did everything but lick the box.

"Dinnae ye ever eat?"

"Sure, but it's the demon metabolism that makes me want to eat and eat and eat." Sean tossed the box down and took a deep pull of his beer.

"Okay, back on track. Let's say you did manage to sneak out, how are you going to disguise yourself as anything but an executioner."

"That's where ye come in. I need to look totally different. I thought ye could snag me a policeman's uniform." Darach hoped Sean would agree.

"All right, that might be possible, but won't Angus recognize you if he gets close enough?"

Darach felt his eyes go molten. "Oh, I pray he does get close. Then I will kill him."

Sean almost dropped the bottle. "Whoa, did I misunderstand? I thought you had to capture the spawn and turn him over."

The halfling's disbelief grew Darach's ire.

"Ye think I could just let the man who killed me family go free?" Darach's tone resembled a caged animal's.

"I get it, but what will you do about Michael's orders not to kill him. You're going to get more than a slap on the wrist."

"Aye."

"Bummer." Sean's green-eyed gaze sympathized with Darach.

"It stinks but..."

Sean sat there and then blew out a breath of air. "Well, Michael could probably hurt him a lot more than you could anyway."

Darach thought about that a moment and then replied. "Nay. I dinnae care. I still plan to kill him. Not only for what he did to Briene and Jamie, but what he would do to Abby if he gets his hands on her."

"We'll make sure he doesn't." Sean held out his hand and they shook on that promise.

"What time do ye have?" Darach asked.

"About eight or so, why? You plan on hunting tonight?" Sean raised an eyebrow.

"Nay, but I need to talk to Michael."

"Abby's got your cell phone."

"There's another way." Darach looked up at the ceiling. "Michael, we need to talk."

When nothing happened, he spoke again. "Now Michael, 'tis about Abby."

A second after his body began to lift off the couch. Sean's mouth flew open, and Darach found himself in front of Michael's desk.

"I see you are feeling much better. You must be to order me around." Michael looked Darach up and down like he was bug crawling on a wall.

"Dinnae be playing hard and furious with me. I dinnae have time to play. And it would be nice if ye asked me how I'm feeling."

Michael threw back his head and laughed. "Sit down, Darach. And just so you know, I have been in touch with the earthly realm on a daily basis. I know that Abby is still worried sick. I also know about your little rendezvous with Sean earlier today and then tonight."

Darach took a seat in the chair that materialized out of nowhere. "Then ye also know why I'm here. I need to find Angus. His demons almost killed me. That is what he wants so he can get Abby. I willna let that happen."

"I agree, the demon has to be stopped, but you

can't just keep fooling Abby. She loves you. And I like the woman, Darach. She would be good for you."

"Until I got her killed or got killed myself."

"Ah…now we come to why you wanted to talk to me." Michael relaxed back in his chair and eyed Darach.

"Aye, but I be sure what your answer will be."

"Why not ask me first?"

Darach drew a deep breath into his lungs and then expelled it. "I want to marry Abby."

"Why?"

The one word question threw him. Darach had expected a full-blown tirade.

"Because, if Angus succeeds in his quest to kill me, I ken ye will do everything ye can to make sure Abby is safe, but I want her to be looked after once this is all over."

"Looked after?"

"Aye, I have money I've saved over the years."

At Michael's raised brow, he explained. "The gifts you gave to help us fit in with the mortals have always been generous. For many centuries, I didnae need much, could be from my background, but I invested some of the coins and now I have more than enough to support Abby for decades to come."

"You can set up a fund to look after her, you don't have to marry her. And might I remind you, that immortals do not marry, and they certainly don't marry mortals."

Darach allowed the blow of Michael's words to flow over him. There had to be a way to get his agreement.

"Then I think ye need to make an exception."

Michael's tight-lipped smile did not make him feel very warm or fuzzy as Abby would say, but he was a MacRath, and they didnae just give up without a fight.

"Why should I ask to have the rule changed?"

"Because if ye dinnae then I'll bed Abby anyway. I willna go to my grave this time without tasting love once more, and I cannae believe ye would ask that of me."

"Good, I was wondering how long it would take you to admit it to yourself."

Darach wasn't sure what had happened, but Michael seemed overjoyed.

"Does this mean…"

"That you can marry Abigail?" The archangel's countenance took on a serious expression. "Yes, but only after I get approval." He stood up and walked around the desk.

"This is unprecedented, and I will have to make sure that by marrying her, you will not be changing events that must occur."

"Any idea when ye will know?"

"Soon. Now back to Earth. I'll be in touch."

Darach landed a lot softer than he did the last time he and Michael talked in person.

"I take it you saw Michael?"

"Aye, and now I think it be time I get back to the hospital. I want to see Abby."

Sean's face showed no sign of shock about what had occurred, only curiosity that would need to be satisfied at a later date.

"Lock up when ye leave, please. And let me know if ye can get the uniform."

Sean gave him a mock salute. "Will do."

****

Abby enjoyed the walk from the restaurant to the lot where the rental car Arianna had leased was parked. The night air was crisp, and the slight breeze carried the combined scents of the gulf waters, pogie boats, and people. She loved NOLA.

"So you ready—"

"Don't look back, but we're being followed." Arianna's words were calmly spoken but still scared

Abby out of her wits. Her heart sped up and the recently awesome food became an unwanted lump in her stomach.

"What do we do?"

Arianna caught her arm in a tight grasp, one that would look like she was holding Abby up.

"Just follow my lead," she whispered. A second later she spoke again.

"Come on, sister, you ain't gonna let a few drinks go to your head like this are you?"

Abby swayed on her heels and managed to act the part of a woman who'd had too much to drink as they moved toward the car, and an encroaching darkness, she didn't like. And she really didn't like not confronting whoever was following them.

"You're doing great. When we get to the car, I want you to slump over, and then when I yell, you get behind the car." The whisper was soft but adamant.

"Why don't we just stop and see what they want?" Abby's question was met with a look of disbelief from Arianna.

"That could get you killed." She whispered again. "Not much farther, then we'll get you home in a flash, sugar." Arianna's attempt at a southern accent was actually good in Abby's opinion and much louder.

"Here we go." The slight push she received almost sent Abby over the hood of the car, but she caught herself with her hands, and played her part.

"Now!" Arianna's voice was loud and clear and Abby darted around to the other side of the red convertible.

"All right, who are you and why were you following us."

"I uh, just wanted to say hello." The thin and reedy voice sounded like…Nate.

Abby popped her head over the hood of the car

just as Arianna put the teacher in an armlock.

"Arianna!"

"Abby, stay back. I want to find out what this guy is doing here." The immortal's red curls shook as she pulled out a pair of handcuffs and locked them around Nate's wrists.

"Arianna, I know him. It's okay."

"Fine, he's human so not much of a challenge anyway."

Nate's eyes grew wide, but he managed a smile as she made her way to them.

"I'm sorry. I saw you leave the restaurant, and I wanted to say hi. I also wanted to know if you'd heard anything about Lance Dumont. We tried to call him but couldn't get him. He was supposed to be in town. We wanted to see if he wanted to help with Cecil's wake." He gave her a slight smile and then turned to Arianna. "Do you think you could take these off? Metal makes me break out."

The immortal's disgust showed in the curse that ripped the air, but she did unlock the cuffs.

"So have you heard anything?" Nate's gaze was on Abby as he rubbed his wrists.

"No, but I'll try to find out."

"Thanks, Abby. I can stop by your house tomorrow if that's okay."

"Uh, I'm not staying at home right now. A friend of mine was—" Abby looked at Arianna.

"Let's go, Abby, we don't want to be late."

"Late?"

"Yes, weren't you planning on being back in a few hours? Well, if we hurry we should about make it."

Abby realized Arianna didn't want her to say anything about Darach. Of course, she should have realized that anyway, but Nate wasn't a demon. He was just concerned about a colleague just like she was now.

"Look, Nate, I'll find out what I can and leave word at the coffee shop we met at the other day. Okay?"

"Sure, Abby, whatever you want to do is fine by me."

Before she could say anything else, Arianna hustled her to the car. The ride back to the hospital was filled with what she should or shouldn't say in reference to Darach. By the time they rode up in the elevator, Abby was more than ready to see Darach.

She pushed the door open and then stopped almost causing the immortal to run into her. Darach wasn't in the bed.

****

Angus looked at the specimen the demon brought him for fun. He would endure better than the last teacher. More muscular, and more able to fight back. It would enhance the torture. And Angus would enjoy the time between now and when he struck Darach a fatal blow.

As soon as he sent Darach back to Earth, Michael allowed himself a big grin. A pat on the back would be nice also, but his wings wouldn't allow it. Of course, he didn't allow them to show all the time but when dealing with mortals or immortals, he'd found it was a bit of a power rush. Yet, he couldn't be more pleased over Darach's attitude. The Highlander might think it was concern over Abby's well-being and lust driving him to marriage but Michael knew better. Now he just had to get permission for a wedding. And if he did, he hoped that would keep Darach from his quest to kill Angus.

Chapter Sixteen

Darach teleported into the hospital room to the open-mouth stares of Abby and Arianna. The sheen of moisture in Abby's deep blue eyes made his heart ache. The condemning look the immortal gave him made him want to look for the nearest rock. However, he was more concerned with Abby's feelings.

"Leave us." He spoke to Arianna, and her cocked eyebrow had him hastily adding, "Please." The immortal had been invaluable in looking after Abby, and in helping him get some time with Sean and Michael.

"Fine, but you upset her again, and I'll show you how much I've learned since you trained me, Darach." She followed her words with action and teleported away.

Arianna's loyalty to Abby was a plus. If

something did happen to him, he'd have no apprehension that Abby wouldn't be guarded like the President of the United States. He stepped closer to the object of his desire.

She moved away.

"Abby, please. I can explain." Darach made a move to get even closer.

She held out a hand to stop him. "Explain what? That all this time I thought you were still too weak to be able to talk to me? That I was scared to death that you could still die?" Abby closed a bit of the distance between them.

"I can't believe you would do that to me, especially after I told you I loved you. But then again, you didn't really say it back did you?"

"Abby, dinnae be this way. I was waiting for the right moment." Darach knew the hole he was digging for himself was getting deeper by the moment. If he wasn't careful, he'd be up to his eyeballs in dirt.

"Moment? I truly don't understand. What makes any moment better than another?" Abby's hurt suddenly seemed to dissipate, leaving behind confusion.

"Abby..." Darach thought about what she said and knew he was wrong for not telling her he loved her when he'd first awakened from the coma. He couldn't be sure if he told her now she'd believe him. Better to wait until he heard back from the archangel.

"Don't bother, maybe I just expected too much from you when I knew better. I'm a job to you, one you can make love to, apparently without remorse."

He reached for her, but she sidestepped away. "That 'tis not true. I do care for ye more then my job."

"Really? Well, then what if I asked you to give up this hunt for Angus? Would you do it?"

"Abby, ye kin I cannae do that. 'Tis part of what I am. I was turned into an immortal to stop evil."

Abby shook off the hand he tentatively laid on her arm. "Yes, but you don't have to go after Angus personally. Let someone else do it."

"I cannae do that. Angus willna rest until he confronts me. If I dinnae find and kill him, he will keep killing innocents. He could kill ye too, Abby." Saying the words tore his heart open, yet he wouldn't lie to her.

"Then I guess there's nothing else to say. Goodbye, Darach."

"Abby, you cannae just go out by yourself. 'Tis nighttime and dangerous. At least wait until Arianna returns."

"I'll be downstairs in the lobby. Have a good life, Darach."

"Abby, please dinnae go. I have made a mess out of this, and I—"

"Save it." Abby stopped on her way to the door, rooted around in her bag, then tossed him both cell phones. "Here, tell Michael I don't need a keeper. I didn't before and I don't want one now."

"Abby, for God's sake. Can ye stop being so stubborn, and listen to reason?"

His answer was her back as she pushed the door open and left.

"Women! I dinnae ken why God made them so contrary." Darach wanted to go after Abby, but he knew she would need a bit of time to cool off, so he paced the confines of the room. He also took some time to look up at the ceiling and yell at Michael.

"Do you still think the woman will be good for me? She's going to be the death of me, Michael. And I think 'tis what ye want. So if ye dinnae want to help me out here, then make sure Arianna is with Abby at all times. I dinnae trust Angus."

He was on what seemed like the thirtieth lap

around the room when the door opened.

"Mr. MacRath, you should not be out of bed. The night nurse who had been like a guard dog the entire time of his stay hurried into the room, grabbed his arm, and tugged him none-too-gently toward the bed.

Darach waited all of two minutes after the woman left the room before he teleported to his house, changed into street clothes and teleported to Abby's. He opted not to try to just land inside the house, he didn't know what type of safeguards Arianna had implemented.

He rang the doorbell and waited. Then he waited more. Were they not home? Darach leveled his fist on the mahogany door and banged several times.

The door flung open a moment later. Arianna stood there looking like she wanted to tear his head off. Her eyes flashed amber, her lips had a snarl on them, and her posture suggested she'd love to kick his arse.

"Look before ye start on me, I want to see Abby."

"That's not going to happen, Darach."

The other immortal stepped over the threshold, forcing Darach to back up. She then pulled the door shut behind her.

"Abby was over-the-top upset when I got back to the hospital. I couldn't get her to talk to me at all. What in God's name did you do to her?"

"I didnae do anything but tell her I couldna stop hunting Angus."

A fractured sigh parted Arianna's lips. "Whew, so that's what got her so upset."

"Aye, and the fact she thinks I dinnae love her."

"Well, I don't know why she thinks that, everyone who is around you two can't help but see you're like a lovesick lamb. Or so I've heard."

Darach would have laughed, but being referred

to as any type of sheep with his Scottish heritage was not exactly a compliment.

"So, any suggestions?"

"You could try groveling." Arianna looked positively excited over that scenario.

"Ye have anything else useful?"

"Talk to her, Darach. She's hurting now, but if she loves you as much as I think she does, sooner or later, she'll listen to reason." She moved farther out onto the porch. "I understand why you can't give up looking for Angus, but I'm not in love with you."

"Thank God for small favors," Darach quipped back.

"Ouch." He rubbed his arm where her small but extremely effective fist connected and stung like the dickens.

"So are you going to go back to the hospital and follow your original plan since Abby already knows or come up with something different?"

"I take it, Sean filled ye in, and aye, for now, 'tis the hospital. 'Tis the only thing I can think of that might make Angus feel secure enough to get careless."

"Right, let's hope he does. Listen, I need to get back to Abby. You want me to tell her anything?"

"Tell her I love her."

"You got it." Arianna turned to go back inside but stopped. "Oh, I don't know if you've heard or not, but a second teacher from Abby's school was killed. Sean dropped by with the news before you got back to the hospital. And before I forget it, someone by the name of Nate, Abby knew him, followed us from the restaurant. Said he just wanted to say hi. He seemed harmless, but I thought you should know."

"Thanks, Arianna…for everything."

"No need to thank me. Just find Angus, I'll protect Abby."

****

Abby watched through her bedroom window as Darach walked away. The fact he'd come after her said a lot, but she wasn't ready to face what he was doing or to forgive him just yet.

Yes, she knew someone had to go after Angus. No telling what the demon, although no evidence pointed to him having killed Cecil, would do next if Darach didn't find him. But she didn't want to think about the toll it would take on him physically and mentally.

He'd barely made it through the last attack. His words their first night together had given her a sense of peace, that he was almost invincible, she'd never truly thought he'd be taken down by a group of demons. Even the vision had not prepared Abby for the horrific way Darach had been attacked and left for dead. Why now after all these centuries? She would have thought it would have been tried before.

Just the thought of it happening again made her blood run cold. She did love him, but she wasn't at all sure she could live with the fact his job would continually lead him into danger.

But then again, he'd been fighting evil for centuries. Did she want to cut him out of her life completely? Or did she want to experience a life that would be rich with love?

Too many questions and her head was beginning to ache.

"Abby?"

"Yeah. I'm in the bedroom, Arianna."

The immortal materialized right in front of her, causing Abby to jump.

"I wish you wouldn't do that. Can't you people use the stairs like the rest of us?"

Arianna laughed and then flopped on the edge of Abby's bed. "I take it you saw Darach leave."

"Yes, thanks for keeping him out for now."

"Oooh, does that mean you might talk to him

tomorrow?"

"I might, why?"

Arianna twirled a length of her auburn hair. "Because it would make him and you happier. Besides, Abby, life is full of risks, if you don't try to find love somehow, then it just sucks."

Abby joined her on the bed. "You sound like you have some experience with that. Care to talk about it?"

Arianna looked away from Abby, before once again meeting her gaze. "I might, but not tonight. I think tonight we need margaritas and chocolate."

"And I think you're right. Come on, I'll get the blender going, if you get the chocolate out of the top cabinet." Abby jumped off the bed and took off for the stairs. She bumped into Arianna when she got to the kitchen. In answer to her raised brow, the immortal laughed.

"Hey, when it comes to chocolate, I don't believe in wasting time."

Abby couldn't help but giggle. "Okay, let's do this right."

Several minutes later they were in the living room, tossing back margaritas, munching down on chocolate, and dissing men. Not a bad way to spend an already horrible evening.

****

Darach laid still as the surgeon who stitched him up in the first place removed his bandages. Sean had been by earlier and glamoured the wounds to show the expected rate of healing instead of the completely healed wounds. If it hadn't been for the halfling, he would have had to wipe the memories of the staff. Which might not be a bad idea anyway. Perhaps he would after he caught Angus. Right now, he needed to stay put for a few more days.

"Well, Mr. MacRath, you seem to be doing much better. The sutures are holding together, and tomorrow we'll remove the ones in your legs."

"My thanks, I appreciate your care." Darach hoped the doctor would take that as a dismissal and leave. He and Sean needed to hit the streets right at dark, and that time was approaching fast.

"All right, then I'll see you in the morning." Dr. Wright spoke as Sean entered the room and then blessedly he was gone.

Darach threw his legs over the edge of the bed. "Do ye have the uniform?"

"Yes, and good evening to you too, Highlander." Sean's sarcastic tone did not match the grin on his lips.

"Sorry, just a bit anxious to get started."

Sean slapped him on the back hard enough to make him falter in getting to his feet. Too much time had been spent pretending to be sicker than he was.

"No more anxious than I am. Angus has a lot to answer for with two dead and possibly a third if he had anything to do with Abby's friend," Sean shot back.

"Aye, Arianna told me about the other teacher."

"Yeah, I meant to tell you myself, but the body was found after we talked last night. Since it was after visiting hours, I got in touch with Arianna. Figured it'd go easier if she told Abby first before she heard it on the news today."

"Thanks, I appreciate that. So where's the uniform?"

Sean pulled it from under the coat he held over his arm. Darach grabbed it, hit the bathroom, and was out a minute later.

"Ready?"

"Yep, let's do it."

****

The uniform felt alien against Darach's skin, the material stiff and new. Sean had *borrowed* one from the supply closet the PD kept for rookies.

Night had fallen and now he and Sean made their way toward Bourbon Street. To onlookers they looked like a policeman chatting up a passerby. Which is exactly the image they wanted to convey. Sean had glamoured himself into a heavier male image with a receding hairline. Totally unthreatening to any demon around. And since for the most part the demon population left the PD alone, Darach was hoping he'd be ignored also.

"So, did you make up with Abby yet?" Sean's question came out of left field, but Darach should have expected it. The halfling had almost become a friend over the last week or so, and he knew his attentions were good.

"Nay. Abby chose not to visit me at the hospital, so I think I will give her until tomorrow. Hopefully, she will forgive me, and be willing to talk about it."

"I hope so for your sake. You need someone to keep you in line." The smirk on Sean's face was a bit overblown with his new look, but Darach let it slide.

"I could say the same about you and Arianna."

Sean caught his toe on a sidewalk crack and almost went flying. Darach steadied him.

"There is no Arianna and me."

"Really? Well, ye could do a lot worse."

Sean's eyes turned red. "And you could mind your own business, Highlander."

Darach would have laughed. The halfling's plight was noticeable only because he was in the same boat. Sean protested too much not to have at least a smidgen of feeling for Arianna.

"The teacher's body you found last night, was it demon-touched?"

"Hard to tell, he was fished out of the canal, but truth, I think it's too much of a coincidence that both teachers worked at Abby's school."

Darach almost missed his step this time. "How? I mean is it possible Angus is behind those two murders if you found no demon touch on the body?"

Sean pointed toward an alley branching off from Bourbon Street. "There are ways to disguise the sulfuric scent. But not usually from another demon, even if I'm only half."

Darach followed the right turn the halfling took into the alley. "So you think there's a serial killer out there who just got lucky with both the teachers?"

"I've seen stranger things. He could have been watching the school. Or he could have been stalking them for a good while and seen both men together. There's no way of telling until we catch whoever committed the crimes, or I could be wrong and it's Angus."

"Why did we stop here?" Darach stood silent next to an equally quiet Sean.

"I thought I saw a shadow slip into the alley. But I can't pick up on anything at all now."

Darach make a circle scanning both open ends of the alley. "Could they have already left?"

"Possible, but I want to look around a bit more."

"Tell me what ye are looking for, and I'll help."

Sean exhaled a breath of air. "That's just it, I don't know. Something feels off. I can't believe you can't feel it."

Darach's sixth sense had pretty much been perfect for the most part in his long second life. The fact he didn't feel anything out of place now was disturbing in the face of Sean's agitation.

"Sorry, I cannae sense anything."

The halfling looked around the alley one more time, shrugged his shoulders, and moved back to Darach. "I have a possible theory about why you can't feel anything, but we need to get out of here, and then I'll see if I'm right."

A feeling of unease did creep over Darach's shoulders at Sean's words, but not that someone was there intending harm, but that something wasn't right inside him. He prayed the halfling was wrong, if he wasn't then his life as an immortal could be in jeopardy.

****

Angus hurled a bottle at the television set. Darach had managed to escape his trap. He knew it would not be easy to kill the immortal, but he'd hope sending in a vanguard of demons would work. Instead, they'd run like little girls when they smelled another demon, one whose aura waxed of old demon blood and magic. But he would have Darach at his mercy once again, and he would make sure that when he died this time there'd be no third chance at life.

Michael didn't know whether to laugh or cry again over Darach's mishandling of his love life. He'd taken his wings in hand, asked for, and received permission for the immortal to marry Abby. Now, the clueless Highlander could ruin his chance at happiness before he even asked her to marry him.

Chapter Seventeen

Abby moved through her house just like she'd moved through the day—sluggish and uncaring of what happened. Darach had not even tried to see her. She thought surely after the evening before last when he'd talked to Arianna he would have at least touched base with the immortal—that hadn't happened.

Now, she was facing another evening and night wondering if Darach had changed his mind about caring for her. Could she blame him if he had—after all she'd pretty much told him to have a good life on his own. And what if he did? She'd managed on her own before and could do it again. *Yeah right, Abby, who are you kidding?*

"Abby, are you just going to stay here and do nothing?"

Abby flopped down in one of the damask-covered armchairs. "Yes, I think I am. Why should I go out of my way to make it easy on Darach?"

Arianna took the other chair. "Well, according to the demon-spawn, he says Darach's miserable."

"Don't call Sean demon-spawn, he can't help it if his mother was raped by a demon."

"Whoa, I had no idea. He truly can't help his nature can he?" Arianna pushed back in the chair and stretched her legs out.

"No, and he's been really kind to me." Abby made a face. "And he probably shouldn't have since I've been such a bitch to Darach."

"Girl, you're not going to just give in are you? I mean, that immortal is hot, but he deceived you."

"Yeah, I know, but he did it to set things up to find Angus. And to protect me he says."

Arianna's lips held a slight smile. And if she wasn't mistaken, her eyes twinkled just a bit.

"You believe him now?"

"You know, I think I do. I just went a bit nuts worrying about him. Do you think he was faking any of it? He says he wasn't but..."

"No, hon. Sean says he was almost dead when he got to him. Which makes little sense to me. Darach is one of the oldest immortals around, and he's never been injured like that."

Abby pulled her legs up under her. "Any ideas as to why now?"

"Not really, but I bet Sean and Darach both are wondering themselves."

"For someone who couldn't stand to even talk to Sean, you seem to be all about Sean-this and Sean-that."

Arianna's pale complexion flushed the color of a pink sunset. "It's business only, Abby."

"Yeah, well, tell that to someone else. You're preaching to the choir here, darling. Remember, I'm in love with an immortal, so I know the signs."

As she watched, the immortal's amber gaze filled with tears. "I can't care for anyone, Abby. It's not going to happen."

"Why?"

"I don't want to talk about it, okay?" Arianna jumped out of the chair and headed for the kitchen.

"If you don't mind, I'm going to strengthen the safety guards, have a drink, and then read a good book."

"I'm sorry...I didn't mean to hit a nerve."

"No problem. You see, in order to care for someone, you have to have a heart. I've been told repeatedly that I don't have one."

Abby sat there wondering what on earth to make of Arianna's words. Someone had hurt her badly, and she was still hurting. She moved out of her chair and headed for the kitchen. A drink sounded pretty good. It might not stop their hurting but hopefully it would dull the sting a bit. Abby stopped. On second thought, nothing could dull how she or Arianna felt.

****

"Okay, tell me when you started feeling this way or when you noticed something strange."

Darach laid on his bed at the house while Sean bent to work his mojo on his wounds. He wasn't sure what the halfling was up to, but at this point he was getting more than a bit desperate.

Sean had tried various ways to test Darach's sixth sense when it came to demons and anything bad happening. One of the traits of an immortal was to be able to know when someone was in trouble. How it happened he didn't know, probably something programmed into his body when Michael turned him into an executioner. Without it, countless innocent lives could be lost, and if he couldn't sense something being wrong, then he could become a victim again. And he wouldn't be able to guard Abby from Angus.

"Highlander?"

Darach brought his mind back from what might happen and to what he remembered.

"I was fine. I didnae have any problems following a sulfuric trail into the alley. I remember there was one demon and then two more showed up.

The first one attacked and then I was hit in the back of the thigh with a blade and the arm, the other thigh, and finally the chest."

Sean sat in the chair next to the bed. "You've fought more than one demon before so it has to be something about the attack that caused you to go down that easily."

"I ken that, but what?"

The halfling leaned forward. "Do you remember anything about the weapons, were you able to see any of them?"

Darach thought long and hard. The only one he'd even had a brief glimpse of was the one the first demon carried. What had it look like?

"It was about eight inches long from the hilt to the tip. The hilt was a scrolled mass of connected figures. I don't know what kind. The blade was serrated, with maybe a red tip?"

"Red tip?" Sean's brows drew together.

"I think so. Pretty much everything that happened that night is a bit fuzzy."

Sean stood up and started pacing the room. A second later, his eyes started glowing a bright red.

"I don't believe it."

"Dinnae believe what? Do ye know what happened to me?"

The halfling stopped mid-stride, turned, and faced Darach. "I could be wrong, but if I'm not mistaken, the blade sounds like one I've heard other demons talk about. It's refuted to have magical properties, or rather black magick properties. I'm not sure where it's supposed to have originated from, but some say Lucifer fashioned the sword from the bones of a dead angel and a sorceress. I have heard of only the one weapon like that, but I suppose there could be others."

"So that might explain why I be helpless when it comes to knowing what I've ken for a lifetime?"

Sean took to pacing again, as Darach sat up and then moved off the bed.

"Yes, unless Michael can remove the spell that seems to be blocking your senses."

"At least now there might be a way to fix what's wrong."

The halfling grinned. "I hope so, 'cause you need to fix what's wrong with you and Abby also."

"I agree, and will do so after I talk with Michael.

"I don't suppose I could talk to him?" Sean's tone was even, but Darach picked up on the tamped down excitement.

"I can ask him."

"Great. Now, what are your plans for tonight?"

"To hunt Angus." Was the halfling daft to even ask?

"Look, don't take this wrong, but you're a liability to me, yourself, and the countless potential victims out there."

Darach wanted to rail at Sean, but he knew he was right. He could get someone killed.

"Do ye have any ideas where to look for Angus?"

"I'm going to look up an old buddy of mine. He use to hang out with some of the more evil species of demons, but now he's more or less a gentle creature."

"What happened?"

Sean's laughter held little mirth. "He fell in love."

"Ye just had to tell me that."

"You asked." This time his chuckle was real. "I'll let you know when I know something."

"All right, I guess since I can't hunt, I might as well go back to the hospital, and from there I'll give Michael a call."

"You do that, and keep me posted on whether or not he's willing to talk to me."

"Aye, I will."

****

Darach teleported back into the hospital room and donned the gown he'd stashed under the pillow. He also retrieved his cell phone. After reclining on the bed, he tapped the icon for Michael and waited for the call to go through. He didn't often contact the archangel this way—he usually yelled for him, but the revelations of the past twenty-four hours had pretty much drained him. If Michael couldn't help him, then he was dead as an immortal. And if he couldn't protect Abby then why on earth would he want to shackle her to him in marriage?

"I assume you have a very good reason for contacting me tonight, MacRath."

"Aye, I do."

Michael's tone wasn't overly friendly but Darach feared it would get down right angry when he disclosed what had happened.

"Then please spit it out. I was in the middle of watching angel football and they—"

"I understand ye might want to watch your winged friends play, but dammit, Michael this is urgent."

The silence on the other end of the phone was so great Darach could have heard angel wings fluttering.

"Since you normally do not take your life in hand by cursing at me, I will let it slide. Now, tell me what's wrong."

"When I was attacked by the demons, somehow one of them or all of them, I don't know, used a magical dagger. Or at least that's what Sean believes. He did some tests, and it seems that my abilities of being able to detect evil or anything bad happening pertaining to crimes is gone. He believes it was an ancient dagger enchanted by a spell that used the bones of an angel and a—"

In less than a tick of a heartbeat, Darach found himself in the presence of Michael.

"What do you mean the bones of an angel?" The archangel's roar caused papers to fly off his desk, and clouds resting outside the window actually moved away with the force of his breath.

"Dinnae yell at me, Michael. That is what Sean said. He'd only heard of a dagger like that, he's never seen it. He figured it to be a myth in the demon realm."

Michael raised his hand and all the papers rested in neatly stacked piles once again. He sat back down in his chair and then just stared at Darach.

Did the archangel know something about the dagger? For a moment, it looked as if Michael would be sick.

"I didn't believe it to be true. Melissande was one of the humblest angels in Heaven. She was gracious, loving, and so innocent when it came to mortals."

Darach remained silent as Michael stared at something he couldn't see.

"She wanted to help mankind. Mel believed that all mortals deserved a second chance. She was under my tutelage. I told her to forget about changing what she couldn't. We argued when she would not listen. She left that day, supposedly to pay a visit to an ailing elderly woman who would soon be joining us here."

The archangel's sigh ruffled the papers, but they stayed on the wooden surface.

"I never saw her again. That was centuries ago. I thought she might have gone over to the demon realm—not because she'd changed sides, but because her culpability would not allow her to know the difference between good and evil."

"Ye think it was this angel's bones that was used to help bind the magick spell?"

"I'm not sure. The dagger was like you said, a

myth, something we here felt was a way to try to frighten anyone with the goal of being good." Michael stood up and began to pace, his footsteps trailed a musical sound as they struck the floor.

"If the dagger is real, then we could have a problem. Explain to me exactly what Sean said."

"He believes the dagger was used—"

Darach stopped when a breath of air whirled inside the room. It grew to the height of a man, constantly swirling until it slowed—and out of its midst staggered the halfling.

A look at Darach opened Sean's mouth. "What the hell—" One moment the lieutenant was standing, the next sitting in a fabricated chair right next to him.

"I would appreciate if you refrained from using that word *here*." Michael's words were couched in a quiet manner, but Darach knew better. The archangel was hunting for answers and it would be best for everyone if he got them.

"Where is 'here'?" Sean looked toward Michael and then back at Darach. "Is this who I think it is?"

Michael smiled. "Forgive my manners. Yes, I am Michael. Your demon heritage and Darach would have told you what status I hold inside Heaven's gates."

Sean looked a bit stunned, but then he pulled himself together. "Nice to meet you, but let's get something straight. I am not fully demon, nor do I embrace that part of my ancestry."

"Right, and for that reason you are here. You have been instrumental in helping my immortal and Abigail. Now, I need your help in deciphering where the dagger came from and if it is real."

Sean crossed one leg over the other at the ankle, before looking around the room. "Nice digs. And of course, I will be happy to do anything I can to help."

"Thank you. Now, tell me what you know of the

dagger. When did you hear of its existence?"

Darach waited, also anticipating, to see if Sean could shed more on the subject of the blade. He needed answers in order to get on with his life.

"It was after I was kicked out of the orphanage that I ran into some demons. After they tried to kick my teeth in, they did not succeed by the way, I hung with them for a while. It was safer being a young demon to immerse myself with older beings. It's been so long, but from what I remember they said they'd heard about it from ancient demons." Sean looked Michael square in the eyes. "From that summary, it would seem the dagger has been in existence since almost the beginning of time."

"So it would seem." Michael waved his hands and a tray of refreshments materialized on a table that also appeared between their two chairs.

"Refresh yourselves. This could take quite a while. I'll return in a few moments. Oh, and if curious, you won't be able to leave this room to explore."

Darach expected the archangel to poof himself out of the room, but Michael's long strides were almost mortal as he exited the room.

"Dude, you have to be kidding me. That's Michael? He looks like the warrior of all warriors ever made."

"Aye, there be a good reason for that. He handles God's warriors." Darach reached out and picked up a glass of liquid from the tray. The rich nectar was a combination of sweet and spicy. After quenching his thirst, he turned to Sean again.

"If ye noticed, Michael is a wee bit upset."

"How can you tell? His face looks like it's carved out of marble."

"Oh, believe me, he zapped me out of my bed at the hospital so fast, I almost swallowed me tongue in the process."

"Well, try being in the middle of a conversation with your boss and the next being zapped out of the only world you've ever seen."

"Been there and done that, remember?"

Sean nibbled on a piece of confectionary he'd chosen from the vast array on the serving tray before answering. "Yeah, I'm sorry. That had to be hard. So, I suppose Michael can fix my boss's memory?"

"Of course I can, Lieutenant Black."

Both men jumped as Michael suddenly appeared back in his chair.

"Thank you, that would be helpful."

"Okay, my boss wants this dealt with as quickly as possible. The dagger must be found."

"And do ye have any idea where we look?" Darach knew his tone was a bit testy, but so far he still didn't have an answer about how to fix his problem.

"You will go back out on the streets with Sean tailing you. As a target, Angus will—"

"Ye think Angus is behind this?"

"Don't you? It was you who was targeted, Darach, and in answer to your question of how to fix your problem. If the spell used was indeed a combination of black magick and angel DNA..." The archangel actually blanched before continuing. "Then the only way to break the spell on you is to destroy the weapon."

Darach opened his mouth to protest but Michael's hand forestalled him.

"I know it's not what you want to hear, but Lucifer's downfall and subsequently dabbling in all manner of magick helped him grow stronger. This dagger is evil incarnate, designed to stop any and all who practice good. Once you find the dagger, Sean must be the one to touch it."

The halfling's protest was also cut off. "You have

to be the one. Only someone with demon DNA, even though it's unwanted by you, can touch the dagger without falling victim to it's spell."

Darach sat forward in his chair. "So, I'm to be on the street with Sean as backup?"

"Not just the lieutenant, I'm bringing in Conner and Ragnor. They are not known by anyone around here. And neither one has had any interaction with Angus back before you two became immortals."

"So when will they arrive?"

Michael glanced at an ornate hourglass sitting on his desk.

"Any moment now. I sent a couple of emissaries to get them."

"What, you didn't want to beam 'em up like you did us?" Sean's question caused a smile to erupt on Michael's lips.

"Since you are my guest, I will answer your question. I decided we needed to finish our talk before they arrived." Michael glanced at Darach who chose not to get involved in the archangel's and Sean's conversation.

Since he wasn't one hundred percent himself then it would be good to have these men at his side. In the days of their training he, Conner, and Ragnor had grown as close as three people could be after being hit with their immortality.

A slight chime sounded before twin dust columns invaded Michael's office. Darach watched as first Conner Douglas, and then Ragnor, who had never admitted to a last name, at least to him or Conner, stepped from the swirling dervishes. Both men were as tall as Darach, both men shook their heads sending in Conner's case chestnut hair, and the Viking's black mane flying. Both sets of eyes, one a green gaze of disturbance, and the other dark blue, also filled with angst turned toward Michael.

"Michael, ye took me away from hunting a

demon I've been tracking for days." Conner threw out the first sentence.

"Yeah, and I was in the middle of a fight and winning when you had your messenger interrupt." Ragnor's tone matched his build, deep, barrel-like, and not at all happy.

Michael merely looked both warriors over before nodding his head Darach's way. "You may thank your brother-in-arms. He is in need of help in tracking down a demon who has fast hit the top of my bad list."

Darach stood to his feet and waited.

Both men's frowns turned into grins when they spotted Darach. Their hearty backslapping almost sent him to his knees, but he grinned and bore it. These men had been just as helpless and confused as he was when they trained under Michael. All having met their earthly deaths with violent endings.

"Darach, ye old dog, I've missed you." Conner's green eyes flashed with a sheen of tears, and Darach felt the same moisture threatening his.

Ragnor's gaze was equally exuberant as he stared at Darach, but there was an underlying sadness in his blue gaze. "Greetings, my friend. I too have missed our talks and fights."

"'Tis been entirely too long since we've tied one on or settle minor differences with our swords." Darach stepped back as two chairs materialized for his fellow executioners.

"Now, if all the greetings are out of the way, I'd like to get down to the reason for this meeting. Sit down, Darach." Michael's tone remained pleasant but all of them, and Sean who had not moved a muscle, knew not to say another word.

"We have a situation where Angus, and yes, he is the man who killed Darach and his family, has come into possession of an old and extremely dangerous weapon. A dagger that has magical components, and after he was attacked with it, Darach lost his ability to sense demons."

"How did this happen?" Conner's question blasted the air with its intensity.

"It happened when a group of demons attacked me. They left me for dead and if not for Sean here"—Darach motioned toward the halfling—"I woulda died again."

"Why is there a demon in your office, Michael?" Ragnor's words were low but vehement all the same.

"I am not a demon." Sean rose from his seat but a wave of Michael's hands pushed him back into the ornate chair.

"Sit. I will handle this." Michael turned to Ragnor. "Lieutenant Black is only half-demon, and that is in no way his fault. Be that as it may, his ancestry has nothing to do with the fact he saved Darach's life and has been helping him hunt Angus." Michael paused, gave all of them a look, and then continued.

"I want that dagger found. When it is, Sean is the only one of you that can handle it without being in danger of having your powers diminished. Ragnor, you will help Darach find Angus. Conner, you will work with Sean. I deem that will not be a problem?" Michael's question was couched more as a command then anything else.

"No problem for me. You have a problem, Sean?" Conner's smile helped to ease some of the tension from Sean's posture.

"None on my part. I want to find that dagger and get it out of commission. The more executioners it harms, the more work there will be for me in trying to keep New Orleans safe." Sean actually dug up a smile. Darach had to give him points for being as conciliatory as he was considering Ragnor's attitude.

"Good, then it's settled. I will send you all back

now." Michael's hand stopped in mid-wave when Ragnor spoke. "No, I can't go."

Darach actually felt his body tense. He also spotted the disbelief on Conner and Sean's faces. Michael's face however remained smooth, although his golden gaze seemed to intensify.

"I do not believe I heard you correctly, Ragnor."

"As much as I hate to say it, yes you did, Michael. I have unfinished business before I can help, Darach. No offense intended, brother." Ragnor looked to Darach.

"None taken." Darach closed his mouth and waited.

"Business that takes precedence over God's business?" Michael pushed back from his desk and stood up. As Darach watched, the archangel seemed to actually grow taller than his usual seven-foot or so frame.

"It's a personal matter that I can't leave at the moment. I'm sure if you look though your window to Earth, you will understand why." Ragnor made no apology for his words, and Darach couldn't help but wonder if Michael would slap him with a lightning bolt or worse.

Instead, Michael closed his eyes and for a full minute there was no sign that the archangel even breathed. Finally he opened his eyes, fixed his gaze on Ragnor, and spoke, "Fine, you are excused, but once this business is concluded, you will report to me. Is that understood?"

Ragnor nodded his head and before Darach or the other two immortals could say a word, Ragnor was gone.

"Sean, you will have to work alone." When Sean nodded his understanding, Michael spoke again. "Are there any questions?"

Darach knew he shouldn't but couldn't prevent the words form tumbling from his lips. "I dinnae expect you to tell us what Ragnor's business is, but can ye tell us why ye didn't know what it was until ye looked?"

Michael's stare made Darach wish he had kept his mouth shut. After a moment, the archangel shrugged his massive shoulders. "It seems my boss didn't think it was something I needed to be bothered with, but"—again he shrugged his shoulders—"that's all right, my boss knows what He's doing. Now, gentlemen, you have your assignments. Take care of them and be careful."

"We will. So what do we do with the dagger once we find it?" Darach wanted to wrap up the chat, he needed time to think about how this new problem would effect him and Abby.

"Contact me. I'll take it from there. Now, if you three are ready, I'll get you back to Earth."

Darach stood up, as did Sean and Connor.

"Lieutenant Black, thank you for your help."

Sean still looked like his mind was muddled from the evening's events, but then a smile crossed his lips.

"You're welcome. I would hazard to say I'm probably the first demon to ever get this close to Heaven since Lucifer's thwarted mutiny."

Michael's lips revealed even white teeth as he returned the smile. "You would be correct on that, but regardless, my boss is very cognizant that you are trying to do good and not evil."

He turned to Darach. "And the answer to your other question is yes. Let me know the time and date, and I'll send a gift."

****

Angus watched the fiery ball of the sun sink below the horizon. Night would soon be upon the city. He loved the darkness. It allowed him to play and tonight he would. After careful consideration he'd decided to hold off on his plan for another kidnapping. Although, Darach had escaped his trap, he was still injured, and if he was lucky could still die. He'd rather wait until he knew for certain before he made his next move. Somehow it wouldn't be as gratifying if Darach was clueless to Angus's plans.

Memo: Research the facts of the dagger, and delve further into Lieutenant Black's parentage. From this point on there needs to be eyes and ears on the demon world. For if correct, Lucifer may have found the perfect way to take down His immortals. Then Hell would rule the Earth in force.

From the desk of Michael/Archangel to God

Chapter Eighteen

Abby was almost sick with worry. She had not seen Darach for almost forty-eight hours. Of course the hospital had told her he was resting, which she found hard to believe since he'd shown up at her door a couple of nights before. How on earth was he fooling them into believing he was still hurt? And why?

Okay, she knew why, but Abby didn't like it.

Tomorrow school would start. They had delayed reopening until after the funerals. Thank God, Jim, Nate, and Meg had handled the arrangements. Abby had decided not to go to either service. She just didn't feel like walking into a place where death was prevalent.

Arianna had already informed Abby she would be walking her to school and walking her home each day. As for her night job, Arianna wasn't anymore pleased with her declaration she would also be working at night than Darach had been Thanksgiving night.

"You know that's just plain dumb, Abby. You could be a target at anytime, and to put yourself out there after dark is nothing short of a death wish."

"If they want to get me, whoever it is, they could do it during daytime. Remember, Cecil was attacked after daybreak. Give me a break, Arianna. I can't just do nothing. At least if I'm out and about, maybe they will make a move. Then you can catch them."

"I wish it were that easy. After what happened with Darach and that bespelled dagg—" The immortal stopped so quickly with her words and her pacing, Abby just stared at her. What about a dagger? Was it the same one that had almost killed Darach?

"Okay, explain. What dagger and does it have anything to do with Darach not getting in touch with me?" Abby tapped her foot.

"I can't answer that, Abby. I'm not even supposed to know about it, but Sean let it…"

"Uh huh. Let it slip did he? Well, if he knows then don't you think I should?"

The consternation on Arianna's face almost made Abby feel sorry for her, but not quite enough to dispense with wanting answers.

"Look, I don't know a whole lot. Just that there's some type of dagger, ancient as all get-out, that could be the reason Darach was taken down so easily."

"And?" Abby strived for patience but it was disappearing fast.

"And nothing, Abby. I can't say anything else. You'll have to ask Darach."

"Fine, that's just what I'll do." Abby followed suite by grabbing her coat and purse.

"Where are you going?" Arianna followed her into the foyer.

"To the hospital. If you want to go with me, fine, but if not, then so be it."

Abby wasted no more breath on words, but headed out the door. She was almost at the trolley stop when Arianna came up beside her. The smile that came unbidden to her lips was discarded just as quickly as it came.

She needed answers and if she didn't get them she and one immortal Highlander were going to go toe-to-toe.

****

Darach signed his discharge papers as Sean and Conner stood waiting. After talking it over, they decided he could be just as out of the way at his home as in the hospital. Sean would take care of wiping the hospital staff's mind, glamouring them into thinking the patient in room 421 was an elderly man with a bad case of pneumonia who had gone home.

As he took his copy of the papers, the door whooshed open to reveal Abby and Arianna.

He thanked the nurse and felt an overwhelming need to sit down. Why was she here and why now? Probably to berate him again on his determination to continue to hunt Angus. She would have a fit if she found out he was incapacitated when it came to his executioner gifts.

"Evening, Abby. To what do I owe the pleasure?"

"I want to talk to you, Darach."

He barely heard Sean greet Arianna and the immortal's barely civil reply. For some reason both the halfling and Arianna struck sparks off of one another and sometimes that wasn't a good thing. As for Conner, he kept silent.

"So talk, Abby."

Abby glanced at the other three occupants, and raised a brow when her gaze hit on Conner.

"Sorry. Abigail Dupree, meet Conner Douglas. He's here to help us find Angus."

Conner smiled. "'Tis a pleasure, Ms. Dupree."

"Oh wow, he has a brogue just like yours, Darach." Arianna threw in her two cents and then introduced herself. “I’m Arianna. Guess you’ve been stuck in Scotland for a while.”

“You could say that. About a thousand years worth.” Conner shook the hand she offered but then dropped it when Abby spoke.

“Darach, we need to talk.” Her tone was tense, he wasn’t sure what bestirred her enough to come to the hospital as upset as she was with him, but one look at Arianna convinced him somehow she was at fault.

“Hey, it’s not my fault. Sean didn’t really say the dagger was a secret, just to keep it quiet.” Arianna snarled.

“Well excuse me, Ms. Immortal. I would have thought someone who is suppose to be as old as you are would know better.” Sean’s sarcasm reeked of ire.

“Look you two, why don’t you take it outside like you did last time.” Abby’s tone carried a bit of ire itself. He couldn’t help but wonder how much of that would be aimed at him. “And if you wouldn’t mind doing the same, Mr. Douglas, I would appreciate it.” Her words were uttered in a much softer tone, and Conner nodded his head at both Abby and Darach before leaving, following the others from the room.

Darach watched Abby. She stood so still, and looked so fragile, he wanted to hold her. Of course, he knew she was a strong woman. She’d proven it when fighting the demon, and with her attitude of helping the needy, not to mention standing up to him. He just wished…

“Darach, I want to know about the blade and what it did to you.”

Damnation! Sean’s mouth had been at work. He should have kept it to himself.

“I dinnae suppose if I say I dinnae know what ye are talking about ye would believe me?”

“Your accent’s worse. That usually means

something's affecting you strongly. Is it my being here or your not wanting to tell me about the weapon that almost killed you?"

To his surprise her words were softly spoken, not at all what he expected. She had good reason to accuse him of keeping things from her. And he had planned on doing just that if someone had kept their mouth shut.

"Abby, I truly dinnae want to have this conversation with ye." Darach clenched his fists to keep from teleporting away.

"I know, and believe me, I really don't want to know anything else that could break my heart, but I need to know what is happening."

The emotion he heard in her voice staggered him. He would have thought she'd wiped her hands of him. Yet, she seemed to still care.

"'Tis not something I can explain in just a few words. Would ye be willing to come to me house?"

"Yes, I'd like that." Her acquiesce warmed his heart. Maybe he could make her understand what this would mean to both of them.

He opened his arms and welcomed the feel of her body as she glided into them. The trust she placed in him touched him deeply, and sparked a kernel of awareness. Abby deserved the truth.

"Are ye ready?"

"Yes." Abby tucked her head into his chest and tightened her arms around his waist as the world dissolved around them.

The disorientation of having your body torn apart and put back together didn't bother Abby as much this time as it had previously. It could be she was more anxious about what Darach would tell her than about the process of moving through space.

However, she did welcome his strong arm as he led her to the settee and sat beside her.

"Now, tell me please." As she waited for Darach

to begin, she remembered the first time she'd set foot in his home. She'd been in disbelief about his story of what he was, and still feeling the effects her fight with the demon.

"I ken ye need the truth so 'tis what ye will get. The night I was attacked, the demon that struck the first blow used a cursed dagger."

"Cursed?" If she were a normal person she'd think him a bit crazy but her life had never been normal, and after meeting Darach it was fast sliding toward surreal. "How can you be sure it was cursed?"

Darach's extended sigh did nothing to soothe her already out of control nerves.

"Because after being stabbed with it, I seem to have lost my immortal ability to feel when evil is near, when a crime is happening, and at the moment, I cannae even scent a demon's signature."

Although, she knew this was a blow to Darach, her heart skipped with happiness. Without these important executioner skills, he could no longer hunt Angus. Now, he would be safe.

"So what does this mean? Will you be giving up your executioner job? Stop hunting Angus?"

Abby knew her questions were almost electric with anticipation.

"Nay, why would ye think that? I still have a job to do." Darach's stare showed his disbelief.

"Well, just maybe I thought you might have come to your senses about finding Angus. Did you forget you almost died? Would have if Sean hadn't saved you."

Darach jumped off the settee. The coldness left behind stung, as did his words.

"I have to find Angus. 'Tis the only way to get our hands on the dagger. It has to be destroyed or all the immortal executioners are in peril."

Abby wanted to scream. Why did the man have

to be such a noble ass? "Why does it have to be you? Couldn't someone else flush Angus out?"

"Nay, he's fixated on me. Abby, please, I willna be going up against him alone. Conner will be with me. He's one of the men I trained with centuries ago, a good man and a skilled executioner." His words were almost a plea, but the look in his eyes boded a no go on changing his mind.

"If you're trying to make me feel better, it's not working, Darach. I can't believe you would think I could just take this without questioning your sanity. I don't want you going after Angus. If you do, I can't watch, I can't live with the fact you could die—again."

Abby tried to shrug off the arms sliding around her waist, lifting her to her feet, and then the lips capturing her own. She didn't want his kisses. Fine, that was a lie, but it wasn't fair of him to make her want him when this discussion wasn't finished.

Darach's tongue caressed and then coaxed her to open her mouth to his. His touch as always ignited a fire that only Darach could quench. Against her will she kissed him back, pressing her body closer to his. She wanted the man and she shouldn't. Abby should run from him. Run fast and far until she could coat her heart against the terror blanketing it. No matter what he said, no matter how much his touch marked her as his, she would not, could not watch his possible death.

She wrenched out of his arms. When he made a move to pull her back, she whispered. "No, please. I can't do this. Please don't ask me to, Darach."

Darach halted Abby's retreat. He feared if she walked away this time, he might never get her back.

"Abby, I would ask this and more of ye. I want ye to marry me. I love you, woman."

She turned toward him so fast, if his hand had not been on her arm, Abby would have fallen.

"No, I can't. I can't even think about marriage to you right now. You have a death wish. I can't condone what you're doing."

"Abby, I be the same man ye first met. Ye cannae judge me for what I am, no more than I judge ye for having visions."

Abby's eyes went wide for a moment. "How can you even compare the two? You actively seek death, I don't. And the fact you want to go out and play Mr. Hero, is not acceptable to me."

He released his grip on her arm when she tried to tug it free but watched to make sure she didn't over balance.

"It's not only the fact you put yourself in danger, although for all the right reasons, but face it, it won't work. You will never look older. I will, and I have to tell you that's not something any sane woman wants."

"Abby..." He knew he was pleading but it was his heart in danger of dying now. "We can work it out. Just give me a chance. Let me finish what I've started with Angus before ye walk out of my life. Please..."

It was as if the word "Angus" ignited a volcanic reaction inside of Abby. "Angus? I'm tired of hearing about him. I'm frightened to death you *will* find him and he'll kill you, and I'll be a frozen Popsicle in hell before I shackle myself to a man who cares more about revenge than he does love."

Abby turned and literally ran out of the room. He heard the front door open and then slam shut. His breath escaped in a frustrated sigh. Without knowing where the house was she would be stuck until someone took her home. Yet, it would probably be best if he didn't act as her ride. She needed space, even though it killed him to acknowledge that thought. Darach speed-dialed Arianna, all the while his heart shattered into fragments of lost hope.

It seemed that no matter what he did, he would lose Abby. Darach didn't know what to do anymore. *Aye, ye do. Ye will hunt and trap Angus and then kill him. For not to do so could mean the death of Abby and others.*

So be it.

Next Darach tapped his phone and waited to be connected to Sean. "Tell Conner I be ready in a few minutes. I'm at the house."

"I figured as much. Arianna got your call and has already gotten Abby home safely."

Darach closed his phone and then flopped back on the couch. He might as well give all his attention to the coming night's hunt. Abby was lost to him, but at least he could make sure she didn't wind up dead.

****

Angus sipped some of the whiskey he'd bought after he left a club. He'd made certain to time his visits, the night before between, Darach and the lieutenant's trips back and forth in the Quarter. A moan from the corner of the room reminded him he'd also brought back his bedmate. After his people had Abigail, he would celebrate. And what a celebration it would be. Not long now and his demons would steal Darach's woman.

Michael truly wished he could snatch Darach bald-headed, or at the very least lock him up until he saw some sense. The man might have been a respected laird in his day, but he knew next to nothing about soothing a woman's feelings. If he didn't get a handle on his relationship with Abby soon, then it could be too late.

Chapter Nineteen

The door to a sleazy bar near the bayou slammed back against the wall. Darach entered first followed closely by Conner. At least fifteen sets of eyes turned their way, the pupils pulsating a deep crimson. He dinnae ken why he was able to see their pupils glow, but he be glad of it. Maybe Michael had given him that gift since his senses were now off kiltered.

Well, in for a penny and all that stuff. He wanted to find demons so he could shake some information loose about Angus, and it looked like he was getting his wish.

"Dinnae move." Darach commanded as a large muscular demon stood up. "We dinnae want any trouble, but if ye dinnae behave we will bring it."

"What do you want, executioner?" The question coming from the creature's mouth showed off a mean set of rancid looking fangs. How did he know what Darach was? He didn't wear a sign and as of yet, his sword remained sheathed inside his coat.

"I want information only. If ye cooperate, then there will be no need for any violence." At Darach's words, Conner moved closer but stilled any further movements.

Hissing erupted from the other demons in the room. "Your kind breeds violence, MacRath."

"He kens your name, Darach. What did ye do to make him so friendly?" Conner's grin did not reach the green of his eyes. His stance, like Darach's, stayed relaxed but cued to move in a flash of light if needed.

"Must be me effervescent personality. A lot of people dinnae like me. I cannae figure it out." Darach's smile didn't touch the hard core of his heart. He wanted Angus, and he would do all he could to extract the demon's whereabouts.

"Again I ask you, what do you want?" The first demon slid a bit closer to Darach. A ploy he was more than happy with.

"I want to know where Angus MacRath is." Darach hated using his clan name in reference to the black-hearted devil, but if it would help jar some memories he'd be happy.

"MacRath, you say. Would he be kin to you?" The demon who shouted it from the back moved forward. Coal-black hair fell in a greasy mess past his shoulders. His reddened pupils glittered with malice.

"That demon spawn has never been kin to me. He stole me clan's name and me birthright." Darach knew he'd allowed his anger to show. Not good, he needed to be more in control.

"Well, I hate to disappoint either one of you Scottish sheep, but if I did know where Angus was, I wouldn't waste my breath telling you."

Conner flexed his fists, a sure sign he was ready to fight, and Darach would be overjoyed to oblige his friend. "Well then I guess we will just have to clean out this nest of vermin. What do ye think, Conner?"

"I say ye take Stringy-hair, and I'll take Fangy

here." Conner didn't glance his way, but Darach knew he waited for his command.

Fangy didn't care for Conner's words, and the sneer on Stringy's lips didn't bode well for a congenial conversation, but Darach could do without the talk. He wanted to pound flesh, to feed the rage of past hurts, to assuage the guilt over what he couldn't give Abby.

"Let's do it." Darach followed his words with a quick right to the throat of the demon nearest him. The strength of the blow took the creature to his knees. His sword did the rest. Demon gore coated his clothes as he continued to work his way through several more of the demons.

He glanced to his right and watched as Conner scored a hit to the midsection of a demon that literally exploded with slime. God above, he hated the mess their disintegrated bodies left behind.

Once again he focused his attention on the demons trying to surround and cut him off from Conner. He kicked out with his right leg and his booted foot met with the soft flesh of a bald-headed demon's face. He finished the job with a short thrust of his sword. Now there was only one demon standing in front of him: the stringy-haired demon who seemed to know a bit about Angus. He wanted information before he dispatched this one.

"So what are you waiting on, executioner? Let's fight."

For some reason, Darach believed the demon in front of him wanted to avoid a fight, why else would he stay back while the other demons were attacking?

"I dinnae think ye want to fight. I think ye want to make a deal. So let's chat, shall we?" Darach kept his tone neutral. He didn't want the creature to know just how desperate he was for that information.

"What about the other executioner?"

Aye, the demon wanted to avoid bloodshed or gore at any cost. Darach motioned to Conner who'd just finished the last of his demon entourage. "My friend willna interfere. Now take a seat."

Stringy-hair did just that, but Darach opted to stand. "Now, tell me what ye ken about Angus. And if ye lie, I will dispatch you back to hell myself, if there's enough left of the gore to send."

"Fine, but I want safe passage out of here if I tell you anything." The demon's fangs came together and he almost bit his bottom lip.

"Tell me something useful, and ye can walk, providing ye get out of New Orleans." Darach allowed his eyes to go flat, the demon drew back a bit but then growled.

"All I know is I heard some big shot from the underworld confiscated one of the warehouses near the Canal. No one I've talked to knows anything about him, but his first name and that he's on some type of mission. Even some of the more aged demons are giving this dude a wide path."

Darach shot a look at Conner and grinned. Just maybe this time he would find Angus.

"And that's all? Ye know nothing else?"

"Nothing, but they say he's got Lucifer's ear and possibly a way to harm executioners." The demon's eyes turned a bit redder.

"So why would ye tell me this? I would think you'd want to see the executioners killed." Darach's puzzlement over Stringy-hair's disclosure showed in his tone.

"Yeah, well, there are executioners and then there are executioners. You've never bothered me before, and you don't make a habit of killing for no reason, so I'd hate to see someone else installed here—someone who would make my life harder to keep."

"Well since you're leaving NOLA it willna

matter will it?"

For a moment the demon looked a bit flummoxed. "I guess not, but I look at it this way, you could have already killed me and didn't. I'm not happy with the life I have but it's the only one I've got, so I guess I owe you one."

"You owe me nothing, demon. Just get out of NOLA and don't look back." Darach waited all of one second before speaking again. "That means now."

The demon looked at Darach, then Conner, before jumping off the bar stool and heading for the door. Before he stepped over the threshold, he turned. "One other thing, I'd watch your woman if I were you. Talk on the street is she's going to be one of Angus's hits."

Before Darach could ask him anything else, the demon disappeared in a ribbon of smoke.

"Well, I'd say we've had a pretty productive night." Conner's grin looked a bit forced, and Darach knew the night had brought back memories of another night when they had stood together after being attacked by a large force of demons. Conner had suffered several injuries, one to his eyes that if not by the grace of God he would have been blind for the rest of his immortal life.

"Aye, I say we did do some arse-kicking. Let's get cleaned up and then we'll meet Sean at the Highlander Bar. I think we both could use a drink."

****

Darach ended up going to the bar alone. After he and Conner got cleaned up, Michael sent a message stating he needed to see the immortal so he'd called Sean, who was more than ready to call it a night.

It'd taken only a moment to ascertain that working both night and day at times was getting to the halfling. And Sean's belief that he now believed Angus was behind all of the deaths, even the prostitute's, was not sitting well with Darach.

“Hi, good-looking stranger.” Rae sashayed up to the booth addressing Darach and Sean. She held her pad in front of her.

“I be the good-looking one, Sean, so get that look off your face.” Darach elbowed the halfling.

“And how can you be so sure I’m talking about you, Darach. I haven’t heard a word from you since Abby ran out of here that morning over a week ago. Thank goodness she had the good will to let me know you were okay.”

“I be sorry Rae, truly. ’Tis been a hectic week.”

“Sure, and now you want me to change the subject, don’t you?” Rae’s smile didn’t quite reach her eyes.

“Would ye mind? We have some business to discuss.”

“No problem, just make sure you stay out of trouble. Abby is a nice woman and doesn’t need to worry about you. And come to think of it, neither do I.”

After taking their drink orders, she left them in peace for a few.

“Speaking of Abby, did you get it straightened out?” Sean grabbed a handful of nuts from the bowl resting on the Formica surface and popped them in his mouth.

“I talked to her, but nothing’s straightened out. I dinnae ken how it will ever be.”

“Well, you might want to try talking to her again, Darach.” Rae sat the drinks down with enough force the glasses thudded on the table.

“Rae—”

“Don’t ‘Rae’ me. The woman loves you and you love her. Nothing can’t be fixed when it comes to that one little emotion. Please don’t make me think you’re not the man I thought you were. Fix the problem.”

Before he could reply, Rae was gone again. Sean

shot him a commiserating look. Darach picked up his drink and downed the contents. Sean did the same.

"So where's Conner, and any ideas as to where to look next to find Angus?" The demon population, other than the group he and Conner had routed, seemed to be hiding out, a situation that sent an alert to Darach and Sean. Something was up, and they needed to find out what it was before there were more bodies.

"Conner's with Michael and we did get one tip after taking out a group of demons near the bayou."

Sean looked toward Rae and raised two fingers. She nodded and then gave the order to the bartender.

"Good, because I have to tell you, never in my existence have I ever seen demons cloak themselves so securely. It's spooky."

"I agree. There's a foreboding in the air that won't go away."

"Yeah, I felt it too…wait a minute, if you felt something then maybe the magick is wearing off?" Sean looked hopeful.

Darach stared at Sean. Could he be right?

"Or I could just be feeling whatever a normal person would feel."

"Maybe, but it's something that Michael might be able to answer."

Darach chuckled. "You like Michael, dinnae ye?"

"Well, yeah, he's an entity that's made demons wet their asbestos drawers forever. Yet, there's something about the archangel that is…"

"Habit forming?"

"Right again. It's like he's almost human in a way."

Darach took his drink from a silent Rae and thanked her. He'd put her tip on the table before he left. She was pissed enough she might refuse to take it from him.

"He does have his moments. Now back to our hunt. We got a lead on a warehouse near the bayou. I plan on checking it out."

"Not by yourself I hope. I have to be there, remember? The dagger?"

"Aye, by myself. I dinnae think Angus will go for me unless I be by myself, and if he dinnae then the dagger is off the table anyway—since I believe he is the only one to have possession of the dagger now."

Sean frowned. "I don't like it. If not me then you need Conner with you."

"I dinnae know how long Conner will be tied up with Michael, and I dinnae want Angus to get word we know about the warehouse."

The halfling opened his mouth but both their phones going off prevented his reply. Darach glanced down and then felt the blood leave his face. The displayed text read ***911 Abby's.***

"We have to go, Abby's in trouble." Darach's voice shook with fear.

"I know. Arianna sent me a message also. I know where our missing demons are. They're at Abby's."

Michael didn't like how events were playing out in the mortal realm. Darach had alienated Abby. Angus was capitalizing on the immortal's and the lieutenant's failure to find any demons at all, and now all hell was breaking lose on Canal Street. With the no-interference rule strictly being enforced, his hands were tied.

Chapter Twenty

Darach waited only a moment after getting outside, before grabbing Sean and teleporting to Abby's house. Several men roamed the front yard. To an unsuspecting mortal they would look just like the casually dressed men they portrayed, but he and Sean knew what shape demons could take. He just prayed they had morphed into the bodies and not stolen them from their rightful owners.

He catapulted over their heads and landed on Abby's porch. "Leave now, and I will allow ye to live."

The first demon smiled, the mortal glamour wearing thin as Darach glimpsed yellow and jagged teeth.

"Did you not learn anything the last time, executioner? I thought you immortals were a smarter breed."

Darach fought the urge to reach out and clamp his hand around the demon's throat. His headcount showed at least eight of them. More than in the alley, but fewer than with Conner, and now with Sean, he figured the odds were about even.

"Smart enough to know ye are the pawn of a demon who does not care if ye live or die."

The other demons snarled their displeasure. Out the corner of his eye he glimpsed Sean who kept an eye on the ones ringing the steps on his side, as Darach looked to the leader and the others.

"And how do you expect to take all of us down, immortal, when you are cursed by the blade of Lucifer?"

Again out of the corner of his eye, he could see Sean, who dropped his glamour, waiting a bit impatiently.

"Cursed is your term, not mine. I still have more than enough strength to kill a few demons. And as ye see I be not the only one who will be fighting this battle."

The leader turned his head and his now reddened eyes bulged. "What manner of demon is this?"

"What's the matter, sulfur-face? Haven't you ever seen a half-breed demon before?" Sean's laughter caused several of the demons to back away.

Sulfur-face stood his ground. "What is the matter with the rest of you? He's just like us and he will die like any demon."

One of the demons near Darach spoke. "And the sooner we kill them both the sooner we can have the women." His evil grin made Darach want to rip his teeth out and crammed them up his unholy ass.

"That's right, my friends, our mentor has promised us great rewards when we deliver the mortal and immortal females to him." Sulfur-face grinned showing his nasty fangs.

The *him* the demon mentioned caught Darach's attention.

"This 'him' ye speak of, is it the demon who is sending ye to your deaths? For if ye touch the women ye all will do more than die, ye will suffer torture like the fires of hell were a candle's flame."

Sulfur-face sneered. "And just what torture could you devise?"

As Darach had been taunting the demon, Sean had edged closer to the one nearest him. The fanged creature seemed to be too enthralled with the exchange between his leader and Darach to notice. Now, if he could keep their attention a bit longer, he and Sean could launch their attack.

"'Tis not me torture ye will suffer but that of the archangel Michael. I believe he has a special way of dealing with those who work in evil. Much the same way he dealt with those who tried to overthrow God."

All of the demons visibly shook at the mention of Michael. Darach had to give the archangel credit, he certainly knew how to incite fear even from a distance.

A barely perceptible nod from Sean and Darach struck. His sword cut a path from the leader's head to his ass. Sulfur-face's glamour fell away leaving behind scaly skin and oozing wounds. At least he had not taken an innocent's body. His sword struck again and the demon disintegrated into particles of air.

His gaze found Sean who was tossing fireballs at his opponent. Darach wasn't even sure Sean knew he could do that before tonight, but he was glad for the skill. It would make the night's work easier.

His sword found a new victim and demon debris flew in the air once again. As he and Sean continued to mow down demons, the previous still air began to fill with a slow but steady wind. It grew stronger, swirling the dust and leftover slime from the demons already dead to encompass the ones they were still dispatching.

As the last one exhaled a dying breath, the wind swirled once more before leaving as quickly as it arrived. Darach thought he heard a faint "Well done". but couldn't be sure.

As he reached to sheathe his sword, and Sean shook his hands in the air, the door behind them opened pouring out first Arianna, followed by Abby.

The immortal moved to Sean as Abby stood watching Darach. He did the only thing he could do—he opened his arms. His heart thudded loudly enough he heard it in his head when Abby threw herself against him. He welcomed the slight weight of her body but hated the tears that soaked into his shirt. She was frightened, something that should not have happened. The demons should never have breached the safety guards of the house and land's perimeters.

"Hush, lass. 'Tis over."

Abby's small fists pummeled his chest. "I'm not crying because I was scared of them, you big ox, I'm crying 'cause I was afraid you would be killed."

"Oh..."

He looked over Abby's head as he patted her gently on the back. Sean and Arianna were staring at the both of them. Darach lightly shrugged his shoulders. A silent but dual "*Talk to her,*" came from both their mouths. He nodded and then gathered Abby even closer.

"I be fine, Abby, love. Now, let's get you inside." Not sure of whether she should lie down or not, Darach decided to err on the side of caution. It had been a traumatic night for all involved, and as the only mortal she might need the comfort of her bed.

The knowledge that Abby hated teleporting had him rushing up the steps to the second floor, his boots making hollow sounds on the stairs. He walked through the open doorway and placed her gently on the unmade bed. For the first time since she'd thrown herself into his arms, Darach realized she was dressed for bed. Of course she would be, it was the middle of the night.

Now, unsure of what to do, he paced the room's circumference. As he moved back and forth he realized he'd done more pacing since he'd met Abby than in the century before.

A slight rustling of the covers preceded, "Darach."

He moved to the bed and sat on the edge. Abby's face was pale against the emerald green sheets, but her tears were now dried tracks on her cheeks.

"I be here, Abby."

Her hand reached out, but instead of taking the one he offered, she plucked at the bedding.

"Talk to me. I promise I will listen."

Abby's gaze lifted to touch his. "Can you promise not to hate me for what I did?"

What on earth was she talking about? Nothing Abby could do would make him hate her.

He caught and brought her hand to his lips. He kissed the soft skin before tucking it next to his heart. "Why dinnae ye tell me what ye did, then we will sort it out."

"I was glad when you told me about the dagger. About how it affected you." Abby's breath hitched and then she sighed. "I thought you would stop the nonsense about Angus, but you didn't."

"Abby, ye already told me this, so it cannot be what 'tis bothering ye."

"You're right, that's not all of it. Earlier tonight while Arianna was getting a shower, I slipped out and went to the club for a few minutes. I just wanted to tell Chaz I would be in to work tomorrow night, and I did leave a note."

Darach tried to control his temper. Yes, she'd gone out when she shouldn't have, and his heart clenched at what could have happened and what almost had, but that wasn't all of it. He needed to find out what she was so upset about and then he'd admonish her for leaving the house.

"Abby, what ye did was not a sin. Foolish, yes, but this 'tisn't what is upsetting ye. Now, what else is there?"

Her eyes filled with tears once more. "While I was at the club, I saw a demon and he saw me."

The pulse inside his body pounded through his blood.

"What did ye do?"

"Darach, you're squeezing my hand too tight."

"I be sorry." Darach caressed the abused limb. "Now, tell me what else happened."

"I talked to him, hoping to get information about Angus."

Darach was staggered. "Abby, do ye have rocks in your brain?" He didn't grip her hand this time. Instead he released it and stood up.

"Please, don't yell at me, Darach. I said I'm sorry. I know what I did was wrong, but I thought maybe if I got the information I could tell Arianna. Once Angus was caught, you'd be able to let go of the past."

Darach wanted to curse, but what good would it do? What she'd done could not be undone, yet he had more questions.

"Do ye know how the demons breached the perimeters?"

"No! How could I? I didn't even know there were any demons outside until Arianna woke me up. I swear the demon was still at the club when I left."

Abby's gaze shone with truth, but if she didn't lead them here, then who had?

"Darach, you do believe me, don't you?"

"Aye, but if ye ever try something that foolhardy again, I will spank ye to within an inch of your life, Abby. Do ye have any idea of the fear stalking me when I found out ye were under a demon attack?"

"Yes, as much as the fear that rides me

whenever I think of you confronting Angus, or you lying in a hospital bed in a coma."

For the first time, he finally realized the terror Abby had being going through. His job was his life, but lately he found that he wanted more. He wanted Abby. If she would have him.

"All right, I understand. I just cannae let it go at the moment." Darach sat back down next to Abby. He knew it wasn't what she wanted to hear but... "Now we need to figure out how they breached Arianna's safety guards."

"Ahem."

Darach looked up and found Sean and Arianna standing at the threshold.

"Can we come in? I think we know the answer to your question." Sean's expression did not give even an inkling of his thoughts.

"Perhaps Abby would be more comfortable if we met downstairs." For the first time since he'd met the immortal, Arianna seemed nervous.

"No, This is fine. Let's just get it over with, okay?" Abby looked at Darach as she spoke and then turned toward Arianna.

"I weakened the safeguards. It was after I found Abby at the club. I could smell demon on her, and she told me what happened. I teleported her back here and she went to bed." Arianna fidgeted with one of her fingernails. "It was a few hours after that, that I decided to walk outside. I saw Sean and you Darach, or at least I thought so. I threw up my hand, and Sean waved. I weakened the guards and before I knew it the front yard was full of demons."

She looked Darach in the eyes before looking down at the floor. "I'm sorry, I never thought. I should have made certain it was you. I'll tell Michael it's my fault."

"No need, Arianna, as much as I hate to say it, drawing the demons out was what we wanted to do anyway. At least there are eight fewer of them now. Add that to the ones Conner and I killed earlier and it's been a decent night's work. And I'm pretty sure Angus is their true leader." Darach rubbed a smudge of dirt off his shirt. "Besides, there is no way ye could have known they would infiltrate this far, nor that they would use glamour to disguise themselves."

Sean inserted, "I agree with Darach, and we were right on the mark about the dagger. It seems to be some type of treasured relic."

Darach took Abby's hand. "Aye, but at least it didn't affect me ability to fight."

"And I'm glad of that fact, Highlander," Sean tossed out.

"I have a feeling ye could have taken them out on your own, halfling. Care to tell me where ye got the fire power from?"

The lieutenant's face went blank for a moment, then his features drew together in a frown. "I have no idea. One moment, I'm wondering if I can kill one of them with my revolver, then I feel a tingling in my hands. My first hit was luck. I was shaking my hands to get rid of the crawling ants sensation, and the next thing I knew fire was shooting from my fingertips."

Arianna flopped onto the bed as Abby's mouth fell open. "Those were the bright flashes I could see when Arianna would let me look out the window."

"Yes, and I thought it was lightning flashes sent by Michael." Arianna looked stunned.

Darach remembered the wind. "Nay, but he did clear away the demon debris.

"So are we square?" Abby's question drew three sets of eyes to her. Darach wanted to kiss the dried tears, but would wait until they were alone. Arianna smiled and then shrugged her shoulders.

"It seems that I was just as much at fault as you

were, so yeah, we're square."

"Hey, Abby, you at least found the demons, something I couldn't do." Sean grinned at Abby and then at Darach.

"And now I suppose ye want me to agree with these two?" Darach allowed his gaze to rove Abby's still features and form as he pointed toward the others.

"Consider it unanimous, but dinnae ever do that again."

Abby threw herself into his arms. "I promise I won't."

"Good, now I suggest we allow Abby to get some rest. Ye do have school tomorrow, aye?" Darach dropped a kiss on Abby's brow and then eased her back to the mattress.

"Darach, I can't sleep."

"Try. Ye will need all your wits about ye if Angus sends more demons."

"What about you? He will send more after you also."

"Dinnae worry about me. I will rest after ye do, and I will be here when ye wake up."

****

The celebration had not happened. His minions were destroyed. Darach still lived and Abigail was beyond his grasp. When Alex had called to let him know they had found a loophole through the immortal security on the mortal's property, he'd anticipated so much more. Now, he would have to find something else to draw Abigail to him, and in essence Darach. It seemed the only way to kill him would be by Angus's own hand.

Michael applauded the success of his immortal and the halfling. He too had been a bit flummoxed to see Sean exhibit signs of being a fire demon, truly one of the strongest and most feared branches of Lucifer's ranks. It would be best to make sure the lieutenant stayed on the side of justice.

Chapter Twenty-One

Darach pushed his boots off his feet, yanked off his coat, and placed his sword in a corner near Abby's bed. He then tugged his shirt out of his pants before lying down next to Abby.

Her wide-eyed stare as he folded his body around hers accordion style caused him to drop a kiss on her open mouth. After he drew away, he turned her pliant and way-too-sensual body away from his. No need to court temptation. Abby needed to rest, and come to think of it, so did he. With Arianna in the house, she would wake him if anything happened. Conner would be back also, and Sean could fill him in on the rest of the night's events.

Darach stifled a yawn and closed his eyes. By the time he dropped off to sleep, Abby's sweet snores filled the room.

****

Darach gazed out Abby's bedroom window, and watched as the sun eased over the horizon. The mingled pinks, oranges, and reds made a beautiful picture. One he didn't always get to see at the crack of dawn. As he waited for the sun to climb higher, he imagined what it would feel like to wake up every day with Abby. Would she be soft and kittenish as he made love to her in the morning, or would she be a tigress giving as good as she got? She'd turn down his offer of marriage and unless he could get her to change her mind, he'd never know. As he thought about never being able to have her for his own, a soft almost non-existent caress slid down his spine. Bringing with it a shiver of goose bumps, and a hard doze of lust.

He held his breath to see what Abby would do next. Darach prayed she'd do more, even if he knew he'd probably catch the wrath of the archangel.

Her hand moved southward and cupped first one butt cheek and then the other, giving them a light squeeze before stopping. When she didn't touch him again, he turned to face her.

"Abby?" His voice was husky with lust.

"Yes?" Her voice was tremulous. Her eyes were wide with, dare he hope, desire for him.

"You ken I be bound not to take ye as I want to. If we start this, I cannae guarantee I willna finish it this time."

Abby looked away and then back. "I know. And I know that if you do you'll hate yourself."

"So, what do ye want me to do?" He hoped she didn't hear the desperation in his voice. Lord, he wanted her. No he shouldn't have her. Yet, he prayed she'd want him to make love to her.

"Make me yours, please." Abby whispered the words. "If we can't be together forever, then please give me tonight."

Before the last syllable of her last word dropped into the air, he pulled her to him. His lips stamped his approval of her answer, and his tongue carried his desire to Abby. His hands found and covered her breast, tweaking her nipples until they were hardened tips.

"Darach..." His name came out on a moan.

He pulled back from her lips. "Aye, I know. This time I plan to love ye all the way, Abby."

"Don't tell me, do it." Abby's tone rose as he replaced his hands with his lips, lightly tonguing her ripe flesh.

Darach loved how she sounded when he touched her. Loved how he could make her moan with pleasure. And yes, he would love sheathing himself deep inside her even more.

His hands slid down the arc of Abby's curves, and to the hidden treasure between her legs. He wanted her ready, and yes, when he thumbed the indenture hiding her female nub, rich cream coated his digit.

Abby's moan this time reached all the way to the tip of his manhood. Blood pooled and then moved through his erection making him harder than a mortar brick.

"Abby, me love, what ye do to me..." He dipped his fingers further into her warmth, slid first one and then another finger deep inside her core. As his blood rose higher, Abby pushed against his hand, her hips undulating in a dance as old as Adam and Eve.

"No more than what you do to me, my love." She whispered the words against his lips.

He welcomed the rhythm, he moved his body in sync, and when she cried out her release, he caught her closer and still closer. One hand went under her knee as he pulled her wet flesh against his aching shaft.

Take her now, his body roared, but he couldn't not like this, Abby deserved at least a bed under her back when he made her his. Darach lifted her into his arms, laid her on the bed, and then discarded his clothes. He followed her down and then spread her legs to his eager gaze. He loved how she wept for him, how her flesh was ripe with her climax.

Now he would find his.

Darach bent Abby's knees and then positioned himself between them. Slowly he inched his way into her core. Her eyes were open but she didn't say a word as he pushed deeper until he breached her barrier.

"Darach!" His name was a bit of shocked exclamation and thrill.

"Did I hurt ye, lass?" He prayed not.

"Only a bit. And it doesn't matter; I need you now, Darach. Please..."

"Soon, Abby, we will both find what we seek."

He continued to push and her hips cradled him as she locked her legs around his waist. Faster they moved and faster still, until a fiery blast of orgasm took Darach over the edge, and he took Abby with him.

****

Darach awoke to find Abby's side of the bed empty. He reached out to caress her pillow and his hand brushed against paper. He pulled the note closer.

Dear Darach,

Thanks so much for keeping me company last night. I know it wasn't easy for me to sleep next to you without us making love, and I thank you. I just needed to be held, and you did a great job.

Love, Abby.

"What the hell?" Darach looked down and found he was still dressed. He raked a hand through his hair. Could it have been a dream? Never had he dream about making love to a woman and the dream be so real. Just thinking about him and Abby like that made him hard all over again. As he thought of the tenderness, the unleashed desire he'd experienced as he'd made love to his dream Abby, he wanted to rail at the fates. Dammit, he wanted her under him for real.

****

Abby rushed up to the front door of her house, and then unlocked it. Arianna stood at her side, and motioned her back until she checked the foyer and the rest of the rooms for unwanted occupants. Once she gave the all-clear, Abby was allowed to move out of the tight corner Arianna put her in. Something about better to see what was coming and give warning instead of being attacked from behind.

Abby headed for the kitchen after she tossed her coat, purse, and briefcase on the couch. She grabbed a pitcher of iced tea from the refrigerator and pulled some cookies out of the cupboard, and placed them on a plate. Chocolate chip was one of Arianna's favorites. She hoped it would pry her mouth open.

All day long, she'd had these crazy thoughts, erotic thoughts, about Darach. She knew nothing had happened during the night. He was still clothed, and her gown was down around her ankles as a granny gown should be. So was it just wishful thinking? Could she have conjured up such a sensual and breathtaking scenario from her subconscious? And if so what was she going to do about it? She needed to see Darach, and that is why she was going to pump Arianna for information.

"Okay, out with it. I know you talked to Darach during the day. What did he say and what are his plans concerning Angus? And did he say anything about me?" Her last question came out in a whisper.

At the immortal's blank look, she changed tactics. "Of course, if you don't tell me, I'll just go to Sean and tell him you have the hots for him."

"Abby, that's a lie." The immortal's words were almost a screech.

"Oh please, you do too," she argued back.

Arianna settled on a bar stool at the counter and swiped a cookie before Abby could stop her.

"No, I don't. And I really don't want to talk about it. I want talk about you." Arianna took a bite of cookie, giving Abby just enough time to wish she had not said anything.

"Oooh, that was good." The immortal looked blissful, but then her features hardened, and her green eyes flashed. "I didn't say anything in front of the guys, but you are one screwed-up woman. It was crazy what you did. And if you hadn't looked so despondent and gone straight to bed, I would have told you so."

Abby took a sip of her tea before responding in kind. "And did you forget who released the safety guards."

"Arrgh! You mortals are insane. And no I haven't forgotten my part in last night's debacle."

"Good, just so you know, you immortals are not much better."

Arianna gave a long woeful sigh and then bit into her cookie. Abby waited impatiently for her to swallow the last bite. She still needed to know about Darach.

"Okay, I said I was at fault, I was, but it wasn't that I have the hots for Sean, I told you I'm not looking for love at all, especially with a…"

"Good, glad you didn't say it. Sean's really sweet."

"Sweet? I doubt it, but he does deserve better than—"

"Don't go there. You would be great for him."

"No, I wouldn't. Too much baggage, and again we are not going to talk about it. Besides, I thought you wanted to know what Darach said."

Abby plucked the red herring offered and decided she'd pounce on Arianna another time about the dark secrets of her past.

"Okay, tell me." She took another sip of tea to wet her suddenly dry throat.

"He plans to continue to hunt Angus."

"Great, I knew he wouldn't change his mind." Her cup landed on the table with a hard clink.

Arianna leaned forward. "Actually, he acted a bit distracted. I'm not sure I've ever seen that type of look on his face when it comes to demons. I know he's worried Angus will continue to come after you. It was just by the grace of God the men got here in time last night. I could never have held all those creatures off."

"Gee, that makes me feel really good having you as my protector."

"Cut me some slack, Abby. I'm good at my job, but eight-to-one odds is not very good even without me worrying about them getting their hands on you."

Abby took the last cookie from the plate and wondered how they'd eaten them all without her noticing.

"Sorry, I guess you're right. Now, what else did Darach say?"

Arianna smiled. "He said that he wanted to take you to dinner tonight before he and Conner went out. Sean and I are to go with you but sit at a separate table. He doesn't want your dinner interrupted by any unwanted guests."

Dinner? With Darach? What would she wear, where were they going, and what would he say?

"Abby, you okay? You went all quiet on me."

"Did he say where we were going to dinner?"

"Antoine's."

"Oh Lord, I have to find something to wear. It's a pretty ritzy place."

"I'm sure Darach wouldn't care if you wore jeans." Abby knew Arianna was trying to be helpful but it wasn't working.

"Look, if he's taking me to Antoine's it's a big deal. I want to look my best."

"Okay, so go get ready. He said he'd be here around seven or so."

Abby's gaze flew to the wall clock. It was almost six now. The staff meeting had gone over.

"Yikes, I've gotta hurry."

She gave Arianna a brief smile and then ran for the stairs. Abby did a mental run-through of formal dresses her closet held and groaned. There was only one dress that would do and it was way too short.

Forty minutes later she stood in front of her mirror staring at what couldn't be lowered or raised.

"I don't know why you're upset, the dress looks great on you." Arianna's support was welcome but how she wished she'd had time to go shopping.

"Are you sure it's not too short…too low in the neck…"

"It's fine, Abby. Darach will love it."

She hazarded another glance in the glass. The silver-blue shade did work okay with her hair, it was just a lot shorter than she was used to wearing except at the club. And that was different, she played a part there. The neckline was a bit lower than what she was used to also.

The downstairs clock chimed seven times and the doorbell rang at the same time.

Before she could plead a case of nerves and back out, Arianna caught her arm and tugged her out into the hall. When Abby tried to retreat, the immortal stared her down. "You either walk down the stairs or I'll teleport you. And I can't promise it won't mess up your hair when I do."

"Fine, let me grab my purse."

Arianna's laughter followed her as she grabbed the clutch bag. "You might want to put a smile on your face. At the moment you look like you're facing a squad of demons."

****

"Lighten up, Darach. You act like this is your

first date."

Darach almost chuckled but his nervous system was rebelling. "Ye wouldna be that far off the mark. 'Tis my first real date. Briene and I only saw one another in the presence of our families. We never 'went out' as mortals call it today."

The halfling made some sort of choking sound. "Shit man, that's rough. No wonder you look like you're freaking out."

He gave Sean a look he hoped would shut him up, but it did the opposite. "Okay, just take some deep breaths. Everything will be fine. Just be yourself."

"Does that drivel work for ye?"

"Hell no, I never tried it. I heard it on a talk show. My track record for dating isn't much better than yours."

Finally another glimpse into the halfling's life. It seemed he had probably been as lonely as Darach was before he met Abby.

Before he could do it himself, Sean punched the doorbell a second time.

"Keep your sword sheathed. We're coming." Arianna's acidic tone finally got Darach's mouth to relax in a smile.

When the door swung open, however he had eyes only for Abby. She literally took his breath. The silver threads of her dress mingled with blue, emphasizing her hair and eyes. Her lips were painted a pale pink, and her eyelids were softly touched with a color similar to her dress. The soft smile she gave him shot an arrow straight to his heart. Not to mention other parts of his anatomy. All day long he'd been semi-hard, the dream always on the back burner of his thoughts.

"Hi, Darach. Evening, Sean." Abby greeted both of them but kept her gaze on him. He should have been more nervous but for some reason all his fears of what tonight might bring disappeared.

"Evening, Abby. Ye look even more beautiful than I could ever imagine."

The blush staining her cheeks made the blood rise in his lower body. Abby's innocence, her beauty, the sparkle in her eyes when she gazed up at him, made Darach want to take her away. So far away no one, not even Michael, could find them. Then he would love her like she'd never been loved before.

"Don't you think we ought to get a move on? Your reservation's at a quarter after seven and it's almost that time now." Arianna's interruption was unwanted but needed, for his only thought was to take Abby into his arms and make love to her for real.

"Aye. We should leave now." He took the coat Abby held and helped her into it. After making sure the house was secure all four of them headed for the trolley stop.

"If ye like, 'tis a pretty mild night, we could walk to the restaurant."

Abby smiled. "I'd love to."

Amidst the grumbling from the other two in their party, Darach caught Abby's hand in his. She gave his fingers a light squeeze, and he pulled her a bit closer. The ever-present scent of jasmine floated in the crisp air sending a shock of lust once again to his manhood. He prayed again that the dinner would go as he wanted. Darach was tired of waiting to make Abby his.

"Thank you."

So immersed in trying to control his desire, he almost missed her soft words.

"For what, Abby?"

"Asking me to dinner. It's nice to forget about everything going on and just enjoy being alive."

Darach couldn't agree more. "Ye've had a hard time, Abby. I hope it will be over soon."

"So do I, Darach. I just wish I knew you were going to survive whatever happens next."

The exterior of the restaurant came into view. "*Next*, we have dinner and enjoy some of the city's nightlife."

****

Darach's last bite of chateaubriand tasted like the peat-bogs in his homeland. At first the succulent dish went down easy, but the more he thought about the rest of the evening and what he wanted to ask Abby, the more it felt like he was going to choke.

"This is delicious, Darach. I'm really enjoying myself."

He tore his gaze away from his plate and turned to Abby. Abby, whose eyes sparkled as brightly as the chandelier shining overhead. It reminded him of how she'd looked in the light of dawn creeping into her bedroom window during his dream.

"I be glad. We both needed a break from all that has been going on."

"Well, if that's the case, why do you look like you swallowed a frog?" Her question wasn't sharp, but he could almost see the wheels turning in her head.

"'Tis nothing to do with ye. Or rather it does, but not in a bad way."

Abby took a sip of the white wine he'd ordered with their meal and then looked back at Darach.

"Care to talk about it? I know that I've been a veritable witch to you. I also know my actions and bad judgment have not helped matters with the demons or Angus, but I think I'm beginning to understand why you have to do it."

So shocked was he at Abby's words, his tongue felt frozen to the roof of his mouth. This was wonderful news, but centuries as an executioner made him leery of just accepting her seeming about-face. He wanted to know why.

"Thank ye, Abby. Now to turn your words on ye,

care to tell me why ye had a change of heart?"

Her smile started the heat roaring back through his blood and finding a home between his thighs. Good thing the tablecloth hung long enough to cover his blatant lust.

"I realized that to do nothing, you would not be the man I care about. You would not be the man who rescued me and that young girl on the night we met. Nor would you have cared so deeply about Cecil and the other deaths."

Her words went straight to his heart. He didn't know what had caused this revelation, but he was glad all the same. It would make the rest of the evening easier—he hoped.

"Again, my thanks. At first I didnae want to embrace the new life I was given, but Michael made me realize that although I couldna save me family, I could save others. And after a millennium of doing so, I cannae see me doing anything else." He leaned forward and caught Abby's hand in his. "There have been so many times I couldna save the innocent. I arrived too late, or they didnae want to be saved, blind to the evil coating their actions with honey. But for all the ones who were stolen from the dregs of Lucifer's clutches, I give thanks to God."

Abby took the linen napkin and as he watched swiped at her eyes. He wanted to hold her but not here. "Will you be wanting dessert, Abby?"

"No, I'm fine."

"Good, then let's walk."

He motioned for the maitre'd, handed him a bill that would more than paid for all of their dinners, and then stood to his feet. As soon as he pulled Abby's chair back, Sean and Arianna were next to them.

"Abby and I are going to take a *walk*."

Sean gave him a look signifying he understood the emphasis on walk. "Okay, Arianna and I'll bring up the rear." The halfling didn't have to tell Darach it would be a very distant rear. Close enough to keep an eye on them but not to interfere.

"Let's go, Abby." He helped her on with her coat, grabbed her hand, and literally stalked out of Antoine's.

"Darach, can you slow down a bit. I can't run in these shoes."

Darach looked down at Abby. Her short breaths made her breasts rise and fall dangerously above the neckline of her dress. God's teeth, he wanted her. Wanted her so badly he could taste it.

"Sorry, I just..." Instead of finishing what would be an embarrassing and inadequate explanation, he scooped her up in his arms.

"Now, ye willna have to run." He tried to slow his own steps but the thought of kissing her lips, exploring the curves playing peek-a-boo with him wouldn't stop. His gaze searched for and found a bench just barely out of reach of a street lamp. He cast a look over his shoulder, nodded toward the seat, and wanted to shout *halleluiah* when Sean stopped Arianna from following them. He knew the halfling would make sure they were safe.

Darach held onto Abby as he sat on the cold iron seat. Before she could even think about saying anything he brought his lips down onto hers. He savored the sweetness of the wine she'd had with dinner, but he wanted more. He eased his tongue inside her mouth, the tempting heat pulled him further into a desire fast rioting out of control—but he couldn't stop. He needed to taste her, to touch her, and he did.

Cradling her against his chest he pushed the edges of her coat aside. His kiss deepened and she moaned as he sought and found the crowning tip of her breast. His thumb and index finger pulled and tweaked it until it rose higher. Abby's whimpers were swallowed up as he explored the hollow of her mouth. Darach's desire manifested into a full-blown hard-on that pressed against Abby's buttocks—seeking to find the honey that would quench its fire.

As he pushed upward, Abby pressed herself against his hardness. The urgency in Darach's eyes had barely touched on what she felt as he'd taken her in his kiss. His hand on her nipple made her weep with wanting him. She pushed against his hold, then turned to straddle his lap. The cool air caressed her thighs but did nothing to beat back the heat pummeling her body. She reached between them and rubbed the hardness rising to touch her aching center.

Darach's groan was music to her soul. He still wanted her no matter what she'd said to him in the past. She continued her strokes through the soft leather of his pants until he snatched her hand away. His breaths were as raspy as hers before he placed a soul-melting kiss on her palm.

"Abby, ye are killing me. We have to stop before I take ye right here in the open for all to see."

"I suppose that would be a no-no?" Her question came out in a husky whisper. She held her breath, hoping he would say no, that he would take her.

"Aye, it has to be. Not only are we drawing a few speculative gazes from some passersby, Sean and Arianna are headed this way."

Heat touched her cheeks as she realized what she must look like, her breasts half out of her dress, her thighs bare and clinging to his like a harlot on the prowl. Lord, he must think her an awful tease.

"Oh God, I'm sorry. I never…"

His quick kiss silenced her apology. "Ye did nothing wrong. I started this, and God's teeth, no matter how much I want to finish it, this is not the entire reason I brought ye out here."

"It's not?" She purposely inserted teasing into

her tone. Darach's expression had gone all stony again.

The smile he graced her with came right before he tweaked her nose. "Ye shouldna taunt a desperate man. Ye could wind up into more trouble than ye want."

Abby couldn't resist. "And who said I didn't want trouble with you?"

Darach caught her close and hugged her so hard he almost squished her ribs. "Enough, Darach, I need to breathe."

His apology was uttered with a chest vibrating chuckle. "All right my love, let's get ye presentable."

Her gasp of alarm as she heard their friends approach preceded her hastily rearranging her cleavage, as Darach eased her off his lap and smoothed the material of her dress over her hips, before pulling her down to sit between his thighs. Almost immediately she felt a hardness growing against her backside.

"Damn. You better sit here." Darach moved her to his side but slung an arm over her shoulder. Making her feel warm and loved.

"Okay you two, it's time to get home." Sean's words were a bit staccato in tone.

"What's wrong?" Instead of answering Abby Sean looked directly at Darach. "We've got about ten demons headed this way. I don't think they know you're here, but let's not take any chances."

"Right. I will teleport with Abby, if Arianna will give ye a ride." The other immortal didn't look enthused about the idea, but she motioned Sean to step closer.

"We will meet back at the house." Darach's words were swallowed up as he pulled her closer and then *poof*! They were off.

****

Angus was at the end of his rope and his

temper. Nothing he'd done had been successful in bringing Darach to him. The ploy to take Abigail from her home would not even be worth trying a second time. He had to get her out in the open, somewhere she would not be on her guard. The club she worked at was a possibility, but he bet she'd be flanked by the woman immortal and Darach. But he would come up with something—he'd come too far to fail.

Michael rubbed his hands together in glee. Finally. The Highlander had done something right. Although, he didn't exactly approve of the physical methods his immortal had used, at least the end results were what mattered. Now, he could ask Abby to marry him again. And even though he didn't put them together in the first place, Michael felt like he deserved a bit of the credit also. Heaven's blessings, he did love a good romance.

Chapter Twenty-Two

The four of them sat around her kitchen table munching on cookies, and for some it was ice tea, for others beer. She supposed Sean had materialized the six-pack. Regardless, Darach was on his second bottle and looking like he wanted to chew nails.

"I suppose the demons can't get through the safety guards." Her answer fell into the silence that had been dominant for the last ten minutes.

"No, they can't. I strengthened them after we got back, and with the old ones already in place, it would take a miracle for them to breach the grounds."

"Thanks, Arianna."

While the men continued to sit there like knotholes on a fallen tree, Abby tried again for a topic. She thought of everything from the weather to her job as she flailed for a conversational piece. Her job! Oh Lord, she'd forgot all about the club. Chaz would kill her for not showing up tonight. The clock on the wall read nine forty-five; she should have been there by eight o'clock sharp. Her boss would never let her excuse of a date stand.

"Listen, I need to call the club. Chaz is going to read me the riot act for missing work."

The trio staring back at her looked confused. "Hello, my second job. The one I forgot all about when I went out with you, Darach."

For the first time since they'd arrived home, the man actually smiled. "Good, ye didnae need that job, Abby."

"I do need it, and what if I just want it?"

"I will not argue with ye over this, Abby. Ye do not need the job." Darach's grin disappeared.

"And just who died and made you my boss?" Abby spit the words out. The evening, which had gone downhill after Sean spotted the demons, slid another hundred feet.

Darach opened his mouth to reply, and Arianna grabbed Sean's wrist and they disappeared.

Abby jumped to her feet, but before she could flee he was at her side. "Abby, 'tis not what I wanted from our evening. Please, will ye just listen for a moment?"

A sigh of air teased her hair before she nodded.

"Good, then come with me, please."

Again a nod. Darach wasn't sure if she was giving in because she wanted to or because she felt she had no choice. In reality she didn't, for he would not leave her another night without speaking his heart and mind.

He towed her through the house until he reached the back closed-in porch. He settled himself into the corner of a lounge rocker, and tugged Abby gently down beside him.

"Now, please hear me out before ye start arguing."

"Fine." Abby kept her gaze away from his.

"Can ye not look at me?"

She faced him and the hurt look in her stare caused another wound into his already abused heart.

"I only want to take care of ye, Abby. I ken I come on like a brutish fiend at times, 'tis a throwback probably from me Highlander heritage, but ye have to ken, I would die for ye. Never, not even with Briene, have I felt love this strongly."

Abby's lips parted and she took the hand he offered. Thank the saints she was listening. After the night he proposed in such a half-arsed way at the hospital, he would need all the help he could get to convince her to be his forever.

"What I did not tell ye earlier was, the years as an executioner hardened me. I grew to not care if the next demon I fought killed me or not. It was not until I met ye I realized how far I'd sunk in despair of the constant battles, the frustration in not being able to help everyone. Only ye touched the hardened shell and began to soften the infernal organ in me chest." Darach kept his gaze on Abby, hoping to see some type of emotion beside hurt.

"Darach, I'm sorry. It seems no matter how hard I try not to be a witch, I still end up one." Abby fiddled with the hem of her dress.

"Nay, 'tis my fault as well. I fought falling in love. I feared to lose what I had before. I didnae realize that to not love at all, meant I had already lost."

Abby all but crawled into his lap and he welcomed the little pats of understanding she rendered to his face, his shoulders, and his chest. Truly, it felt good to be soothed like he was a babe. He allowed her ministrations for a moment longer before capturing both her hands.

"Abby, I love ye. I want to make ye my wife. I know ye said nay when I asked ye the first time, and I did out of desperation—"

Her gasp made him rethink his words. "That 'tis

not what I meant. I feared ye would leave and I would never get a chance to hold ye again."

"Okay, I can live with that explanation." She giggled softly against the pillow she'd made of his chest.

"Aye, but can ye live with me?" His breath held, and his chest hurt waiting on her response.

Abby's laughter stilled, she tilted her head back, and then looked him in the eyes. "Yes."

"Aye?" He almost choked on his question.

"Aye, Darach."

His roar of happiness echoed throughout the house. A bare second later, both Sean and Arianna materialized. Sean with his hands held out like weapons, and the immortal with her sword raised and ready.

Darach had a hard time making himself heard over Abby's unrestrained laughter. Not to mention Sean's "What's going on?" And Arianna's "Are you two okay?"

"Put away your weapons. There be no battle to be fought tonight, unless ye count the one already waged and won."

At his words, Abby laughed harder amidst the confused looks of the halfling and Arianna.

"What are you talking about, Highlander?" Sean frowned his confusion.

"Simply this, halfling. Abby has finally agreed to wed me."

Sean grinned while Arianna looked bored. "Is that all? I thought there was a hurricane blowing in off the gulf." Her words were tart but the smile she sent his and Abby's way was one of congratulations.

"I suppose now we have to plan a wedding?" The immortal's nose turned up like she smelled something rancid.

"No worries, Arianna. It will be simple. If Darach agrees, we can be married right here at the house as soon as it can be arranged by a justice of the peace. No frills. I don't think my new fiancé will want a long engagement."

"Ye got that right." He'd marry her right now if they could get a preacher.

Darach stopped resisting the lure of her lips and kissed her again. When he raised his head a few minutes later, Sean and Arianna were gone again.

"Abby, when does the Christmas break start for your school?"

"In about three weeks, why?"

"I be thinking, although ye didnae want to hear it before, I have more than enough money for us to live on for several lifetimes. Would ye consider giving your notice and not going back after the first of the year?"

Since Darach had phrased it as a request and not a command, Abby thought about what he said. So far, her immortal usually had a pretty good explanation to back up what he said, unless it came to romance, then he was all thumbs and toes, but she could deal with that since he was so cute when he made an idiot of himself.

"Why?" She raised an eyebrow.

"Well, 'tis like this: I have been here in NOLA for almost a decade. So far no one has remarked upon the fact I dinnae seem to age. Sooner or later, I be sure, Michael will send me somewhere else. I would want ye to go with me."

Abby knew he was right. His ability to not age had been and still would need to be addressed in reference to how they would live their married lives.

"All right. I can do that. The school system won't have any problems in filling my spot with the economy like it is. Do you want me to quit sooner?"

She welcomed another kiss from his lips, although it was way too short for her satisfaction.

"Only if ye want to, lass."

"Okay, I'll give my notice starting the Christmas break, and if they can get a temp admin until then, I'll quit sooner."

"Thank ye, Abby. Now, do ye have any idea when ye want to marry?"

"The weekend's almost here. I vote for Saturday if we can get the license and blood work done. Oh...will you have a problem with them drawing your blood?" Abby bit her lip, she hoped not.

Darach laughed. "Nay, and there willna be a problem with the license either."

"Oooh, you're going to do something you shouldn't, aren't you?"

"If ye mean using mind thoughts to help our cause along, then aye, I'll do what I have to."

"Darach you're so bad, but I love you. So Saturday it is?"

"Aye, now give me a kiss and get upstairs."

Abby did as he asked but didn't move away. "What if I don't want to leave?"

"Abby, I have been pretty much celibate for centuries. The fact that ye have agreed to be my wife is making my lust for ye grow even more." The pained look on his face, and the redeveloped hardness near her hand almost caused her to laugh. Except it wasn't that funny. She too wanted him like there was no tomorrow.

"Okay, I'm going. Will I see you after school tomorrow?"

"Aye, as soon as ye get home, I will pop in."

"I love you, Darach."

"I love ye too, lass. Ye be my heart."

****

It was only after she left his side and went upstairs that Darach could actually let out a sigh of relief. Not just because his lust didn't beat at him so much with her out of sight, but the fact she'd actually agreed to marry him.

Just a few more days and she would be his. Then he would make sure she never regretted saying yes.

"Hey, you coming out tonight or staying in?"

"Out." Darach answered Sean who evidently had been popped back in the house by Arianna. A happening he should have heard, and he would make sure in the future his thoughts did not get in the way of Abby's safety. It could have been a demon if the guards were down.

"Any idea where to look tonight?" Sean propped against the doorway.

"I want to check out those warehouses on the other side of the bayou." Darach stood up. "Ye want to walk or teleport?"

"Let's walk. I'm kinda like Abigail. I'm not overly fond of that type of travel." Sean eased out the door in front of Darach.

"Where's Arianna?"

"Upstairs with Abby. She'll check the guards again after we leave. I told her we would probably be out hunting."

"Thanks." Darach closed the doors and then both he and Sean moved away from the porch light and out into the dark shadows of the front yard. They then made their way to the industrial section of Canal Street. Four dilapidated structures sat at fifty-foot intervals away from some of the more sturdy buildings.

"Ye want to take a couple and me a couple?" Darach looked around as he waited for an answer.

"Naw, let's check them together. I really don't want to run into a demon pack without backup." Sean's grimace reminded Darach all too well of their encounter the night before.

As they entered the first warehouse, Darach withdrew his sword and held it ready. He wanted no surprises, but if they came, he would be ready.

Sean grinned, held up his hands, and then his face went somber as they search the first floor. They found nothing out of the ordinary. Boxes with old shredded paper, a few sealed fifty-gallon drums, and several rodents. It went that way for the next three floors.

Outside once again, Darach brushed off cobwebs and jerked his head toward the next object on their list. This warehouse had a bit more debris scattered around, but no demon trail.

The third was the same and they moved to the last building.

The moment they entered the interior, Sean jerked his head toward Darach. His mouthed *Demons* stirred Darach's blood. Just maybe this time they would find Angus, if nothing else the dagger. Since the demons did not have the weapon with them when they engaged them in battle, he believed the weapon must be back with Angus or hidden somewhere.

Their steps were steady and silent as they used the stairs to climb to the upper floors. A nod from Sean pinpointed where he thought their quarry hid. Darach didn't like that he couldn't smell the demon trail, but at least Sean could ferret them out.

As they traversed the third floor, the halfling's eyes began to glow red. Darach's heartbeat picked up a bit of speed. The adrenaline that accompanied the anticipation of a battle pumped blood through his veins at a dizzying rate.

Sean motioned toward a stack of wood piled almost to the rafters. They skirted around the obstruction and found a door. A lock hung in the metal hasp. Darach moved nearer to the halfling. "Do we go in together or one at a time?" His whisper was so low he barely heard his question, but Sean's demon ears picked it up. He held up a finger pointed to himself and Darach. Good—a frontal combined attack would hopefully give them the element of surprise needed to dispatch the creatures back to hell.

Darach kicked the door with his foot, and they charged over the threshold. His sword swung in a circle but he brought it to rest at his side. The room was empty. He turned to Sean who shrugged his shoulders.

"They were here."

"I believe ye, but when?"

"By the smell, no more than a few hours ago. It could be they're coming back."

A sigh so full of frustration escaped Darach, that he followed it with a fist to the wall. The fissures began to close immediately. Thank God, the dagger had not damaged that part of his immortal makeup, and his healing process seemed to be getting back on track.

"So do we wait?" Sean looked at his watch as Darach studied the room. For a building on its last legs, this one cubicle seemed to be in almost pristine condition. He couldn't imagine run-of-the-mill demons not leaving it in a frenzy.

"Sean, this place is too neat for demons like the ones who attacked us last night. Someone with a sense of order made sure this place was maintained. I wonder if Angus used this as a headquarters?"

Darach circled the room. "I wouldna put it past him to use this as a front, and keep his real hiding place a secret, even from his minions."

"You've got a point. Let's see what else this room holds besides questions." Sean joined Darach in his perusal and both of them began moving the neatly stacked boxes out of the way. They did the same with several barrels and pieces of moldy plywood. Only when the obstruction was out of the way, did they find a door.

They used the same precautions as they did the

first time, but still no demons. However, this time the room looked like Darach thought it should. Litter consisting of bottles, cans, paper, and half-eaten food dotted the floor. An old scarred desk sat to one side, with an equally antique rolling chair.

Darach moved to the desk. At first it looked like another bunch of papers, but then a corner of color caught his eye. Darach laid his sword across the wood, and pulled the stiff paper loose. An image of Abby jumped out at him. He pushed more papers aside, and found various poses of Abby going to school, at the club, standing in her front yard, and even with him at the restaurant the night before.

****

Angus watched as Darach and the half-breed entered one of the warehouses. He hoped they would find the office he used now instead of the antebellum home he lived in. He also hoped Darach found the pictures of Abigail. It would fuel his rage, and could be used against him. Too bad he wouldn't get a chance to see the results of their hunt, but Angus had to pay a visit to the underworld and give his report to Lucifer.

Michael glanced at the gift he'd sent another immortal to purchase for a wedding present. Darach would be pleased. He also wanted to get something special for Abby. And although, he'd rather have Ragnor helping Darach also, he felt better after talking to Conner. Too much was at stake and until Angus was caught, his immortals, their loved ones, and the city of New Orleans was in for a dangerous and as much as he hated voicing the thought, deadly ride.

Chapter Twenty-Three

Darach's roar of rage startled Sean who turned and immediately fell into a fighting stance. His gaze traveled to the photos spread out on the desk.

"Damn, Darach, they've been following Abby for quite some time."

"I ken, and I will kill the son-of-Satan when I find him."

"And I'll help. I think we need to check on the girls."

Darach gathered up the photos. At Sean's confused look, he snarled. "I will be damned before I let those demons keep these. They have done enough to violate Abby already."

"I agree, and I think I'll let you give me a ride back to Abby's."

Darach stuffed the sword back inside his coat, the photos in his pocket, and grabbed Sean by the arm. He welcomed the dissolution of his molecules. He needed to be with Abby.

****

Abby pattered into the kitchen. After Darach left she'd fallen asleep only to wake up abruptly. Before she could determine what had awakened her, the vision hit.

The woman was so young, so beautiful, and so dead. Blood dripped away from her limp body to pool on a concrete floor. Abby knew there was no way she could help her, but it didn't keep her from bemoaning that fact. Nothing she did would make a difference at this point. Usually when the visions struck she could see what was happening in the present, and if this vision followed on course, then the woman was already dead, before Abby went to bed.

Now she couldn't sleep. Maybe a cup of hot tea would help. And until it did, now would be a good time to make notes of what all she needed to do before the weekend. While the water heated she gathered some index cards from her briefcase and a pen.

By the time the kettle hissed she'd drawn up a list she could make work in the time left before the wedding. She got up, popped a teabag into her mug, and drowned it with hot water. As it steeped, she got out the phone book and looked up justices of the peace. She'd prefer to get the minister from her grandmere's church, but Pastor Evans was out of town.

Abby wrote down at least four names, and was sipping on her tea, when the room wavered and Darach and Sean sorta fell into the kitchen.

"Geez, you could give a girl some warning." Abby wiped spilled tea off the front of her robe, and blotted her notes.

"Sorry Abby, I thought ye would be fast asleep."

"Not with me giving up my job at the school and a small ceremony to plan. I needed to get everything in order, so I wouldn't forget anything. Which reminds me..."

She grabbed one of the cards and held it up. "What time should we get married? I don't know if you...either of you have to sleep during the day for your jobs. And Arianna seems to be up every time I am."

Darach dropped a kiss on her lips and laughed. "I can sleep anytime, what about ye, Sean?"

"Same here. I never know when I'm going to be called out. Second shift is my primary but as you know, crime doesn't play favorites. So you pick the time and I'll do my best to get someone to cover if I get called in."

"Great. I'm thinking maybe five or six. I know it might cost a bit more to do it after hours, but I really would like to have the service here. Just us two and Sean and Arianna, oh yeah and Conner too, to act as witnesses if ya'll and she agrees."

"Agrees to what?" Arianna came strolling into the kitchen with a leopard print robe flapping around her ankles and bare feet.

"To being witnesses when Darach and I get married."

"Well, duh. When do you two plan on doing the leg shackles?"

Arianna grabbed the cookies out of the cabinet.

"Saturday, if I can hook up a preacher." Abby stole one of the cookies off Arianna's plate. Her movement galvanized Sean in doing the same.

"Hey, get your own. I'm hungry."

"Yeah, I bet it takes a lot to fuel a leopard." Sean's teasing tone as he eyeballed Arianna's robe met with a reaction Abby would never forget. The immortal grabbed him, locked her lips to his, and kissed him until Sean actually looked like his legs didn't work.

"Get a room, you two." A chuckle of laughter

rolled from Darach.

Abby knew her face was burning, and the arm Darach slid around her waist just heated her up more in all the right places.

"Now you can quit wondering and leave me alone." Arianna's snappish tone turned Sean's eyes a bit red.

"Maybe we should leave these two alone?" Her whisper was met with Sean's equally sharp words.

"No need, I've decided I don't like jungle kitties."

Arianna put up her hand, whether to ward off Sean's rude words, or to slap him, Abby didn't know. Talk about television drama come to life, daytime soaps had nothing on the immortal and Sean.

"Okay ya'll, settle down. I want to hear about the hunt tonight. Did you find anything?" Her question resulted in a variety of reactions. Arianna stepped away from Sean and crossed her arms over her chest. "Good night, Abby, I'm going back to bed."

Sean looked Abby's way as the immortal left the room and then at Darach who's bronze skin lost some of its color. He gave an almost imperceptible shake of his head.

"Nothing to tell, Abby." Sean edged toward the door.

"You seem to be in a hurry, Lieutenant. Are you sure nothing happened?"

Before he could reply, Darach spoke up. "We explored some empty warehouses on the other end of Canal Street, Abby. No demons showed up."

She wasn't sure if she believed either man, but at least Darach's color had returned.

"Well, I guess I'll see you tomorrow night, huh, Darach?" Sean was at the door with his hand on the knob.

"Aye, and I want to start earlier, say about seven? Conner hopefully will be back by then."

"Sure, works for me. Good night, Abby."

"'Night, Sean." She smiled at the good-looking lieutenant. Nice looking to begin with, but when he dropped his glamour as he did when hunting, he was downright hot. Of course, he was no Darach. She also gave a smile to the man standing at her side.

"You gotta run off too?" She hoped her wistfulness that he could stay didn't show up too badly. But then again they were going to be married in a few days, and now that she knew Darach loved her she just didn't want to let him out of her sight. And then there was that dream. So hot it still made her burn thinking about it.

The wistful look in Abby's eyes mirrored how Darach felt. No, he didn't want to leave, but if he stayed he wouldn't be able to keep his hands to himself. The dream from the night before came flooding back sending a spark of desire to his shaft.

"Aye, I do need to go and let ye get some sleep. 'Tis almost three in the morning."

"Will you be by before you go out to hunt?"

"Count on it, darling. Now, give me a kiss."

Abby pressed her body next to his, stood on her tiptoes, and pulled his head forward. Her lips were a hair's breadth from his when a slight crackly sound interrupted his anticipation of her kiss.

"What's this?" Before he could stop her, Abby reached into the outside pocket of his coat and withdrew the wad of photos.

"Darach?"

"Give those to me, Abby. Ye dinnae need to see them."

She held them close to her breast, her eyes wide and questioning. "Where did you get these?"

His sigh only made his angst worse. He should have destroyed them outside the warehouse and not brought them here to her home. But in their haste to make sure she and Arianna were safe, he had forgotten them.

"Please let it go, Abby."

"No, these are pictures of me and..." She laid them on the table, and flipped through all six of the photos, smoothing the last one out. "This is of us together, at Antoine's. I want to know where you got them...please."

It was the insecurity and the fright in her eyes that turned him into a wimp. He needed to reassure her there were no more pictures of her.

"I found them when Sean and I searched the last warehouse."

"I thought you said nothing turned up."

Darach crossed his arms over his chest. "Nay, Sean said that. I didnae say much of anything, remember?"

Abby's brows drew together. "As I recall that's about the same time you turned a bit pale." She stamped her foot.

"I want to know what else happened and I want to know now."

"You're going to be the death of me, woman."

Abby's snarl was unexpected. "It's your job that will be the death of you, Darach."

For the life of him he wanted to laugh. Not at her upset, but the picture she made standing there in a fuzzy pink robe, with matching animal face slippers on her feet. Her hair was all over her head, and her eyes gleamed with emotion.

"I swear, Abby, there be nothing else to tell. There were no demons at the warehouse, and we came straight here. Now, come on and kiss me. I have to get in touch with Michael and will probably catch a couple of hours of sleep myself."

"Why not sleep here? I promise to keep my hands to myself." Finally a small smile slipped over Abby's lips.

"But, I cannae promise to do the same."

"Then don't, Darach." Those three whispered

words almost dropped him to his knees. Yes, he wanted her. Yes, he wanted her now, but he didn't think it would be a good thing to talk to Michael if he made love to Abby. The archangel would read his mind, then all hell or heaven would break out for taking her innocence before the wedding.

In truth, he still couldn't believe Abby was to be his wife, his in every way.

"Abby, don't make this any harder than it is."

"Do I make it hard on you, Darach?" The bold look she gave him stiffened his member even more—an aching awareness that roared release. Before he thought twice he yanked her against his chest, tugged the robe opened and baptized her breasts with his lips. Her moans were pure bliss to his ears, but he wasn't finished. His little Abby needed to learn not to play with fire until he could finish the game.

His hands roamed her hips and then he pulled the silken material of her gown up her legs, past her knees, and to her thighs. The first touch of her hot flesh almost caused him to lose his mind not to mention his seed.

The wetness greeting him was a bonus to the whimpers coming from Abby's throat. He loved that she wanted him as much as he wanted her. His fingers found and caressed her woman's nub and then he slid one digit into her female center. Her flesh grasped his finger and pulsated as he pushed and then pulled his finger out. He continued the motion until Abby strained against his hand, her thighs like a vise as she trapped him with her zest for fulfillment. When she threw her head back, he nipped the skin at her throat, then slid his tongue over the soft contours. Her mouth opened in a moan that would have awakened the immortal sleeping above stairs if he hadn't captured it in his mouth. He savored his kiss and welcomed Abby's weight as she slumped against him.

Darach broke off his kiss and then placed another on Abby's forehead.

"Wow, that was almost as good as the dream." Abby's whispered words caused Darach to jerk back.

"What's wrong?" Now his beloved's slumberous eyes glowed with concern.

"Nothing, ye just surprised me is all." Darach almost stumbled over his inadequate explanation.

"I don't get it, why would the mention of a dream throw you into a panic?" Abby slid back from his touch and waited on Darach's answer.

Darach's eyes went all silvery, and his normally tanned face tinged with red. Abby frowned. Something was definitely up with her immortal.

"I told ye, nothing, Abby." Darach's gaze slid from hers.

"Okay, the one thing you always told me, you don't lie, isn't that right?" She moved closer to him.

"Aye." He moved back. It reminded her of the first time they met, but now the roles were reversed.

"I don't believe you. Now tell me." Abby crossed her arms over her chest and gave Darach a look that he could not misinterpret.

"Did anyone ever tell ye that ye are a very pushy and obstinate woman?" He growled his words.

"Not until you came along. Now seriously, what gives?"

Darach let out a long breath, but he did look her in the eyes. "Ye probably will think this is crazy, but…"

"Darach, the entire scenario since we met has been crazy, so go ahead."

"I think I had the same dream." His words were a mere imitation of his usual deep baritone, but it's what he said that made Abby hear every syllable crystal clear.

"Explain, please." Abby couldn't wait to hear his

explanation.

"I think it happened because I slept with you..." Darach's words trailed off, when Abby gave him a look.

"I mean when I stayed with you the night of the demon attack. I be not sure what happened. As I told ye before, I have never been able to project any thoughts into your mind." A slight smile touched Darach's lips. "Your stubborn nature, probably, but I had the most realistic dream about us making love."

"Did the dream start with you standing at the bedroom window, and then end with..." Abby broke off her question. If he said yes, then she wasn't sure what to say. The dream had plagued her since she'd awaken. Its content was not something she'd ever forget.

"Aye, and we made love in the dream. Completely, uninterrupted, hot love, Abby." Darach's words came above her ear. So lost in her thoughts she hadn't realized he'd closed the slight distance between them.

"Oh..." Her breath left her lungs as he caught her close. "Uh, how do you think we dreamed the same thing at the same time?"

His breath caressed her hair as he answered. "I be not sure, possibly with ye being asleep and your defenses down, I might have projected my dreams into your head."

"Wow, that's..."

"Unbelievable?" Darach questioned.

"Actually, I was going to say it was so erotic, I couldn't get it out of my mind all day." Abby clutched at his shoulders.

"Then we be even; neither could I." Darach closed her open mouth with a kiss that took her back to the dream and every time he'd actually touched her for real. Her knees went weak, her body heated to the scorching point, and Abby did nothing to stop either reaction. She welcomed his touch as always.

When the kiss was over, Darach lifted her in his arms.

"Time for ye to be in bed, my love." He decided to teleport Abby to her bedroom for he didn't trust his arms to hold her without dropping her while mounting the stairs. His body trembled with lust and love and the memories of their shared dream.

After tucking a vocally protesting Abby into bed, he walked down the hall to the guestroom, which now had been cleared out for a guest, and lightly knocked on the door.

"Abby?" Arianna opened her door and then stepped back.

"Sorry to wake ye, but I be leaving now. Just wanted ye to know."

"Thanks, I'll take care of Abby."

"I know ye will. See ye tonight, Arianna."

****

Angus extinguished the candles he preferred to use and prepared for bed. The day had been fulfilling. His pawn had brought him the information he needed to flush Abby out. And when he finally took her, it would be doubly hard for his cousin to swallow the rape and murder of a second loved one. Atlas, he wished he would have more time with her, but Lucifer said to wrap it up as soon as possible before the Christmas holiday—a holiday when angels came to Earth to deliver Yuletide cheer and blessings. He hated Christmas.

Michael admired the shine of the stars over the Crystal Sea. Their brilliance upon the water was blindingly beautiful. A miracle of what his God could do. So many times since he'd been created by God's divine hand, he'd not stopped to enjoy the beauty surrounding him. As he gazed at the silver twinkling on the sea's surface, it reminded him of how simple life's pleasures could be. And in that moment, he realized there was only one present he could give Abby on her wedding day.

Chapter Twenty-Four

Darach awoke in his own bed sometime after the noon hour. He'd slept longer than he had in several days—in fact, since he'd met Abby. Abby, whose skin was like the finest silk, lips that were sensual weapons ready to bring him down, and laughing eyes that touched his heart and soul.

He be not sure why he'd been blessed to receive her love, but after centuries of being alone, tortured by thoughts of death and the past, Darach was more than thankful.

It was a miracle they had even met. If Abby's vision hadn't led her to the demon that night, he might never have met the woman who changed his lonely existence into a new blessing every day. Albeit if you discounted Angus, a cursed dagger, and demon spawn jumping out at every turn.

Aye, his life had changed in a lot of ways, some painful, but he would not trade Abby for a millennium of peace. Her love sustained him when before he had seen only the darkness of the coming ages. Now instead of hating his immortal life and not caring if he met death, he embraced his immortality.

Darach sat up and scrubbed a hand over his bristled face. He couldn't wait until they were married. To commit himself to Abby for whatever earthly time they had together. After that he would ask Michael to allow him to die. Yes, he looked forward to sliding a ring on her—

His body shot out of the bed so fast, if he'd been a mortal he would have suffered whiplash. A ring—he didn't have a ring and he doubted Abby had given that aspect of the service any more thought than he had. Tomorrow was their wedding, and today he needed to find the perfect ring. Should he buy a set of rings? One that she could place on his finger?

Darach rotated his neck, then stretched his body into a series of exercises to limber up muscles that were stiff. Being an executioner for a millennium did have its drawbacks. A smile pulled at his lips—of course if he didn't have his job, he would never have met Abby.

He padded naked into his oversized bathroom. The house was a perk that he truly liked. Large rooms and a master bath he could move around in without knocking into the sink or toilet. And the shower with its roomy walk-in space was a luxury with numerous built in jets. Darach accessed the jets and reveled in the hot water cascading over his body. The heat reminded him of loving Abby last night and their shared dream. Although not as fulfilling as the real thing, he loved making her moan with pleasure. Loved touching her wetness, loved holding her in his arms as she exploded with passion.

His shaft rose with the memory of how her eyes had glazed with wanting and then went wide when her release was upon her.

God's teeth, he prayed he would make it through tonight and then the day tomorrow until he could take her to bed and keep her there for infinity.

Blood pounded through his erection making him hurt with need. His hand hovered over his flesh, but he pulled it back. Nothing but sinking himself deep into Abby's center would assuage his desire.

Soap ran off Darach's body in rivulets as he rinsed and then turned off the shower. He needed to go shopping, not a recreational activity he usually welcomed. A ring for Abby would top any and all purchases he'd made in his lifetime.

He got dressed and then left the house. The early afternoon sun warmed him a bit in the crisp air. His steps were light, his mood that of a man who was still amazed he'd found the miracle of love for the second time.

His first stop was a big name jewelry store where he browsed the wedding bands with the help of an overzealous clerk. Nothing looked like Abby.

"Sir, I have some nice—"

"Thank ye, but not at the moment." Darach left and then hit the next stop on his mental list. He wanted something special, something Abby would love.

An hour later he wanted to beat his head against the wall. Still no luck! As he stood with his back against the concrete, literally, he spotted a small sign across the street. *Rings For Romance.* Darach decided to check it out. When he stepped into the quaint shop, a woman approached him.

"Could I be of assistance, sir?"

He planned to say no, but the older woman's eyes twinkled with an inner zest Darach could relate to today.

"I dinnae ken if ye can or not, but I be looking for wedding bands. My fiancée and I are to be married tomorrow."

"And you forgot to buy the rings?"

Darach smiled. "Something like that. Do ye think you can help me?"

Quick as a wink and doubly graceful, the auburn-and-silver-haired woman moved to a wooden box sitting on top of one of the few counters.

"I believe you will find something in here." She opened the box and then pushed back the lid.

Gold, silver, and jade colors winked back at him, but then a heather-colored stone caught his eye. The band was etched with what looked like a thistle design. A matching ring with the same silver band drew his eye.

"How much for this set?"

"You have good taste, sir. These rings were in a shipment that came to me from Scotland. The cost is trivial compared to the elegance of the rings."

Darach figured the rings were going to be expensive, but he didn't care. He had the money and he wanted Abby to have the rings. He tried on the man's ring, which fit perfectly and by the looks of it, the woman's ring would fit Abby's slender finger. After paying the woman she enclosed both rings in plush jewelry boxes, placed them into a bag which she handed to him, along with his receipt.

"Thank ye for your time."

"My pleasure, sir. If in the future you are looking for something special, please remember my shop."

"Count on it." Darach nodded his head and then left. The entire exchange had taken less than ten minutes. He had time to pick up a bouquet of flowers for Abby. His first courtship had been a long one. Romance was not at all something he had time for back then, but Briene understood the duties of a laird. Abby also had a knowledge of his life and duty now, but he couldn't wait to see her face when he gave her the roses. Twenty minutes later, the rings were stowed in his safe at home and he prepared to walk to Abby's.

The long-stemmed roses were resting in a tissue-shrouded box, and he wouldn't take a chance on something happening to them if he teleported.

As he drew near Abby's home, he saw a man's form move through the front of the yard, and then around the side of the house near the canal. With the safeguards in place, it had to be the halfling—he prayed it was or that would mean someone had breached the perimeters.

Darach placed the roses on the rail of the porch and then tracked the man who was fast moving toward the water's edge. Suddenly he lifted his head, sniffed the air, and turned toward Darach.

The halfling threw up his arm and motioned toward the high grass bordering Abby's property. Darach made his way toward Sean. The closer he got to the canal's edge the more a scent of something rotten teased his nostrils.

"I didnae think ye would be here this early." Darach spoke first.

"Neither did I, but I thought I'd see if you wanted to go ahead and get started. I mean since you're getting married tomorrow and might want to quit at a reasonable hour," Sean explained.

"'Tis fine, but why are ye sneaking around in this spot?"

The halfling's nose wrinkled. "Almost as soon as I got inside the safeguards Arianna opened for me, I could smell demon spawn."

Darach's growl stirred the air.

"I didn't find any, but I did find this." The halfling knelt in the grass, and Darach moved closer. A woman's nude body lay amid offal from the canal. Her long slender arms and legs were posed in a fetal position, her hands under her bruised chin as in prayer. Light brown hair, snarled with blood and other fluids he didn't want to speculate about, rested across her shoulders and back.

"God's teeth. 'Tis more brutal than the other prostitute's death." Darach clenched his fists.

"I know. It seems to be an outlet for someone's rage. Why they dumped her here, I can only guess. Did they know it was Abby's property or not? I don't know, Darach, but I don't like it one little bit."

Darach tamped down on the gorge rising in his throat. He didn't like the coincidence either.

"The women are okay, I checked." Sean's assurance helped, but not a lot. No one should have been able to get on the property.

"How did they dump the body?"

"Since the safeguards were intact, I'm thinking they tossed her from a boat. Some of the bruises look post-mortem."

"I dinnae want Abby's house turned into a crime scene, Sean."

"Neither do I. I think we can contain it to this section here. I'll call in a favor or two." Sean's voice conveyed the rage Darach felt. The halfling's eyes turned red.

"I would appreciate that and if we could keep it from Abby."

For the first time since he'd spotted Sean, the halfling smiled. "I'll leave it to you to distract your bride-to-be. Why don't you go on up to the house and I'll see to this matter."

"I owe ye one. Not only for this but for standing up for me and Abby tomorrow and all your help." Darach held his hand out.

Sean took it. "Hey, we're both on the same side of the law, and if it means I get to kick some demon butt, I'm all for it. And look, I know you and Conner have been friends forever, if you'd rather have him as your best man, I'd understand."

"Thanks man, but I'd be tickled pink, as Abby

would say, if you'd do it."

Sean grinned and both he and Darach shook hands, before Darach teleported back to the porch where he retrieved Abby's roses, and then knocked on the door.

"Darach! You're early." Abby's face glowed with an emotion he was fast learning was contagious.

"Well, I be hoping ye wouldna mind, but I could leave and come back."

"Get in here, you. I want to tell you about all I got accomplished today." Abby tugged on his hand and after he allowed her to pull him over the threshold, he held out the other one.

Abby took the box and then slid the ribbon off. She took one look and grinned.

"Roses! Oh they're beautiful. Thank you. I'll just go and put them in some water."

He watched as she almost ran, he assumed to the kitchen, and then he walked to the living room. Arianna sat curled up in a chair and Conner took up a good bit of space on the sofa.

"Hey, Conner. When did you get back? And what did Michael want?"

Conner's smile was a slash of white as he nodded to Darach's greeting. "Aye, everything's fine. Got back a few minutes ago, and Michael wanted me to do a quick job for him. I hear ye had a bit of trouble while I was gone."

"Aye, ye could call it that, but Sean and I handled it."

"He seems like a good man." Conner placed the newspaper he'd been reading when Darach walked in onto the coffee table."

"He is. He'd been a godsend." Darach looked toward Arianna. "Evening Arianna, I didnae mean to ignore you."

"Evening, Darach." She smiled but the vibrancy he was used to seeing was missing from her gaze. He hated adding to her mood, but she needed to know about the dumped body.

"Sean found a body at the edge of Abby's property."

Arianna sat up on the couch. "When?"

"Just a bit ago, after ye let him through the guards."

"Oh…that's why he didn't come in. So who and how?" Arianna's eyes went flat.

"A young woman, murdered, and dumped here. Sean said he smelled demon spawn after he got to the house." Darach arched a brow.

"The safeguards?" Arianna's agitation showed in the way she clicked her long nails on the back of the couch.

Darach knew how she felt. Once an immortal set the guards they should hold. The fear they wouldn't could put the executioner and those in his care in jeopardy.

"Your guards held, Arianna. She was dumped from the canal side. No way ye could have known."

"Thanks, but not sure that makes me feel any better. I should have gone all the way to the edge of Abby's property." She continued to tap the couch.

Darach heard Abby's footsteps heading their way. "Forget about it, and I dinnae want Abby to know—not now anyway."

"All right."

Abby entered the room with a vase filled with his gift. Her smile lit up the blue in her eyes, and he loved seeing her happy. He'd do anything in his power to keep that light in her eyes.

"Again, these are gorgeous, thank you."

"You are welcome." Darach needed to get her out of the house. "I be thinking, what if we go to dinner and ye tell me all about the plans for tomorrow. I need a time so I can show up."

Abby's mouth fell open before words spewed out

of her mouth. "Oh my gosh, I'm sorry. I guess you do need to know that."

Darach stood and crossed the room. He took the vase, placed it on the coffee table, before pulling Abby into his arms.

"Oh please, I hope you two are not going to be kissing in here. I want to watch television."

Darach grinned at the immortal. "Nay, I will be saving me kisses for somewhere more private, but—"

Arianna groaned. "Oh no, I hate buts."

"I be going to say, I will need ye to go with us to dinner." He gave her a look she couldn't possibly misunderstand. With the latest demon development, and his senses still off, he didn't plan on going out without back up.

"Sure, give me a minute to freshen up." Arianna jumped off the couch and headed for the stairs. "Oh, now you can kiss," she tossed over her shoulder.

Darach's lips hovered above Abby's. He wanted to savor his first kiss of the day with her, but before he could Sean came through the front door.

"Ahem, Darach, could I get a minute with you and Conner?" The halfling's gaze looked at him and then over at the other immortal who was looking anywhere but at Darach and Abby. So taken up with Abby's happiness, he'd forgotten Conner was still there.

"Hi, Sean. When did you get here?" Abby's smile was briefly returned by the halfling.

"Just arrived."

Darach knew the lie probably went against Sean's grain; he hated lying also, but both of them wanted to do what was right by Abby.

"Well, I'll see all of you later. Darach and I are going to dinner, and I want to change clothes." Abby stood on tiptoe and brushed her lips lightly against his. He resisted the urge to pull her so close she could never leave.

Once she did, Sean took several deep breaths. “Okay, just gonna spit this out. You’re not going to like it.”

“What is it?”

“When the medical examiner came to get the corpse, there was a note under the body.”

“What did it say?” Darach knew it was about Abby, he felt it in his heart.

“Here, I saw the note and got it before the doctor noticed it. I’m not going to enter it into evidence.”

At Darach’s look, he continued. “There’s no point in telling my captain. He’d think I was crazy for even talking about demons.”

He took the note and read: “Next time it will be your woman.”

****

Angus listened as his minions gave their report. The body had been dumped right where he’d instructed. From a secluded distance away and off the Dupree property, they had watched through a pair of binoculars as the half-breed demon and then Darach studied the body. Yes, it had been a stroke of genius to violate the sanctity of Darach’s woman’s home. And he would so enjoy violating her body even more.

Note to myself: Do not forget to look in on Darach and Abby's wedding tomorrow. Although he could not be there in person, he wanted to see the looks on their faces when they opened his gifts. In the meantime he needed to clear his desk of other matters. Christmas would be upon them soon, and he planned to take pleasure in the joyous occasion.

Chapter Twenty-Five

The note was signed simply with an A. Darach wanted to rip it in half, wanted to find Angus and tear his heart out. He felt so helpless. His nemesis would not stop until one of them was dead, and Darach planned to live.

"Angus will get his punishment. I just wish Michael would let me dole it out."

"He does need to be killed. I could do it." Conner's habitual smile was absent. "That demon is nothing but trouble."

"You've met Angus?" Darach questioned.

"Not in person, but I have seen some of his handiwork after he finished. Women raped, men disemboweled, children stolen away and never found." Conner hissed the last part. "I ken Michael wants him captured, but I have to tell ye, if one of us gets the chance to kill him, I will look the other way."

"I plan on taking his miserable demon life meself. I do need all of ye to promise to look after Abby if I get zapped by Michael for disobeying a direct order."

"Would Michael truly kill one of his executioners?" Sean's question caused both Darach and Conner to turn his way.

"I dinnae know, but I want Abby looked after regardless. Angus will never fight fair, and too many things could happen to me, but I will do all I can to revenge my family's deaths."

"Don't blame you, Darach. Hopefully that will happen soon." Conner moved toward the door.

"So…what now?" Sean's question was not out of place, but Darach wished he knew what to say. Other than continuing to hunt his cousin, there wasn't a lot to be done.

"When I get back from dinner with Abby, we will start our hunt. I know we probably willna find him, unless he wants us to, but…"

"We'll try any way." Sean gave him a salute and went to the kitchen, which reminded Darach he should probably bring both men back some food.

"I will be back in time to go hunting with ye also, Darach." Conner gave a brief wave of his hand before disappearing. Darach looked back in time to see Abby standing in the doorway, now dressed in jeans and a sweater instead of the suit she'd worn to school.

"I'm ready to go. Just let me grab my notes." Abby detoured to the kitchen, said hello to Sean again, and then met Darach in the foyer.

"Do you have a preference where you want to go?"

"Somewhere quiet if that's okay with you." Abby truly didn't care where they went as long as it kept him from hunting for a while longer. She didn't care if he did have back up in the form of Sean or Conner. Too much could happen and she did not want to lose him.

Darach leaned over and kissed her.

"What was that for?" She wasn't complaining

but he looked a bit relieved.

"For reading me mind. I would prefer some quiet time with ye also." His words melted her heart all over again. In less than twenty-four hours, hopefully, they would have several blocks of time to be together without a crowd.

Darach opened the door, bowed a bit at the waist, and with his arm extended in a slight flourish, he ushered her out into the night.

A while later, they sat in a bistro sharing creamy spinach dip as they sipped tall glasses of iced tea.

"So tell me about our wedding plans." Darach wiped his mouth on a linen napkin and then smiled. His black eyes resembled polished onyx in the light from a cozy fire.

"Well, the minister will be at my house around six. I ordered a small cake and champagne for afterward." She grinned. "I also placed an order for pizzas to be delivered. I know Arianna and Sean will probably be a bit…"

"Starved, as usual?"

"Exactly. And Conner too if I'm not mistaken. And I did have a question. I didn't know if you wanted to stay at my house or go to yours for…uh…afterward." Abby's tongue twisted around itself at the thought of their wedding night. She couldn't wait, and then there was a tiny part of her that was a bit apprehensive. So far, Darach seemed satisfied with her attempts at partial lovemaking, but what if she did something he didn't like? And of course the dream was just that. Could she satisfy him as she did in their fantasy?

"You mean for our wedding night?" Darach's eyes twinkled.

"Yes." Abby's one word reply came out in a whispered confirmation.

"Well, if you be all right with it, I would like to

take ye to my home. There are a lot of rooms you didn't see." Darach's words weren't a whisper but instead a distinctive rumble of sound.

"I'd love that. Will Arianna be coming with us?" She glanced toward the immortal who'd caught up with them before they got to the trolley stop earlier. Arianna had been the perfect guard, staying way behind them on the walk from the stop to the bistro. She'd parked herself on a bar stool and stayed put ever since.

"Nay, I think she will be more comfortable at your house. And since I usually teleport to me home, and I bought it under another name, there shouldna be a problem with demons finding us."

"Will we be displacing Conner? I know he's been staying here." Abby hoped her wishful thinking didn't show through.

"Conner will sleep anywhere. He'll stay at your house."

"Good. I mean..." Abby looked away.

Darach reached across the table and grasped her hand. "'Tis okay, Abby. 'Tis not wrong to wish for our first time as man and wife to not be disturbed."

The waiter brought their entrees and for a bit they were both silent enjoying steak and sides. Over dessert Abby brought up a subject that would need to be addressed sooner or later. Where they would live in the future.

"Darach, once Angus is caught, will Michael send you somewhere else right away?" She watched the strong line of his jaw work as he chewed the last bite of his chocolate cake.

"I dinnae ken, but I think he will allow me a few more years here in NOLA. I can always use artifice to age a bit."

Relief flooded Abby from the inside out. She didn't want to leave her birth home, but she would when it was time.

"Okay, that's good to know. I guess my next question is where do you want to live?"

This time Darach took a sip of tea before answering her.

"That be up to you, Abby. I have had many temporary homes since I became an executioner. I will be happy to live wherever ye are the most comfortable."

"I think I'd like to split our time at the houses."

Darach's smile was a gleam of white as he gave her a wolfish look. "Then I cannae wait to introduce ye to the shower at my house. It's large enough for two."

He adored the blush coating Abby's cheeks. Marriage to this woman would be an adventure each day. His smile faded just a bit. If only Angus wasn't a thorn in his side. Abby deserved better than to have to be worried about a mad demon on the prowl.

"You better behave or I just might take you up on that offer." Abby smiled back.

"'Tis what I'm counting on, me love."

****

On the walk back to the trolley, Darach listened as Abby told him about her day at school. She'd told the principal she would be leaving after Christmas. Her boss had been sorry but understood.

"And guess what? He said his niece could fill in until they get another secretary. I don't have to go back as of today."

"Are you sure you be okay with that?" He prayed she was, he truly didn't want to let her out of his sight for more than a few hours at a time.

"I'm sure. I've enjoyed working with the teachers and getting to know the students as they enroll in classes, but I'm so looking forward to being your wife."

He pulled her closer and dropped a kiss on the top of her head. "What made you decide to become a receptionist?"

"It was my grandmere's idea for me to take business in college. She wanted me to have an education I could make a living at, but I've always wanted to try my hand at art."

"Painting?" He was curious about Abby. So much time had been spent worrying about the threat of demons, dead bodies, and his stay in the hospital. He wanted to know more about what she wanted out of life.

"Maybe, I don't know. You know after my parents were killed, when I was a baby, Grandmere gave up a good job to take care of me." For a moment, Abby's eyes glistened before she blinked back her emotion.

"She loved me so much, as I did her. In fact, without me knowing it, she pawned her and Grandpere's wedding rings to pay for my education. I never met him, but she told me they met on a trip she took to Scotland. She said she fell in love with him almost immediately. I tried to get the rings back from the pawnshop after she told me, but by then a couple of months had gone by and the pawnshop was out of business. I wished Grandmere could be here tomorrow."

Darach squeezed her hand. "I ken you do."

The house came into view and Darach waited as Arianna, bringing up the rear, with a few take-out orders in her arms, eased the guards. Once they were in the front yard, she tightened them again before leaving them alone. Darach walked Abby to the porch steps but didn't climb them with her.

"You're not coming in?"

"Nay, Sean, Conner, and I be going—"

"I know, hunting. Well, at least I'll have you to myself tomorrow night." Darach's breath hitched as Abby slid into his embrace. Her body pressed his in all the right places.

"Aye, that be a promise. Now, get inside. The quicker I leave the faster I can return. I dinnae plan on sleeping at all tomorrow night."

Abby's cheeks began to glow. He couldn't wait until he could make her blush that way all over.

"I don't know what you're thinking, but please do hold that thought until tomorrow night."

It was his turn to feel heat creep onto his cheeks. While he was trying to come up with a reply, the minx laughed at him and then walked into the house.

"That woman is going to give you fits, my friend." The halfling had crept up on Darach again, and it was something he wished would stop. After sensing something in the warehouse, he'd hoped his abilities would return.

He turned to Sean. "I ken, but I be looking forward to it."

"Can't say I blame you. While you and Abby were at dinner, I paid a visit to the medical examiner. The young woman wasn't a prostitute like I thought originally. She is or was a student at the university. Before she died, she was raped and tortured."

Darach steeled his emotions. Angus's legacy of violence was still intact, but soon, God willing the man or demon would go down.

"What about demon signature, could ye identity any of them?

"No, it seems Angus is using new people every time he kills. It makes it harder to know who it is, since demons don't have fingerprints or DNA on file."

"Too bad. I would bet my sword Angus's signature was prevalent."

Sean kicked at the concrete foundation. "He needs to be stopped. At the rate the demon's going, there will be more bodies to count."

"Aye, and I'd fight the devil himself to keep Abby's from being one of them."

The halfling exchanged a look with Conner who came out of the house. "I'm with you. As I said before, we'll just have to make sure it doesn't happen." Sean started off, but Darach hesitated a moment. "Look, Conner, I ken you are supposed to go with me, but I would feel a lot better if ye stayed here. I know Arianna's good, but she seemed a bit off this afternoon."

"Whatever you need I will do it. But if ye do find Angus, I want to know." Conner's tone was serious and for good reason. What he hadn't disclosed in front of Sean was Angus had been dominant in starting a clan dispute that had wiped out Conner's family. Something the immortal had not known until after he'd been changed into an executioner.

Darach clasped arms with Conner and then moved off the porch to catch up with Sean. "I know ye will do your best to keep Abby safe, and I appreciate it more than ye know. Without some of my abilities, I be a sorry help mate." He berated himself for not being more careful that night in the alley. His ego at being able to dispatch demons had been his downfall.

"Cut yourself some slack, Highlander. There was no way you could know you'd be stabbed with a cursed dagger. Now come on, before we go hunting, I want to talk to some of our murder victim's friends."

****

"I never saw this guy before. Lila and I always go together to whatever club we want, when we party." The young woman's brown eyes teared up, as she looked at Sean. "We just wanted to have some fun."

Sandi pushed a strand of dirty-blonde hair back behind her ear. "Lila was so sweet. We had a pact. If we met someone and wanted to spend time with them, then we signaled the other one."

"So was this something Lila did often?" Sean queried.

"Oh no. In fact since we started this a couple of months ago, Lila never ever used the signal until the last time I saw her."

Darach couldn't stand it any longer. "What did the man Lila dance with look like?"

"Wow, let me think. She talked and danced with several guys that night, as did I, but I remember she came over to me when I was at the bar. She pointed him out and said he was such a gentleman and so hot." Sandi pushed at her hair again. "I didn't believe he could be all that hot, you see Lila's idea of hot was anyone who looked like something from a romance book. I figured the drinks we'd had were doing the talking, but when I saw this guy, he was something else."

Sean pulled a pad from his pocket. "Please describe what you remember about him."

"He was way tall, sorta like your friend here." She pointed to Darach. "His hair was a light blond and he wore it long—almost to his shoulders. His eyes were a bit odd. Sometimes they looked green and then it had to be the lighting at the club, they seemed to glow."

"That's good, can you remember anything else about him?"

Sandi used the back of her hand to wipe the tears from her eyes. "Yeah, I do. The man had an accent. Something you see on television. You know, like in that Scottish Highlander series. A brogue."

Darach clenched his fists. The man she described was Angus.

"Thank you, Ms. Miller. If we need anything else, I'll be in touch."

"Lieutenant." She caught Sean's sleeve. "Please catch this guy, I mean, if he killed Lila. I know ya'll are keeping it hush-hush because of her parents, but I have a friend that works at the medical examiner's office. No one deserves to suffer like Lila did." This time the tears cascaded down her face.

"Don't worry, when we catch him, he'll pay for his crime."

****

Angus walked through the house and wanted to gnash his teeth. The silence was deafening. He didn't care for being alone or inactivity. His plans of enjoying another tender New Orleans morsel had failed. He would have gone hunting himself, but felt it more prudent to keep his distance from any public gatherings. The television news channels had been full of the demise of poor, sweet, and delightfully innocent Lila. Although no mention had been made of where the body had been found, he knew Darach was suffering torments about Abby meeting the same fate. And that was what mattered. He wanted him to suffer and suffer dearly until the time came he could dispatch his cousin to death.

Michael ushered the last angel out of his office. He was more than winding down his workload for the day. And although he could not be there in person, another forbidden no-no on his do-not-violate list, he was looking forward to viewing Darach's and Abby's wedding from on high. In the meantime, he needed to handle a problem in the Middle East and then he would report to God. After that he was taking the rest of the day and night off.

Chapter Twenty-Six

Abby hit the floor almost at a run. Today was her wedding day, and she didn't plan on missing a minute of it lying in bed. She still had several things to do before their six o'clock date. Darach had not returned last night, but he did send her a message by Sean to Arianna. The small note was now pressed between the pages of her Bible. The brief, *I am counting the moments. Love, Darach* would be a memento she would always treasure.

She made short work of the stairs and headed for the kitchen. Caffeine was the first item on her list, and then a shower. After that she planned on going shopping. After looking in her closet, she realized she had nothing to wear for the ceremony. And she refused to wear the dress she wore to Antoine's. She wanted her wedding day dress to be a surprise for Darach.

Abby put on water to boil and pulled out a pack of tea. She also made a quick breakfast of toast and jam. Once the tea was ready, she sat down and scarfed down the toast while her tea cooled somewhat.

She wondered if Arianna was up yet. She knew she shouldn't go out without the immortal, but she wanted to make a run on the stores before they became too crowded with holiday shoppers. Christmas was less than two weeks away. That reminded her, she needed to do some holiday shopping herself. From all she gleaned from Darach, he had not really celebrated much of anything since becoming an executioner.

And with everything going on, there was no way of knowing how long Arianna would be in NOLA. Abby liked the idea of having a Christmas spent with friends and she wanted to decorate both of their homes with all the glorious props of Yuletide.

However, that would have to wait until after their wedding and honeymoon. Abby couldn't fathom how she went from being single to almost married in less than two weeks. Thoughts of what would happen tonight had teased her dreams. She was more than ready to be Darach's wife, lover, and soul mate.

"Hi, what are you doing up so early? I figured you'd want to sleep in a bit." Arianna's question was thrown over her shoulder as she made her way to the coffeepot the immortal had readied the night before. The aroma of crushed coffee beans and almond did smell good, but Abby preferred her flavored tea this morning.

"I have so much to do today. I need to go shopping."

"Shopping? As in for what?" Arianna looked a bit panicked.

"A wedding dress, a nightgown, among other things."

Arianna took a seat opposite Abby. "Okay. I guess it won't kill me to go with you."

"Well don't sound so happy about it. Besides, you know Darach would kill me if I went shopping on my own, or for that matter, left the house period without a guard."

"I know. Don't mind me. I didn't sleep much last night."

"Care to talk about it?" Abby held her breath. Arianna hadn't had a lot to say since the night she kissed Sean.

"No, but thanks anyway. What time do you want to do this thing?"

Abby laughed. "Well, as soon as we get showers and get dressed. It's about..." She looked at the clock. "Seven now. Most of the shops will open around nine. I plan on having all my shopping and errands finished and back home no later than noon. And if you're a good little immortal, I'll buy you an early lunch."

Arianna's eyes lit up for a moment. The woman could eat like a pro-wrestler, but of course she never gained a pound. Not fair at all. All Abby had to do was look at food and it jumped on her hips.

"Okay, I'm in. Let's do this thing."

"Great." Abby stood up and dumped her plate and cup in the sink while Arianna finished the last of her coffee.

"I'll be ready in about thirty minutes."

Arianna waved her hand as she got up to pour another cup of java. "Okay, I'll meet you back here in the kitchen."

Abby's foot was on the first step of the stairs when her phone rang. She started to just let the answering machine pick it up, but it could have something to do with today's events. She backtracked to the living room.

"Hello."

Silence met her greeting before someone cleared their throat. "Abby, it's Nate. I hate to bother you, but I didn't get a chance to talk to you before you left yesterday."

Abby tapped her slippered foot on the floor. Nate was a sweetie, but time was ticking away.

"That's okay, Nate. Everything happened so quickly. I had no idea the school would be able to get someone to cover for me right away."

"Well, I just wanted to let you know, I'll miss you. And to tell you some of us are planning a party for you. It's gonna be like a retirement/Christmas bash. Jim is handling the details, but we really want you to be there."

Although Nate sounded sincere, Abby couldn't forget the night he followed her and Arianna to the car. Then she shook her head. She'd known the teacher off and on for the last several years. He'd never said anything out of the way to her, so it must be the demon happenings making her nervous.

"That's awfully sweet of you guys. At the moment, however, I'm kinda tied up. I'm not sure when I'll be free so why not make it just a Christmas party."

Nate's sigh came over the phone line. "If that's what you want, Abby, sure, but if you change your mind, will you let me know?"

Abby's sigh wasn't as vocal but she felt it all the way to her toes. "Yes, I will. Please thank Jim for the idea also, and thank you, Nate. Merry Christmas early to you both."

****

Darach looked at the wildlife sniffing and then finding the food he'd put out. Squirrels scampered, rabbits hopped, and the occasional deer meandered up to feed their hunger. His house sat off the beaten path of tourists. One of the reasons he bought the place, and the other the large acreage in back of the house. The wooded area reminded him a bit of his old home.

Arianna had phoned him with the news she and Abby were going shopping. She wouldn't say much more but he figured the smile in her voice had to be the result of a bribe of food from Abby. Most executioners did have hearty appetites. His, however, had been reduced by his fears for Abby. As the last creature bounded away, Darach pulled out his cell phone. He had some shopping to do also, but he would deliver his order verbally and then wait on the items to be delivered.

Food was a must. As were the bottles of champagne coming from Antoine's. He'd placed the order for those the day after Abby said yes. As he now ordered furnishings for the rest of the house as well as rugs to cover the granite floors, he couldn't help but wonder if their wedding would go off without a hitch.

Angus would stop at nothing to get at him through Abby. Which reminded him he needed to have Sean check out the minister doing the ceremony.

Darach's cell phone rang. Speak of the devil, or the halfling, he wondered why he was calling so early.

"Hello."

"Morning, Highlander. Wanted to let you know Lila's death hit the news."

Darach sucked in air.

"Don't worry, they didn't have the exact location of the body dump. They were told somewhere in the area of Canal Street, and since that covers a great deal of territory, no one will know it was Abby's."

"Thank ye. I dinnae want anything to ruin this day."

"Or tonight I bet." The halfling's smirk came across loud and clear.

"Right ye are and ye can help me with that."

"You need my help with Abby? Just say the

word." He didn't have to see the halfling's face to know he wore a grin.

Darach's snarl ripped through his house as well as finding its target in Sean's ear.

"Hey, you almost deafened me."

"I dinnae need your help with Abby. What I need is for ye to stay with Arianna at Abby's tonight."

"Oh no, not me. Get Conner to do it." The halfling's panic was more than apparent to Darach. He wondered why Sean was so dead set against staying with Arianna.

"Conner is going to be out scouting for Angus."

"That's a low blow, Highlander. I suppose I could stay far away from her in the house."

Darach laughed. "It might be for the best since she cannae seem to decide to kiss or slap you."

"Okay, on that note, I'm ringing off. I'll see you tonight before the ceremony."

Sean hung up before Darach could reply. It felt good to rattle the halfling's cage just a bit. And although he knew his remarks about Abby were just his form of teasing, he still didn't much care for the idea of anyone helping him with Abby in that way.

****

Abby sat watching Arianna shovel food in her mouth like there was no tomorrow. Of course, the immortal's table manners were impeccable, but she would give a man a run for his money when it came to eating. Abby on the other hand had long since finished her salad and the bowl of soup she'd ordered and turned down Arianna's offer for half of her second hamburger.

Between them they'd picked up the cake, some bottles of wine, and a few table decorations for the wedding. Abby had found the most delectable dress in a pale cream, street-length with a short matching jacket. She'd also picked up a small bouquet of pale peach roses and other flowers with baby's breath. The only other woman there would be Arianna. Abby wondered what the immortal would do if she threw her the bouquet. Probably drop it like it was a baby alligator.

"I'm finished, Abby. You ready to go?"

While she'd been wool-gathering Arianna had chowed down the rest of her lunch.

"Yeah, I'm ready." Together they gathered up Abby's purchases. She kept possession of the covered dress-hanger with her wedding apparel and the small package containing her newly purchased nightwear. The combination of colors was beautiful. She just hoped Darach thought so also.

Once back at the house, Abby threw it into high gear. She covered the dining room table with a lace cloth that had belonged to Grandmere. She also sat out goblets for the wine. Darach would be bringing the champagne. Counting the minister, if he stayed for the quaint reception, there would be six of them. She would love to invite Rae from the bar, but didn't want to pull her into the hedge of trouble she and Darach seemed to be under. Abby prayed Angus would be stopped soon.

She pulled out china plates, silver cutlery, and linen napkins from the china cabinet. The roses Darach had given her the night before were still beautiful, and she placed them in the center of the massive table.

Candles! She needed candles for their wedding. Since there was a fireplace in the dining room, it would give off additional light, and the ivory-colored pillars she'd also unearthed from the cabinet would make the room twinkle with their flames.

Their wedding cake with a bride and groom standing sentinel on top sat on a tea cart with a knife for cutting the first slice. There had been no time to have napkins printed but she'd grabbed a couple of bride-and-groom goblets. A twenty-dollar incentive convinced the shopkeeper to engrave them with both their names and the date.

Abby surveyed the room and gave a sigh of relief. It looked beautiful. She would light the candles right before the wedding and get a fire going in the cold hearth. The clock chimed four times, galvanizing her into reality. While she'd been setting up and admiring the room time had literally flown. She needed to get herself ready.

****

Darach arrived at Abby's the same time Sean did and they both walked the pathway to the house. He'd called Arianna earlier and told her their arrival time, and she'd lifted the guards right on time.

The immortal met them on the porch and sealed the guards once again. That must mean the minister and Conner had already arrived. Reverend March had been investigated and given an all-clear by the halfling.

Now, God willing, nothing would interfere with their wedding.

"Immortal." Sean's greeting to Arianna was clipped.

"Halfling." Her response was delivered in the same manner. Darach hoped both their friends would put their animosity on a back burner.

"Come on in, Darach. Abby's still in her room, but the preacher and Conner are here."

"Thanks, Arianna. I appreciate ye taking care of making sure all is safe."

"Hey, it's my job, besides, I like Abby. For a mortal she's pretty cool."

"Aye, she is." Darach followed Arianna to the dining room that now resembled a fairyland of lights. Abby had done wonders in the short time she'd had to get ready. Everything shone with the ambiance of romance. He actually liked it.

He nodded to Conner who stood out of the way, before taking his place next to the minister. As he greeted the clergyman and gave his thanks for doing the ceremony on such short notice, the clock chimed six times. Sean moved to stand next to Darach.

Darach's heart picked up a bit of speed. The moment was at hand. Soon Abby would be his in the truest sense of the word.

A slight sound at the threshold caused Darach to turn his head. His breath caught and held before he remembered to breathe. Arianna walked into the room first and when Abby followed, he lost his breath again and still again when she smiled. Never in his two lifetimes had he beheld such a beautiful sight as his bride-to-be. He took her hand in his and tucked it gently against his body. Darach knew he would never forget this moment—not even if he lived another millennium.

Michael looked through his porthole to Earth. The view of Abby's house cleared and he found the couple. Good, he wasn't too late. A bulletin had arrived about one of his immortals stationed in an earthquake-ravaged area, and he'd had to handle that first. As he watched, Darach took Abby's hand in his...

Chapter Twenty-Seven

Abby welcomed the warm touch of Darach's hand. She was more than a bit nervous, but oh-so-happy.

"Now repeat after me..." Darach turned to Sean who handed him the rings. Darach had told her he'd taken care of the rings, so she hadn't even seen the circlet that would bind their love for an eternity.

His large hand held her finger gently as he slid the band on her hand. "With this ring, I thee wed..." Darach's fingers still covered the ring blocking her view, but her glance at his face as he repeated the vow to love, honor, cherish, until death do us part, almost brought her to her knees. As it were when it was her turn to place the ring on his finger, she had to blink several times before she could see to slide it in place.

"I now pronounce you husband and wife. You may kiss your bride."

The moment the preacher finished the ceremony, Darach caught her to him in a grip that would have been bruising if he hadn't gentled his touch. Abby looked up into his face and for a moment she saw his eyes go silver before his lips locked on hers.

The tantalizing taste of Darach assaulted her senses. More so because he now belonged to her. She would fight to stay with him and to save him if the need ever arose.

After much throat clearing, he raised his head, leaving her feeling bereft. He took her hand and raised both of theirs together. It was then she finally saw the ring he'd chosen.

"My grandmere's ring!" Abby's exclamation brought his attention back to her from the back clapping from Sean and Arianna's congratulations.

"Abby, what be ye talking about?" His puzzlement seemed sincere. Could he actually not know the ring had belonged to her grandmere? She turned his hand over and gasped out loud.

"Darach, I don't know how you did it, but these are my grandparents' rings. The ones my grandmere pawned years ago.

Darach couldn't have been more surprised than if the Loch Ness monster had materialized right in the dining room.

"Be ye sure? I bought these at a shop right here in NOLA."

Abby looked a bit uncertain, but then she tugged the ring off his finger and looked on the inside. "Oh Lord, it is his. See the inscription?"

Darach looked at the tiny etching inside the circle *Ian, I will love you forever. Love, Mimi.*

"What does yours say, Abby?"

She pulled her ring off and then looked at it before handing the small circle to Darach. *"To my Mimi. Love always, Ian."*

"How did you find them?" Abby pushed his ring back on and took hers back.

"I dinnae ken. I was shopping for rings and found a small shop I have never seen before." Darach retrieved the ring boxes Sean had placed on the table prior to Abby's appearance.

"See here's the name of the..." His words trailed off. The logo inside the box was no longer there. Instead the words Michael/Archangel to God stared him in the face.

Before he could say anything else, the preacher announced he had to leave. An early dinner his wife had planned. Abby walked him to the door but returned quickly.

"Okay, did you find the name of the shop? I'd love to thank them, even if they don't know what they did."

"Trust me, the person who finalized this deal knows exactly what he was doing."

"Darach?" Instead of answering he handed her the box. Abby's laughter pealed forth and filled the room with its musical sound.

"I want to thank him. Darach, hand me your phone, please."

"I didnae bring it. I mean, 'tis at home in meother pants."

Abby's eyes were shadowed for a moment, and then she shrugged. "Oh well, I guess I can thank him tomorrow."

The evening wore on, the cake was cut, the champagne poured, and Abby was wishing they could leave. She'd packed just a small overnight bag to take to Darach's.

"Are you ready, me love?"

Ready to step into the arms of her new husband? To make love with him, and to give herself to him forever? Yes, she was ready.

"Yes, I just need to get my bag." Abby made a move to leave.

"Don't bother, I have it right here, Abby." Arianna's grin preceded the hug the immortal gave her. "God's blessings on your marriage.

Sean was next to step forward. "May you always be as happy as you are at this moment." He clapped Darach on the back and amidst a mock growl from her husband, kissed Abby on the cheek.

Conner bade his good wishes also and then stepped back. Abby clutched the small bag Arianna handed her, and then Darach grabbed her. A moment later she stood inside his home. Wait…it was now her home also.

Darach took her bag and then stood looking down at her. If she didn't know better, she'd swear he looked a tad nervous.

"I could show ye around if ye like."

"I'd love that." Abby glanced around the large room they stood in. It looked different; there was actually furniture in the room. As she followed Darach to each of the lower rooms and then upstairs, she realized he'd furnished the entire house.

It all looked great, but when he stopped in front of two double doors, she knew it was his room without being told. Darach opened the door and gave a bit of a flourish with his hand. Abby stepped into the room and just stared at the bed.

The bedposts stretched almost six feet in the air before they connected making a perfect rectangle. She applauded the decision not to add bed curtains. They would have ruined the majestic view of the almost floor-to-ceiling windows. The moon shone into the vista and Abby felt as if she could reach out and touch each strand of silver.

One wall held a dresser, and a small table displayed a lamp. A rug graced the granite floors, it's price tag barely tucked under the edge. The walls were a deep purple and screamed royalty. Yes, this was a room for a laird of old.

"If you dinnae like it, ye can change anything you want."

"I love it, Darach. It's beautiful."

His sigh as he looked down at her brushed her cheek.

"Well then that be good. Would ye like to see the bathroom?" Darach looked almost excited.

"Uh, yes, that might be a good idea." She smiled back at him.

He strode across the floor and then pulled open an oversized single door. She followed him and then gasped out loud. "Oh my! This has to be one of the most fabulous rooms I've ever seen."

A shower nestled against one marble wall, its length stretching almost to the center bay window. In front of the window sat a sunken tub with candles on the uplifted edges. Empty of water, it looked at least three feet deep. You could almost float on your back in the thing. An open cabinet filled with fluffy towels of all sizes and washcloths stood near another door.

"What's in there?"

Darach's face turned just a bit red. "'Tis where ye take care of personal business."

"Oh, okay, I think I get the picture." She patted him on the arm. "And it's okay to say toilet around me."

"It dinnae sound very nice." His voice was gruff. Abby wanted to kiss him. Who would have thunk a man his age would still be a bit archaic when it came to bodily functions.

"I love you, Darach."

The gruffness in his voice stayed but his frown disappeared as he leaned over, caught her under the arms, and lifted her to his height. "I love ye too, Abby."

The kiss he gave her fairly scorched her lips, but then he pulled back and put her back on the floor.

"I will go and check the safety guards if ye want to take a bath or something."

Before she could tell him to come back, he was

gone. Oh well, maybe he was a bit shy. Lord knew she was a bit nervous about what was to come. Not even the most explicit dream could rival the real thing. Abby opened her overnight bag and pulled out her gown, toiletries, and hairbrush. No time like the present to try and make herself seductive.

****

Darach wanted to rip his tongue out. After a millennium of immortality he would have thought he'd be a bit more at ease. Instead he babbled about the bathroom and then left his bride just standing there.

The truth was now that the moment was upon them, he was a bit fearful that he might not be able to hold back his lust. Abby was a virgin; he needed to go slow with her. And there was the undisputable fact it'd been decades since he'd made love to a woman. He just hoped he hadn't forgotten how.

He checked the guards and glanced at the clock. How long would Abby need to bathe? He didn't want to disturb her privacy, yet the thought of her in his home, in his bath, caused a spear of lust to fill his shaft.

God's teeth, he couldn't wait any longer. Darach ran up the stairs and down the hallway to the master bedroom. The door was partially open, allowing a crescent of light to shine through. He'd left it open all the way. Was she out of the bath? Feeling like a green, untried lad, Darach pushed the door forward.

Abby stood at the dresser, her back to him as she brushed out her hair. The moonlight highlighted her silhouette and outlined every lush curve of her body under the ice-blue material. Darach's shaft grew harder, his jewels tighter, as he took several breaths, and then moved forward.

He slid both arms around her silk-clad body and took the brush from her hand. Abby's eyes opened and she caught his gaze in the mirror.

"Your beauty takes me breath away."

Darach molded her body back against his. His hands teased the straps down her shoulders until the material caught on her breasts. The thrust of her now aroused nipples inflamed his blood. He wanted her so badly his teeth ached.

"Abby, I dinnae think I can wait any longer, but if ye need more time..."

Abby turned in his embrace. "And I don't want you to, husband," she teased back.

As she looked up at him, his pupils turned to silver discs. He lifted her in his arms, and the hardness she felt before now pressed against the vee of her thighs. Abby's center grew wet with her desire for this man who'd changed her life in one moment of time.

He strode to the bed, pulled the coverlet back, and then placed her gently on the mattress. He nudged her legs apart and stood between them. Darach's hands smoothed over her gown, circling over her hips, over her mound, and then back to her breasts. Finally when she thought she couldn't stand it any longer, his hands sought and found her aching nipples. Even through the material the caress of his fingers made her want to claw her way out of her gown.

Darach's touch as he tweaked the hard crests sent a wave of desire straight to her female center. When his hands left her she wanted to weep with frustration, but then he tugged her gown down to her waist and his mouth renewed the torture.

Abby's upper body left the mattress when his mouth closed around one nipple and his hand grasped her other breast. His teeth grazed her swollen peak, and then his tongue soothed the ache before making her ache even more as he swirled and laved the tip. He changed sides and her desire grew.

His hands touched her hips and she tensed with anticipation. Cool air bathed her lower body as he slowly pulled her gown down and then off her unresisting flesh.

Darach stopped his sensual administration and she wanted to pull his head back to her breast.

"I dinnae think in all me years of living I have ever beheld such beauty. Ye spellbound me."

"Then it's only right, for I fell under your spell the first night we met."

"Abby…" Words failed Darach as he realized how fickle fate could be and how he could have missed meeting Abby or…his heart almost stuttered to a stop, failed to stop the demon from killing her.

So horrified at what could have happened he pulled away.

"Darach, whatever you're thinking, stop."

The stern look and frown marring her beauty gave him pause.

"You be right, me love." He slid back over her succulent curves and leaned forward to tease her lips. The press of her desire-ripened breasts against his chest stirred his blood once again. Abby's arms slid around to his back and she pulled him closer.

He deepened their kiss and then released her lips.

This time he moved completely off the bed.

"Darach, where are you going?"

Instead of speaking, he pulled the shirt loose from his pants and stripped it off. Abby's eyes went wide. Darach unbuttoned his leather pants, unzipped them, and pushed the material down his legs before stepping out and kicking them to the side. Abby's mouth flew open.

Darach dressed always took her breath away, but it was nothing compared to the immortal in the flesh. The dream had only touched on the possibility of what he looked like. His chest was wider, and a small spattering of ebony curls narrowed down to his belly button and beyond.

It was the *beyond* that caused her mouth to fly open. His arousal stood tall and angled toward his lower belly. The sac below hung heavy and full. Lord, the man was built like a god from mythology, his bronze skin an enticing contrast to the cream-colored sheets as he lowered himself to the bed.

"I be not going anywhere, wife. I plan to make love to ye until the dawn wakes the sleeping sun. After that until the moon rises to bathe a tired Earth."

His tone as well as his words pulled Abby further into the spell of his desire. She reached up, grasped his shoulders, and pulled him down.

"Promises, promises. Now prove it my, immortal Highlander."

****

Angus wanted to rip the heart out of the demon that brought him the message. He didn't often allow one of his underlings access to his home, but he'd said it was urgent and about Abigail Dupree.

"Get out!" The demon ran from Angus's sight leaving him alone to engage his rage. Darach had married the woman. Even as he stalked the length of his chamber, he knew it was too late. Abby would lose her innocence to his cousin. Once again Darach had beaten him to the prize. But Angus would be the victor in the end.

Michael strolled up the steps of his mansion. The evening had been a testimony of what God's love could do. Darach and Abby were married and for a few days they would enjoy the peace they deserved. He just wished he could make the looming tragedy go away, but he couldn't. He'd already interfered to the point of having his boss tell him to step back or he would be barred from anything to do with Darach and Abby. Now, he would have to wait and see how fate dealt with the newlyweds.

Chapter Twenty-Eight

Darach planned to prove to Abby he was a man of his word. He nudged her legs apart again and rested the weight of his arousal against the soft flesh of her womanhood. Her eyes were wider now than when he'd stripped off his clothes.

His hands found her breasts and palmed them as he leaned forward and left a trail of kisses from her lips, down the side of her neck, and ending at the delicate shadow of her collarbone.

Abby's whimpers fed his ego and his lust as he licked and suckled her nipples. Her body squirmed beneath his, bringing her beckoning opening closer. His shaft stretched even more with the blood pulsating beneath its surface. He wasn't sure how much longer he could hold out before taking her, but he wanted Abby to be ready for his loving.

Darach placed his hand against the heat of her feminine core. Desire coated his fingers, and he slid one slowly inside her wet channel. Abby bucked against the mattress.

"Darach...please..."

"Nay, this time will be for real, I want ye ready to accept me."

"I am, believe me, I am."

His laughter came out harsh. She had no idea what she was doing to him, but soon he would show her.

He slid two more fingers deep inside her warmth, searched, and found the spot he sought. As he manipulated her trembling flesh, Abby stiffened and then let out a keening cry. Her release drenched his hand in hot liquid desire. He continued to caress her as he bent again to taste her breasts.

Abby's movements finally stilled and Darach guided his aching erection to the haven it craved. Slowly, one excruciating inch at a time, he pushed forward. The barrier guarding her treasure stopped him from going further.

"Abby, me heart, this will hurt ye just a bit."

Her breasts rose and fell with her rapid breaths. Her eyes glowed with her climax, and her face was flushed with fulfilled desire. If he could capture Abby in this pose then he would treasure the portrait for all time.

"It will hurt me more if you don't take me. I've waited a lifetime for you, and I don't want to wait any longer."

He dropped a quick kiss on her trembling lips and then with a quick thrust he breached her virginity. Darach forced himself to hold still until Abby was able to accommodate his length.

Darach's flesh filled Abby, stretching her feminine walls until she thought they would burst. The pain had been minimal when he'd claimed her, and the slight burning sensation ebbed leaving her with an ache she needed healed.

She wrapped her legs around Darach's hips and

pulled him closer. The look of delight in his now silver gaze warmed her heart, and she wanted him to burn her with his touch.

Slowly he withdrew and then pushed forward again. This time there was no pain, only an incredible tingling deep inside her womb. Again he repeated his actions. Abby met his movements by lifting her hips. Now the tingling grew stronger. When the tip of his erection touched a spot she didn't know she had, the spirals of desire began again—stronger than ever before.

Darach's eyes scorched Abby with their intensity. His upper body was a taunt column of bronze strength. His corded arms rippled with muscles as he pressed harder and deeper. Abby closed her eyes against the vortex of desire pulling her closer and closer to the edge of ecstasy. Her hips became pivots as she met each of his thrusts and rotated her body against his.

A groan parted his lips and he thrust faster. Abby's world began to melt as did her insides as he continued his torture. Finally when she thought she could stand no more he gave one hard push, and she fell into the beckoning grasp of desire's flame.

Darach's roar as he obtained his release was the last thing Abby heard before she too succumbed to the arms of fulfilled rapture.

****

Abby wasn't sure what had awakened her, but it took only a moment to realize the exquisite torture was Darach's tongue rasping against her lower spine. She tried to turn over but a hand on her buttocks held her still. As she sucked in air and then released it, Darach spread her legs apart.

Surely he wouldn't? Abby again tried to turn on her back.

"Lie still, lass. Our first time was just a prequel for all the ways I want to make love to ye."

"And are there many ways?" Abby's whisper was caught against her pillow casing, but Darach heard it anyway.

"Oh aye. Many ways for many pleasure-filled hours. I have waited several lifetimes for another chance at love, and I dinnae plan to rush."

His lips skimmed down the cleft of her butt, and Abby squirmed against the mattress trying to scratch an itch that just got worse. Darach's feather-like touch was sending her over the edge as he brought his lips to bear on the sensitive skin of her inner thighs. The first touch of his tongue against her most feminine place sent shockwaves of eroticism straight to her womb.

She fought to turn over. She needed him inside her, but the desire pooling deep within only made her body a useless puddle of need.

Her flesh burned with his touch, she twisted this way and that trying to reach the pinnacle of fulfillment. When his mouth closed on her heated and sensitive flesh Abby felt the spirals of heat pull tighter, then expand out to draw her into the most mind-blowing organism of her life.

Before she could recover, Darach pressed his hardness against her and then slid deep inside—igniting her passion once again. She rose to her knees and felt the slap of his scrotum against her backside, she welcomed the swift slide of passion as he moved in and out building a friction that she knew would take both of them into a world of ecstasy. Abby pressed back to meet each thrust with her backside, she could feel the slightly chilled bedroom's air caressing her nipples. The blast of heat from below collided with the sensation of having her nipples kissed, and then when she thought she could endure no more, Darach bit her buttocks and shouted his release. Abby collapsed on the bed as she fell into the mindless void of lust and love, and welcomed the press of his body as he followed her down to the mattress.

****

Blood coated the insides of her closed eyes. Abby tried to open them. To stop the vision but couldn't. The metallic scent made her stomach churn. Someone had died. Who? She crept closer to the middle of the tin building. Chills barreled down her spine. Her hands shook, and her lips trembled. She didn't want to know what happened. Yet she could not stop her steps from going forward. Several people were gathered around a form on the floor. The two immortals, Sean, and she also saw her own body standing stock-still. Where was Darach? Why couldn't she see him? The closer she got to the tight circle, the more she screamed inside. Abby watched the looks of horror, sadness, and rage on the faces of her friends. She witnessed the tears running down her own. The group parted for her, and she moved through to gaze at the body lying in a pool of blood. Darach! It was Darach, and he was dead. As her vision form begin to fall, Abby's physical form broke from the tight hold of the vision.

She felt Darach's arms around her body, his warm breath on her face. He was alive. Yet, how long would that last? She thought after the attack in the alley that her first vision had come true, only the outcome wasn't death. Could she be so blessed again? Not sure what to do, and knowing she couldn't allow Darach to know what she'd seen, Abby snuggled even closer to his broad chest. She feared to close her eyes and prayed her sleep would be dreamless.

****

Darach woke to the soft press of Abby's lips against the side of his neck—his shaft already thick with need. They'd fallen asleep facing one another, her head resting on his chest. All he could think of was no dream could equal the night he'd just spent.

"Morning, wife."

"Morning, husband." Abby giggled just a bit, and he wondered if she was nervous. He couldn't fathom why since they'd made love once more after their first two bondings. His innocent bride had a vixenish side, and he loved it and her.

His arousal pressed against her hip, and he wanted to make love to her again, but Abby was certain to be tender in all the wrong places for that to happen. Later today would be better after he bathed her and rubbed her with healing oil.

The idea of stroking his hands down her body, finding all of her erogenous zones again made him ache harder. He needed to distance himself from Abby or he'd take her now against his better judgment. Darach gave his wife another kiss, and then reached over her to pick up the watch he'd taken off sometime during the night.

Impossible. He never slept until three in the afternoon. It looked like later was already here, and despite his desire to stay in bed with Abby, he needed to check on her house, and for any news of Angus.

Not to mention, now that his mind was almost off of sex, he needed to relieve himself.

"I'll be back in a few. You rest."

"What time is it?"

"Three o'clock, me love."

Abby shot up so fast she almost clipped him on the chin.

"What's your hurry? You don't have to be anywhere, right?"

"No, but I had planned to check with Arianna, and then fix dinner for you."

Darach pulled the sheet that had fallen down to her waist back up. The temptation of her luscious body could prove to be too much for his forbearance.

"What about this? Ye rest for now, and then we will cook an early dinner together."

"Are you going to talk to Arianna?"

"Aye, I planned to talk to her and Sean. I also want to check in with Conner." Darach hoped she would not want to go, but he feared she might have ideas of her own. So far she'd hadn't heard anything about the last body, not with all the rushing around for their wedding, and he would prefer to keep it that way.

"Good, then would you ask her if she has enough food in the house? I sorta feel responsible for her."

"I will ask her. You do ken she be a lot older than ye are and can take care of herself, don't ye?"

Abby pinched his arm. "Of course I do. Just like I know you are several times older than me." She abused his arm again. "Now, go get ready, old man. You might need a bit more time to shower since your bones are so ancient."

Blue eyes shone with mischief as she waited on him to respond which he did by leaning down and running his hand over her now peaking nipples and downward to caress the flesh between her legs. "Ancient I might be, but I still be young enough to make ye moan."

Abby's face took on a blush that almost matched the dark crimson striped in the robe he seldom wore.

"You are a beast, immortal."

"Right, and dinnae ye forget it, wife."

Darach left to the accompaniment of his pillow hitting him in the arse and Abby's laughter.

****

Several hours later, after a long, luxurious bath, and moments of anticipation awaiting Darach's return, Abby had given up waiting on her husband's return. She stood in the kitchen stirring a pot of jambalaya. Six-thirty and still no immortal. The man should have taken his watch.

She refused to allow the unease of her vision to disturb her. She wanted to be upbeat when Darach returned. She just wished she knew when that would be. And while she was wishing she should wish for a way to get back to her house. Not knowing where she was in reference to her new home was more than a bit troublesome.

Abby sighed and turned down the stove burner to simmer, before popping the rolls she'd cooked earlier into a warming pan. The kitchen, for a confirmed bachelor, was well stocked. She'd also found the fixings for an instant Key lime pie that she'd thrown together and put in the fridge.

What to do with herself now? Maybe she'd watch some television. Abby decided to turn her entrée off completely and then covered it with a lid. Surely it wouldn't be much longer until Darach returned.

The living area now offered a variety of electronics and what looked like would be a very comfortable sofa instead of the Spartan furnishing of before. She grabbed the remote control and flopped down on the forest green material.

She was right, the back and seat of the couch felt like bliss against her sore body. Making love with Darach had been the ultimate pleasure, but she wondered if she'd be able to keep up with him tonight.

The channels rolled by as she flipped through them. A documentary on the mating habits of snakes didn't do a thing for her, a historical program on the rites of murder in the Middle Ages was also a no-no. Finally she settled on a local news channel.

"And in headline news today, we have a late breaking bulletin in about the body of Lila Carnes, only daughter of Walter Carnes, whose ancestry denotes one of NOLA's most prestigious and oldest families."

Abby sat forward on the couch and ignored the

slight ache in her lower region.

"Ms. Carnes's body was found the night before last tossed onto riverfront property abutting Canal Street. We are awaiting a statement from the property owner."

The scene panned in on the property, and Abby sat up straighter on the couch as she spotted the back of her own home.

Someone had dumped a body on her land, and Darach had kept this pertinent information from her. Why?

Almost numb, she watched the image of a young girl flashed on the screen. She knew that face. She'd seen the eyes open in death. Her heart thumped overtime. The vision she'd had about the girl's death had come true. Immediately her vision of Darach imploded into her brain.

No, she couldn't think of that, she would not allow him to die. Somehow she would make sure he didn't. No matter what she had to do, her vision would not come true.

Tired, and more than a bit frightened, Abby switched off the TV. She needed to think. Putting the vision aside, she thought about the newscast.

Darach had kept Lila's death from her. She could imagine why he did, not to ruin their wedding day, but she would not, could not live in a bubble. He should have told her. Abby stood up and began to pace, her arms wrapped around her waist.

That poor, poor girl. Had Angus killed her? Just the thought made her sick at her stomach. The demon indeed lived up to his name. She knew he had to be stopped, but her heart bled at the thought Darach would be in the line of fire in order to bring him down.

She stopped her pacing and glanced toward another new item added since her first visit. The clock now showed six forty-five. Should she be worried? And why hadn't she kept the cell phone she'd flung at Darach? Maybe he still had it.

Abby began pulling out drawers, searching on top of all the appliances, and even in the numerous closets. Finally after much frustration, she found the cell phone sitting on a battery cradle in the bedroom. She grabbed a seat on the bed and punched Darach's icon.

"Abby?"

"And who else would it be?" She knew her tone was tart, but fear rode her hard, and the man had a lot of explaining to do.

"Be everything all right?" She ignored the warm caress his tone invoked and went for the jugular.

"Yes of course it is, except you have been gone hours, not minutes, and there was a body found in my backyard. Care to tell me about it, immortal?"

She heard his hurried explanations, she assumed to Arianna and Sean, and then while she waited for him to come back to the phone, he materialized in front of her.

"And that's another thing. You have to stop just appearing without warning." Abby knew she sounded like a petulant child, but dammit, he should have told her someone violated her property—again. Not just violated, but also left her a horrendous gift.

"Abby, I..." Darach sat down beside her.

"I know, you're sorry. I understand why you didn't want to tell me before the wedding, but why didn't you tell me this morning?"

"And when would ye have liked for me to do that? After ye woke up so warm and sensual in my arms? Would ye have wanted me to defile our marriage bed with talk of death?"

Put that way, Abby couldn't disagree with the man, but still...

"Fine, but do you know how hard it was to see it on the news?"

"Aye 'tis why I have been gone so long. Arianna filled me in as soon as I got there. Sean arrived shortly after, and together, he and I, Conner, and Arianna put together a press release if needed. We plan to keep your name out of this."

"And you didn't think I wouldn't find out?"

"Nay, but I wanted to pick the time." Darach's tone was reasonable, and Abby's temper began to cool somewhat.

She followed to where he now stood at the window. "Look, I'm sorry for jumping on you, but it was just not a good afternoon. I missed you, and then finding out about the murder. You know I can't teleport. I have no clue where your house actually is since I've not traveled here by car, and I kinda felt..."

"Abandoned?"

"Yes, and believe me, I know that sounds selfish in the wake of that poor girl's death. Do you think Angus killed her?"

Darach remained silent. He didn't want to tell Abby the truth, but she needed to know.

"Darach?"

"Why dinnae we talk about this over dinner? Whatever ye fixed smells good." He hoped she'd agree.

"Fine, but don't try stonewalling me anymore. I'm your wife, I'm in the middle of this, and I'm vested in your safe-keeping." Abby led the way to the kitchen.

He hid his grin at her words. His ever-resilient Abby bounced back from a blow with the determination of an immortal.

"I promise. Now, can we eat? I be starving."

****

He speared a piece of pepper from his bowl and savored the spicy flavor. Abby's skill as a cook far surpassed his own. He wondered if it would be chauvinistic to ask her to do all the cooking.

"So, now that you've gotten somewhat full"—Abby gestured at his second bowl of jambalaya—"do you think you could tell me about the body?"

The bite almost became lodged in his throat. So much for thinking she might forget. Once the pepper found haven in his belly, he spoke. "Aye, I will tell ye."

"Good, then I'll give you the dessert I was going to toss to the deer if you didn't."

Despite the dread of telling her Angus was behind Lila's death, he wanted to laugh. How could she know he had a sweet tooth that would be a dentist's delight if he were not immortal?

"Sean found the body the other night. He said he smelled the demon signature as soon as he drew near your porch."

Abby's lashes flickered for a moment, before she gave him her attention once more.

"I arrived and found Sean edging around the side of your house. It was too dark to know if he was a demon or not. Although…" He held his hand up to ward off her chastisement that he could have been walking into a group of demons. "I felt sure no one had breached the guards. Sean was at the canal's edge. The young woman had been tossed from a boat and from the first examination Sean determined she'd been dead for several hours before her body was dumped."

He took a sip of tea to wet his throat. "The halfling tried to keep the media away, but… The one thing ye need to remember is ye are safe here. Only a select few can get inside without me allowing it. I want ye to stay here until Angus is caught."

His wife looked like she wanted to argue but instead just nodded her head. He wanted to hold her, tell her it would be all right, but she busied herself cutting him a slice of pie. Abby didn't cut one for herself.

"And I suppose you will be out hunting the demon without a regard to your own safety?" Her words were low, but still stung his heart.

Abby turned away as if she didn't expect him to answer, which was a good thing. He be not sure if he could.

Darach forced himself to finish the slice of pie. Afterward he watched her load the new dishwasher and then wash her hands. Her facial expression was smooth, but he didn't care for the frozen look in her eyes.

God's teeth, he hated she was blaming herself when if anyone was to blame it was him. He should have already found and killed Angus.

"Come, Abby, 'tis time I make good on at least one of the promises I made ye this afternoon."

****

Angus was happy. Not a state he was used to being. The news had finally shown a bit more of where the body was found. It was good that Abigail, on the first day of married life, would be haunted by death. It would make the murder closer, and in essence she would think of him—as would Darach.

Events were in play Michael couldn't stop. He wanted to, oh yes, how he wanted to play...not God, there was only one God, but archangel with a vengeance. But, vengeance belonged to his boss, and unless something occurred that would endanger more than the players already in place, he would step down for now.

Chapter Twenty-Nine

Abby gasped as water cascaded over her flesh, and Darach raked her body with nips and kisses. She thought he might want to make use of the swimming pool he called a tub, after the decadent and sensual massage he'd given her, but instead, he'd stripped her to her skin, turned on the shower, and then tugged his own clothes off. Her offer of help was discarded when she kept caressing his engorged shaft. So much man and so much loving went a long way to turning her thoughts from murder.

Now she surrendered to the touch of his skillful mouth and wished she could return the favor. Darach, however, had trapped her hands over her head. Her breasts were thrust out like a sacrificial offering and she liked it—no, make that loved—being his captive.

She opened her eyes and watched her husband. Darach's skin looked delicious with water droplets hugging the muscles in his arms and the wide expanse of his chest. Abby wanted to do the same and more.

Her gaze followed the wet tendrils of hair

leading the way to his impressive erection. She didn't think she would ever get enough of watching him as he made love to her. The wolfish look in his eye as he tongued her breasts, nipped her nipples, and then kissed his way toward her abdomen, weakened the stiff posture of her legs. If she eased her control she'd land on the tile floor.

Instead she slid out of his soapy grip and down to her knees. Her hand found and caressed his erection. She welcomed Darach's groan. She shrugged off his attempt to pull her to her feet. "No, I want to love you like you loved me."

His hands fell down to his sides, and she once again ran her hands over his impressive sex.

"Abby!"

"Hush, I'm not finished." She placed her lips against the soft but firm texture of his skin and then sent her tongue exploring from the base of his shaft to the tip.

Darach's knees bent, his hands found a haven in her hair as she gave him what he wanted. He grew larger, the blood vessels more prominent as she loved him. Finally when she ached so badly from knowing he was close to climax, he tugged her to her feet.

"Enough. Now we will finish this together." Darach's words were an erotic growl. She loved how she could make him lose control.

One strong thigh forced her legs apart and rode her center as she now rode his leg. The motion of his mock lovemaking sent her body into overload. She could feel the wetness of desire push pass her woman's center. And she knew when Darach felt it also. His eyes went the molten silver she loved, he grunted as if trying to retain control, and then he did exactly what she wanted him to do. He lifted her by the waist and slowly lowered her onto his shaft. His fullness stretched her sore spots but she didn't care. She wanted him, all of him, and still that would never be enough.

She used his shoulders as a handhold and raised her body up and then slid back down. "Abby, ye be killing me."

Abby wanted to laugh. She loved making her immortal lose control. He'd changed so much since their first meeting, and she never wanted him to go back to the stony-hearted warrior she'd met in that alley.

"Yes, I know, but you love it."

His chuckle seemed to be ripped from a throat hoarse with desire, but she welcomed it all the same as she did the accelerated movements of his hips.

Her head tilted back against the tile wall. Her mouth opened to emit a scream when his finger slid over her swollen nub. When he tweaked the instrument of her desire, she was lost.

Abby's scream ripped through the bathroom and beyond. As if waiting for that one sound, Darach's thrusts became stronger, faster, and again she felt the stirring of desire. Her body, weakened by her first climax, began to peak again as he withdrew and then pushed forward again and then again. One last deep thrust and they both reached the pinnacle of ecstasy.

Darach caught Abby close to him, and still buried deep inside her, he turned off the water and stepped out of the shower. He walked them both to the bed and then collapsed on top of the cover, careful to make sure Abby stayed on top of his body.

"Darach, I don't think I can do that again." Abby's words were a mere whisper.

"And why is that, my love?"

"Because…you almost killed me."

Darach laughed so hard his ribs hurt. "If it helps, me darling wife, ye almost did the same to me."

“Well…it might help some.” Abby’s voice was a bit stronger but her lids began to cover the lovely azure of her eyes.

“Rest, wife.”

Abby struggled to open her eyes as she grasped his arm. “Will you be here when I wake up?”

“I have no plans to go anywhere.” Darach allowed her to slip off his body and then turned on his side, pulling Abby with and then against him. He brushed her cheek with his lips, and flipped the cover they weren’t lying on over them. No, he had no plans to leave her side. Holding Abby in his arms while she slept was almost as wonderful as making love with her.

****

Abby woke before Darach did the next morning. She cradled her head on her arm and watched him sleep. His face, even in slumber, was a sensual painting. Dark lashes fanned over his bottom rim. Women would kill for what came naturally to him. His lips were relaxed almost in a smile. She reached out, traced their curve with her fingertip, and found herself flat on her back—Darach’s face above hers, his lips pulled back in a snarl. As she held her breath, he shook his head, looked at her again, and then released the grip he had on her throat.

“Abby, I didnae know it was ye. I be sorry.”

“It’s okay, just try not to do it again.” His actions had startled more than frightened her and even with his hand on her throat it had been more like a protective instinct instead of a threat.

“I dinnae know what happened. I guess I be not used to waking with someone in my bed.”

That bit of information made Abby want to shout with joy.

“Well, I was in your bed yesterday morning too.”

“Aye, but I woke before ye did. ’Tis been a long time since someone touched me while I slept.” His tone remained apologetic.

"Well, do you think you could get used to it? I love doing it. You're beautiful when you sleep."

Darach's face as well as his ears took on a red hue. "I will see what I can do."

Abby pulled his face down for a quick kiss before rolling to the edge of the bed.

"Abby?"

"I'm going to the bathroom, and then I think I'll fix breakfast."

"So the honeymoon's over?" Darach sounded like a small boy denied a toy.

"No, so quit whining. I want to go over to my house today and grab some more clothes. That is, if you'll beam me out of here."

"Of course, but then again, ye could stay naked and I would like that better." His teasing voice turned her bones to mush, but she really did want to bring some of her own things over.

"Not a chance. If I did, I'd never get to the house, ever."

"Ye could be right, so go do what ye have to do. I will look forward to breakfast in bed." His grin was contagious.

"Who said you were having breakfast in bed? I thought we could have it on your back terrace if the weather cooperates."

His smile became a crestfallen pout but she'd make it up to him later. Breakfast in bed with Darach would definitely lead to other things.

****

Abby knelt and laid the bouquet of roses Darach had given her a few days prior on the spot Lila's body had been found. Thanks to a couple of aspirin in the water, they were still beautiful. She bowed her head and said a prayer, ignoring the media who still hung out on boats stirring up the poor woman's death on a daily basis.

Darach took her arm and helped her to her feet. He'd been against the idea of her coming to the canal's edge, but she'd argued it was her property, and she was not going to let what happened keep her from walking the grounds.

Sean met them before they were halfway back.

"Hi, Abby." He nodded to Darach.

"Hi, Sean. Please tell me you didn't drop by to tell us there's been another killing?" Abby wasn't sure she could handle much more. As much as she loved her home, she couldn't wait to get back to Darach's.

"Actually, it's been quiet. A bit too quiet for my liking." The lieutenant exchanged a look with her husband. One she didn't particularly like.

"I can't believe you two. Quiet should be good, right? I mean if there's no bodies then that means Angus is not doing anything at the moment."

Darach kept her hand in his as they skirted the house and then mounted the steps. "Abby, Angus never does nothing. There be a reason he is staying quiet for the moment. A reason I be sure none of us want to find out."

"I understand that, Darach, but sooner or later you're going to have to quit talking around me like I'm wrapped in cotton. I'm his target, as well as you. The more I know the better I'll be able to watch my back." Abby turned to open the door.

Darach tugged her back to face him. "I will be watching your back. As will Sean, Arianna, and Conner. Ye are to stay safe. Do ye understand me?" His tone was abrupt, almost violent.

"Darach, let go of Abby's arm." Sean stepped forward and touched his sleeve. Only then did he realize how hard he gripped Abby.

"God's teeth, Abby, I be sorry!"

Instead of backing away from him, she moved forward and locked her arms around his waist. "It's okay. I know you didn't mean to hurt me. I promise I'll do what you ask. Just promise me one thing." Abby looked up at him. "Please guard your back too."

Tears burned his eyes. He still couldn't fathom why she loved him, but he was so glad she did. He brushed her hair with a trembling hand before turning to the halfling. "It seems I owe ye again. Me thanks."

"No need. Emotions run high when you care about something or someone." Sean opened the door and they walked in and through the house. It seemed the kitchen, with its homey atmosphere, peaceful vibes, and now the smell of pizza wafting through the air would be their meeting place again.

"Hi, all finished outside?"

"Aye, and Abby wants to pick up some clothes." Darach pulled a chair out for his wife, and then seated himself. Sean chose to stand instead of finding a seat next to Conner.

"Want some pizza? I ordered extra."

Darach and Abby passed on the offer, but the halfling took a couple of slices and chowed down like his life depended on his next meal.

"So, do we have a game plan for tonight? Will you two be out hunting?" Arianna's gaze raked Sean as she asked the question, before she shifted her gaze to Darach.

"Yeah, I plan on going out. What about you, Darach?"

"I uh, I will stay with Abby tonight. Conner you can go with him, right?"

"Sure thing. I have a few ideas of me own I want to explore," Conner mouthed around a bite of pizza.

"Don't blame you. If I had a woman, I'd stay home too." Sean gave Arianna a look that couldn't be misconstrued.

"Well, don't hold your breath, if you're waiting on me. I don't do halflings."

Darach opened his mouth to say something at the same time he heard Abby gasp. Sean, however, walked right up to the immortal.

"I don't recall asking you to." The lieutenant did an about-face. "I'll keep you posted if I find out anything."

He left before Darach could say anything in return. Conner followed him out after grabbing another slice of pizza.

"Arianna! That was just plain mean. How could you do that to him?" Abby's tone was filled with disbelief.

"Abby, I like you, girl, I truly do, but this is none of your business." Arianna tossed her uneaten slice of pizza back in the box and then left Darach and Abby alone.

"Well, that was a bit awkward." Abby stood up and began to clean off the table.

"Leave it, Abby. Arianna can clean up her own mess. Grab your clothes and we will return home."

"You're right. I'll be right back." Abby flew out of the kitchen. He hoped she hurried. Darach was more than ready to get back home.

"Darach, I—"

He met Arianna's chastised look. "Dinnae say a word. Ye are here to do a job, as is Sean. Ye both need to treat each other with dignity—at least until after Angus is caught. After that, I dinnae care if ye go at it with fisticuffs."

"You're right. I allowed myself to get angry. It won't happen again."

Darach took Arianna's chin in his hand and raised her head. "Dinnae promise what ye cannae deliver. We all feel anger for whatever reason, but as an executioner ye have to retain control."

He released her chin. "Now go. Find something to do this evening, and if ye run into Sean, try to be civil."

"I will. Thanks, Darach. I don't suppose we could keep this from Michael?" Her expression was hopeful but resigned.

"I willna tell him, but I figure our archangel already knows what happened."

"Yeah, me too." Arianna's dismay showed in her gaze.

"I'm ready." Abby tugged an overly large suitcase across the kitchen threshold. She looked a bit harried, but the smile she sent his way made the overcast day a bit brighter.

"Are ye sure ye have enough?" Darach's grin was returned.

"Well, I figured if I packed more you might not be able to teleport it. You being such an ancient personage and all."

Arianna's laughter joined Abby's and Darach decided he couldn't win and wouldn't even try.

"I will take ye and then come back for the bag."

"Whatever you say, old wise one."

Darach teleported Abby back to his house with the sound of Arianna's laughter ringing in his ears. Hopefully her good humor would last for a bit.

After he returned with Abby's case, he found her in the kitchen. It seemed even here this room would be a center for Abby.

"Hi, you. I thought you might be hungry since I don't think you ate anything after breakfast."

Abby was right, he was hungry but not for food. The horror of having her loose in a city without a guard, taking care of herself, had terrified him to no end. Now he wanted to love her like there was no tomorrow, no dead bodies, and no Angus.

"I be hungry but not food." Darach stalked Abby as she closed the refrigerator.

"And what is it you want?"

"Ye, my love, forever and always ye."

****

Angus was in a good mood. Soon he would have what he wanted. Word had reached him earlier that his human contact had arranged a meeting with Abby. Once they met, Angus's demons would have her. She would be the pawn to bring Darach to his side, of that he had no doubt. His cousin would do anything in his power to rescue Abby. His penchant for playing the knight errant would be his downfall. Then and only then would he use the woman before he drove the dagger straight into Darach's immortal and miserable heart.

Michael shook his head. Why couldn't his immortals behave like the adults they were? Arianna had been added to his executioners when she'd given her life to save a small child during the Renaissance era. The fact that she'd been running from a cruel husband made her decision to stop and help the child even more extraordinary. The action had resulted in Arianna being beaten to death. It was her inability to forget the past hurts that made it hard for her to trust too many people today. Yet, she had thrived on protecting others from the cruelties of Earth.

Chapter Thirty

Abby was ready to pull her hair out and kick Darach to the curb. He'd pretty much kept her with him twenty-four-seven for the last four days except when he went to the little boy's room. It was amazing how he could make love all night long, walk naked around the house (not to mention he expected her to do the same), yet he couldn't tinkle in front of her.

At least she could take the few moments while he attended to personal needs to grab his phone and call Arianna. Without the other immortal, she would be clueless as to what was happening. Whenever she got near the television set, it magically didn't work. She was more than ready to go out in the real world.

"Abby, where are ye?" Darach's yell made her jump and she dropped the cell phone. Great.

"I'm in the bedroom." She went down on all fours and stretched her hand under the bed. If she hurried maybe she could get it back on the battery charger before he noticed it was gone.

It wasn't that she was trying to deceive him, but his male ego just wouldn't understand she needed to breathe. Not a lot mind you, she loved him, but after being used to doing her own thing for years, it was hard to sit back and let someone else coddle her.

Her fingers touched the small cylinder and she began to drag it toward her. Of course, Darach wasn't used to having a wife either. Maybe if she talked to him.

"Abby!" She jerked so hard her head hit the edge of the bed frame.

"Ouch!" She got slowly back on her knees, and with the help of his hands she found herself standing and facing her husband. The telltale evidence of her deception of being happy as a pig in sunshine resting in her hands.

"What were ye doing?"

"Is it important?"

"It could be if 'tis something ye dinnae want to tell me." Darach sounded more curious than anything.

Abby decided she might as well tell him the truth and see where it got her.

"I was calling Arianna. I've been calling her every day to see what's going on." She sounded like a small child but for the life of her, she felt like one at the moment.

"Why didn't ye just ask me?"

"Because, every time I ask you anything about what's going on in the world, you tell me nothing. I feel like you want to pat me on the head and say 'Good Abby, good Abby. Now lie down and go to sleep.'"

Darach looked like she'd shot him out of a cannon. So real was his shock she felt terrible. She should have kept her mouth shut. "Look, forget it.

I'm fine. I love it here."

"I didnae realize ye would want to get out a bit more. I thought ye were content."

"Darach, I am content. I love you." Abby sat on the edge of the bed and tugged him down beside her.

"It's like I had work before, you know, and I saw Arianna on a daily basis, kept up with what was going on outside my own door, and now I feel like I'm wrapped in a cocoon. I know you want to protect me, but couldn't you lengthen the leash a bit?"

In less than a second her handsome confused husband turned into an unreasonable male. "Forgive me, I didnae realize I had ye on a leash, period." His words spoken in a harsh tone put Abby's back up.

"Well, you do. I want to be able to come and go. I don't even know where I am when I'm here. I can't teleport. I have to wait on you to beam me over to my house." Abby got off the bed and walked to the window. "I know you don't mean to, that you want to keep me safe, but I don't even have the freedom those animals have." She lifted her arm and motioned toward the wildlife in the backyard.

Darach's anger dwindled back down to the hurt that caused it in the first place. He had no idea Abby felt that way. All he wanted to do was protect her. Did she really think he was heartless? Had he been that uncaring and selfish?

"Fine, wife, if ye want to go see Arianna, I will take ye." Despite his restraint, he knew his words still sounded harsh. Hurt feelings were not something he was used to as an executioner.

Abby turned to him, and her eyes shimmered with tears. He admired her determination. She didn't allow not one to fall.

"Great, I'm ready to go now." Her voice was a faint echo of before. Gone was the straightforward woman he knew. Standing in her place was a woman who looked miserable.

Darach could fix it by telling her he was sorry, but he wasn't sure he was. His reasons for wrapping her up safely were good ones. She would have to learn that there would be times he knew best. After all he was an executioner and had centuries of experience. He ignored the small voice reminding him it had also been centuries since he'd been married.

Instead of pulling Abby into his arms as he normally did to teleport her, he caught her hand. A hand he wanted to bring to his lips and kiss, but if he did then that would be backing down, right?

A moment later, they were in Abby's home. His wife rushed off to find Arianna, and he stood there like a block of wood. It was only mid-afternoon, and Sean probably would not be around for a bit. He might as well go out himself. It wouldn't hurt to hunt a bit during daylight, and once Abby had her girl-talk with Arianna, he'd take her home before dark and smooth her ruffled feelings.

Darach teleported to the kitchen. "Arianna, I will be back to take Abby home." As for his wife, Abby just looked at him, not offering a word. He repaid her the same way by leaving without saying goodbye.

Five minutes later he stood on the street where the little jewelry shop had been. It wasn't there anymore. Somehow he'd figure it wouldn't be. Michael would have taken care of making sure no one else walked into the shop by accident. He owed the archangel his thanks for giving Abby what he wouldn't have been able to without Michael's help. His boss definitely knew what he was doing.

Darach stalked down the street and then decided to go visit Rae at the bar. He had a sketch of Angus that Lila's friend had given them, but one that they did not air to the public. Maybe Rae had seen him. And if not, Darach needed to tell her about the wedding.

The Highlander was quiet. Deserted in fact, but then again most of the regulars were still home, probably sleeping off the previous night's brew.

"Darach, you're here early." Rae's eyes sparkled and the smile she sent him warmed his abused heart.

"'Tis a beautiful afternoon and I wanted to get out."

Rae sat across from him in his regular booth. "Then why are you here and not out in the sunshine? And how is Abby?" Her questions poked his brain with their truth. Why wasn't he with Abby?

"I wanted to see an old friend and tell ye that Abby and I were married a few days ago."

At first the waitress's face fell with the news then she extended her hand across the table. "Congratulations. I'm not surprised. I just thought you would tie the knot sooner."

Darach took the hand she offered and squeezed it. "Why are ye not surprised?"

"I told you a while back the woman loved you, and it was very apparent you loved her also. So if you're still on your honeymoon, I repeat: what are you doing here?"

Darach blew out several deep breaths. Maybe if he talked to another woman he could make sense of Abby's feelings.

"I warn ye, 'tis a long story, and it dinnae make me out to be a good person."

Rae laughed. "I've got time, the regular customers won't be here for a bit, and my boss stepped out. And honey, men are never good when it comes to figuring out women."

****

Abby drained the last of her latte, the third she'd had since she and Arianna arrived at the coffee shop. Elle had been happy to see her, and even more joyous when she told her she and Darach had gotten married.

Now after being plied with questions about how, when, and where the wedding had happened, Elle was waiting on other customers.

"So are you having fun yet?" Arianna's droll question broke into Abby's thoughts.

"And if I say yes, will that make you happy?"

"I'd have to call you on that one, hon. You'd be lying between your teeth. So..." Arianna popped another bite of pastry in her mouth, and chewed it, all the time making moaning sounds. "Sorry, I just couldn't resist. These things are sinful. If I wasn't an immortal I'd be big as a barn."

"Don't rub it in."

"Okay, you want to tell me what you and big mad Darach fought about?"

"How do you know we had a fight?" Abby reached out for one of the raspberry delights but pulled her hand back. She did have to watch what she ate.

"Girl, the man's face was like a brick wall. And you didn't look much better. All pale and fragile looking."

"Oh great, our first big fight since we got married, and I come off as the proverbial female."

"Hey, it takes one to know one, so dish. What happened?"

Abby took the question as an offer to spill her guts. "The man won't let me breathe. It's like he's terrified if I go anywhere without him something will happen. I know he has reason to be cautious, but Arianna, it's driving me crazy."

"I'm sorry, I have to side with Darach on this one. He has every right to feel that way. He's frightened. More than I've ever seen him in the last five hundred years. He doesn't want to lose you like he did his first wife, and with his senses running amuck, I think he's doubly afraid he won't see the threat until it's too late."

Arianna's words blasted Abby with a kernel of truth. She should have thought about Briene. The tragedy of his family's death would have made him more anal about keeping her safe.

"Do you think ya'll will ever catch Angus?"

"Truth?" Arianna's gaze caught Abby's.

"Yes." Abby answered although she dreaded the answer.

"I don't know. He's been around almost as long as Darach. He's a mean SOB and he wants Darach dead, and he'll use anyone he can to make that happen."

"I've been an idiot. Do you think we could go back and find Darach? I want to tell him I'm sorry."

Arianna grinned. "Yeah, we can do that. Nothing worse than a pissed off or hurt man. They mope around for days. Just let me run to the little girl's room."

"All right." While Abby argued with Elle over accepting her money (the woman wanted to write it off as a belated wedding gift), the bell over the door jangled and in walked Nate.

"Abby, what a nice surprise."

Abby wasn't so sure about that, she wanted to get home to Darach, but she had brushed Nate off rather abruptly last time they spoke.

"Hi, Nate, how are you?"

"Fine, how remarkable to run into you here. I was going to call you. Jim's got everything set up for your party. Won't you reconsider and make an appearance?"

Abby looked toward the ladies' room. What was taking Arianna so long?

"I really appreciate the thought and all ya'll's consideration in wanting to throw me a party, but I can't."

Nate's face fell, and Abby felt like a heel. As she wondered again what was taking Arianna so long, Nate's eyes began to sparkle. "Well, if nothing else, let me and Jim take you for an early dinner."

Abby sighed. "No, really, I can't. I already have plans."

"Bummer, but won't you at least come out and say hi to Jim? He's waiting on me to grab a latte."

Again she looked toward the back of the shop and again no Arianna. Would it do any harm to just say hello? Arianna would surely be out in a moment.

"Okay, I'll say hi to Jim. Elle, would you let Arianna know I'll be right out front?"

"Sure, Abby." Elle threw up her hand in goodbye and continued to tally up her customers' orders.

The late afternoon sun cast a feeling of warmth over Abby as she looked around for Jim.

"I don't see Jim. I thought he was right outside."

Nate looked confused. "I left him here. Not sure where he got off to." He looked around and then grabbed Abby's hand. "Look, there he is right across the street. Come on."

"I'd rather not. I left word I'd be right here for my friend."

"Abby, please. It won't take but a moment. Jim will be upset if you don't."

"Fine, but only for a minute." Surely it would be all right. It was broad daylight, and she knew both men. They crossed over to the other side of the street. The smile Jim gave her looked a bit pained.

"Hi, Jim, I want to thank you about your party idea, but I can't go. Now, I need to get back to my friend."

Instead of saying a word, Jim locked his hand around Abby's arm. "I have someone who's been dying to see you again, Abby."

"Jim, you're hurting me. Let go. I told you I can't go anywhere."

Jim ignored her and Nate's added entreaties to let her go as he hustled her between two buildings and into an alley. The sight greeting her eyes chilled her blood to below zero. Demons of various sizes, numbering ten in all, waited.

"Jim, how could you?"

"How could I what? Oh, you mean these guys. They're here to take you to your brother."

"I don't have a brother. These are evil creatures. They're demons." Abby's fear escalated. She knew where they were taking her.

Jim laughed. "That's crazy talk, Abby. They won't hurt you. Your brother is a nice guy."

"And just how much did this supposed brother pay you to do this?"

Jim wouldn't meet her eyes as he spoke. "It's not like that, Abby. I got in some trouble gambling, and he offered to bail me out if I set up a meeting."

"What you've done is sign my death warrant not to mention my husband's and probably yours."

One of the demons spoke. His eyes glowed so red even the men with her noticed. Nate stepped back, while Jim stood there with his mouth open. "She's right, now that we have the woman, we don't need you."

The demon motioned with his arm and two of the creatures rushed Jim. The man she thought was her friend fought them and in the commotion Abby grabbed Nate's arm. "Run!"

Nate did as he was told and took off, sprinting toward the alley opening. Abby was right behind him when two clawed hands attached themselves to her arm. Her scream bellowed out and Nate stopped. "Keep running, Nate. Find Arianna. Tell her what happened."

Before the demons could grab him also, Nate put on a burst of speed and exited the alley.

Abby stopped struggling and faced her captors.

"I suppose now you're going to take me to the asshole you work for."

The head demon leered down at her. "Yes, and when he's finished with you, and your husband is dead, I'll enjoy Angus's leftovers.

Abby spit at the creature. His words frightening her into showing courage she didn't have.

His reply was a fist in her face and a clap on the side of her head, and then blackness engulfed her vision.

Michael wanted to hurl his angel paperweight out the window. Abby was kidnapped, Arianna couldn't find her, and now they couldn't find Darach. Oh what a tangle his people had made of things. If one hair on Abby's head was harmed he'd, he'd...

Do nothing! He could not interfere. The word that left his mouth wasn't a curse word but close enough he would be answering for it anyway.

Chapter Thirty-One

Darach teleported into Abby's house into the midst of chaos. Arianna stood over a man he thought was called Nate. Sean was also there firing questions. Conner gave him a look that chilled him to the marrow of his bones.

"What is going on?"

Arianna's face was white as cotton when she turned to face him. "Darach, I didn't know where you were. Abby's missing."

Terror almost drained the blood from his body.

"What do ye mean, she's missing?"

"We went to the coffee shop. We were getting ready to leave and I went to the bathroom. Abby was still sitting there." The immortal wrung her hands. "When I got back, Elle said she'd stepped outside with *him*." She jerked her thumb at Nate.

"When I went to find her she was gone. Then this person runs out of an alley across the street yelling like all get-out."

The scrawny man in question was gesturing with his hands. "I told you, I didn't know."

Darach's steps were quiet as he walked to the man. Nothing like the rapid beating of his pulse screaming in his ears.

"What didnae ye know?"

"That it was a trap. Jim said I was to bring Abby to him for a surprise going away party." Nate's eyes glistened. "I should have listened to her, she didn't want to go, but I truly thought she would enjoy the party. Only Jim wasn't just outside like he said he would be, he'd walked across the street. Me and Abby walked over. She said hello and was going to go right back to the coffee shop, when Jim grabbed her by the arm."

Tears poured down the mortal's face. "They killed Jim and took Abby."

"Who took her?" Darach was fast losing his grip on his retreating control.

"These creatures. They had red eyes and fangs and claws. Abby and I ran when they attacked Jim. They caught her and I turned back to help."

Nate ducked his head. "I'm sorry. I should have stayed, but she told me to find her." He motioned toward Arianna.

Darach wanted to kill the man, but it seemed he too was a pawn of Angus. Angus. God, his heart wanted to burst with the agony of knowing his sweet Abby was with that monster.

"Do ye have any idea where the demons might take her?"

"No…but wait, I know from what Jim said right before they killed him, that he'd been dealing with a man who said he was Abby's brother. I truly think he believed it."

"Think mon, did Jim ever say anything at all about this man before?" Darach tried not to let his desperation show.

"No, nothing. I'm so sorry. If I hadn't convinced Abby to talk to Jim, this wouldn't have happened.

Abby would be safe and Jim alive."

Sean looked at Darach before leveling his gaze on Nate. "Jim signed his death warrant when he delivered Abby. You're lucky you aren't dead also."

"If Abby hadn't fought with them when they caught her, I would have been."

Darach barely noticed when Sean ushered Nate out nor did he realize Arianna had left the room until she returned with a shot glass full of whiskey.

"Here, drink it." Arianna handed him the glass. "Now forget about blaming yourself. Abby loves you and wasn't upset with you when she left the coffee place. We'll find her. And just in case you can't forgive yourself, I should never have left her."

Darach lifted his head, his first instinct was to tear into the other immortal, but he didn't. It seemed that whatever the reason, Angus had Abby. Now he would have to wait for the demon to contact him. And that he would, Darach had no doubt. Angus loved to gloat and for him this would be a shining moment, not to mention a nail in Darach's coffin.

"No, ye are not to blame."

"Thanks Darach, I just wished I could believe it. What do we do now?" Arianna moved closer to Darach.

Darach tossed back the shot glass of liquid. "We wait. Angus will contact me. Of that I am certain." He accepted the clasp on his shoulder Conner issued and then prayed the demon didn't kill Abby first.

****

Abby roused to the taste of blood in her mouth. Her arms felt as if they were being pulled out of the sockets. She lifted a swollen eyelid and glanced around. She was alone, thank God.

The demons had brought her here, and it seemed locked her up with a multitude of chains. As if she could have broken free from even one of her new silver bracelets. She wished she knew how long she'd been out. And she prayed Darach would stay away. Abby could take what Angus dished out, she closed her mind to the memory of the bodies he'd discarded, as long as Darach remained safe.

A clink of a lock and then the slightly squeaky door signaled the arrival of a visitor. She could just guess who that was.

The man, or demon, that strutted in had blond hair and green eyes for the moment. She was sure they would turn red when she got through telling him off. His build was okay, a bit impressive, but he was nothing like Darach and never would be.

"Angus, I assume." Abby manage to get out through the swelling in her split lip.

"Yes, and you are the evasive Abigail Dupree."

"That's MacRath, you asshole."

"My, my, it seems this time my cousin married a lioness instead of a mouse." Angus followed his words with several steps toward Abby. She wished he'd go away. She decided to remain silent and see what he had to say. Any ammunition she could use against him would be welcomed.

"I applaud his taste, but then he always had exquisite taste in wives. The beautiful Briene, although not much of a fighter, was a most rewarding rape." Angus looked as if he wanted her to applaud what he'd done.

"Well, I suppose rape is the only way you can get a woman of your own. Although, I would think that would become old after a few centuries." Abby spit out with a drop of blood.

His snarl preceded the change in his pupils. Yep, they were glowing a bright red. Abby guessed she shouldn't tweak his chain, but if it would buy her time to hopefully escape on her own, then Darach could remain safe. She didn't give a rat's ass if he ever got the dagger and destroyed it. She just wanted him to stay alive.

"You take your life in your hands, woman. If I didn't need you to draw Darach to me, I'd kill you right now after I tortured you."

"Oh pooh, that goes to show just what a poor excuse of a demon you really are. How it must grate to have to use a woman to do your job."

The blow rocked her head back against the concrete wall. Stars exploded behind her closed eyelids. She wondered if she would get a chance to tweak him again. When the second fist connected with her face, she decided she didn't care.

"Now since you have first hand knowledge of what I can do, I will be taking this." Angus grabbed her left hand and began to twist off her wedding ring.

"No, leave it alone. You can't have it." Abby knew it was a lost cause but she didn't want the demon touching the bond of her and Darach's love.

He ignored her protests and wrenched the ring off. She bit back the cry of pain his action caused. She just prayed he hadn't broken her finger. Abby wanted to have all of her fingers intact to claw his eyes out if she ever got the chance.

****

Darach ran shaky hands through his hair. It'd been exactly four hours and thirty-one minutes since his world exploded. No word on Abby at all. God only knew what was happening to his wife. Why didn't Angus get in touch with him? How long could he endure this torture before slowly going out of his mind?

"Darach, try to settle down. I'm sure we'll hear something soon." Arianna's voice wasn't as calm as he was sure she wanted it to sound. She and Sean had stayed with him during the grueling hours of torment, while Conner went back to the club he and Darach had busted in hopes he could get a location on Angus.

"I just wish I could be sure." Darach had even tried to call Michael but got no answer. What kind of archangel didn't answer his phone?

Sean walked back into the living room and closed his cell. His face was grim. Darach jumped up. "Is there any news?"

"No. I just got off the phone with Michael. He says he can't help. Something about interfering with the order of events that need to take place. I told him that was bullshit. Guess that's why he hung up on me."

"Thanks, Sean. At least we now know not to expect help from that quarter." Darach began to pace, his steps short and furious as he thought about all the times he'd obeyed the edicts of Heaven. Now when he needed help the most it was withheld.

"Why don't I order us something to eat? We're going to need our strength whenever Angus does contact you."

"I dinnae think—" His words were interrupted by the doorbell.

He couldn't say who made it to the foyer first but when he opened the door, Sean and Arianna stood beside him.

"Special delivery for a Mr. MacRath."

Darach grabbed the package and left Sean to sign for it. He ran back to the living room and tore the envelope open. A single white sheet of paper fell out followed by the pinging sound of metal.

He bent over and picked up the flash of silver. Abby's wedding ring glowed back at him. Oh God. Oh God. All his hopes, although he knew were ridiculous, that maybe Angus didn't have her were destroyed.

"What is it?" Sean's terse tone only made matters worse. The halfling was almost as upset as he was over Abby's abduction

"Angus does have her. He sent me her wedding band."

Arianna moved up beside him and rubbed his arm. "What does the note say?"

His hands shook like he'd had too much to drink as he unfolded the paper.

Meet me at the warehouse where you found the pictures. Midnight. Come alone or you will find your wife's body in pieces. Angus

Darach's vision grew dark as spots danced before his eyes.

"Here sit down." Sean guided his body backward until his legs touched the sofa. "Get him some water, Arianna."

Darach took the glass she offered and welcomed the grip aiding his hand as he tried to drink. The water tasted like bile to him, but it did help to still some of his dizziness.

Sean picked up the paper he'd dropped, read it, and handed it off to Arianna.

"Don't worry, we'll get her back."

"Nay! Ye read the note, he will kill her as soon as he sees ye."

"Be reasonable, Darach, Angus will kill her anyway." Conner's appearance into the room had gone unnoticed by Darach, but his words scared the hell out of him.

"I willna let him. I will bargain with him. He can have me, not Abby."

"And just how do you expect to pull that off? If he does kill you, he's not going to let her go. You need backup."

"Sean's right, Darach. You can't do it alone." Arianna inserted.

Darach stood to his feet and prayed his earlier weakness would not return. It was almost midnight now. Angus must have paid a pretty penny to have the package delivered after hours.

"I dinnae know what to do." His hair stood on end as he raked his hands through it several more times.

"Why not trust us? Arianna or Conner can teleport me to the warehouse after you've had time to arrive. We'll stay back and wait."

Darach tried to think. Should he allow it? If they were there then maybe between them they could get Abby out alive. It was worth a chance. He would not lose another loved one to Angus.

"Verra well. Just make sure ye get Abby away. I dinnae care what happens to me. She must live." Darach saw but did not decipher the looks exchanged between the halfling and the immortals.

"Good, then this is what I think we should do." Sean began to spell out his plan.

A half an hour later Darach prepared to teleport to the warehouse. His backup stood ready to do the same.

"If this dinnae go as planned, then I want ye all to know how I value your friendship. Please take care of Abby for me."

Sean snarled, "Shut up and transport, Highlander. You can take care of Abby yourself when we get her back."

Michael felt the weight of Darach's pain on his shoulders. It threatened to break his resolve not to interfere. He hated this part of his job. He didn't like standing still and allowing someone else to fight evil, but alas, his boss had been adamant again about certain events having to occur. He just prayed those proceedings did not result in the loss of Darach and Abby.

Chapter Thirty-Two

A slap brought Abby back to consciousness. She opened her eyes and stared into the face of evil. Angus grinned as he motioned for two of his demon buddies to unlock her chains. Her arms felt like dead weights when they dropped. The only thing holding her up now was a chain around her waist.

She shuddered as one of the fanged creatures leaned in way too close to unlock that barrier also. She shook her hands and tried rotating her arms—grimacing against the pins and needles attacking her limbs.

"Well, it seems we will see in a few moments whether or not Darach loves you as much as he did Briene. Will he fight for you, Abby? Or will he leave you to me?"

Abby reacted without thinking. Her leg shot out and she kicked Angus in the balls. "Well, at least he's willing to fight, and not let others do it for him. You coward."

Angus recovered far more quickly from her blow than she would have liked. His hand grabbed her hair and pulled her neck back at a painful angle.

"I can hardly wait to have you under me, my dear. I will revel in breaking your spirit and then bathed in your blood."

A glob of spit hit him in the face and then he struck her with his fist. "Let's see if your Darach will want you after he sees your face. You're not so pretty anymore."

Abby fought the pain threatening to pull her under. "Darach loves me for me, not my looks, and because I love him."

His laughter caused the hair to rise on her arms. "Well, that remains to be seen. Bring her!"

Angus's henchmen grabbed her by the arms and tugged her out of her small prison. The moonlight almost blinded her as she was hurriedly marched to a waiting car. Their shove into the trunk was not gentle, and the last view she had was of Angus's snarling face as he slammed the lid shut.

Great, if he didn't kill her beforehand, she could die from lack of oxygen. Abby rooted around in the dark and tried to find anything she could to jiggle the trunk open as the car started up and moved off. After several minutes of searching, her uninjured hand clutched a screwdriver. Her thank God turned into a prayer when the car began to slow.

Lord, she needed to hurry!

The screwdriver slipped with the rough pavement they rode on, but then she found the latch. She wiggled the flathead into the slight opening and turned it. Abby tried again and was rewarded with a faint click. She reached out to push the trunk open and the car stopped.

She was too late.

Several crunches of gravel heralded the arrival of her kidnapper. She held her breath and the screwdriver close as the trunk was flung open. Abby waited only a second before stabbing the screwdriver into one of the demon's eye and then swung her legs over the back of the car, praying she could get away before Angus caught her.

So much for hope.

Again her scalp was assaulted as Angus wound his fingers through her hair. Damn, she was tired of this.

"Going somewhere, my dear?" At her nod, he backhanded her. "I think not. We have an appointment with Darach."

She struggled but succeeded in only tearing out several strands of her hair. Angus and the two remaining red-eyes, one with blood streaming down his face, flanked her as she was pushed toward the warehouse.

Once through the door, her eyes took a moment to adjust to the dimness. Angus dragged her to a steel beam, and his two goons wrapped her in chains once more. The building seemed eerily familiar. Then her vision about Darach raised its head and her fear. This was the place where Darach would die. And if he did, she would surely die with him.

She reached out to claw their eyes but Angus only grinned maniacally as he grabbed her hands and squeezed so hard she just knew he'd broken another bone. "It's midnight. And if I'm not mistaken, your husband has arrived.

****

The Darach that arrived at the warehouse was a far cry from the shaking, terrified immortal of before. Abby could be saved, but it would take him calling upon all his skills and concentration to do so. Not to mention the help of his friends.

His stride was sure, his form straight, as his gaze found and identified Angus and two other demons. Darach sought Abby, and when he found her he almost lost it. Her beautiful face was swollen, bruised, and one eye almost closed. The other blue orb looked toward him, and he swore he saw a glimmer of a smile on her abused lips.

The rest of her body, except for a ring of bruises around each wrist, looked untouched. He prayed Angus's habits had not changed and that he would want an audience before raping her.

"Darach." His name was a croak of sound from Abby. He bowed to her and then stiffened his shoulders against Angus's laughter. His cousin walked to Abby and touched her face. As Darach watched he ran his clawed finger down the side of her cheek, opening a furrow of blood.

He steeled himself not to react. It would do Abby no good if he allowed his rage to take control. Only calm would win the night against Angus and a lot of luck.

Angus left his torture of Abby and moved closer to the center of the warehouse floor. A position Darach had taken when Angus touched Abby.

"So it seems we meet again, cousin. I hope you plan to die without sniveling this time."

"How I die and where I die is none of your concern. I be not a trusting soul any longer, Angus. It will take more than ye to kill me."

Angus's lips pulled back to reveal his fangs. Thank God he had not used those on Abby. "Well, we shall see about that. And since you did come alone, I will allow your wife to live so she can watch you die."

Abby's whimper hurt Darach, but he could not look at her or calm her fears. His attention must stay on Angus at all times. The demon had been tricky as a mortal and would be more so now.

"And will ye be brave enough to do your own fighting this time?" Taunting Angus could backfire on Darach but he wanted him as far away from Abby as possible.

The demon did move closer to Darach. "I don't need anyone to fight my battles now. I am one of the strongest demons around."

Darach kept his tone derisive. "Oh, so that's why ye were kept as a lackey in hell for so long."

"Why you miserable..." Angus stopped and motioned for one of the demons to come forward. He took the proffered wooden box, lifted the lid, and pull out the cursed dagger. Well, at least Darach knew where it was now. Not that it would help any. If Angus struck him with it, there was no telling what it would do to his fighting skills.

"Let's see what you have to say when this dagger cuts you from throat to ass."

"I say 'tis time ye quit stalling and fight me, Angus." Darach withdrew his sword. "My blade has not tasted the flesh of demons for several days. It will welcome a chance to feed its hunger."

While he baited Angus he watched three shadows take shape behind the demon's henchman, as well as Abby. A quick thrust through their hearts and they turned to slime. Sean made eye contact with Darach and then moved to stand next to Abby. Arianna did the same. Conner held her up as the others released her bonds. At least if he met his death this night, Abby's freedom would be guaranteed.

"Kill him!" Angus's cry roared through the warehouse echoing off the metal beams.

"Who are ye talking to, cousin?

Angus looked behind him. The rage his flesh gave off sent sparks dancing in the air. Oh yeah, he was pissed, but so was Darach. With Abby no longer in danger he could do what he did best: kill a demon.

"As ye see, the fight is now between us only. Prepare to die and meet your judgment." Darach waited as Angus seemed to hesitate, then the demon rushed forth, the dagger held high.

Darach blocked the blade before it connected with his heart. He spun and brought his sword down to cut a hole in his opponent's chest. The ooze stank like a nest of maggots before it began to slowly close up. Not a good sign. Someone had doctored Angus's demon makeup. He would not be easy to kill, but Darach was determined to do his damnest to send him back to hell—regardless of Michael's orders to turn him over to him. As far as he was concerned, even if he'd changed his mind about killing Angus, Michael's refusal to save Abby rent him of any promise he'd made to the archangel.

Again and again Angus lashed out, and each time Darach sidestepped him. Every blow he dealt the demon danced away and each time Angus laughed. There had to be a way to win this match. Perhaps...

He needed something to slow Angus down, to get him to drop the dagger, and then he would chop his head off. Hopefully that would do the trick. If not, then it would take himself, Sean, Conner, and Arianna to bring the demon down.

Darach started a frontal assault, slashing at Angus like a madman. His cousin began to back up. Good. The closer they moved toward the group waiting all the better. Sean stood poised, as did Conner. Arianna would make sure Abby stayed out of harm's way.

Angus cast a glance sideways. Sean cursed. "You son of a goat. That's my mother's medallion."

"Really? Then she must be the slut I raped centuries ago. I have to tell you, *son,* she was a tasty bit of flesh. I wondered what happened to her. She left before I was finished with her."

Sean moved toward Angus. "Because of you my mother was an outcast. She worked her fingers to the bone to take care of me. I will kill you for that."

The halfling's hands fisted. Darach knew what would happen next. He could allow Sean to kill him. Dead was dead, and the man had a good reason to want Angus dead also, but the demon had struck Abby, hurt her, and would kill her if possible. No, Darach wanted the pleasure of taking Angus out. Then he'd answer to the consequences of his actions if he was still alive.

"You would kill your own father?" Angus looked a bit proud at that thought, but Sean's words vanquished the smile on the demon's lips.

"You may have sired me, demon, but you are not my father."

Sean's fingers extended, and it looked as if the halfling had taken the choice out of Darach's hands. He moved to get out of the line of fire, and slipped in a combination of blood and ooze on the concrete floor. He went down on one knee. Angus turned his back on Sean, grinned, revealing his fangs, and slashed out with the dagger. The hot feel of copper raked Darach's face, blinding him.

He swiped his coat sleeve across his eyes in a desperate attempt to clear his vision. Angus cut him again, his arm this time, and against the fiery blaze of pain, Darach tried to lift his sword to block what would be a deathblow.

"No!" Abby's voice rang out a second before her protector's cries.

"Stop!" Sean's command ripped through the building.

"Abby, stop." Arianna's plea was an anguished cry.

"Abby, wait." Conner's desperation caused Darach to turn his head. Abby ran the distance between them, her arms out in front of her, her mouth open again to scream.

Darach tried to pull himself to his feet, to place his body between Abby and Angus, but his body would not cooperate.

Angus's blade completed its downward arc just as Abby threw herself in Darach's arms. He felt her body shudder as the blade cut through flesh to bone. He heard her breath catch as pain lanced her bloodied form.

"Nay!" Darach's roar echoed in his ears and settled in his heart. He barely realized when Sean picked up the sword he dropped and swung it at Angus's head. The demon shrieked and then his body exploded into fragments of bone and gore.

"Is she?" Arianna dropped to her knees by Darach.

"I dinnae know." He frantically searched for and found a pulse.

"What can we do?" Sean and Conner both now crouched by Abby's almost lifeless form.

As Darach watched her breath began to slow. And then her eyes flickered open. He had to lean his ear close to her lips to hear her whispered, "Darach."

"I be here, me love. Hang on. We will..."

"It's too late, my beloved immortal." Abby lifted her head just a fraction. "Arianna, keep him safe and be good to Sean. And Sean, no matter what Darach says, please continue to be his friend."

Abby's body shuddered. "Darach, I'm cold. I am so cold."

Darach held her so close to his body he could feel the point of the blade still buried inside her body.

Rage and pain bellowed forth in one yell. "Michael! Ye owe me, angel. I have given my service to ye. Take me life back and give Abby hers. Hear me, Archangel, dammit; she dinnae deserve to die! Why have ye and God turned your back on me?"

****

Tears poured from Michael's eyes as he watched the scene below unfold. Never in his wildest imaginings had he expected this conclusion. Darach's cries caused the roses outside his window to weep also. The dew from their petals fell onto the paved pathway. He should not, would not interfere.

It could cause him to lose his position as an archangel. If he did so then who would help his immortals, who would teach them to fight the demons so intent on taking over earth? Michael shook his head—he had no answers.

Yet, he found himself stepping outside and then he caught a shooting star's light to earth.

****

As Abby took her last breath a golden light filled the warehouse. So bright, Darach squinted his eyes swollen lids against the glow. As he watched a form stepped from the light.

Michael!

Arianna gasped, the halfling stepped back, and even Conner backed up as Michael strode toward them. "Give her to me, Darach."

"Nay, ye cannae have her."

"I want to hold her." Michael's tone was patient and kind. As he looked full into the archangel's eyes he saw a sheen of moisture. Reluctantly Darach handed Abby's body to him.

Michael pressed his lips to her forehead, all the time whispering something Darach could not hear, as he lay her down on the concrete. He then gently withdrew the cursed dagger from her body, and with a flick of his wrist it shattered into pieces so small they would never be detected by human eyes.

Darach turned his attention back to Abby. Was Michael going to help her? Would removing the dagger bring her back? The questions stumbled through his mind as he fought against the inner and outer pain threatening to take him. He kept his gaze trained on Abby and the archangel.

So faint it was at first, he dared not hope that her chest rose and fell with life. His gaze shot to Michael who picked Abby up and returned her to Darach's arms.

The archangel smiled.

"She is yours now for eternity. You both will fight against evil." He stood to his feet, his seven-foot plus frame a daunting sight. "And you." He motioned to Sean. I would have you work as an executioner also."

"Me? I'm not worthy to do that, angel. I'm half demon, remember?"

"Yes, but it was your mortal soul that chose to deliver justice when Darach could not."

Darach dared not take his eyes off of Abby but he had to know. "I thought you wanted Angus alive? You warned me not to kill him."

"That would have been the best thing, but when he killed Abigail, I knew he would die, I just wasn't certain who would render the death blow." He nodded at Sean, and then looked at Arianna. "You have done well, Arianna. Conner, you will stay here for the time being." Michael then glanced again at Darach. "I will handle the paperwork. I'm sure my boss will understand. After all he is a loving God who understands more than anyone what love means." Michael pressed a hand to Darach's shoulder and then strode away, only to stop. Without turning around he spoke again.

"Darach, do not curse at me again. I told you there were events that had to occur, although I didn't know Abby's death was one of them, and therefore you need to earn patience."

Before Darach could reply, Michael was gone.

"Darach?" Abby's eyes fluttered open. Confusion ran rampant in her gaze, but the look of pain she'd had earlier had disappeared. Gone also were the wounds on her face.

"Shush, my love. Everything is all right…now."

"What happened?" Abby began to sit up, the blood on her clothes the only evidence she'd ever been wounded and died.

"You ran between Angus and me and he stabbed

you."

Abby looked down at her body. "Oh, God in Heaven. I remember, but I thought he was going to kill you just like in my vision. And if he stabbed me, why am I not dead?"

"Well..." he replied as he helped her to stand. "Michael paid us a visit."

"Yeah, after Darach literally called him out of Heaven."

"What?" Abby stared at Sean.

"It's true, Abby, Michael actually made an appearance. You were dead. I can hardly credit what I saw, and I have seen a lot of things. And Highlander, your wounds have disappeared also." Sean's eyes still contained the shock of the last few minutes.

Before Darach could think about how Michael had healed him, Abby asked, "So what happens next?"

"Ye will be my wife for eternity, and I guess you dinnae have to worry about growing old anymore." Darach said the words, but still felt the shock of the last several hours.

"You're kidding. Michael turned me into an immortal?"

"Aye." Darach thought Abby would be upset, instead she smiled.

"That's great. Can you teach me how to teleport? Fight?"

Darach caught her up into his arms. "Slow down, Abby. Let me just get ye home for now."

"Fine, but I want to know everything that happened. Sean are you and Arianna coming? And what about you, Conner?"

"Not right now, Abby. I need to..." Sean kissed her on the cheek and then took off at a run.

"It will take him some time to come to grips over Angus being his sire." Darach felt the halfling's pain.

"I agree. Arianna?"

The immortal grinned at Darach and Abby. "Naw, I think you two need some together time. Besides, I found a great restaurant I want to try out. I'll stop by and pack later. You wanta go, Conner?"

"You're leaving?" Abby's question was echoed in Darach's mind.

"Well, I'm hoping I can stay here for a bit, but if I do I want to find my own digs." Arianna flashed them a smile and then she and Conner flashed away.

"Well my love, ready to go home?"

"More than ready, Darach, but first I want my ring back. That vicious demon stole it to send to you."

Darach withdrew the ring from his coat pocket and placed it on Abby's finger. He followed his action with a kiss to finger and then her lips.

****

Abby rested her head against Darach's chest, after they'd spent several hours making love, a position she would utilize for the next millennium or longer. She still couldn't believe she had died and now she was an executioner. How blessed she was to have found love and friendship in the last few weeks. To think if she'd never gone out that night, none of this would have happened.

"What be ye thinking, wife?" Darach's baritone rumbled inside his chest and tickled Abby's ear.

"How much I love you. How blessed I am." Abby entwined her fingers with his before giving a shout.

"What is it?"

"I just realized I missed meeting Michael! That is so not fair!" Abby didn't care if it sounded as if she pouted. She really wanted to meet the archangel in person.

Abby and Darach heard laughter at the same time a piece of parchment floated through the ceiling and landed on the bed.

Darach unrolled it and felt tears burn the back of his eyes. The deed to MacRath Castle was made out to him. A small sticky note was stuck to the paper. "Sorry it didn't arrive in time for the wedding."

"What is it?" Abby's curious tone and gaze met Darach's. He handed her the paper. It was the deed to Darach's family's property in Scotland. They both looked at one another and grinned before speaking at the same time. "Thank you, Michael."

****

Michael finished his notes on the night's activities. All in all it had been a splendid end-result. Darach got Abby. Abby would be working for him, and he'd guaranteed Sean Black would be dedicating his skills for the good of Heaven. And another demon had been destroyed.

The reprimand he expected from his boss never came and for that Michael was grateful. It wasn't as easy as he'd first supposed centuries ago to make his executioners do what they should. While being immortal, they still maintained some of their mortal qualities. Some he approved of like embracing love, and Michael had discovered while working with Darach and Abby that he liked that emotion and his part in their matchmaking. Now he would send Arianna to Scotland to see if indeed absence would make her heart grow fonder of Sean, but although he had his own opinion about whether they would end up together, he would have to wait and see.

Conner would fill in for Darach and instruct Sean in the ways of executioners, while Darach and Abby got some well-deserved time off.

Michael blew out the candle on his desk, put his quill pen back into the ink, and then walked out the door. A moonlight stroll by the Crystal Sea would help him finalize his plan for his executioners.

As he made his way toward the sandy beach he

smiled. Michael hoped God would be as pleased with his plans as he was. While he watched, a moonbeam danced on the placid surface of the sea and he smiled. Yes, it had been a very good night indeed.

A word about the author...

Faith started her journey to publication when she joined the Romance board at iVillage.com, where she became a community leader. She has written book reviews for *Bridges* magazine, MyShelf.com and for Romantic Times Book Reviews. She also pens a column for a local magazine. Her dream of having her own work published is a blessing and an honor. Faith resides in the South with her daughter Amanda, memories of her now-angel husband Rick, and a special zoo crew of furry babies.

Visit her at www.faithvsmith.com

Other books by Faith V. Smith:

Beware What You Wish
Kensington's Soul
Dunbar's Curse
Viking, Go Home
Semper Fi Magick
Gideon's Heart

To my readers...

Some of you have been with me from before I ever became published, and some of you are new fans. Thank you so much for making me love my work. I appreciate each and every one of you!

Look for "Hawk's Salvation," Hawk Sherwood's story of love, book four in the "Bound By Blood, The Legends" series, as well as "Tiernan Punishment" coming soon from The Wild Rose Press

Thank you for purchasing
this Wild Rose Press publication.
For other wonderful stories of romance,
please visit our on-line bookstore at
www.thewildrosepress.com.

For questions or more information
contact us at
info@thewildrosepress.com.

The Wild Rose Press
www.TheWildRosePress.com

To visit with authors of The Wild Rose Press
join our yahoo loop at
http://groups.yahoo.com/group/thewildrosepress/